Cy▮▮▮▮▮▮▮▮▮▮▮▮▮▮▮▮▮▮▮▮▮▮▮ hugely popular
Mo▮▮▮▮▮▮▮▮▮▮▮▮▮▮▮▮▮▮▮▮ and enthralled
readers for decades. She is also the author of the War at Home
series, which is an epic family drama set against the backdrop
of World War I. Cynthia's passions are music, wine, horses,
architecture and the English countryside.

WITHDRAWN

By Cynthia Harrod-Eagles

The Bill Slider series

Orchestrated Death
Death Watch
Necrochip
Dead End
Blood Lines
Killing Time
Shallow Grave
Blood Sinister
Gone Tomorrow
Dear Departed

The Morland Dynasty series

The Founding
The Dark Rose
The Princeling
The Oak Apple
The Black Pearl
The Long Shadow
The Chevalier
The Maiden
The Flood-Tide
The Tangled Thread
The Emperor
The Victory
The Regency
The Campaigners
The Reckoning
The Devil's Horse
The Poison Tree
The Abyss

The Hidden Shore
The Winter Journey
The Outcast
The Mirage
The Cause
The Homecoming
The Question
The Dream Kingdom
The Restless Sea
The White Road
The Burning Roses
The Measure of Days
The Foreign Field
The Fallen Kings
The Dancing Years
The Winding Road
The Phoenix

War at Home series

Goodbye Piccadilly:
War at Home, 1914

Keep the Home Fires
Burning: War at Home, 1915

The Land of My Dreams:
War at Home, 1916

The Long, Long Trail:
War at Home, 1917

Till the Boys Come Home:
War at Home, 1918

Pack Up Your Troubles:
War at Home, 1919

Blood Lines

Cynthia Harrod-Eagles

sphere

SPHERE

First published in Great Britain in 1996 by Little, Brown and Company
Paperback published in 1996 by Warner Books
This reissue published by Sphere in 2019

1 3 5 7 9 10 8 6 4 2

A CIP catalogue record for this book
is available from the British Library.

ISBN 978-0-7515-7537-8

Typeset in Plantin by Palimpsest Book Production Limited,
Falkirk, Stirlingshire
Printed and bound in Great Britain by Clays Ltd, Elcograf S.p.A.

Papers used by Sphere are from well-managed forests
and other responsible sources.

Sphere
An imprint of
Little, Brown Book Group
Carmelite House
50 Victoria Embankment
London EC4Y 0DZ

An Hachette UK Company
www.hachette.co.uk

www.littlebrown.co.uk

1

A Scar is Born

In the canteen queue Detective Inspector Slider came up behind DI Carver.

'Hullo, Ron. You look as if you've been up all night.'

Carver, a balding man with a perpetual grudge, grunted. 'Had a call-out last night.'

'Must have been something serious to get you out of bed,' Slider said blandly. The night shift in the Department consisted of one DC, who called up a DS in the case of something he couldn't handle. Only really serious crime warranted telephoning the Ops DI, who was likely to be just a teensy bit tetchy if disturbed for what he regarded as trivia. 'The big one, was it? Murder? Armed robbery?'

Carver looked a snarl. 'Attempted burglary. Big house in Stamford Brook.'

'Oh, bad luck,' Slider said with brimming sympathy. Ron Carver had sometimes said things about him behind his back. 'Open window, opportunist thief?'

'The window was shut, as a matter of fact,' Carver corrected loftily. 'Bloody sash window,' he added savagely. 'Child's

1

play – two seconds with a five-bob penknife. It don't matter how often you tell 'em, they won't fit locks. And it's not as if this one couldn't afford it – she was loaded.'

'Much missing?'

'Nah, she frightened him off.' He glanced sideways at Slider and began to unbend. One couldn't waste a good story, after all. 'She didn't reckon he was after her Renwahs. Oh no. And she was ready to defend her honour to the hilt – literally. Gilbert says she come to the door brandishing a bloody great knife. Sacrificial dagger, apparently, real Abraham and Isaac job, souvenir of Tel Aviv.'

'Sharp?'

'As a lemon. Apparently, she's sat in the lounge in the dark thinking about going to bed when she's heard the window going up in her bedroom, so she's grabbed the knife off the coffee table, tiptoed in, and there's chummy on the drainpipe with his leg over the sill. Well, she reckons that's not all he wants the leg over – though to look at her you'd think it was more hope than fear – so she's only gone for him, hasn't she? Hacked him in the leg with this bloody pig-sticker, and he's gone. Near as damn it fell off the bloody drainpipe – first-floor window and a concrete strip at the bottom. But anyway, he shins down and has it away across the garden, and she's straight on the dog to us. Keeps the number on her phone pad – reckons it's quicker than nine-nine-nine.'

'A doughty female,' Slider commented.

'I haven't told you the best bit yet,' said Carver. 'Benny Cook feels it's his duty to warn her about the consequences, should chummy have broke his leg or his neck falling off her drainpipe. So he says, "You really mustn't go about hacking at people's legs like that, madam," and she comes back like the Queen Mum, "Young man, I was aiming for his genitals."' Carver's haughty falsetto was worth coming in early for, Slider thought.

2

Carver went off with his breakfast into the guv'nors' dining-room, but Slider preferred to mess with the ORs, and exchanging friendly nods with some of the sleepy night relief just coming off, who had stayed for a cuppa and a wad, he took his tray to a window table. A few moments later his bagman, Detective Sergeant Atherton, appeared beside him, dunking his teabag at an early morning andante. 'How long have you been here?' he asked.

Slider looked up. 'Who's Prime Minister? Pass the tomato sauce before you sit down,' he said.

'Dear God!' Atherton stared unwillingly at Slider's tray: two fried eggs, double fried bread, sausage, bacon and tomato, tea an' a slice. 'I see you've plumped for the Heartburn Special,' he said. 'Last train from St Pancreas.'

Slider chuckled. 'You're such a gastro-queen. How did you ever come to be a copper?'

'I was switched in the cradle by gypsies,' Atherton said, sitting down opposite him. 'Why are you breakfasting here? Oh, of course, Joanna's gone down to Glyndebourne.'

'She left early to miss the traffic. And she's got a couple of morning orchestra calls, so she's staying down tonight and tomorrow,' Slider said, trying to sound indifferent about it. But the fact was, sleeping in her bed in her flat when she wasn't there made him feel uneasy. He anticipated restless nights. 'What's your excuse?'

'I'm not early in, I'm late out,' Atherton said, extracting his teabag by the tail, like a drowned mouse, and laying it carefully in the ashtray where it would later infuriate the smokers.

'With?'

'One Nancy Gregg. A little blinder. Met her last week on that house-to-house in East Acton.'

'What about Sue?'

3

'Sue?' Atherton said as though it were a word in Urdu, of meaning unknown to him.

'Sue Caversham, violinist, friend of Joanna's,' Slider reminded him drily. 'I thought you and she were a big thing.'

Atherton sipped, at his most superb. 'No commitment has been made on either side.' And then, 'She's down at Glyndebourne as well, you know. You can't expect a healthy, red-blooded young male suddenly to become celibate. We 'as urges, guv.' He dropped into a whine. 'I dunno what came over me. It's all a blank. Summink must of snapped—'

'Yes, yes, I get the picture.' Slider folded a piece of wonder-bread and carefully mopped up tomato sauce. Atherton watched him in dilating horror. 'So, did you hear, Mr Carver's firm had a sleepless night?'

'Yes, I was talking to Hewson about it,' Atherton said. Hewson was the DS on call. 'Modest bit of excitement. He quite took to the intended victim – told me she had balls.'

'Surely not?'

'She's one cool dame. You'll be able to meet her later on if you like. She's coming in to see if she can pick anyone out from the mugshots. Apparently she caught a glimpse of chum-my's boat, though it was dark, of course, and it all happened quickly. Hewson isn't too hopeful, but it would be nice to nail one of our persistent offenders.'

'Did she actually wound him?'

'Apparently. There was blood on the blade of the knife,' Atherton said. 'Even if she can't pick anyone out, it might be worth tugging a few of our best customers and see if anyone's limping. A known section-nine-er with a matching cut on the thigh ought to be convincing enough even for the CPS.'

'And how would you propose discovering this cut? Ask them to take their trousers down?'

4

'That is one difficulty,' Atherton admitted. 'Not least because there's a few who'd agree to. Still, I understand Mr Carver intends putting the word out on the street that the villain ought to sue this woman for assault.' He shrugged. 'I can't believe anyone'd be daft enough to come forward. It means putting his hand up for burglary.'

'It never does to underestimate the stupidity of the criminal,' Slider said. 'I remember the time One-Eyed Billy got nicked because he took a stolen Magimix back to Currys to complain one of the attachments was missing.'

'I never know whether to believe your stories,' Atherton complained. 'And I've never understood why he's called One-Eyed Billy, when he's got two perfectly good ones.'

'Because his father was called One-Eyed Harry,' Slider said, serene in the knowledge that he could only add to his own legend. 'It's like a family name. Harry's wife was always known as Mrs One-Eye. It was perfectly respectful – everyone liked her. When she took her teeth out she could fold her lower lip right up over her nose. Broke the ice at parties.'

Atherton felt it was time to raise the tone. 'Reverting to the subject of that break-in last night, the lady in question, interestingly enough, is someone you'll have heard of quite recently: Christa Jimenez.' Seeing Slider's blank expression, he added, 'She sang in that *Don Giovanni* you went to at Glyndebourne.'

'Oh? Which one was she?'

'Donna Elvira. Don't you know? Don't tell me you slept through it all!'

'Of course I didn't,' Slider said indignantly. 'But I'm not an opera buff, the names don't mean much to me. She was the dame with the very low-cut dress, right?'

'I'll take your word for it,' Atherton said drily. 'I haven't seen the production.'

'You haven't missed much,' Slider grumbled. Joanna was playing in two operas down at Glyndebourne this year, and orchestra members were allowed to bring two guests each to the pre-dress-rehearsal. Though there were many who'd have given their eye teeth for the privilege, and Slider was not unappreciative, it was still small compensation for the amount of time she had to spend away from him. Besides, though he didn't like to admit it in front of Atherton, he wasn't *all that* keen on opera – especially a modern, minimalist production which offered him nothing to look at while he listened. 'If I'd paid seventy-five pounds for a ticket,' he said in sudden wrath at the thought, 'I'd have expected at least some nice scenery and costumes, or my money back.'

Atherton didn't quite keep his smile under control. Slider gave him a suspicious look, and he straightened his face. 'It did have terrific reviews,' he mentioned, 'from some very serious critics.'

'You think I'm a philistine,' Slider said, a little ruffled. 'But I don't believe those critics really like all that modern stuff. They just pretend to so as to make themselves superior to the rest of us. Anyway, they get paid to sit through it. Something that's put on for the public, and paid for by the public, ought to aim at pleasing the public.'

'Ah, there you have the whole dilemma of arts funding in a nutshell,' Atherton said. 'Well, I'd better go and have a shave and change my shirt. Mustn't be late for work, must I, especially now we're short-handed. I wonder if we'll ever get a replacement for Beevers.'

Detective Sergeant Beevers had left three weeks ago. Slider said, 'Who ever would have thought of him entering the Church?'

'It's only a Baptist ministry,' Atherton said.

'Snob! A priest is a priest is a priest. But I'd have thought

Beevers was in The Job for life. It isn't as if he had any outside interests—'

'Except the Church.'

'Well, yes, obviously. But if it had been one of the others, now – take Norma, for instance—'

'I've often taken Norma in my dreams,' Atherton said tenderly, 'but I'd never dare try it on in real life.'

There was a moment's reverent silence. Woman Detective Constable Kathleen Swilley was blonde, athletic and slim – every man's erotic dream. She could also shoot the eyebrows off a fly at fifty paces and packed a punch like an army mule, and because of her machismo was generally known as Norma. She hated her given name so much she didn't even mind.

Atherton sighed, coming down to earth, and stood up. 'I suppose one of these days we'll get a new super, too. That'll be something to look forward to. Not that Mr Honeyman's any trouble.'

Since Detective Superintendent 'Mad Ivan' Barrington had committed suicide, they had only had a night watchman at the crease: Det Sup Honeyman, working out his time until retirement and hoping for a quiet life.

'I hear McLaren's started a book on who we'll get,' Slider said.

'He says that according to the grapevine – alias his mates at Kensington – nobody's very anxious for the job. With the last two supers dying in harness, they reckon Shepherd's Bush is a poisoned chalice. That's why we've had the night watchman so long.'

'They're a right bunch of Hans Andersens down at Kensington,' said Slider. 'Obviously now Mr Honeyman's here, they aren't going to replace him until he retires, and he won't have done his thirty years until next month.'

And a man on the brink of completing his thirty in an increasingly dangerous profession was not going to do anything to risk his life, health or reputation, which was why Eric Honeyman was 'no trouble' almost to the point of catatonia; but out of respect for the chain of command, Slider didn't say so aloud. 'I don't suppose it's possible ever to stop coppers gossiping,' he complained, pushing back his chair and standing up, 'but it'd be nice to break McLaren of the habit of phoning Kensington twice a day for fresh rumours. But he just doesn't seem to take to training.'

'Hit him with a rolled-up newspaper,' Atherton suggested, following him to the door.

Slider had stayed on at the end of the shift, clearing desultory bits of accumulated paperwork and trying to rearrange his 'pending' pile into stuff he was likely to do something about eventually, and stuff he was hoping would simply die of old age. Even as he tried to be conscientious about it, part of his brain knew that he was sitting at his desk because it was preferable to deciding what to do tonight. *Ain't you got no home to go to?* enquired a thread of song ironically. He had the key to Joanna's place, ten minutes away in Turnham Green, but despite his shaving gear in the bathroom it was still Joanna's place and not home, especially when she was not in it. When she was there it was a dear and familiar haven; without her it seemed as cosy as a 1950s seaside boarding-house.

The ex-marital home in Ruislip, from which his wife and children had decamped, he had never loved even when his family lived there. It was now fulfilling a secondary role as an albatross hanging round his neck. The idea was for him and Joanna to buy a place together once he had sold the albatross and paid Irene her half; but with the housing

8

market suffering from clinical depression, even the estate agent had passed from cautiously jaunty to defensively evasive. All the same, a good number of his possessions were still stored there, and he supposed if he were stopped by the police, it would be the address he would give as his. It was where Irene thought he still lived: she didn't know about Joanna yet.

But he only went there when constrained; which left staying at work as the only alternative. It made him realise how few friends he had. Detective Inspector was a lonely sort of rank. Too much blokeing with the lads undermined authority; and in any case, he'd never been fond of football. Socialising above his station was even more out of the question: he was not ambitious enough either to ingratiate himself with his seniors, or to be welcomed by them as an aspirant. Besides, up there in the stratosphere internal politics and golf were the reigning interests, and he'd never really got the hang of intrigue. As to golf, he had met many golf-club members during his years of living in the suburbs. Most of them were dull, and many of them were called Derek.

Atherton was his only close friend. Atherton had no ambition and no nagging doubts about himself, so Slider had nothing to prove to him and nothing to fear from him. His intellectual curiosity made him the ideal partner at work, and his hedonism ditto at play. Moreover, Atherton liked Slider, and made it plain enough to reassure without embarrassing a solitary man with the usual difficulties of his age group in expressing his feelings.

In the feelings department, Joanna had been an earthquake to Slider. She had burst in on a lifetime's reserve and obedience to duty with revolutionary ideas about one's duty to oneself and the nature of happiness. She had turned his life upside down, and he had to admit he hadn't made a very good job of coping with it. Coming alive at his age was worse than pins and needles, and it was hardly surprising if he had periods of reaction, especially when she was not there to reassure him. But the boats were burned now, anyway. Irene had run off (well, sauntered off) with another man, taking the children with her, so there was no way back into his old life. A life with Joanna, some time in the future when everything had been sorted out, glittered like the distant prospect of the Emerald City. He told himself everything would be all right; it was the limbo of the present that was so uncomfortable.

'Sir? Mr Slider?'

Slider looked up, coming back from a great distance to find standing in his open doorway a man about whom much was familiar: a strong, fleshy, broad-bottomed man in a brown suit which original cheapness and subsequent hard wear had rendered shapeless, especially about the overworked pockets. He wore an off-white shirt with the sort of tie men choose for themselves, and thick-soled shoes scuffed at the toe and worn down at the heel. He wore a large, elaborate but cheap metal-braceleted watch on his right wrist, and a large, plain gold signet ring on the third finger of his right hand. The first and second fingers of his left hand were amber cigarette holders. He had detective written all over him.

He was in his mid-to-late thirties, dark-haired, dark-eyed and moley; his lower face had the bluish shading that went with really black hair and white skin.

'DS Mills, sir,' he said helpfully when Slider failed to respond.

'What does the DS stand for?' Slider asked. 'Dark Satanic?'

'Detective Sergeant, sir,' Mills corrected, deadpan.

'Are you being funny, lad?'

'No, sir. Would you like me to be?'

Both men broke into a grin, and Slider got up to stretch out his hand. 'Good to see you, Mills. How are you?'

'I thought for a minute you didn't remember me,' Mills said gratefully. 'It's a long time since the old Charing Cross days.'

'Ten years at least, I should think. So you made your stripes? Well done! And what are you doing here?'

'I've just transferred from Epsom.'

Slider raised his eyebrows. 'Nobody told me. I've been a sergeant short for three weeks. I thought I was never going to get a replacement.'

Mills looked embarrassed. 'Oh, no sir, I'm not for you. I'm joining Mr Carver's firm tomorrow, but when I heard you were here I thought I'd drop in as I was passing and see if you remembered me.'

Carver had been agitating for extra manpower for months, but he hadn't actually lost anyone. If anyone ought to have got Mills, it was Slider; but Ron Carver was on the square. Slider swallowed his disappointment and his paranoia. The ways of the Met were passing strange but there was no future in pissing into the wind.

'How are things in Epsom?' he asked instead.

Mills made a face. 'Quiet. Except on Saturday nights. You know what these outers are like, sir.'

'Ah well, you won't get bored here.'

'I'm from Shepherd's Bush originally,' Mills said. 'I mean, I was born here.'

'Were you? I suppose someone has to be.'

'We lived in Oaklands Grove,' Mills confided. 'I've been walking about the last couple of days, though, and the place has changed a good bit. I passed where the Congo Church used to be, and it's gone!' He sounded quite indignant. 'It's a block of flats now. I used to go to scouts in the church hall there when I was a kid.'

'Got any family here?'

'My mum, she's in sheltered in Hammersmith. And my auntie lives in Ormiston Grove.'

'Sir Robert Mark would have a fit,' Slider murmured. It had been that great man's contention that detectives should not get to know their ground too well, or corruption would inevitably set in, struggle how one might. 'Are you staying with her?'

'No, sir. I've got a temporary place just round the corner, Stanlake Road. I'll be looking for a flat a bit further out once I've got settled.'

'Well, I'm sure you'll be a great asset to Mr Carver, even if you do have to relearn the geography. I wish you were joining my firm. I've lost a DS, and the holiday season's always a problem. Have you had your holidays?'

'Yes, sir.'

'Where did you go?'

'Rhyl, sir.'

Slider was unable to think of a single thing to say about Rhyl. Possibly no one ever had. 'You haven't taken up DIY, have you?' he asked suspiciously.

'No sir,' Mills said with faint surprise.

Slider was relieved. 'Better steer clear of DC Anderson, then,' he advised. 'He's just built his own sun-lounge extension.'

'Thanks for the warning, guv,' said Mills grinning.

The White Horse wasn't much of a pub, but it was open all day and the nearest to the police station, so it received more patronage than its efforts to please deserved. Slider pushed open the door of the saloon bar and a friendly fug embraced his head, an all-senses combination of cigarette smoke, cherry-coloured nylon carpeting, the smell of institutional gravy and the pinging and gurgling of a fruit-machine. Along the bar in front of him was a row of broad dark-blue serge behinds topped with a variety of anoraks and leather jackets: B Relief must have been on overtime. He imagined he could hear the steady sound of sucking, as when a team of plough horses, just turned out, nudges up to the water-trough.

One of them, alerted perhaps by the unnaturally fresh air that had wafted in with Slider, turned his head, and then smiled welcomingly. 'Hullo, sir. I'm up – can I get you one?' D'Arblay said. The others looked round as well, and their expressions were not wholly unwilling, but Slider felt shy of imposing himself upon them. They had been sucking in grateful silence, and if he joined them they'd have to make polite conversation.

'Oh, thanks, you're very kind, but I'm going to get something to eat,' he excused himself.

'You're a brave man, sir,' said Elkins, his moustache heavy with froth like a hawthorn bush in May. Before them on the bar were four opened packets of Pork Scratchings. Courage is all relative, Slider thought as he made his way to the food counter.

Mein host was a tall, fat, cold-eyed man who resented the fact that the coppers from across the road didn't like his pub, and got his own back by making them feel as unwanted as possible. Slider's request for food pleased him because it gave him the chance to disappoint.

'At this time of day? You must be joking. I can't keep kitchen staff hanging about just on the off-chance.'

'A sandwich, then,' Slider said as firmly as he could on an empty stomach. The landlord's face registered a brief struggle. He hated customers, and especially policemen, but their constant presence on his premises meant he had very little trouble from drunks or vandals. Besides, policemen spent well. His overall aim was to make them feel miserable without actually driving them away; compromise was sometimes necessary.

'Only rolls,' he said at last.

'Two ham rolls, then,' said Slider.

'No ham. Only cheese.'

'I see you studied at the Hobson school of catering,' Slider said politely. 'Two cheese rolls, then; and a large scotch. And a packet of crisps,' he added, throwing caution to the winds. What the hell? You have to splurge sometimes.

'What flavour?' the landlord asked with the light of battle in his eye.

'Vanilla,' said Slider, staring him down; and after a moment he walked off, thwarted. The food, when it came, was as miserable as it could be rendered, the sort of rolls that were soft on the outside and hard on the inside instead of the other way round, scraped over with margarine instead of butter, with one thin square of processed cheese in each, whose four corners, poking outside the circumference, had gone hard and greasy from exposure. When Slider opened the rolls to inspect them, he found as a final insult a single wafer-thin circlet of tomato stuck to the marge in each, damp, anaemic and smelling of old knives.

And the crisps weren't crisp. Slider ate and drank almost with a painful pleasure, a sense of supping life's dregs, after which things could not possibly get worse. As if to prove the point, the landlord approached, and said with offensive indignation, 'Phone call for you.' Slider made his way round the bar to the public telephone at the other end, and could only think it must be Irene; if it was business or Joanna they'd have used his bleeper.

It was Joanna. 'You forgot your bleeper again, didn't you?'

'I left it on my desk,' he discovered.

14

'So I've been told. Luckily someone saw you go across the road, or I'd have had a long search. What on earth are you doing there?'

'Making myself suffer. Nothing's any fun without you, anyway. Where are you?'

'At the Trevor,' she said through a blast of background hilarity. 'Can't you tell?'

He thought of the Trevor Arms, the nearest pub to Glyndebourne, the one the orchestra always patronised. He thought of a pint of Harvey's – mahogany nectar – and the house ham, egg and chips – the greatest trio since Schubert.

'What's the weather like?' he asked, hoping for relief.

'Terrible,' she said cheerfully. 'It's pissing down. I do feel sorry for the punters, all togged up and nowhere to go. If it doesn't stop by the interval, they'll all have to squeeze into the marquee for their picnics.'

'What you might call loitering within tents,' Slider said.

'What? I missed that, there's so much noise here. What's it like there?'

'Noisy.'

'The weather, I mean.'

'Oh – terrible. I don't know, really. Not raining, I don't think.'

'Darling, what's the matter?' she asked anxiously.

He searched for some succinct way to tell her, but the distance between them was too great, and the line wasn't good enough for delicate expositions. 'It's Thursday,' he said. 'I've never really got the hang of Thursdays.'

'Oh,' she said, wanting to get to the bottom of it, but feeling, like him, that the effort over the phone was too exhausting. 'Well, only another one and a half horrible *Dons*, and then it's lovely *Traviata*. You'll like that – frilly dresses and damask drawing-rooms. You will come to the pre-dress, won't you?'

'If I'm off, of course I will.' He thought of telling her about the singer whose house was broken into, but he couldn't remember her name. While he was hesitating she went on.

'I've got some good news.'

'Yes?'

'The BBC's going to do a television recording of the *Don*, and we're being booked for it. Best of all, they're not just taping a performance down here. It's going to be a studio recording. That means nine sessions.'

'That's wonderful.' He roused himself to enthuse: he knew what that meant to the finances. Then he frowned. 'Nine three-hour sessions? But the opera's only about three hours long, isn't it?'

'That's my detective, scenting the anomaly,' she said, and he heard her smile. 'The running time's about two hours fifty – depends a bit who's conducting. But you're only allowed to record twenty minutes of finished product per session.'

'Why?'

'Union rules, silly. We've got to eat. All the same, by the time you've run through, polished up, done a few takes, and hung around for the engineers to decide if it's good enough, you wouldn't get more than twenty minutes taped anyway.'

'Well, I'm glad for you,' he said. Work had been a bit thin on the ground lately.

'Be glad for yourself, too – the sessions are bound to be in London, maybe even at White City. We'll be able to have lunch together.'

She sounded so simply pleased at the idea that the words 'I miss you' were surprised out of him, with hardly a thought for the surroundings or the possibility of being overheard. 'When are you coming back?'

'Well,' she said, and he knew it was bad news. 'We've got two calls tomorrow for *Traviata*, morning and afternoon, and the last *Don* is on Saturday. So I thought tomorrow evening I might go and see my parents and stay over. It's my mother's birthday on Saturday.'

'Oh,' he said. Her parents lived in Eastbourne, which wasn't very far from Glyndebourne.

'Well, you see, I thought I could take them out for dinner tomorrow night, and then spend the day with her on Saturday, take her out for a drive somewhere maybe. I don't see them very often, and as I'm down here anyway—'

'It's all right, you don't have to ask my permission,' he said. He tried to say it neutrally, but he was afraid it sounded petulant all the same.

'You don't mind, then?' she asked doubtfully.

The question peeved him, because even if he said he did mind, she wouldn't change her plan. And why should she? It wasn't as if they were married. She could do as she liked – and did. 'It isn't for me to mind or not mind. You're a free agent,' he said.

There was a pause. It went on so long he thought she might change her mind, but at last she said, 'Well, as long as you'll be all right—'

Disappointment was mingled with a feeling of guilt for trying to spoil her evening, with resentment for being put in a situation where it was possible to feel guilty, with exasperation for his own feebleness in being so tied to her apron strings. She mustn't think he was going to be moping at home and waiting for her reproachfully. 'It's all right,' he said, and unthinkingly added what had just jumped into his mind, 'I've got to go and see Irene anyway.' Stupid, stupid! In the context that sounded like *sucks to you*.

But she only said, 'Of course you have,' and for the life of him he couldn't tell how she'd taken it. Then she said, 'Listen, I've got to go, there's a queue for this phone.'

'Have fun,' he said.

'And you.' She hung up, and he felt like forty-seven kinds of idiot. This love business was fraught with potholes. He hadn't even asked her if she was coming home on Saturday after the show. Surely she would? But if it was her mother's birthday and he had made her feel uncomfortable, maybe she'd spend the night in Eastbourne again rather than risk a chilly welcome. It was undignified to be cast in the role of reproachful, stay-at-home spouse, and ironic after all the years he had been failing to turn up in Irene's evenings. Boots and other legs didn't half alter your perspective on things.

He wandered back aimlessly to his end of the bar and tried to catch the landlord's eye for another large Bells. But, he thought, anomaly-spotting again, why hadn't she told him yesterday before she left that it was her mother's birthday and that she might go and visit? Come to think of it, she hardly ever spoke of her parents at all. So why this sudden flush of dutifulness? As far as he knew, she had never marked their birthdays with a visit before, not while he had known her.

Maybe she wasn't going to Eastbourne at all. Maybe there was someone else down there – another man.

At that point he actually made himself laugh. Someone else? She was playing in an orchestra of sixty musicians, the vast majority of them men; and male musicians were the most sexually irresponsible animals in the universe, next to policemen. It was the old unsocial hours syndrome, plus propinquity and being in a discrete group with its own esoteric language and experience. Just like policemen again. He reminded himself painfully how he had met her in the first place.

The monster of jealousy boggled at him round the corners of his mind, and like all monsters it was ludicrous and fright-

18

ening in equal proportions. He took a pull on himself. If she was down there, out of his sight and unaccountable, he was up here equally unaccountable to her. You had to trust someone if you loved them; and jealousy was most unattractive behaviour. But of course there was still the old dichotomy between the mind and the balls. Even while his intellect was explaining everything to him rationally, his hormones were prowling up and down with a baseball bat, looking for a fight.

2

Knife Work

For once Slider beat Atherton to a call. In fact, he was so quick off the mark that when he reached the TV Centre at White City, there was only a single jam-sandwich parked in front of the main reception hall. Inside it was a forensic nightmare, with a milling crowd jostling around three tables set up along the left side, where they were apparently being checked in and badged, before moving slowly up the staircase at the far end. The main reception desk to the right was besieged only in a minor way by bored couriers, and as soon as Slider held up his ID a worried-looking young woman detached herself from a telephone conversation and hurried over to him.

'Detective Inspector Slider, Shepherd's Bush CID,' he said. 'There's been an incident – a body found?'

'Oh yes, it's on the fourth floor, in one of the gents' loos. I'll get someone to show you up.' She grew confidential. 'It's such a terrible thing – I mean, it isn't a *natural death.*' She pronounced the words in a voiceless whisper. 'No-one knows quite what to do – you see, it's a live programme, with an audience and everything. I do hope you can sort it all out. Do you think they'll have to cancel the show?' She raised hopeful eyes to his face.

'I expect so,' Slider said. 'What programme is it?'

'*Questions of Our Time.* Roger's one of the panellists. Well, was.'

'Roger who?'

'Oh gosh, didn't they tell you? Roger Greatrex. He's the one they found. Well, I don't know all the details, but apparently he's killed himself in some ghastly way. Poor Fiona's in a terrible state—'

'Is this the audience?' Slider cut her off, indicating the milling mob.

'The last of them. The rest are in the exec canteen, or on their way up to it. It takes ages getting them all in. We thought, as we didn't know what was to happen, that we'd better carry on as usual, rather than tell them to go home.'

'I'm sure that's right. Can someone show me upstairs now?'

'Oh, sorry, yes, of course. Kate, can you come here a minute?'

In a moment Slider was following a young woman who scurried like the White Rabbit up stairs, along a corridor, through some swing doors, up more stairs, along another corridor, without ever looking back to see if he was keeping up with her. At last she deposited him, completely disorientated, before a small worried knot of people standing before a closed door which bore the familiar straddling peg-man silhouette, the UN-approved International Idiot Icon for the gents' loo. A uniformed constable – Baker – was guarding the door and some bloody footmarks in front of it. To Slider's surprise, DS Mills was also there.

'What are you doing here?' Slider said.

'Oh, I just happened to be passing,' Mills said vaguely.

'I intercepted the call, and I thought I might be able to help.'

Slider said, 'I wouldn't be a bit surprised. What've we got?'

'He's in there, sir.' Baker gestured towards the closed door.

'He is dead?'

'As a fish,' Mills reassured him. 'I had a quick shufti. Looks like suicide.'

'You've got blood on you,' Slider noted with disapproval. Surely after all this time Mills hadn't forgotten the basics?

'It's off the bloke that found the body. He was hysterical, sort of threw himself at me,' Mills explained.

'Morley's taken him away, sir,' Baker intervened. Morley was his partner. 'Giving him a cup of tea.'

'Name?'

'Philip Somers. He's the assistant producer for this programme that apparently the deceased was going to be on.'

Slider nodded, worked on a pair of gloves, and opened the door. It was a small, white-tiled room with off-white ceramic tiles on the floor. There were two stalls straight ahead, of the usual grey melamine and stainless steel construction, their doors open onto innocent untenanted sanitary ware. Three urinals occupied the far right hand wall, and a row of four washbasins with mirrors above the left-hand wall immediately inside the door. The door opened to the right, but in the mirrors Slider could see the reflection of the wall behind it, which supported an electric hand-drier and a condom slot machine.

That was the easy bit. The unpleasant bit was the blood, spattered across the mirrors, streaking the water in the washbasin, smeared over the washbasin rim, and puddled on the floor. The body was lying with its feet towards him, crumpled on its side. Even from here, he could see how Mills could be sure life was extinct: the neck had been severed so determinedly that the head was almost off. It lolled back at an unnatural angle, exposing the butchery aspect of severed vessels. Slider felt the familiar sense of pressure behind the eyes and had to look away for a moment and fix his gaze on something neutral; behind him Mills was breathing hard and swallowing rapidly. And then he heard Atherton's voice saying, 'If only blood were some nice unassertive colour, like grey or pale green, it wouldn't be half so bad. But red . . .!' Slider managed a smile, and the pressure behind his eyes evened itself out.

'Boss?' said Mills into his ear. 'Over there, on the floor, by the end stall.'

A knife with a bloodstained blade, an old-fashioned clasp-knife of the sort dreamed of by boy scouts in Slider's youth, with a leather-wrapped, steel-capped handle and a steel cross-guard, and a slightly curved blade about eight inches long.

'Suicide, you think?' Mills prompted.

'Mmm,' Slider said non-committally. He stared around a few moments longer, memorising the layout, and then closed the door. Atherton was a little way off, chatting to a young woman, his hands in his pockets, the curve of his back at its most languid. Slider knew that pose, and left him to it.

He said to Mills, 'This man, Somers, who found the body – he raised the alarm?'

'Apparently he stayed on guard here while he sent someone else – a female, Dorothy Hammond, one of the assistants – to tell the producer – that's the top bod in this set-up. Somers said once he knew this bloke was dead, he realised he had to stop anyone else going in there and touching anything.'

'An intelligent member of the public,' Slider commented. 'How rare, Who's the producer?'

'Fiona Parsons – female over there in the suit.' The one Atherton was chatting up. No, had been chatting up – he had left her now. Slider met him halfway.

'It seems there's a bunch of celebs in a room along there,' Atherton said, gesturing with his head, 'who will be growing restive. Miss Parsons wants to know what to do with them. I suppose we'll have to interview them?'

'Even if it is suicide,' Slider agreed.

'If?' Atherton said.

'Better safe than sorry. You can go and pacify them in a minute. You've a light hand with demigods.'

'Years of practice in the CID.'

'But fill me in first on this programme.'

'*Questions of Our Time*. Haven't you ever seen it?'

'Of course I've heard of it, but I've never watched it.'

'You haven't missed much. Well, you know the formula – panel of experts, studio audience, chosen topic, audience put questions, panel exercise egos. They put it out live, in an attempt to inject some excitement into it. It's cheap telly, of course, because the audience isn't paid, and as long as they pick publicity-junkies, the panel do it for nothing as well.'

'And what was today's question?'

'Right up your street, guv. Funding of the arts – elitist, or essential? Bringing culture within reach of the masses, or subsidising middle-class taste with working-class money? A question that is no question, really,' Atherton added provocatively, but Slider wouldn't be drawn.

'So who are these celebrity guests, then?'

'Well, Roger Greatrex, music critic and opera aficionado, alias the deceased, you know. Then there's Sir John Foster, Director of the Royal Opera House; Jack Mallet—'

'The Heritage Minister, yes.'

'Dame Barbara Frankauer – novelist, Islingtonite and token woman,' Atherton went on. 'And Sandal Palliser. You know who he is?'

'Of course I do.'

24

It would be hard to categorise Sandal Palliser, except to call him a Media Star. He had done crits, written columns, presented programmes on television; he was frequently to be seen at awards dinners making speeches, and at film premières escorting the nubile and famous under the barrage of flashing lights. His opinion was sought on discussion programmes, his *bonhomie* on game shows, and his showbiz anecdotes on chat shows. He had recently even written a novel, a surprisingly slushy love story set in his native Derbyshire Peaks, which had reached best-sellerdom – partly, so Atherton said, on the strength of Palliser's famous name, but mostly on account of a much-talked-about sex scene in chapter eight, in which the heroine encountered the hero after hours in a porcelain factory and did quite surprising things to his person with china clay before being bonked to within an inch of her life on a heap of packing straw. Since the book was assumed to be autobiographical, That Chapter had been the talk of the dinner-party circuit for weeks, while the Groucho seethed with speculation as to who the heroine really was.

'I should have thought with Sandal Palliser and Roger Greatrex on the panel, they'd hardly need anyone else,' Slider said.

'They're a debate on their own,' Atherton agreed.

Recently Palliser, who liked to pose as a champion of the people, had conducted a printed slanging match with Roger Greatrex on the subject of the unacceptably esoteric nature of the modern arts. Palliser had cited in particular the latest Booker prize novel that no-one would ever want to read, the Turner prize winner that only a regurgitation fan would want to look at, and the Glyndebourne *Don Giovanni*. It was the latter which had actually sparked it all off, for they had happened to be at the same performance and got into an attention-grabbing row in the foyer during the interval. The following day Greatrex had praised the production in his review column in the *Guardian* as 'daring, innovative and thought-provoking', while Palliser, in his commentary page in the *Mail,* had castigated it as 'pretentious adolescent clever-dickery'.

Greatrex had responded in *The Sunday Times'* Arts Supplement by accusing Palliser of 'pseudo-blokeism', and Palliser, perhaps a little unfairly, had brought out the big guns by devoting a whole edition of his *Arts and Minds* programme on ITV to the proposition that the whole modern arts machine was an exclusive back-scratching club paid for out of tax-payers' money.

All this had stirred up quite a lively ongoing debate in the letters columns of the national dailies. Slider had followed it at first because he had seen the *Don Giovanni* production which had started off the row – with Joanna playing in it, it was almost a family concern. But the argument had become blurred by a number of letters complaining that the DG production was blasphemous, on account of the Act Two supper-room scene taking place, for no adequately explained reason, in a church, where the Don had done a number of sacrilegious things around and on the altar. Even at the pre-dress which Slider had attended, there had been disturbed murmurings from the audience, and though Slider had merely thought it silly, it had obviously upset some people. After a couple of days the correspondence in the papers had wandered off into the byways of what constituted blasphemy and whether it should still be a criminal offence in the nineteen-nineties, and Slider had lost interest.

But he could quite see why any discussion programme about the arts at this moment in time would have to include Sandal Palliser and Roger Greatrex if it wanted to be topical.

'All right,' he said to Atherton, 'you go and pacify the great and famous. As soon as reinforcements arrive they can give their statements and go home.'

'What about the audience, guv? There's a couple of hundred bods penned up in a canteen upstairs with nothing but sandwiches, tea and the daily papers to keep them quiet.'

'Someone had better go up and talk to them. Mills, find Morley and send him up. He's to tell them as little as possible, but keep them quiet.'

'Right, guv.'

'Aren't we going to let them go?' Atherton said in surprise.

'Not yet. I might want statements, and you know what people are like once you let them get away. I want their names and addresses, anyway.'

'All of them?'

'All of them. You'd better contact the factory and ask the Super politely for some more uniforms. We'll need a few just to keep this area clear of sightseers, let alone all the interviewing. This is going to mean a bit of overtime, I'm afraid. What are you smirking about, Baker?'

The duty police surgeon had been sent for, but it was the forensic pathologist who arrived first – Freddie Cameron, the man for whom the adjective 'dapper' might have been invented. Slider had been distributing his troops when he arrived, and hurried back to the scene of the crime to meet him. Cameron was engaged in putting on a set of overalls to cover his light grey Prince of Wales check suiting; Atherton was with him, holding a plastic cup of something that steamed, Cameron's clipboard under his arm.

'Hullo-ullo-ullo,' Freddie said jauntily. 'The hounds of law on felon's traces, eh?'

'Come again?' said Slider.

'My words exactly,' Atherton said.

'Which, mine or his?' Slider asked. 'No, don't answer that. How did you get here so fast, Freddie?'

'I was only down the road at Hammersmith Hospital. Just finished a post when the call came, so here I am.'

'You've beaten the surgeon to it.'

'Where's he coming from?'

'It's Prawalha. From Fulham.'

'Oh well you can forget that,' Freddie said effortfully as he hairpinned his foot up within reach and tugged on a plastic overshoe. 'Fulham Palace Road's solid – accident at the junction of Lillie Road. I'll do the necessary, if you like.' He met enquiring stares over his arm and said simply, 'Heard it on the car radio. On Classic FM Roadwatch. Don't you coppers know anything?'

Atherton grinned at Slider. 'I'd better see if I can turn Dr Prawalha back. He won't like coming all this way for nothing.'

'Right, all togged up,' Cameron said. 'Let's have a look.' He opened the door, stepped carefully over to the body and examined it in silence for a moment. He looked at his watch. 'I pronounce life extinct at – eight-oh-six p.m. Forehead still warm; warmth in the axilla. Death within the last three hours, probably two.'

'We know he was alive within the hour,' Slider said.

'Good. That's a help. I hate doing all that mental arithmetic with temperature readings. Well, not much doubt about the cause of death.' He examined the wound. 'Single clean incision from under the left ear across and downwards to the right. All the structures through to the anterior spinal ligament completely severed. Death due to anoxia caused by severing of the windpipe – more or less instantaneous.'

'More or less?'

'Depends on your point of view. Who can say how long an instant of terror lasts, subjectively?'

'You're a great comfort,' Slider complained. 'Anything else?'

'No superficial cuts or haggling around the wound – a sign of great determination or great strength, or both. No apparent bruising or other wounds. Clothing a little rumpled, but no signs of a struggle.'

He stood up and looked at the basins and mirrors. 'Now you see there, across the mirror, the typical spread pattern of droplets from the arterial pumper? He went straight through the left external carotid with the first cut. Lovely work.'

'So he was facing the mirror,' Slider said.

'Yes, or had his head slightly turned to the right, as you'd expect if it was a suicidal cut. And the blood in the basin and the smears on the rim suggest that he collapsed slightly forward and then hit the rim, or brushed against it, as he fell. Blood on the hands, under the nails, on the cuffs and sleeves, as you'd expect. Both hands. Two-handed action for extra penetration, perhaps. Blood on the cheek, too, but that's from resting in it on the floor.' He pondered.

'So it looks like suicide, then,' Atherton said from the doorway.

'The wound is consistent with a right-handed suicidal cut,' Freddie said. 'And he was right-handed, by the look of it. See the writer's bump on his right middle finger? Don't see so many of those in this world of the word-processor, but in my day every school-kid had a whopper of a one. He must have been a nice old-fashioned sort who liked to write longhand,' he finished regretfully, as though one fewer of those in the world was a real loss. 'On the other hand, it could have been a homicidal cut by someone standing behind him. No way of saying.'

'Doesn't the lack of other superficial cuts suggest homicide?' Atherton asked.

'Not necessarily. I've known a homicide case where the

29

murderer slashed away like a mad salami-slicer before he got through to the business parts. You never can tell. Deceased's quite a tall man, though, by the looks. If it was a homicidal cut, you want a tallish murderer. Or a short one with his own set of steps.'

'What about the weapon? There's a knife over there,' Slider said.

Freddie turned and looked. 'Yes. I'll have a closer look when it's been photographed, but from a cursory glance it's certainly consistent with the wound, and there's plenty of blood on it.'

'Yes,' said Slider, frowning thoughtfully. Freddie looked up and met his eyes, and an intelligence passed between them.

'There's something else,' Freddie said quietly, and reached for the corpse's jacket. 'Look here.' Slider looked. 'And here. You see what this is? Might be nothing, but—'

'As you say,' said Slider, 'but. Well, if that's all you can tell me for now,' he went on, straightening, 'I'd better strike while the iron's hot.'

Reinforcements were arriving all the time, and over Slider's shoulder Freddie saw the photographer shoving his way to the front. 'Ah, there you are, Sid. About time. I can't do anything until you've recorded this little lot for posterity.'

'Traffic's bloody terrible,' Sid grumbled. It was his usual mode of communication. 'And no wonder, with every bloody copper in West London hanging around in here. Why don't some of you lot go and do something useful for a change, and sort the bloody traffic out?'

'That's a new one,' Atherton said mildly. 'We generally get asked why we don't solve murders instead of harassing motorists.'

'Well come on, come on, let the dog see the rabbit,' Sid hustled his way into the doorway. 'Oh, bloody hell, it's a wet one! If I'd known I was going to go bloody paddling, I'd have brought me bloody wellies. I suppose you want this lot in bloody colour? Who's got the plastic shoes?'

Slider left them to it, and eased himself away from the door of the gents.

'What next, guv?' Atherton asked.

'I want to talk to Miss Parsons,' Slider said.

'I don't think you have any choice in the matter,' Atherton murmured. 'She's determined to talk to you.' He gestured with his head to where Fiona Parsons was lingering just to one side with her eyes fixed on Slider.

'I'll do her first, and then Philip Somers. And I want someone to talk to this Dorothy person, see if she can pin down some times. Oh, and see if you can get me a drink, will you?'

'A drink drink?'

'Some hope. What's the coffee like in the machine?'

'All right, if you don't swallow,' Atherton said.

Atherton moved away, and Slider allowed himself to be waylaid by Fiona Parsons. 'Do you have to leave him lying in there like that?' she asked indignantly, looking towards the rest-room door. 'I mean, in that place of all places. It seems so – unfeeling. Can't he at least be put somewhere more, well, dignified?'

'I'm afraid we can't move him for the time being,' Slider said gently. 'It's a matter of collecting evidence, you see. I really would like to have a word with you. Is there somewhere quiet nearby we can go and talk?'

'There's a dressing-room just along here,' she said. 'Will that do?'

The dressing-room was small, windowless and bare, containing a padded bench fixed to the wall, a broad shelf with a mirror over it for a dressing-table, and a small table

31

and hard chair. Fiona Parsons sat down on the bench, so Slider pulled out the chair and sat down facing her. It was no hardship to look at her. She was tall, athletic, and tanned, with a clear, freckled face and short, heavy fair hair cut in a bob and held off her face with a black velvet Alice band. She was wearing a severely cut, but very short-skirted pinstripe suit with three-quarter sleeves, over a plain white shirt with an open neck, from which her throat rose somehow fragile and vulnerable, encircled by a fine gold chain. Legs to rival Princess Di's in the sheerest of hose and plain, flat-heeled shoes; the manly cuffs on her jacket contrasted with a delicate gold watch on one wrist and a narrow gold bracelet on the other. Everything about her was a mixture of the businesslike and the feminine, which Slider assumed was deliberate, but was nonetheless intriguing.

There was no doubt that she had been shaken by the event. She was pale under her tan, her face wore the numb look of shock, her eyes were pink-rimmed, and she fiddled constantly with a handkerchief crumpled in her strong fingers. But she was determinedly under control, and looked straight into Slider's face with a directness that rather disturbed him. It reminded him of Joanna.

'This must have been a shock for you,' he began. 'I won't keep you too long, but I want to get an overall picture of the events of the evening, and I believe you are in charge of the programme. Am I right?'

'Except for Martin Fletcher – the editor. But he's more of a policy-maker. The day-to-day, hands-on running of things is down to me.'

Slider smiled. 'I've never been quite sure what a producer does.'

'The short answer is everything. But a programme like this is pretty easy compared to, say, drama, where you've got studio sets, outside shots, VT, actors, costumes, all the hoo-ha to keep track of. Properties alone can give you grey hairs – practicals, for instance, always go wrong. I started off as a properties buyer, so I know a bit about it. And actors are the very devil. But with *Question* you've got one set and five guests and that's that.'

'Yes, I see. So, then, can you tell me what time Mr Greatrex arrived?'

'Half past six. I went down to meet him at reception and took him up to green.'

'Green?'

'Sorry, the greenroom. Sometimes called the hospitality room.'

'Ah. For drinks?'

'And briefing,' she corrected with a faint smile. 'Not that Roger needed briefing, really, he's been on the show so often.'

'Has he?'

'Well, yes.' The question seemed to embarrass her for some reason. A slight pinkness appeared in her cheeks. 'He's one of our leading critics and columnists,' she said as if justifying herself. 'And besides that, he's such an all-round man, with so many interests, we've had him for several different topics. He's a great communicator, too. We always get a lively discussion going when we have him, that's why we—' Her voice faded and her face drained as she remembered. 'I can't believe he's dead. I can't believe he would do a thing like that. He was laughing with me only—' She stopped and shut her lips tight.

'He was quite happy when he arrived? Relaxed, nothing apparently on his mind?'

She nodded, as if speaking was too risky.

'Was he the first to arrive?' She nodded again. 'And you met all the guests in the same way?'

33

She took a deep breath. 'No, my assistant, Phil, went down for the others.'

'And they were all taken to the greenroom?'

'Except for Jack Mallet. Martin took him away for a private drink – politics, you know. Martin always has to be thinking about budgets. The others had drinks and sandwiches in the greenroom. Dame Barbara was the last to arrive. I didn't actually see her because I had to go back to the studio while Phil was fetching her.'

'Leaving them alone?'

'Gosh no, Dorothy – one of the production assistants – was there all the time, and Phil was in and out. It's an absolute rule that the guests mustn't be left alone at any time. It is a live show, you see.'

'So just before Dame Barbara arrived, you went to the studio. What time was that?'

'Oh, about sevenish I suppose,' she said vaguely. 'I don't know exactly.'

'And at that point Mr Greatrex was in the greenroom having drinks and sandwiches, and seemed quite happy and relaxed?' She nodded; her eyes shone suddenly, and she blinked hard. 'Did you go back to the greenroom?'

'No, I was busy in and around the studio then, until Dorothy came and told me—'

'Yes?' he prompted gently. 'What did she tell you?'

'It was awful. She was white as a sheet, and shaking. I couldn't understand what she was saying at first. I told her to calm down and speak slowly. Then she told me she met Phil in the corridor. She said he was covered in blood, and he just said to her, "Roger's dead. He's killed himself," and told her to run and fetch me.'

'And what did you do?'

'I said to her, "Are you sure?" or something like that. And

then I told her to telephone for the police while I went back to Phil.'

'You didn't tell her to call for an ambulance?'

'No.' She stared at him as though the question made no sense.

'You were quite sure he was dead, then?'

'Oh! But I—' She frowned, and shook her head, looking confused. 'Phil said he – Dorothy said he was covered in blood. Phil was, I mean. I didn't think—' She paused. 'It never occurred to me that he might still be alive. Phil's terribly sensible. I suppose I just took his word for it.'

Slider left it. 'So where was Phil when you found him?'

'Where Dorothy said, at the door of the men's room. He looked dreadful. He said, "Roger's in there. He's killed himself. He's c—"' She stopped, swallowed with a dry click, and tried again. 'He said, "He's cut his throat."' Her eyes filled again, and she shook her head slowly from side to side, staring sightlessly at the floor.

Slider saw she needed steadying, and gave her a practical question to answer. 'What time was it when Dorothy came to fetch you?'

She breathed deeply and managed to answer. 'I'm not sure to the minute. Twenty, twenty-five past seven, something like that. I didn't look at my watch.'

'And did you go into the men's room?'

'No. Phil said he'd been guarding the door, and no-one had been in except him, and no-one else must go in until the police came.'

Slider didn't comment on that. He asked, 'So you didn't actually know that it was Mr Greatrex in there?'

She licked her lips. 'I just – just looked in. For a second. Phil didn't want me to, but I had to.'

Bluebeard's Castle, Slider thought, not without sympathy.

Of course she had to. Wouldn't anyone? And this was her punishment, that she would never be able to erase from her memory the picture of what she saw.

'Can I go now?' she asked. 'I've still got a lot of sorting out to do for the programme.'

'What do you do about that?' Slider asked out of interest. 'It was supposed to be live, wasn't it?'

She put her hands to her cheeks in a curious, unfinished gesture, and then said almost absently, 'Oh, we have one in the can for emergencies.'

'Here's one I prepared earlier?' Slider said, trying to lighten the atmosphere.

'Yes.' She pulled herself together. 'Of course, it puts the schedule out. This *Question* was announced last week. But I suppose it will be all over the papers by tomorrow morning, and everyone will know why it was changed.' She looked into his face, bravely. 'Will someone have told his wife?'

'That will be dealt with by the local police. Someone will go round from the nearest station.'

'I see,' she said. 'Poor Caroline.' It was the most natural thing for anyone to say, but there was something about the way Miss Parsons said it that puzzled Slider a little, though he could not immediately decide what.

3

Brief Encounter

Philip Somers was a tall, gangling man in his twenties, dressed, as was the fashion, in clothes of various shades of beige that looked too big for him, and with floppy, toffee-coloured hair which kept slipping forward to hang like a pony's forelock over his brow, giving him a somewhat daft look. His cheeks were lardy with shock, which seemed with him to be taking the form of anger: his indeterminate-coloured eyes were glazed and shiny with it. Beyond that, or underneath it, Slider thought he looked drawn, as though from a long illness or constant pain: there were those deep, fine creases like hairline cuts under his eyes that you see in people who have been sick unto death in their recent past.

He was sitting on the bench in another of those spartan dressing-rooms, a red blanket draped over his shoulders, and his stockinged feet set one on top of the other, as if they felt vulnerable without their coverings.

'When am I going to get my shoes back?' he demanded as soon as he saw Slider. 'It's ridiculous, taking them away.'

'I've told him, sir, that we didn't want him to make bloody

footmarks which might confuse the investigation,' Morley said over his head.

'Well, when can I have them back?'

'I've brought you a cup of coffee,' Atherton intervened, holding it out. 'I hope you take sugar – I had to guess.'

'Yes – thanks – but—'

'I'm Detective Inspector Slider, and this is Detective Sergeant Atherton. I'd just like to talk to you about finding Mr Greatrex.' Even a cursory inspection showed that Somers had a great deal of blood about him. There was blood on his hands, under his fingernails, in his ears and around the edge of his face, flecks of it in his front hair, a smear under his jaw, and stains on his sleeves, on the lapels of his jacket, and on the front of his trousers. 'You seem to have got yourself into a bit of a mess.'

'That was lifting him up to see if he was dead. And I must have wiped my hands down my front.'

'You seem to have blood on your face, too.'

'I suppose I must have put my hands to my face – the shock, or something.' He imitated the gesture. 'I tried to wipe my face on my hanky. They wouldn't let me wash. You try to do the right thing, and this is all the thanks you get!'

'I won't keep you very long. There's just a few things I want to ask you while it's all fresh in your mind. I'm trying to build up a picture of Mr Greatrex's exact movements this evening.'

'Well, it's no good asking me,' Somers said petulantly. 'I don't know where he went. I was the one who went to look for him.'

'He was lost? Missing?'

'Not really lost, of course, but he wasn't where he was supposed to be. You see, everyone was asked to come at six forty-five, but they all arrived at different times, and Dame

Barbara was late. Typical! I mean, the only woman, so naturally I wanted to get her to make-up first, but I couldn't hoosh her off the moment she arrived, so I asked Roger if he'd go first, since he was the first to arrive – for a wonder – and he never has more than just the shine taken off. He said okay, and I said I'd take him in a sec, as soon as Fiona came back, because I couldn't leave Dame Barbara alone, not when she'd just arrived, and bloody Dorothy had disappeared again. But Roger said not to bother, he knew the way all right, and he'd go on his own, so I said okay, and he went.'

'What time was that?'

'Just after seven, I suppose. Well, anyway, about ten past he hadn't come back and I thought I'd better go and fetch him, because if he got chatting to Sylvia – the make-up designer – he'd be there all night – she talks like a train – and time was getting on. So I went up to make-up—'

'Up?'

'Oh, yes, didn't I say? There's been a burst pipe and our make-up room can't be used because the electrics aren't safe, so we were using number five upstairs. It's all right, I had told Roger, he knew where to go. The layout's exactly the same on five as down here, he understood that, he only had to go up one floor.'

'I see. So you went upstairs to make-up,' Slider prompted.

'Yes, and Sylvia said he'd never turned up. Then I got worried.'

'Worried? Why worried? What were you afraid had happened?'

'Nothing, I don't mean that,' he said irritably. 'But he was one of our panellists. You can't go mislaying your panellists like that, not on a live show. And I shouldn't have let him go alone. So I went looking for him.' His mouth pulled down. 'If I'd known–! Well, I didn't really know where to look. I popped my head round a few doors, and then I thought of the loo. We had one guest once who was so nervous he got sick and I showed him to the loo and then I couldn't get him out, he just kept throwing up. Of course, I didn't think Roger was nervous like that. But anyway, I went and looked and just pushed the door open on the off-chance and – and there he was.'

'That was the nearest lavatory to the greenroom, was it?'

'Yes – well, on this floor, anyway.'

'What does that mean?'

'The gents and ladies are alternate, on alternate floors,' Somers said, and seeing he had not explained himself sufficiently, began again. 'On this floor, if you turn right out of green and go to staircase four, there's a ladies by the lift, and immediately above it, on the fifth floor, there's a gents. But if you turn left out of green and go to staircase five, there's a gents on this floor and a ladies above. D'you follow me?'

As far as I'd like to, Slider thought. 'And which way is the make-up room?'

'From the greenroom? You turn right, and it's past staircase four and on the right.'

'So if Mr Greatrex had been going up to the make-up room, he would have passed a men's room upstairs, on the next floor.'

'Yes, I suppose so.' Somers did not seem to see where that was leading. 'But I told you, Sylvia said he never arrived at make-up.'

'Quite so. But considering where he ended up, perhaps he never actually meant to go there.'

'Oh,' said Somers. 'Well, I don't know. Maybe he just had to *go*, you know,' he added delicately, 'and decided to go first.'

Slider moved on. 'What time was it when you found Mr Greatrex?'

'About twenty past, I suppose. I didn't look at my watch, but I'd been looking for him for about ten minutes.'

'You opened the door, and saw him – what, lying down?'

'Yes, of course. What do you think, he was dancing a jig?'

'Lying down how?'

'He was crumpled up, more or less face down.'

'And what did you do?'

'There was blood everywhere. I knew he was dead straight-away, but I had to be sure.' His voice was toneless. 'So I went and lifted him up. I thought at first maybe he'd slashed his wrists, but when I took him by the shoulders to turn him over, his head – his head sort of flopped and – and rolled backwards—' He put his hands to his face, dragging at his cheeks with his knuckles. 'It was horrible. Like a mouth opening. I dropped him and got out as fast as I could. I thought I was going to be sick. I wanted to run and run, but as soon as I was outside I realised I had to stay there and stop anyone else going in. But I had to get help. I didn't know what to do. And then Dorothy came round the corner, and I told her to run and find Fiona and tell her that Roger Greatrex had killed himself, and to call the police.' He seemed suddenly exhausted now, and looked greyly at Slider as though asking for mercy.

Slider pressed on. 'So you stayed there outside the door until the police arrived? You didn't go back in?' He shook his head. 'And no-one else went in?'

'No-one. When Fiona came, she wanted to see him. I tried to stop her, but she insisted, so I made her just look from the door. One quick look was enough.'

'Just one more thing, Mr Somers,' Slider said, leaning forward confidentially, letting his hands dangle between his knees. 'It's rather important. When you first went in, where was the knife?'

'The knife?' Somers said blankly. Exhaustion or prevarication?

'Yes, the knife. Whereabouts was it? Under the body, beside it, where?'

'I don't know. I didn't see it. I didn't see any knife.'

'You must have seen it, Mr Somers,' Slider said, giving him a chance, 'because you threw it across the room. Or did you kick it out of the way? An automatic gesture of revulsion, perhaps – quite understandable in the circumstances.'

Somers looked frightened. 'I didn't touch it. I tell you I didn't see any knife!'

Slider straightened up. 'Very well, Mr Somers, thank you. I'll leave you in peace for a bit. But I will want to talk to you again later.'

Outside, Atherton said, 'What was all that about?'

'I had my doubts from the beginning about suicide, but I wasn't sure.'

'And now you are?'

'Somers says he didn't touch the knife. He's quite forceful about it. So what was it doing on the other side of the room?'

Atherton thought it out. 'Greatrex didn't cut his throat over there, because the blood's all by the basins.'

'Right.'

'Maybe he threw the knife away after he made the cut?'

Slider shook his head. 'With a cut like that, he'd have collapsed instantly. He'd have dropped the knife where he stood.'

'Well, let's say it's likely. So – either someone else went in there and moved the knife – or Somers is lying and he moved it—'

'Or the murderer threw the knife aside after making the fatal cut,' Slider concluded.

'That sounds logical, captain. But you said you had doubts from the beginning?'

'The basin was full of soapy water. If Greatrex was standing facing the mirror with a bowl of soapy water before him, what do you suppose he was doing?'

'You think he was disturbed while washing his hands?'

'Only an obsessive would wash his hands before killing himself; and someone that obsessive would surely empty the basin first. I think someone came up behind him, yes.'

'I wonder why the murderer didn't pull the plug out? It would have made it look more like suicide.'

'I don't suppose he even thought about it. I think he had other things on his mind,' Slider said.

'Specifically?'

'There was something else that Freddie pointed out to me – there was blood on the *inside* of Greatrex's top inside pocket, and a corresponding smear on his shirt. Someone with bloody hands was looking for something in that pocket. I wonder if they found it?'

Atherton was thinking. 'Well, if it was murder, there'll be no shortage of suspects.'

'You mean all that lot upstairs?'

'No, I mean everyone he's ever given a bad review. He was a critic, don't forget – the most hated creature on the planet, after the housefly.'

WDC Swilley had never been self-conscious about her height, feeling it was an unalloyed advantage to be able to see over the heads of a crowd and get things down off shelves without needing a chair. There were occasions when close encounters with members of her own sex made her wonder how they coped with life way down there, and this was one of them. Being shut in a dressing-room with Dorothy Hammond, Production Assistant, made her afraid to move too quickly for fear of crushing her.

43

Dorothy Hammond was a tiny person with a neat, sharp face behind large gold-wire-rimmed glasses. Her dark hair was cut short and layered so that it looked like soft feathers; her mouth was curving and tender; her little pointed fingers were tipped with pale-pink nails that looked as unused as a baby's.

She didn't seem particularly upset by the events of the evening – more cheeringly stimulated by the novelty. 'Well, I'm sorry to have to say it,' she said briskly, 'but I didn't like Roger, and as far as I'm concerned he'll be no great loss. Not that I'd wish him ill, of course, but—' She let it hang. 'I couldn't be more surprised that he's killed himself, though. I wouldn't have thought he was the type.'

'Is there a type?' Norma asked.

'Oh, I suppose that sounds a stupid thing to say,' she said, not as if she believed it. 'But he wasn't a bit depressed, from what I saw – quite his usual chirpy self. And I'd have thought he liked himself too much to want to deprive the world of his wonderful presence.'

'Conceited, was he?'

'Oh, one of those who think that anyone who isn't a celebrity is dirt. Calls you darling all the time, but can't be bothered to remember your name or say please or thank you. Always arrives late, never mind who he's inconveniencing – leaves his rubbish around for other people to clear up. I had no time for him. I don't like Sandal much either, but at least he knows his manners. I mean, I don't expect them to fawn over me, but I do expect common courtesy. I could never understand what—' She stopped herself abruptly, and as Norma looked enquiringly at her, she blushed a little, and said hurriedly, 'I suppose it was suicide? I mean, I didn't see the body, but they say he cut his throat, is that right?'

'His throat was cut, yes,' Norma said.

'That's a rotten way to go,' Dorothy said. 'No wonder Phil

44

was in such a state. I've never seen so much blood. I thought he'd cut himself. It was on his face and everything.'

'There was an awful lot of blood around,' Norma said. 'His throat was cut right through.'

Dorothy looked away. 'Well, I'm sorry. I wouldn't wish that on anyone,' she said. 'But really, I would never have thought he was suicidal. Everyone else on the programme, maybe.'

'What d'you mean?'

'Oh, I knew it was going to be a bad evening before we started. Everyone was in a rotten temper. Having Roger Greatrex and Sandal Palliser on the same panel was a big mistake in my opinion. I suppose Martin – Martin Fletcher, the editor – was hoping for a verbal punch-up to boost the ratings, but to my mind you don't take that kind of risk on a live programme. I think that's why Fiona was in such a state.'

'What do you mean, a state?'

'She was like a cat on hot bricks all day. Speak to her and she wouldn't hear you the first three times, or else she'd jump like a kangaroo. And she couldn't speak a civil word to Phil. *He* didn't want Roger on the show at all. It was his job to book the guests, and when it came up I heard him saying to her something about, if she wanted Roger she should phone him herself because he didn't want it on his head, and she said don't be stupid, all you've got to do is pass the message, it isn't up to you, and he said if it was up to him he wouldn't have that man on the same planet, let alone the same programme, and they'd all live to regret it.'

'What do you suppose he meant by that?'

'Well, Roger and Sandal hated each other. Everyone knows that.'

'Because of this debate in the newspapers?'

'What, that thing about the arts?' Dorothy laughed derisively. 'God, no! That's a put-up job to boost circulation.

They're both on the same side, really. Sandal might pretend to be Essex Man, but he's as middle-class and elitist as Roger. You couldn't put a fag-paper between them. They'd both be horrified at the idea of the Royal Opera House losing its subsidy.'

'Their livelihood depends on that sort of thing?' Norma suggested blandly. 'It's a gravy train, the whole arts bit, isn't it?'

'You're telling me! Well, not Glyndebourne, because that's private, but the rest of it's a disgrace. The Opera House soaks up millions in subsidies every year, but let some inner-city school ask for a couple of hundred to mend the roof, and they're told there's no money in the kitty.'

Norma took a tug at the reins, before she was galloped away with. 'So what is the trouble between them, then, if it isn't that?'

Dorothy looked blank for a moment. 'Oh. I don't know exactly. Something personal, I don't know what. All I do know is they can't be trusted not to go for each other. I mean, they even had a row tonight while I was out of the room for a second.'

'What about?'

'I didn't really hear anything, only the raised voices, and of course they stopped as soon as I came in. All I heard was as I opened the door, Roger was saying something like, "He doesn't even know what day it is," and then Sandal said something I didn't hear, and Roger said, "It's none of your bloody business anyway," and then they saw me and stopped. But Roger's face was really red, and Sandal looked like thunder.'

'Who else was there at the time?'

'No-one,' she said. 'You see, Fiona brought Roger up and left him with me, and then Phil brought Sandal in, and we

46

four were there for about ten minutes, chatting, until reception rang to say Sir John had arrived. So Phil went down to meet him, and I – well, I just popped out for a minute to the loo, and when I came back, I heard them at it.'

'Do you think Roger Greatrex was really upset by the quarrel?'

'What, enough to want to kill himself?' she asked. 'No, I'd have said he was more mad than upset. Like I said, I couldn't have been more surprised that he did it. The last time I saw him, he was looking really cheerful – like the cat that got the cream, really, which was his usual expression.'

'What time was that?'

'About seven, I suppose. I was just going back to green, and he must have just come out. I asked if I could get him anything – we're not supposed to let them wander about on their own, really, in case they get lost – but he said he was going up to make-up and he knew the way, and he made it quite plain he didn't want me around so I left it at that and went back to green.'

'And he went up the stairs?'

'I suppose so. I didn't watch him go. He was heading in the right direction.'

Norma nodded. 'And what about Sandal Palliser? Do you think he was upset by the quarrel?'

'It's hard to say. He doesn't show his feelings really – always polite on the outside, whatever's happening. You can't really fathom him.' Something obviously struck her. 'Oh, but he—'

'But he what?' Norma prompted when she didn't go on.

Dorothy blushed again. 'It's nothing really. But after I passed Roger in the corridor, after I went back to the green-room, Sandal said he had to go out and make a phone call. I said he could use the phone in there, but he said he needed a bit of privacy, and he had his mobile with him, and he'd only be a minute. Well, I couldn't stop him, could I? And he said he'd only be a minute. And after five minutes I went out to look for him – and that's when I met Phil, all covered with blood.'

'You didn't see Sandal, then?'

'Well, no. But he was there with the rest when I went back up after phoning the police.'

It was, Norma thought, like one of those tiresome farces where the characters keep going in and out of different doors and just missing each other, for no apparent reason except to further the misunderstandings of the plot.

Though the post mortem did not promise any great surprises, there was the usual crowd of onlookers with their hands in their pockets and the Trebor's Extra Strong Mints energetically a-suck, just in case. Lying on its back, the corpse didn't look quite so bad. Slider looked into the face, and examined the hands. Roger Greatrex had been tall, lean, blue-eyed, and with artfully tousled, possibly streaked fair hair. He had a long, rather melancholy face, prominent nose, high cheekbones, a wide, thin-lipped mouth, a strong chin. His hands were long, large-jointed and veined – that's where the age always showed, Slider thought – his nails were well-kept, and he wore no rings.

'Would you call him good-looking? Attractive to women?' Slider asked generally.

'Except the mouth,' Atherton answered him. 'That's a bad mouth. From what I can see of the teeth, they weren't too good either. Didn't take care of them when he was a lad.'

'His clothes are expensive,' Slider said. And stylish: a light-biscuit-coloured double-breaster, hanging fashionably loose from the bony shoulders, trousers with pleats and turn-ups, brown moccasins – expensive but not well-polished. All of course were now spoiled with blood – the tie was so stained he had to turn it over to see the design: a blue and lilac Matisse, very 'in'. Along with the streaked hair, it spoke of a man for whom appearance was important, a man who wanted to be younger than his age.

Freddie was preparing to undress the body, and Mackay was standing by with the evidence bags, having tossed Anderson for it and lost. 'I say, guv,' Mackay said suddenly, 'the dirty bugger's left his flies undone.'

'Fly,' said Atherton automatically. 'Flies are what you have in theatres or on dead meat.'

'Well, what d'you call him?' Mackay protested.

'Was that how he was found?' Slider asked Freddie.

'No-one here's touched it, if that's what you mean,' Freddie said.

'Probably doesn't mean anything,' Slider said. 'He wouldn't be the first man to forget.'

'Those pleat-fronted trousers hang better anyway, so you don't notice so much,' Atherton said.

Freddie drew open the inside top pocket with forceps. 'See what I mean about the bloodstains?' he said to Slider. 'I'll cut some pieces of the fabric for the lab.'

'If someone's had a hand in there, it's just possible we may get a fingerprint,' Slider said. 'Can you cut the whole outside of the pocket away?'

Freddie grunted and complied, and removed from the exposed pocket a very battered leather wallet. It contained a number of credit and other cards, two hundred and fifteen pounds in cash, and three wrapped condoms.

'Not robbery from the person, then,' Slider said. 'What's that?' A piece of card, about four inches by five, had fallen out from behind the wallet onto the corpse's chest. Freddie passed it over.

It was blank on one side; on the other side a plain black cross was embossed at the top in the centre, and below it was printed in Letraset:

When the righteous turneth away from his righteousness, shall he live? In his trespass that he hath trespassed and in his sin that he hath sinned, in them shall he die. Ezek. 18:24.

'Very nice,' said Atherton.

'Ezekiel,' Slider said. 'Nice warlike book – lots of smiting and swords and wrath-of-the-Lord.'

'You wouldn't have thought he'd be religious,' Mackay commented. 'Not dressed like that.'

'What's dress got to do with it?' Anderson asked.

'Well, he's not got sandals on, or a beard.'

'He doesn't have to be religious, anyway,' Anderson said.

'Then why's he carrying that card?' Mackay said with triumphant logic.

'Hasn't it occurred to you,' Atherton said kindly, 'that perhaps the murderer put it there?'

'If he was murdered,' Mackay returned. 'There's no blood on it, anyway.'

'Maybe he had gloves on. Or it could have been sent to him earlier as a threat.'

'So why would he carry it around in his pocket?'

Atherton rolled his eyes and left Mackay to his triumph.

'Send the wallet and the card for fingerprinting too,' Slider said. There was nothing else in the inside pocket. The other pockets revealed nothing of more interest than a used handkerchief, a handful of change, a stick of lip salve, a key-ring with car and house keys on it, a two-week-old tube ticket from South Kensington, and a very crumpled small paper bag containing five Pontefract cakes, two of which had stuck to the paper.

'There aren't many places you can still get sweets weighed out and put in a bag,' Slider said. 'I wonder how long he's had these?'

'Probably prophylactic,' Atherton said. 'He looks the type. Muddy complexion – dead giveaway. No personal things, you notice. No letters, photographs, anything like that.'

'Not everyone carries them,' Slider said.

'But if they do, they often carry them in the wallet or the inside pocket. Maybe that's what the pocket-fumbler was after.'

'It's possible,' Slider said. The rest of the clothes were of no particular interest, except that the socks had holes in them, and the toenails were long and not over-clean.

'I'm liking this man less as we go along,' Atherton complained.

'Maybe he had a touch of arthritis and couldn't bend down that far,' Slider suggested kindly. Atherton snorted derision.

There was a moment's respectful silence, however, as the underpants were taken off. 'Well, that accounts for his popularity with women,' Anderson said at last, rather wistfully.

'No wonder he wore pleated trousers,' said Mackay.

'You'd have thought he'd have trouble balancing,' Anderson said. 'I mean, with all that forward drag—'

Freddie was examining the equipment in question with rather closer attention than might be thought necessary. 'Look at this, Bill.'

'It's not easy to look anywhere else,' Slider complained.

'No, but look – here, and here. Smears of blood.'

'That's more than I need to know.'

Freddie snatched back the purple bikini briefs which Mackay was in the act of bagging. 'Yes, look, and here, on the waistband. Now what do you make of that?'

'I'd rather not make anything of it,' Slider said. 'But if you force me to, I'd say somebody with bloody hands has handled it. Please don't ask me why.' To Mackay, 'Bag the pants and the trousers separately. We might get a lift off one or other of them.'

'It's more evidence that it was murder and not suicide, though,' Atherton commented. 'Unless Philip Somers – or somebody else – found him dead and interfered with the body.'

'Yes, I'm afraid there's always that possibility,' Slider said.

'If somebody was looking for something in his inside pocket and didn't find it,' said Atherton, 'maybe he went on to look in his underpants as well. No, scrub that, it's stupid. What would a man keep in his underpants instead of his pocket?'

'Maybe he wanted to check if he's Jewish,' Mackay said. There was a short silence. 'He was circumcised.'

'So are lots of people,' Atherton said. 'Anyway, he's a blue-eyed blond. What's to check?'

'Here's another little problem to add to the collection,' said Freddie, who had been re-examining the trousers through a magnifying glass. 'There doesn't seem to be any blood on the tag of the zipper.'

'So maybe he had just forgotten to close it,' Atherton said.

'And chummy just couldn't resist a peek?' Mackay suggested. 'If he was famous for the size of his salami—'

'I'll make it the first thing I ask everyone who knew him,' Atherton promised.

4

Definition of Character

Detective Superintendent Honeyman was a small, tidy man with a pale face and a repressed expression, which always made Slider think of Richmal Crompton's William scrubbed clean and pressed into his Eton suit for a party he didn't want to go to. Honeyman parted what was left of his hair low down just above his right ear and drew it carefully over the bald top of his head in a Robert Robinson to meet up with the side-linings on the left. Did he really believe it would convince onlookers that there was a full head of hair all present and correct? Slider pondered. Or was it a more complex form of self-delusion, or even self-hypnosis carried out in front of the looking-glass? It was very dark, shiny hair, and Honeyman oiled it into place, so that from the front it looked rather as though he was wearing a crash helmet. The worst thing about it was trying not to look at it; concentrating on the effort meant Slider frequently missed things that Honeyman said.

'Ah, Slider, there you are,' he said. He had a small, high, rather fluting voice, which must have been a terrible handicap to him when he was a uniformed PC out on the wicked streets of London – even if villains were more polite in those days. 'This Greatrex business.'

'Yes, sir,' Slider said, fixing his eyes on the point between Honeyman's eyes. This meant looking down rather, since Honeyman standing up was shorter than him; and perhaps subconsciously Honeyman compensated by tilting his head back so that he could look at his subordinate from under his eyelids, like a small mistress of the house trying to subdue a tall housemaid by the power of personality.

'I suppose it's suicide,' Honeyman said hopefully.

'I don't think so, sir,' Slider said, and an expression of dissatisfaction overspread the little features.

'Oh dear. And why not, pray?' Slider told him about the knife, and Honeyman's suffering lightened a little. 'I can't see your difficulty. It is possible deceased threw the knife away himself, isn't it?'

'Possible but unlikely, sir. The pathologist says death would have been instantaneous.'

'Ah, the pathologist. Expert witness and all that. Well, personally, I wouldn't hang a dog on scientific evidence. I think we need more than that, don't you?'

'There's the religious text card, which sounds rather like a threat.'

'No reason to think it wasn't his.'

'And the bloodmarks on the inside of the pocket—'

'Well, deceased could have made those too – fumbling for something in the confusion of the moment.'

'—and on the underpants.'

'Oh dear, I don't like what you're suggesting. You think the body has been interfered with?'

'It certainly does seem so to me, sir.'

'Still, even if someone else did go through the pockets and – et cetera – it doesn't rule out suicide.'

54

'He was remarkably cheerful that evening, apparently.'

'Ah well, they often are, you know. And in any case, a mood can change in a moment.'

'But appearances are more on the side of homicide than suicide. There are too many anomalies for me to be happy with writing it down.'

'Oh dear,' Honeyman said again, and lapsed into silence like an overstretched personal computer. Slider waited. At last the screen flickered again. 'It's a tricky one. I don't know that we would be justified in setting a full-scale investigation in train on the strength of your not feeling happy about it.'

He made it sound like PMT, Slider thought. 'Well, sir, it's still a suspicious death. There has to be some sort of investigation.'

Honeyman looked at him sharply. 'I'm quite well aware of that, thank you.' It was like being savaged by a goldfish. 'But I can't let you monopolise all this manpower indefinitely. There's a crime wave out there on the streets, you know, and I am responsible to the public for the way we use our resources.'

'There are an awful lot of people to interview, sir,' Slider said. 'It's important that we find some witnesses before memories cloud.'

'Oh, yes, yes, yes,' Honeyman said testily, 'but it's ten to one that it *was* suicide, and the press will be following every detail of this one, and the BBC. We can't afford to look foolish, and be accused of throwing money about recklessly.'

'If it turns out later that it wasn't suicide, we'll look even worse,' Slider pointed out. Honeyman gave him a goaded look. 'Greatrex must have been somewhere in the building during those ten minutes, sir, and somebody must have seen him. There were hundreds of people wandering about. And he was a striking-looking man.'

'Oh, very well,' Honeyman said disagreeably. 'I'll let you have the extra men for a week, but if you haven't come up with something by then, I shall have to cut you down to just your own squad. I'm perfectly certain in my own mind,' he added pathetically, 'that it was suicide, so do make it your first priority to look for a note. There's bound to be one somewhere – he wouldn't have missed the chance to tell his public all about his state of mind. These media-types are notoriously self-obsessed, they like nothing better than to talk about themselves. And,' he added severely, 'they blow their own little problems up out of all proportion. Can't see the wood for the trees. I can't waste my budget on that sort of thing. I'm answerable to the Commissioner, you know.'

Talk about pots and kettles, Slider thought glumly, trudging dutifully out.

'Things always look better in daylight,' Atherton said, sitting on his desk and contemplating the shine on his shoes. 'There was something almost surreal about the TVC. I began to think I was in something by Stendhal.'

The CID room was crowded with the extra personnel so begrudged by Honeyman. Mills, on loan with other members of Carver's team, was clipping his nails into the wastepaper basket. 'What about the post mortem, then, eh? Is that right, they found bloody fingermarks on his old man?'

'Why do you men always have to bring everything down to the lowest level?' Norma said, busy writing.

'I could explain it to you, if you'd like to meet me after,' Mills offered.

'Oi! There's a queue, you know,' Atherton said. 'Get thee behind me.'

'In your dreams,' Norma said, going on calmly writing. 'Anyway, what about that nice woman you were going out

56

with, Jim? I thought you might be going to settle down at last.'

'I do settle down,' Atherton protested. 'Just not in the same place every time.'

McLaren, who was reading the *Sun* and eating a bacon roll, called across, 'Eh, Atherton, have you ever had two women at the same time?'

'At the same time as what?' Atherton enquired.

Unfortunately, McLaren didn't know a rhetorical question when he heard one and answered, which made Norma look up at last, severely. 'You disgust me, Maurice,' she said.

'Oh he has,' Atherton agreed. 'Certainly with everyone here.'

Mills finished snipping, put down the bin and dusted off his hands. 'Does the guv'nor really think it's murder?' he asked Atherton. 'I can't see it myself.'

'He has a feeling about it,' Atherton said. He remembered the Radek case, when it all looked sewn up, except that Slider felt something was wrong about it. 'When he's got one of those, it's best to go along with it.'

'If the guv'nor says it's Christmas, we all sing carols,' said Hewson, another of Carver's team.

'He's not like that,' said Norma, beating Mills to it.

'They're all like that,' Cook, Hewson's partner, contradicted. 'It's just some show it sooner than others. You'll find out.'

'I've been with him for six years,' Norma said firmly. 'He's the least dogmatic man I've ever worked with.'

'It's there underneath all the same,' Hewson said, unconcernedly, looking over McLaren's shoulder at the page three tits. 'Stands to reason. A guv'nor's a guv'nor, spelt gee-oh-dee. You can't get away from it.'

'I've met a lot of people in my life,' Norma said icily. 'You two are not amongst them.'

57

Cook looked annoyed. 'Don't give me that. Are you telling me—'

'Brass at twelve o'clock,' Mills warned as Slider appeared in the doorway, and a sudden silence fell.

Slider looked round curiously, caught Atherton's minute shrug, and strode front and centre. 'Right, the Greatrex case. Suspicious death. Let's have some views. I know you're for suicide,' he added to Mills, 'in which you have the great and good on your side. Mr Honeyman sees no reason to suppose it's anything else. But if it was suicide, someone at least interfered with the body. Either it was Philip Somers, and he's not admitting it; or someone was there before him, and is keeping quiet about it.'

'To me, it's murder,' Norma said. 'There was definitely something funny going on. I had all sorts of hints from Dorothy Hammond—'

'Oh, women are always gossiping, trying to stir up trouble,' Mackay said easily.

Norma sailed straight over him, '—about a row between Fiona Parsons and Philip Somers over whether Greatrex should even be on the show or not; and then about a row between Greatrex and Palliser. And Palliser left the greenroom just after Greatrex, on a flimsy excuse.'

'My money's on Somers,' Atherton said. 'If you're covered in blood, what better way to explain it than to be the one to discover the corpse?'

'I can't see it,' Mills said. 'You'd have to be pretty cool to think of that, and carry it off, and the last thing he was when I arrived was cool. He was nearly hysterical.'

'He struck me as so wet, he'd never have the balls to cut someone's throat,' Mackay said.

'He's still got to be favourite,' Anderson put in. 'He's the only one with blood on him. And he was out of sight for the crucial ten minutes, by his own admission looking for Greatrex.'

'But Dorothy Hammond said he didn't want Greatrex on the show at all,' Norma said.

'Because he hated him, maybe.'

'But if he wanted the chance to kill him, he'd have argued to have him on, not the other way,' Norma said.

'If it was planned ahead,' Anderson said. 'Maybe he just hated him so much it came over him on an impulse, and he was left trying to cover up the best way he knew.'

'That sounds very nice,' Slider said, 'except for the knife. If it was impulse, why did he bring the knife with him?'

'We've got to try to tie the knife in with someone,' Mackay said.

'Oh, did you think of that all by yourself?' Atherton murmured.

'It could have been Somers, it could have been Palliser, it could have been Fiona Parsons for that matter,' McLaren said. 'It could have been anybody at all – if it was anybody.'

'McLaren's right,' Slider said into the stunned silence. 'The difficulty is that we don't know where Greatrex went or what he did in the missing fifteen or twenty minutes. We've got a situation where an unknown number of people are wandering around a large building, and nobody knows where anybody is at any given moment. Nobody's accountable, nobody can be pinned down to exact times. Our particular problem is that until we can find some witnesses, we can't prove it was murder and not suicide, and we can't get the manpower to do the sort of investigation we need to find witnesses until we can show that it was murder.'

'Catch twenty-two,' Mackay said triumphantly.

'So we're going to have to start at the other end,' Slider said, 'with motive. We've got to find out all about this man

Greatrex, who loved him and who hated him, who wanted him dead – and if it turns out that he hated himself most of all, well, so be it.' He gazed round them at his blandest. 'I'm not dogmatic.'

Norma and Atherton exchanged a look. Was it possible he had heard?

'And in the meantime, we've got to talk to everyone who was in the building at the time, and that includes all the members of the audience of the show – telephone work there for everyone with bad feet or a poor excuse. And I want two teams to comb the immediate area around the exits from the building for anything that might have been dumped, because if it wasn't Somers, somebody must have had some blood-stained clothing to account for. Start outside and work your way back in. Mills, as you were in at the beginning, I'm going to make you office manager. Right, there's a lot to organise, so let's get busy.'

The room broke into a buzz of talk and movement, amongst which one voice came out clearly saying, 'Overtime all round, then.' That was Honeyman's concern, of course; but Slider had a moment of doubt as he looked at the pleased faces following the remark. For when all was said and done, the fact that the body had been interfered with did not mean it wasn't suicide, and if that's what it turned out to be, Honeyman was not going to be happy with Slider. Slider liked to keep Det Sups happy – that was the route to a long and untroubled life.

Slider had long wanted to see the inside of one of those houses in Pelham Place, and Roger Greatrex turned out to have lived in one of them.

'Ah, I know where he got the liquorice,' Atherton said in sudden enlightenment as they approached the wedge of South

Kensington Station along Harrington Road. 'There's an old-fashioned sweet shop just outside the station, by the Thurloe Street exit. They do sherbet lemons and acid drops and toasted teacakes and all that sort of tackle.'

'I'm so glad we've cleared up that point,' Slider said. 'What's the wife's name?'

'Caroline, formerly – and I ask you to believe this – a Miss Fiennes-Marjoribanks, daughter of Viscount Chirnside.'

'Money?'

'Dunno. Somebody has, though, to live in Pelham Place. I suppose a media honey like Greatrex must have been pulling down big biccies, but I'd be surprised if it was enough for a house like that. Be sure to wipe your boots before entering. And curtsey while you're thinking. It saves time.'

The house – white, elegant, shapely – smiled in the sunshine across its railings and semi-basement with a century and a half of assured beauty. Slider sighed with satisfaction. The terrace led the eye away kindly and then bent to the supple curve of Pelham Crescent, in all the loveliness of perfect proportion. Ah, they didn't write 'em like that any more. 'Didn't they use one of these for the outside of the house in *Upstairs Downstairs?*' Slider asked.

'Before my time,' Atherton said cruelly. They trod up the steps, and he ostentatiously wiped his hand down his trousers before pulling the bell. Caroline Greatrex received them in the drawing-room, which was chilly with the spaciousness and quiet of real wealth. Atherton, disposing himself elegantly on a brocaded settle, took a quick inventory of the age and value of the appurtenances. It reminded him of that line from the *Goon Show* – the curtains were drawn, but the furniture was real. Though in this case, it was the widow who was drawn – and pale, even through her perfectly applied make-up. Her hair, ash-blonde over natural ash, was arranged as carefully

61

as if she had been to the salon that morning, in the rather bouffant page-boy bob that a certain section of Society favours, drawn back in a curve to show the ears, decorated with large pearl studs. Three rows of pearls around the neck, and if they weren't real, Atherton thought, he was a monkey's uncle. A black roll-neck sweater showed off the pearls; below that she wore a grey-and-white-fleck tweed skirt and black court shoes. All very plain and suitable; and no other jewellery except a rather ugly collection of rings on the wedding finger: a broad gold band, a three-stone diamond engagement hoop, a diamond-studded eternity ring, and a keeper of thin gold with clasped hands filled all the space between knuckle and first joint. She had ugly hands, Atherton thought, stubby and pale with fleshy joints, and the sort of nails that shouldn't be drawn attention to, and were painted bright scarlet.

'May I offer you sherry?' she asked. 'Or are you not allowed? I never know whether that's pure fiction or not.'

'Thank you,' Slider said. He liked to give them something to do if they were likely to be ill at ease, and she ought to be, though she was outwardly completely composed. The English upper classes in adversity, Slider thought: there's no-one like 'em. As a farmer's son in a wealthy county he had had more experience of them than Atherton, for all the latter's urbanity. Town gentry are not like the old county families.

When she had brought their glasses and sat down opposite them, Atherton could see what Slider had already noted, that her composure was only outward, and liked her better for it. Death should never be a matter of no moment, he felt. She turned her sherry glass round slowly in her fingers, and at rest her mouth trembled. She looked much older than the corpse of Roger Greatrex had done – sixty, perhaps, to his fifty – but then death smoothes away lines while bereavement adds them.

'I'm sorry to have to trouble you at such a time,' Slider said, 'and I'm very grateful to you for seeing me.'

'That's quite all right,' she said bleakly. 'You have to do your job, I understand that.'

'I have to ask you first if you know of any reason why your husband might have wanted to do away with himself? Was he depressed? Unhappy? Worried about anything?'

'No, not at all,' she said firmly. 'I can't believe that he would do such a thing. He was at the height of his career, he had no financial worries. In fact just lately he has been particularly cheerful.'

'Why is that?'

She looked chilly. 'I have no idea. He did not discuss it with me.'

She paused reflectively. Her eyes wanted to take a look at Atherton, but Slider held her glance and said, 'I can assure you that anything you tell me will be held in confidence if it possibly can be.' Atherton noted with faint surprise that his boss's usually regionless voice had taken on a very slight country softness – hardly an accent, more a cadence. But something in Mrs Greatrex seemed to respond to it. Atherton saw her begin to relax, as a nervous dog does with assured handling, and could only admire. He could not have done that, he knew.

'I think I should tell you, then, that my husband and I have for a long time gone our separate ways. Our marriage is more a formality than a union of any intimacy. We have separate suites upstairs, we each follow our own activities – though we keep up appearances for the sake of the family, and there are still occasions when we appear as a couple. *Appeared,* I should say.'

'You were on friendly terms?'

'Oh yes, it was not a rancorous arrangement. But I didn't

63

care for some of Roger's media friends, and he was utterly bored by mine.'

'Did he have any enemies?'

She raised an eyebrow. 'He was a critic, and not generally a benign one. I should say he had many enemies – but I can't believe anyone would kill over a bad review. That *is* what you're asking me? Did anyone hate Roger enough to kill him?'

'Did anyone?'

'I don't know. I can only say, not that I know of. But I can't say what would be enough, can I?'

Slider let the question slip past his ear. 'Did he have any relatives?'

'His parents are both dead now. He has a sister, Ruth. They were always very fond of each other, but she's married and lives in America. They write to each other once or twice a year, but we haven't seen her since – oh – it must be four years, if not five.'

'What about your family? Did he get on with them?'

Her mouth made a wry movement. 'Oh yes, we all got on with each other. He didn't like them and they didn't like him, but on family occasions we would all turn up and be polite. That's what happens in civilised society. I shudder to think how much time we all waste being polite to people we don't much care for.'

'Why didn't they like him?'

'*Not good enough.*' She sipped her sherry, scanning Slider's face for comprehension. 'My parents thought I made a disappointing marriage. Roger wasn't one of us. But they tried to make the best of it. The trouble was that Roger resented being made the best of. He wanted to be judged on his own merits. I'm afraid Daddy's generation wasn't very good at that.'

Slider nodded gently, the quiet stream into which she might slip her painful confessions. 'Have you any children?'

Her eyes hurt. 'Just one. Our son, Jamie.' She looked, for his benefit, towards a framed photograph on the sofa end-table, of a smiling, gap-toothed, very ordinary-looking boy with tousled hair, in an open-necked shirt. 'That was taken when he was nine.'

'How old is he now?'

'Mentally he's still nine. Chronologically he's twenty-five.' She held Slider's gaze, as though for support; Atherton she had clearly forgotten. 'He's in a home, in Sussex – near Petworth. He's very happy there. It's a very nice old house, large grounds, even a lake. We go down three times a year to see him – at Christmas, Easter, and on his birthday.' She seemed on the point of adding something else, and then didn't.

Was that part of the not being good enough? Slider wondered. He looked into her naked face and could only be silent in the face of the world of hurt revealed there. If her husband had been murdered, life had already dealt her a worse blow. He moved a foot, scuffing against the floor, and she drew back into herself a little, enough for him to be able to put the next question.

'Do you know Sandal Palliser?'

Her expression grew veiled. 'Yes, of course I know him. He's one of Roger's friends.'

'Friends? I was told he and your husband didn't like each other.'

'Who told you that?' she asked, but warily.

'They had a violent quarrel at the television centre the night he died. I was told it was not unusual. And they did have a long-running dispute in the newspapers.'

'That had nothing to do with it. That was merely a professional debate,' she said unwarily.

'So, what was the cause of the enmity?'

She hesitated, as though she contemplated not answering.

Then she answered in a voice which was suddenly harsh, 'I don't know what, specifically, they quarrelled about the other night. But I imagine it had something to do with a woman. My husband – well, you'll find out sooner or later, I suppose – my husband had other women. At one time he and Sandal used to go out together and get drunk and pick up – women, girls, call them what you will. There was rivalry between them as to who could do best at it, but it was friendly rivalry at first. Then I believe Roger "stole" one from Sandal, and after that it became hostile. They would do each other down if they could. I thought it was all very silly at first, but then it seemed to get nastier. I don't know why – except that Sandal was always jealous of Roger, because he'd done so much better in his career. And financially, of course,' she added. 'Sandal is a great believer in money. He would love to be rich, and failing that, he likes to be with the rich. And old money, of course, is more desirable than new. He hated the fact that Roger had the entrée into that sort of society, while he didn't.'

'Through you.'

'Through me, yes. But Sandal would have married well if he could.'

Slider glanced across at Atherton, and Mrs Greatrex, seeing the eye movement, remembered where she was and drew the perfect composure back over her face. Slider stood up.

'May we see his room?'

There was a bedroom, dressing-room, bathroom and sitting-room, all interconnecting, on the second floor. The maid who showed them up explained that Mrs Greatrex had a bedroom and bathroom on this floor, but used the morning-room down-stairs as her sitting-room. All the rooms were expensively carpeted and furnished with antiques, and also expensively cleaned. The wastepaper basket in the sitting-room was empty, and all the surfaces were clear. The fireplace contained only a log-effect electric fire in an elaborate iron basket, almost comical in its inappropriateness. It went to show, Slider thought, that everyone has their blind spots.

The room had been done yesterday morning when Mr Greatrex left, the maid said. He had returned in the late afternoon to shower and change before going to the BBC, and the room had then been tidied again, and the towels changed. If there had been a note, it would have been found and given to madam, but there was no note. He seemed, the maid said, very cock-a-hoop when he came back to the house for the last time; not at all depressed or sad.

But there was a small bureau in the sitting-room, and a lowboy in the bedroom, both stuffed with personal effects. 'We'll have to go through them all,' Slider said, opening drawers without enthusiasm. 'We'd better get someone sympathetic on the job. Anderson's a nice, clean-living lad.'

'Pity the maid's so efficient. These rooms are as unrevealing as a hotel.'

'Oh, I don't know,' Slider said. 'There's negative evidence: if his clothes are taken away to be washed when he takes them off, the only way he could get holes in his socks would be by not changing them.'

'Dirty boy, eh?'

Slider opened another drawer, lifted up some neatly folded shirts, and found under the lining-paper, two pornographic magazines. 'You might say.'

'What's that? Oh, hygiene publications. I'm beginning to build up a picture of this man in all his loveliness.'

Slider was now in the sweater drawer, and found, similarly hidden, a black-and-white photograph in a very old leather frame, of a girl of about fifteen, with short fair hair pulled back at one side by a slide, and a cheerful grin. On the back the photographer's name was stamped in curly Gothic print, and an address in Pulborough.

Atherton looked over his shoulder. 'The sister, do you think?'

'Could be. But why is it hidden? Mrs G said he was fond of his sister.'

'Maybe it didn't go with the decor.'

Slider stared at the photograph, frowning, and then slipped it into his pocket. Atherton noted the action and forbore to comment. His boss, as he knew, often had trouble with photographs. They upset him, in the same sort of way that dead people's shoes upset Atherton.

On their way out, they approached Mrs Greatrex again to ask permission for someone to come and go through the papers. Then Slider produced the knife. 'Have you ever seen this before?'

She looked at it, and her face seemed to turn a shade paler, almost yellowing. 'Was that –? No. No, I haven't seen it before. It's not Roger's.'

'To your knowledge.'

'Why would he have such a thing?' she countered.

'Was he ever in the Boy Scouts?'

'Really, what odd questions you – oh. I see. No, I don't think so. It wouldn't have been in his family's tradition. And Roger was never a joiner. He liked to be different from everyone else. He wouldn't have cared for the uniform.'

'One other thing,' Slider said, remembering, 'was your husband religious?'

She raised her eyebrows. 'Not particularly.'

'He wasn't a churchgoer? Fond of the Bible?'

'Good heavens, no!'

Slider explained about the card.

'I don't know where that would have come from,' Mrs

Greatrex said, 'but I knew very little of what he did day by day. But he wasn't a Christian. His father's name was Grossvater. They changed it when they came over, when Roger was a little boy.' She looked quizzically from one to the other. 'I thought you realised, that was what I was saying earlier. I come from an Old Catholic family. It was largely why my father thought Roger unsuitable.'

Front wheel skid, Slider thought. Well, who'd a thunk it?

'But he was fair-haired and blue-eyed,' Atherton said, unable to withhold a faint protest.

She looked at him blankly, as though the table lamp had spoken. 'Sephardic Jews often are,' she said after a moment, as if he ought to have jolly well known that.

5

Who Dragged Whom?

Sandal Palliser's house on Addison Road had been a semi-rural villa when it was built in the eighteen-forties, but the countryside had retreated like the tide fifteen miles further west and left it stranded. Now it stood on the one-way system which was the southbound extension of the West Cross Route, and traffic thundered or coughed past it all day, wreathing it in noxious fumes and making its walls shake. Flats and houses pressed up close on every side; but it slept in its secret, unkempt garden behind the high brick wall as though entranced, and amongst the overgrown shrubs and trees city birds found a green haven which must have surprised the socks off them.

Slider's practised eye took in the signs of neglect. 'Either Palliser's not doing well enough to pay for the upkeep,' he said as they walked up the path, with twigs tugging at them like fractious children seeking attention.

'Or he doesn't care,' Atherton finished for him, 'and spends his money on something else.'

'That roof wants looking at. And the guttering. I hate to see a lovely house let go.'

Inside, it was as different as it could be from Greatrex's pampered surroundings. The walls had a long time ago been painted magnolia, and then left to get on with it. The furniture was old, some of it antique, some merely ancient, and there was an awful lot of it, which at least helped to hide the deficiencies of the decor. There was clutter everywhere, books, sheet-music, toys, bicycles, china, clothes, plant pots, an art-deco naked lady lampstand with a broken flex, a footstool only half re-covered with a petit-point of pansies in a vase, a Royal Standard typewriter, an ancient record-player and a tottering heap of 78s, a scooter with the front wheel missing, a pair of leather riding-boots on wooden trees, a headless teddy bear, a wooden high-chair with the reddish paint worn off in patches so it resembled brawn – it was as though the house had been visited in the fifties by a huge family of cousins, and never tidied since.

Easing his way past a battered Utility sideboard loaded with vases and jam-jars, which was almost blocking the passage, and tripping on a hole in the carpet, which seemed to be made of off-cuts, Slider was led into the kitchen where he was able to take stock of Mrs Palliser. She was a surprise, too, after the steely glamour of Mrs Greatrex. She was a comfortable, motherly-looking woman with a kind face, iron-grey hair pulled back into an unfashionable and rather unsuccessful bun at the nape of her neck, and unexpectedly dark eyes. She was wearing a flowered smock over a shapeless brown skirt, and the sides of her forefingers were deeply ingrained with the sort of stain that comes from a lifetime of peeling vegetables. She seemed to have been making soup, and there was a complex smell of food in the air.

She scanned the faces of both men while Slider introduced them. 'You've come about Roger, I suppose. That's a terrible thing, isn't it?' She had the hint of a Scottish accent. 'It said in the paper this morning that he committed suicide, is that right?'

'It looks as if it could be suicide,' Slider said cautiously.

'I can't believe that,' she said firmly. 'He wasn't the sort. Sandy doesn't believe it either, I know that for a fact. Roger had everything to live for. I suppose you want to talk to Sandy, don't you?'

'Yes, please.'

'He's up in his study, working. He doesn't like to be disturbed when he's writing, but of course this is an emergency, isn't it? I'll just show you up. Can you wait a moment, I was making his coffee, and you can take it up with you. I dare say you'd like a cup of coffee? How do you take it?'

Shortly afterwards they were following her upstairs, Atherton in the rear carrying a tray with coffee and a plate of shortbread and trying to keep watch round it for hazards: the stair carpet was as full of holes as the hall, and there was in addition the problem of the books stacked on both sides of each stair, leaving only a narrow space in the middle. Mrs Palliser climbed like a stayer, using her hands to push down on her thighs to boost her upwards, talking breathlessly the while.

'We've been here since nineteen sixty-five, bought the house with the money Sandy got for his first book. It cost two thousand pounds, can you imagine that? Of course, it was in a terrible state.' Behind Slider, Atherton snorted and changed it to a cough. 'We'd to do it up ourselves, bit by bit, for we hadn't a bean in those days. Years it took us. It's worth half a million now if we wanted to sell it. When we first moved in, there weren't even any floorboards in the hall. It had been empty for years. The garden was like a jungle. Well, we've been happy here. It's a good house, a happy house. Oh, mind the step-ladder on the landing. We keep it there for changing the light bulbs, the ceiling's so high, and they seem to pop every five minutes. They

72

don't make them to last the way they used to. Sandy says we ought to get the wiring looked at. I dare say it might be that.'

Slider dared say so, too. The light switch he was just passing, skirting the step-ladder and a standard lamp with a split shade and a trailing flex, was a round, dark brown bakelite one with the little nipple-like protrusion in the middle, the sort he remembered from his childhood. Hitler still wanted to be an engine-driver when this house was last wired.

'I suppose it's a bit cluttered, the house,' Mrs Palliser said without apology as she embarked on a second flight, 'but you tend not to notice your own messes, do you? And you never know when something might come in useful. Sandy! Here's visitors.'

She had reached a door on the half-landing and pushed it open. It opened only part way, stopped by some further foot-hill of gubbins concealed behind it. Through the doorway Slider saw a man sitting at a vast desk which bore a personal computer at the centre with piles of books and notepads all around. The rest of the room contained nothing but a side table, a red leatherette-covered armchair with curved wooden arms, and some bookshelves on metal supports fixed to the wall; but almost every inch of surface was covered in heaps of books and papers. The large, beautiful sash window looked out over the avian paradise of the garden; and the naked light bulb dangling before it on a pre-war plaited fabric cord had been hitched across by a piece of string tied to a nail in the bookshelf so that it would hang over the desk.

'This is the police,' Mrs Palliser announced. 'And here's your coffee. I'll leave you the while, then.'

Sandal Palliser swung round to look, and then got up and came to take the tray from Atherton. Slider had not expected him to be so tall, or so old. He had thick white hair which sprouted upwards from his head and only bent over at the ends from its own weight. His face was deeply lined, his eyebrows bushy, his large nose spread and coarsened with age and hard living, his neck chicken-skinned. He wore old-fashioned glasses with brown plastic rims, and behind them his eyes were an unexpectedly bright blue, which made them somehow look completely round and rather blind. But his movements were vigorous and his voice powerful; probably, Slider thought, he was not as old as he looked – late fifties, perhaps.

'You've come about Roger, I suppose,' he said. He put the tray down on top of the papers on the side table. 'Chairs, now. You'd better have the armchair,' to Slider. 'Shove all that stuff on the floor. It's all right, it won't hurt. And if you,' to Atherton, 'go into the next room, you'll see a kitchen chair just behind the door. Bring that in.'

When the arrangements were complete he took up his coffee and sipped it, and passed the shortbread around. 'Phyllis makes it herself. She's a wonderful cook. No bloody use at anything else, and eccentric as a parrot, but she can cook. I've been married to her for thirty years, and she gets more like Princess Fred every day.' He looked from Slider to Atherton and back with a quick, appraising glance. 'Are you an historian?'

'Architecture's my interest,' Slider answered. 'But there are overlaps.'

The round blue eyes reappraised in the light of that information, but he only said, 'Perhaps you'll know who Princess Fred was, then. So, Roger Greatrex. I didn't kill him, if that's what you're thinking.'

'It says in the paper it was suicide,' Slider said blandly.

Palliser grinned without humour. 'Oh no, you don't catch me with that little game! I know perfectly well it wasn't. Roger loved himself much too much to want to deprive the world

74

of his presence. And since you can't cut your throat by accident, he must have been murdered. No big surprise, really.
There must have been a waiting-list of people wanting to kill
him.'

'Who was at the head of the queue?' Slider asked.

'Don't ask me. That's for you to find out. I should look
amongst the women, if I were you – there were a few with
grievances. God knows what they saw in him, though. He
was a dirty little bastard. I don't mean sexy, I mean dirty.'
He caught Atherton's eye and grinned again as he looked
around the room. 'Oh yes, it's untidy here, all right. I have
a theory, that there are people in the world who are untidy
but clean, and people who are dirty but tidy. Roger was
immaculate on the outside, but it was all a façade. Whereas
me – you could eat your dinner off me. And many a woman
has done so, but that's another story.'

Atherton gave a tight smile, and seeing Slider's dreamy
expression, gathered he was to ask the questions this time.
Briskness, he thought, was the order of the day. 'You had a
quarrel with Mr Greatrex in the greenroom. Would you mind
telling me what about?'

'Oho, that's it, is it? Amazing how predictable you people
are. *Ay* quarrel, followed by *ay* murder, ergo – not that you'd
know what ergo means – the quarreller must be the murderer.
Ha! Well, not this time, chaps, sorry. *Cherchez la femme,* that's
my advice to you.'

'Mrs Greatrex says you and he used to compete over how
many women you could pick up,' Atherton said, obligingly
changing tack.

'Dear Caroline! Serves her right for marrying Roger. If
she'd married *me* instead – but that's yet another story. Oh
yes, Roger and I used to haunt the streets together. You
wouldn't think we were the same age, would you? He had

75

the body of a twenty-year-old – several times a week if he could get it.' He laughed at his own joke. 'Phyllis says he must have had a picture in his attic.'

'Would that be a reference to the novel by Oscar Wilde, sir?' Atherton asked ponderously, making pretence to lick a pencil.

Palliser laughed, more naturally. 'All right, one up to you! Very well, I'll grant you so much, that I disliked Roger cordially, even though we were once friends, and no, I am not going to tell you why. I admit we had words on Thursday night, but I'm not going to tell you what about, because it's none of your bloody business. I didn't kill him, though I half wish I had – there would have been an artistic symmetry to it. Trouble is, he probably would have enjoyed it, and it wasn't my business to pleasure him, thank God. It's not my business to sort out your problems, either. In short, I have nothing to say to you about myself – but I will tell you one or two things about Roger that you may not know, and that probably no-one else will tell you. That's my bargain. How about it?'

The narrative was long, made longer by the evident fact that Sandal Palliser liked the sound of his own voice. He was a gifted narrator, and though the story was not an edifying one, it at least cleared up one question: the identity of the hidden photographee of the sweater drawer. According to Palliser, Greatrex had had two sisters – Ruth, five years older, and Rachel, two years younger than him. He was fond of them both, but being closer to Rachel in age, was particularly attached to her. As they grew up together, they became inseparable, so much so that when Greatrex was seventeen and due to go up to university, the parents had difficulty in persuading him to leave her. He went unwillingly; and shortly before the end of his third term Rachel became ill with leukaemia. Greatrex came home, missing his exams, and through the summer holidays watched his sister die slowly and in agony. When she was gone, he refused to go back and resit his first-year exams, without which he could not continue at university – for this was St Andrews and the Scottish system – and instead left home and went to London – as far away as he could get, according to Palliser – to seek his fortune. After drifting through the various jobs the unqualified could get in 1960, he found himself in Fleet Street and was lucky enough to catch the eye of the editor of the *Daily Express*. Thus started his apprenticeship to journalism and his ultimate stardom – and, for reasons yet to be discovered, his bloody death in a loo in the TVC.

That was also when he first met Palliser, who was working for a publisher and freelancing for the papers when he could get the work; and drawn together by their both having been brought up in Scotland, they became friends.

'I don't think Roger ever really got over Rachel's death,' Palliser said, lighting a Gitane. 'My mid-morning indulgence.' He proffered the pack. 'Do you—?'

Atherton shook his head, and Slider said, 'No thanks, not while I'm breathing.'

Palliser gave a tight smile. 'A policeman with sense of humour. I thought that wasn't allowed.'

'Some of us slip through the net. Do go on.'

'Where was I? Oh yes, Rachel's death and Roger's obsession.'

'Why do you suppose he hid her picture, if he was so fond of her?'

'He never spoke of her. It was all too painful, I think. It forced its way out in his obsession with young women. Well, that's what it amounted to – always markedly younger than him, though fortunately they got a bit older as he did. I

77

suppose he was maintaining the differential – the latest one probably seemed to him at fifty the way Rachel had seemed to him at eighteen.'

'You aren't suggesting his relationship with Rachel was incestuous?'

'Not physically – good God, no – but mentally, isn't it always? If you love your siblings at all, that is?'

'I'm an only child,' Slider mentioned.

'Ah, then you'll have had the Oedipus bit instead,' Palliser said easily. 'Roger spent his life trying to find his lost sister in other girls. He couldn't keep his hands off them. Luckily, most of them didn't want him to. He was a good-looking sod, sort of like a young Peter Cook. You know, fair, clean-cut, terribly English – if only they knew! He went especially for suburban dollies, "up west" for the evening with stars in their eyes. They had no resistance, and Roger was always one to go with his best stroke. They took him for public school, and he didn't bother to disillusion them. It was a great pulling line. And then of course the sixties started in earnest, and he couldn't go wrong. Dear God, what a picnic that was! I remember my father saying the same thing about the Great War – a holiday from the normal rules of decency and decorum. Every now and then, civilisation needs to be let off the leash for a run—'

Palliser paused at that point, and his face went blank for a space. Writing his next article, Atherton thought, not without envy – a nice little quasi-historical, cod-psycho-social analysis for those who like their thinking done for them. And he'll get a couple of thousand for it.

Then the animation faded back in, and Palliser said, less flippantly than hitherto, 'Except that it was all wrong for Roger. Underneath it all there was a streak of suburban prude, a longing for lace-curtain propriety. He could never be a whole-hearted hedonist – he was too middle-class for that. I think what he really wanted from the dollies was just to be with them, talk to them, maybe pet them a bit. He wanted someone to be a big brother to. But he was a healthy lad, and they were looking for excitement, so it never stopped there. And after a bit I think he forgot why he was doing it – not that he ever knew, not consciously. The ambivalence, the conflict, resolved itself in that streak of dirtiness – not washing his feet, not changing his underpants. He was punishing himself for his inner loathsomeness, you see – and he did like punishment. That was another manifestation of his bourgeois soul. Yes, now I come to think of it,' his round blue eye, satirical as a parrot's, roved from Slider to Atherton and back, 'he was just the sort to commit suicide after all. Gentlemen, I have solved your case for you.'

Slider let all this pass him by with a policeman's patience. 'What happened when he married?'

'Oh, it didn't make any difference to his habits. Caroline would never make a fuss. That's the advantage of marrying into the aristocracy.' An expression of displeasure crossed his face. 'The Honourable Caroline Fiennes-Marjoribanks – Christ, what a name! Do you know Chirnside? The old boy's still hanging on to life, God knows how, he must be ninety-something. Sheer stubbornness, I wouldn't wonder. Stiff upper lip – stiff upper everything, solid wood from the neck up. You know these old Lowland titled families, more English than the English.'

Slider nodded as if he did. 'Mrs Greatrex said that they were married in the face of family opposition.'

Palliser's expression hardened. 'Oh, you've spoken to her, have you? Well, yes, I suppose you'd have to. Not that she'll have told you much. Never complain, never explain, that's the motto of these old families. That's why they decided in the end to make the best of it and accept Roger. Worst thing they could have done all round, as it turned out.'

'How did it turn out?' Slider prompted, at his most inscrutable.

'The union wasn't blest,' Palliser said harshly, 'and it turned out to be Roger's fault – chronically low sperm count. The Chirnsides were devastated – they were longing for grandchildren. I knew the family – grew up in the same part of the country. And then when Caroline did sprog down at last, the kid turned out to have mental problems.' Palliser looked away for the first time, turning a blank gaze onto the garden, where a blackbird was ducking and running along the line of the bushes, pausing to rummage with those familiar, abrupt movements, amongst last year's dead leaves. His voice became strained. 'Fact of the matter is, it wasn't Roger's kid. We all knew that. The whole thing broke him up. And Caroline – you can imagine what a strain it was on her. After that he and Caroline came to an *accommodation*' – he made a moue to show he knew the word, though old-fashioned, was nonetheless necessary – 'and he went back to his old pursuits. I think you probably met his latest conquest. Nice-looking girl, but horribly earnest. I think he was getting in over his head there. I believe the dreaded M-word had been mentioned. Of course, Roger would never leave Caroline in a million years, even if he could – she's his security blanket – but I doubt whether he will have told *her* that.'

'Her?'

'The female in question.' Palliser grinned mirthlessly. 'And no, I'm not going to tell you her name. You can work it out for yourself or go hang. I don't kiss and tell, even when it's someone else doing the kissing.'

Slider reverted to the question of the quarrel with Greatrex, hoping that with the better atmosphere generated by Palliser's

80

self-satisfaction, the cause of their enmity might be forthcoming. But Palliser was quite determined, though also quite cheerful, about refusing.

'I don't have to tell you anything, and I'm not going to. My private life is none of your bloody business.' He said it with a grin, but Slider felt there was a tenseness under it, and that the eyes were wary behind the shielding glass.

Even the old 'by the way' ploy chalked up a big fat zero. 'By the way, I understand you left the greenroom alone shortly after Roger Greatrex left it for the last time. Would you mind telling me where you went?'

'I went to make a telephone call,' he said, and cocked his head consideringly. 'Now who told you I left the room? One of those daffy girls the Beeb is infested with, I suppose. That's where our licence money goes – from our pockets straight to Monsoon and The Body Shop, merely filtered by all the Emmas and Katys and Sarahs. It's social work, pure and simple. No-one else'd give them a job.'

Slider refused the enticing flicker of the lure. 'There was a telephone in the greenroom,' he said. 'You could have used that.'

'Ah, but I wanted privacy,' Palliser grinned. 'And no, it's no use looking like that, I'm not going to tell you who I telephoned.'

'If you won't tell me, I may draw my own conclusions from your refusal,' Slider warned.

'You can do what you like – I can't stop you,' Palliser said almost gleefully. 'I've told you I didn't kill Roger, and unless you want to charge me with it, that's all I am going to tell you.'

The inner man needed fortifying after that, notwithstanding the coffee and shortbread.

'Do you fancy a pint?' Atherton asked tentatively.

'Does Carmen Miranda wear fruit?' Slider responded; so they drove back to the Crown and Sceptre in Melina Road to collate the information over a pint of Fullers and a plate of pasta.

'So what do you think of all that, guv?' Atherton asked. 'Likes listening to himself, doesn't he?'

'A practised performer,' Slider said. 'He was putting up smokescreens, watching himself do it, and watching us watching him.' Too many layers of overlapping consciousness for the truth to be obvious, which was the purpose of the exercise. 'He was hiding something, but what, and why?'

'Maybe just for the hell of it,' said Atherton. 'Another one of those clever dicks who think it's amusing to mislead coppers by concealing perfectly innocent information.'

'Maybe.'

Atherton looked at him. 'You liked him,' he discovered.

Slider looked up. 'That doesn't mean I don't think he was capable of doing it. He's a clever man, a thinking man, and if he did kill Greatrex he'll be one step ahead of us all the way.' He sipped his pint. 'And if he did kill him, he'll have had a very good reason.'

'He's got to be up there with the star suspects,' Atherton said, and told off on his fingers. 'There's the acknowledged enmity between them, the quarrel on the night itself, his being missing at the appropriate time, and the fact that he's concealing things from us. And,' he remembered, 'he's tall enough, and he looks strong enough.'

'There's one big objection,' Slider said.

'How did he manage to cut Greatrex's throat and return to the greenroom without a speck of blood on him?'

Slider nodded. 'Protective clothing, perhaps, which he concealed somewhere before going back to the greenroom.'

'And probably meant to collect afterwards, but which might still be hidden somewhere?'

'Maybe,' Slider said.

'After all,' Atherton reasoned with himself, 'whoever killed Greatrex had the same problem. He'd have had to have protective clothing, or wander about the Centre covered in blood and have someone notice it. How would he explain it away?'

'By saying he got it all over him when he examined the corpse,' Slider said. 'It's good psychology to be the first to find the body. If you raise the alarm, no-one's going to think it was you that did it – everyone expects a murderer to make very long tracks – and if you're bloodstained, you've got the perfect excuse.'

Atherton thought about it unwillingly. 'But you'd have to be a very cool customer to brass that out. Your average person, even if they meant beforehand to kill, would instinctively want to run away and try to conceal everything afterwards. You're talking about a cold, ruthless cunning, calculating the odds. Did Philip Somers strike you that way?'

'No,' Slider admitted. 'And there was the mistake about the knife. If he was a calculator, he'd have taken my hint about the knife.'

Atherton grinned. 'I love the way you always see both sides.'

'But a man doesn't have to be completely consistent. You can have a degree of calculation intermingled with unforeseen panic. He could have planned it all beforehand, but not have reckoned on how upset he'd be afterwards; clung to his original plan without being able to adapt as he went. And certainly he stuck to his post, guarding the door and preventing anyone else from going in. Don't you think that was an odd thing to do?'

'Unusually self-controlled, anyway,' Atherton granted. 'Well, Somers certainly had the opportunity – and he is the one person who didn't have to explain the blood away. But what would his motive be? Did he know Greatrex?'

'We have Dorothy Hammond's story that he said he didn't want Greatrex on the show. For reason or reasons unknown.'

'And then there's Palliser's hints about a woman in the case,' Atherton said. 'If Greatrex was a womaniser, there could have been any number of jilted lovers and cuckolded husbands after his blood.' He sighed. 'Let's face it, it could be absolutely anyone.'

'Yes. We have so little to go on.'

'Who dragged whom at the wheels of what, how many times round the walls of where?' Atherton said. 'Ah well, it's early days yet.'

'Quite. We have lines to follow up, so let's follow them. Palliser, to begin with, I think. His wife may have some interesting information, if she can be got to open up.'

'Me for that,' Atherton said. 'I'm good with old ladies. It's my old-fashioned courtesy mixed with my boyish good looks. They always want to pet me and give me toffees.'

'And we might trace the knife, or find witnesses, or more forensic evidence. If it wasn't Somers, there must be more blood somewhere.'

'Blood will out,' said Atherton. 'I'd settle for a nice thumbmark somewhere – Palliser's print and Greatrex's blood-group.'

Slider ignored the taunt. 'If only it had happened somewhere more private and confined. I hate to think of all those hundreds of people coming and going and trampling about. A nice little domestic where you can seal it all off would be a piece of cake compared with this.'

'That's why we get the big money,' Atherton said cheerfully. 'Want any pud?'

6

The Bridgers of Kensington County

Norma was looking for him when he got back to the factory. 'The Lab phoned, guv. Mr Arceneaux. Wants you to phone him back.'

'Right, thanks.'

She followed him into his room. 'Any luck?'

'Lots of interesting stuff about Greatrex. He and Palliser were friends from thirty years ago, but there was a lot of rivalry between them. Palliser won't say what their quarrel was about, but all the indications are that Greatrex was an inveterate womaniser, and Palliser reckons we should be looking for a woman. But if it was a woman that killed him, she'd have to have been tall and strong – like you, in fact. Any offers?'

'As a matter of fact,' she said, 'I have. It struck me as odd that the only guest Fiona Parsons went downstairs to meet in person was Greatrex. And, after what Dorothy Hammond said about her quarrel with Somers, I checked with the editor, and it was actually Parsons who suggested Greatrex for the show. Martin Fletcher, the editor, was doubtful about having

85

Greatrex and Palliser at the same time, but she persuaded him.'

'It was a topical choice,' Slider pointed out. 'After all, they had been having a newspaper argument about the very subject of the show. It might have been no more than that.'

'Yes, guv, but it was Parsons who suggested the subject as well. Maybe she was having an affair with Greatrex, and wanted the chance to be with him – what d'you think?'

'If she was having an affair with him, surely she'd have wanted to be alone with him, not see him in a public place like that? After all, how much time could she hope to spend with him in those circumstances?'

'But he was married,' Norma said, and then, seeing he hadn't followed the point, elaborated. 'A woman who's having a secret affair with a married man jumps at any chance to be with him, whether alone or in public, for however short a time. Those are the crumbs from the table she lives off.'

Slider felt uncomfortable to be reminded of this, and said, 'Even if she was having an affair with him, why should you think she murdered him?'

'I don't think it,' she said, offering him his own customary words back, 'I'm only looking for anomalies.'

'And have you found any?'

'I think so. Parsons says she was in the studio at the time of the murder, and that that's where Hammond found her to tell her of the death, but after I spoke to Hammond I went and talked to some of the people in the studio, and there's not one who can say exactly where Parsons was at any particular time. And when I checked with Hammond again, she said she had to look all over the studio before she found Parsons.'

'Go on,' Slider said.

Encouraged, she perched on the edge of his desk. 'Well,

guv, you saw the studio: it's not as if it was a brightly lit open space. There's the set in the middle, with the panellists' table and a sort of backdrop screen behind it. A person could be standing behind the screen and not be seen by the rest of the studio. And all the lighting is focused on the set, so everywhere else is dim and shadowy. Then there's the tiers of audience seating, set up on scaffolding – you can walk right under that. And then there's the control box and the lighting gallery, and all sorts of little rooms off the studio floor – props and make-up and dressing-rooms. What I'm saying is that there's any number of places someone could be in the studio without anyone seeing them. So what better excuse, if you actually *weren't* there at the time? Parsons can't prove she was there—'

'But no-one can prove she wasn't,' Slider said.

'Exactly. And she was dodging about all evening, which could have been her way of making sure everybody remembered seeing her around, but nobody knew where she was at any given moment.'

'Is that all?'

Norma made a face, which meant it was. 'She's tall and strong. She plays basketball for the BBC team. And she insisted on having a look at the body, even though Somers tried to discourage her. Maybe she was making sure the scene looked right for the police.'

'If he was her lover, why would she want to kill him?'

'Any number of reasons. Love and hate, jealousy, frustration—'

Slider smiled at her. 'You know you've got nothing, don't you?'

'All we've got is nothing,' she pointed out boldly.

'However, on your side, Sandal Palliser said that we had already met Greatrex's latest female fancy, which suggests it was someone at the BBC. So it's quite possible it was Fiona

Parsons. While that doesn't make her the murderer, it can't do any harm to find out a bit more about it. She might have some light to throw on the situation. So you can go and talk to her—'

Norma jumped up. 'Thanks, guv!'

'—carefully.'

'I'm always careful,' she said indignantly.

'I've heard that.'

When she had gone, he picked up the phone and dialled. Tufnell Arceneaux was a scientist at the Met Lab, whose specialist field was forensic haematology; a life-loving man with whom Slider had spent some memorably Byzantine nights when they were both younger and his head was harder.

The handset roared, and Slider held it back hastily. Tufty's voice was as large as his appetites. 'Hello, Tufty, it's Bill.'

'Hello, old fruit! How's it hanging?'

'Symmetrically, thank you. How are you?'

'Bloody awful, thanks for asking. I haven't been to bed for two days – feel as if some bastard's borrowed my body and been careless in it.'

'What was the celebration?'

'Burns night.'

'I thought that was in January?'

'I'm talking about that fire at the fertilizer factory in Cricklewood,' Tufty roared triumphantly. 'I've just spent the last thirty-six hours tissue-typing the victims. Identified all but one, though – had to send that one off to the tooth fairy. However, all that aside, I've got some good news for you. Your culture vulture who cut himself shaving—'

'You've managed to look at that, with all you've had to do? I'm touched.'

'Had a sleepless moment to spare. Couldn't let my favourite dick down – does that all by itself these days!' Tufty chuckled massively at his own humour. 'Anyway, I managed to get a lift off the wallet – quite a nice one – a thumb. Good enough to identify, I should have thought. I'll send the print off to you.'

'That's terrific. Thanks, Tufty. Oh—'

'No, no it's all right, I thought of that. It isn't the corpse's. But I've got something else for you as well. I got a whole forefinger and thumb off that holy card jobbie you sent over—'

'The Bible text?'

'That's the chap. There are all sorts of marks on it, but one finger and thumb – ordinary greasers, not bloody – have come out a treat. And in my humble op, the thumb's not the same as the one on the wallet. Here's the thing, though – it's not the corpse's either.'

Slider thought for a moment. 'Just one finger and thumb?'

'Just one identifiable.' Slider was silent, thinking. 'Does that help?' Tufty howled anxiously.

'Like a hernia,' Slider said. 'I've no idea what it all means.'

'You mean, before you hadn't a clue, and now you haven't a clue?'

'Nutshell.'

'Life's a bugger, isn't it?' Tufty sympathised. 'Tell you what, I'm just off in ten minutes or so. Handling flame-grilled factory workers doesn't half give you an appetite. Why not join me somewhere and we'll have a meal and a drink or two, make a night of it. You need the oils wheeling, old horse.'

'I've still got the hangover from the last time we did that,' Slider said, 'and that was two years ago.'

'Time you let go again, then. You introverted types get your pipes clogged up – too much thinking and not enough drinking. What say?'

'I'd love to, really, but I've got to go and see Irene this evening. I promised. She wants to talk about the divorce and everything.'

'Christ,' Tufty said, awed. 'Well, best of luck, old chum. If you survive it, give me a bell, and we'll get together some time.'

Atherton was lucky – quite a short vigil rewarded him with the sight of Sandal Palliser leaving the house alone. He watched him walk up to the main road and turn left, and a few moments later was ringing the doorbell in hope. He had armed himself with an excuse, but it wasn't needed. Mrs Palliser expressed no surprise or curiosity on seeing him, but simply bid him come in, and padded before him towards the kitchen.

'Sandy's away out, you just missed him,' she said over her shoulder. 'He'll not be back until late. It's his night for bridge with the Frasers – they live in Kensington Court, just a step up the road. D'you know them? She writes the society column in one o' those glossy magazines, and he writes plays no-one can make head or tail of.'

Atherton knew who she meant. 'Too rich for my blood,' he said. 'I'm just a humble copper. Don't you play bridge?'

She turned to him, and her eyes crinkled with amusement. 'I do not. There's nothing so daft as a card game – except those who play them. But Sandy likes being with his own sort of people now and then; and I like an evening doing what I like.'

'And what do you like?' Atherton asked, obediently taking his cue.

'Being left alone in the house with a handsome young man can't be bad at my age. What's it to be, now? Tea, coffee, or a drop of something?'

She sounded positively roguish. Atherton plumped for safety and tea.

'We'll stay in here, if you've no objection,' she said, pulling out a chair from the kitchen table. 'It's the only warm room. When Sandy's out, the central heating goes off.'

90

Atherton didn't know whether she meant he turned it off, or she did, whether he was supposed to sympathise or approve of the thrift. However, the kitchen was cosy, with a four-oven Aga sitting fatly under the chimney throwing out heat, and the smell of recent baking in the air. There was an ancient bakelite wireless with an illuminated dial half-hidden in the clutter on the dresser making conversational sounds just below the level of comprehension; and an enormous black cat, which had been curled up looking like a fake-fur cushion on a high-backed wooden chair by the range, unfurled itself and hopped lightly down to come and wipe its nose politely on Atherton's trouser, purring like a food-mixer. It was no hardship to sit in here amongst the amiable clutter. Atherton lolled at his ease at the table, the cat now heavy on his lap, and watched while Mrs Palliser made a pot of tea, and buttered a plateful of oatcakes and decorated each with a slice of cheese. He had a sense of absolute comfort and safety, and he wondered if Palliser knew how lucky he was.

Mrs Palliser brought everything to the table, sat down catty-corner to him, and put the plate between them. 'Help yourself,' she said. 'I see Gordon's taken to you. You like cats.'

'I have one myself,' he said, and told her about Oedipus as he watched her put milk into two enormous teacups and fill them with strong orange-brown tea from the fat black earthenware pot. Then she reached for the bottle of Teacher's she had put down nearby, unscrewed the cap, and poised it over his cup. 'You'll take a nip,' she said, and it was hardly a question. 'Or do you like it separate?'

'I'll have it your way,' he said, fascinated.

She poured a good slug into each cup, screwed the cap back on the bottle, and drew a hearty sigh. 'Ah,' she said, as though he had passed some test, 'you're a good boy. Here's how!'

'Good health,' he found himself replying. It didn't taste half bad, actually, almost perfumed; and since he was ravenous, he followed her example and took an oatcake, and found the combination faultless. Soon, elbows on table, they were talking cosily. Mrs Palliser would have been happy to indulge his curiosity on any subject – 'Chatting's my best thing,' she told him at one point – but it was easy to bring her to the subject of Roger Greatrex, which must have been on her mind in any case.

'Of course, Sandy and Caroline were goan out together at one time, did you know that?' she said. 'Before she married Roger, of course. As a matter of fact, it was through Sandy that Roger met her. It's queer to think about that now,' she added reflectively. 'How things happen, and you can't see the end of them. That's how it's meant to be, I suppose.'

'It seems that way sometimes,' Atherton said encouragingly.

'Sandy'd known the family from boyhood, you see – Caroline's, I mean. His father was a solicitor, and he did some work for the old lord, and that's how Sandy met the young folk. They lived nearby, and Sandy used to get invited to make up the numbers.' She gave a wicked little smile. 'That's where he got his taste for the high life and the County Set. Of course, it's different there in the lowlands.' She poked her chin up. 'Me, I'm from Deeside. We don't bow the knee to anyone.'

'I can't imagine you ever needed to,' Atherton said gallantly, and she rewarded him by pouring him more tea. 'You must have had the world at your feet.'

She didn't deny it, only looked at him with a wry smile and crinkled eyes. 'Well, Sandy was a handsome young man, and as clever as a knife,' she resumed, 'and he was popular with the younger ones, and the old lord quite approved of him too. Anyway, after Sandy came to London, Caroline came down too – not for his sake, you understand, but for a bit of excitement and change, to see life and so on. But of course, knowing Sandy was there, and maybe feeling a bit lonely, she got in touch, and he offered to show her the sights, and one thing led to another, and so they started to walk out. I don't know how serious it was on her part – it was before my time of course – but I know Sandy wanted to marry her. But then he got friendly with Roger, and introduced him to Caroline, and before he knew where he was, Roger'd taken her away from him.'

'How did he take it?' Atherton asked.

'Oh, well, Sandy would always put a good face on it. He'd not let Roger know he minded – that'd be letting him win. But to my mind there was always a tension between them. A rivalry, you might say. They were friends, right up to the end, but underneath they watched each other like two cats. Maybe that's why the friendship lasted so long,' she added with a little nod. 'It mattered too much to the pair of them, d'you see, ever to drift apart. And Sandy was always devoted to Caroline. Devoted.'

'Didn't you mind?' Atherton asked, intrigued by the lack of rancour in her voice as she said it.

'Mind? Why should I mind? It was me he married. I've half an idea the old lord asked Sandy to keep an eye on her. Poor Caroline hasn't had an easy row to hoe. Married to Roger was no picnic – and then the child being not just right in the head, and there was never another. I dare say they were afraid to risk it. No, I wouldn't have swapped places with her for anything. But Sandy would always do her a good turn if he could. Not that she ever said anything. It wasn't in her to complain, and I liked her better for that, I can tell you. Except just the once—' She paused, though it may only have been to concentrate on pouring. 'Will you have a piece of my Dundee cake?'

Atherton accepted, since she obviously wanted him to, and watched her in silence as she pottered about the kitchen fetching the huge, nut-studded cake, the cheese, a knife and two small plates. She cut him a dark cliff of cake, laid a matching wedge of cheese against its side, and passed it over, and waited while he sampled and pronounced. It was excellent, and she smiled at his praise as though it genuinely pleased her.

When at last she was settled again, he prompted her. 'So what happened, that one time that Caroline complained?'

She looked at him quickly and then away. 'Oh, it was a long time ago. Before the baby was born. The marriage was in trouble, and for a while there Sandy thought they might be going to split up. Caroline wanted a baby, you see, her family was pressing her about it, and Roger – in defiance, maybe, I don't know – was flaunting this young woman at her. He'd always had a roving eye, but this time it was blatant. Anyway, Caroline broke down for once in her life and ran out on him, she actually moved out, to a bedsitter in Earl's Court. Shocking it must have been for her to do that, and her a Catholic. Sandy went and saw her, of course. He said she was in a desperate mood. I think he thought she might do something silly. But he talked to her and he talked to Roger, and finally they got back together and it was all hushed up.' She paused, just a breath, but Atherton felt he could hear the wings of the Kindly Ones beating the air around them in the moment of silence. 'And then she found she was pregnant.'

She looked at Atherton, and he nodded very slightly as encouragement to go on. She sighed, as though he had given her the wrong answer, and looked down at her hands again. 'Well, that sorted things out. Roger dropped the young woman, and it all looked set fair. Then the baby was born.'

'And that was the—?'

'The poor simple boy, yes. Jamie, they called him. After that, I don't think it ever really worked between Roger and Caroline, but they always kept a good shop-front, as they had to, really, since they couldn't divorce. I think it suited them, really, to have their separate lives. But Sandy always thought Roger treated her badly.'

'Do you have any children?'

'No. We've none. We'd have liked them but – Sandy can't.' The last words were almost swallowed, as if she felt she shouldn't tell him, but wanted to too much to stop. And then she looked up suddenly into Atherton's eyes, and he stared down into thirty years of silent disappointment. 'But I've plenty nephews and nieces. And we've had a good marriage, Sandy and me,' she said defiantly. 'We understand each other. He has his little ways to put up with – but then, so have I. And he'll never leave me. I've always known that.'

And that was what she had to be grateful for, what she settled for? he wondered. He felt hugely, horribly sad. The ramshackle, cluttered house suddenly became a gigantic metaphor, a neglected opportunity, at the heart of which this shapeless woman cooked huge vats of nourishing, tasty food – for whom? He wanted to ask her but didn't dare. He didn't think he could bear the sadness of her answer, whatever it was.

He met Slider in the White Horse for a quick one before going off. 'So there you are,' he said at last, when he had told everything.

'Where am I?'

'There's our suspect. No alibi, suspicious behaviour, won't answer questions, is obviously hiding something – and has the cast-iron motive. The Big Green One. As the Southern planter said about the bougainvillaea, it's all over my jalousie.'

'Because Greatrex pinched Palliser's bird?' Slider said discouragingly.

Atherton was hurt. 'Why not? A lifetime of dissembling, hiding his hurt and jealousy, pretending to be friends with this despicable nerk, just so as not to let him get the better of him. Seeing Greatrex swanning around making a bigger and better name for himself, succeeding everywhere just that bit more than Palliser can manage. They have a long debate in the newspapers about modern art, and Greatrex even wins that one—'

'Does he?'

Atherton was confused. 'Does he what?'

'Does Greatrex win the debate?'

'Well of course,' Atherton said impatiently. 'No-one could take Palliser's position seriously – all that guff about art being elitist, and the arts subsidies ought to be spent on welfare instead. It's hackneyed – the wealthy liberal's guilt-trip. No-one really believes it. He probably only took up the argument to be on the opposite side from Greatrex.'

'You think so?'

'He earns his living from it,' Atherton pointed out. 'And all he achieves by being contrary is to make himself look like a plonker, while Greatrex, who is still a handsome son-of-a-gun, gets the pole position, the praise and the totty. Then he comes face to face with him at the TVC, and it all becomes too much. Thirty years of resentment boils over, and he tops him.'

'With a knife he's brought with him for the purpose?'

'All right, it may not have been absolutely spontaneous. But he knew he was going to be on the same panel with Greatrex.'

'Did he?'

'Oh yes. Anyone in the country could have known, because they announce on the programme the week before who's going to be on next week, and it was in all the TV listings. But anyway, Palliser knows. He arrives early, hoping for a moment alone with Greatrex, and when the opportunity finally presents itself – when Greatrex leaves the room alone to go to make-up, Palliser follows him.'

'Lures him into the gents – with the offer of sweeties, perhaps?'

'Greatrex probably went of his own accord. After all, it wasn't essential to Palliser's plan to kill him in that particular place, was it? Whoever killed him,' he added, seeing Slider about to object, 'it's hardly likely to have been the chosen spot.'

'Fair enough. But then we're back to the problem of the bloodstained clothes, or lack of,' Slider said, sighing. 'Did you try Mrs P with the knife?'

'Yes – no go.'

'Still, it's better than Norma's theory,' he said, 'and worth following up. Since the motive for the murder wasn't robbery from the person, it must have been someone who knew him, and Palliser seems to be the one who knew him best. We'll have to get him to volunteer some fingerprints. Somers too. Even if only for the purpose of elimination.'

'As long as you can keep Mr Honeyman sweet. He still wants it to be suicide.'

'Ah, on that subject – I had a telephone call from Freddie. Good news from our point of view – he's found subcutaneous bruising on the chin and jaw, including one very fine finger-mark on the right side just below the ear.' He watched Atherton visualising it. 'So that gives us the murderer coming up behind him, grabbing him with the left hand under the chin—'

'To force his head back,' Atherton supplied, 'and pull the neck taut.'

'Right. Freddie says he thinks it was inflicted immediately

prior to death, which accounts for it not spreading to the upper layers.'

'Well, Mr Honeyman can hardly argue with that. Congratulations, guv.' Atherton looked at his watch. 'I'd better go. I've got a hot date.'

'Oh?'

Atherton grinned. 'Sue isn't playing in *Traviata*, remember.'

'Lucky you.'

'Where are you eating tonight? Why don't you come round later, have some supper?'

'I've got to go and see Irene.'

'Will she be feeding you?'

'Absolutely not.' Slider shuddered at the thought.

'Well, then, come round. Look, you don't have to commit yourself. I don't suppose you know how long you'll be. Just come round if you want to. I'll be cooking something that doesn't spoil, just in case.'

Slider was tired and his mind was full of little jumping bits of information, like a dog with fleas, which was not the best state to be in for an interview with his future ex-wife. Not only that, but he had to go and see her in the house of the man she had ambled off with, which made him feel awkward and see red. The place was large and overstuffed and dull, like Ernie Newman himself, and it had a funny smell about it, which he couldn't pin down, but which reminded him depressingly of visiting aunties when he was a child – in particular Aunty Celia, who was ferocious about children being seen but not heard, and who always made him kiss her, instead of contenting herself, like other relatives, with kissing him. The texture and taste of her Coty face powder was all woven into the nightmare which began when Dad rang her doorbell. Ernie Newman's house had the same door chimes as Aunty Celia's.

The children had been allowed to stay up to see him, but he was so late that they had been scrubbed and pyjama'd and were waiting for him in brand new dressing-gowns and slippers which they wore with the air of lamb chops wearing paper frills. Matthew in particular was pale with shock, and after staring at Slider with his lower lip under his teeth for an agonising moment flung himself into Slider's arms to whisper passionately, 'Oh Dad, can't we go home? He bought us these slippers, and he calls them *house shoes.*'

Slider's heart lurched with sympathy. In such small things does true horror reside. When he was Matthew's age, there had been a teacher at school who had filled him with crawling dread because she pronounced the name Susan as Syusan. There was no arguing with that kind of aversion. The person concerned might be the paradigm of every kindly virtue – it was still garlic flowers and stake-through-the-heart time.

Kate was not stricken, but even her bounce was less ballistic. 'They don't do Nature Study in my new school,' she complained, 'they do Eartha Wareness. And Melanie took the gerbils home, even though it was my turn. It's not fair.'

'Didn't you say anything to the teacher?' Slider asked.

Kate's tiny chest swelled with indignation. *'I couldn't.* Because Mummy said I couldn't have my *turn.* Because *he* gets *assama.'*

Irene caught Slider's eyes and looked flustered. 'Don't call Uncle Ernie *him,* it's rude,' she rebuked her daughter.

'He's not my uncle,' Kate returned smartly, and forestalled further rebuke by grabbing Slider's hand. 'Come and see my room, Daddy. I've got four new horses in my c'lection, and I'm going to have a shelf over my bed to put them all.'

Matthew reddened and glared at her. 'Shut up,' he hissed. 'Dad doesn't want to see your bedroom.'

'Shut up yourself,' she retorted, clearly getting out of hand.

'Daddy, don't you think I'm old enough to wear a bra? Stephanie at school's got one, and Melanie's getting one next week.'

'You'll have to ask your mother. How are you getting on at school?' Slider asked Matthew hastily. 'Settling in?'

His son regarded him with troubled eyes. 'All right,' he said guardedly. 'I wish I didn't have to go on the bus, though. If I had a bike I could cycle there. It's only six miles.'

'Not on that main road, Matthew,' Irene said, plainly treading a path that had been trodden before. 'I've told you.' She appealed to Slider. 'He'd have to go part of the way on the A412. You know how the cars zip along there. It's too dangerous.'

'What's wrong with the bus?' Slider asked, trying not to get sucked in.

Matthew blushed again and chewed his lip before admitting, 'The others get at me.'

'What for?'

Even more reluctantly, Matthew said, 'They say the police are the fascist lackeys of state repression.'

Slider was impressed. 'They use longer words than the boys you used to mix with. There's something to be said for private education after all.'

'Don't joke, Dad,' Matthew said. 'Can't we—' He flicked a glance at his mother, which proved he had been going to say, *can't we go home,* and changed it to, 'Can't I go back to my old school?'

'No you can't, Matthew,' Irene said angrily, 'and I wish you'd stop asking that.'

I wish I could help you, Slider thought sadly, but I can't. Sometimes you just have to bear things. 'You'll get used to it,' he said instead, uselessly. 'Everything seems strange at the moment. Just give it time.' And Matthew looked at him in silent reproach, just as he would have done in the same situation.

After such soul-searing, it was quite a relief to be left alone with Irene, even if it was in Ernie Newman's best parlour. The three-piece suite was covered in white and gold brocade, the shagpile carpet was off-white, and the occasional tables had green onyx tops with gold rims. He looked to see what Irene had been doing before he arrived, and saw on the table nearest the dented cushions Irene's reading glasses lying on top of a book called *The Acol Method and After* and next to it a shorthand pad on which notes had been made in Irene's small and careful hand.

'What's the Acol method?' he asked, and refrained from adding a joke about birth control, which would have gone too near too many sensitivities.

'It's bridge,' she said, almost irritably. She knew what he thought about the game. 'As you know very well. I'm brushing up on my bidding.'

'Is he giving you a hard time?'

'Of course not,' she said. 'Everyone gets frustrated sometimes when their partner misses a signal. In fact, Marilyn says husbands and wives shouldn't partner each other – but she's only joking, of course,' she added hastily, perhaps fearing Slider might say something about her not being Ernie Newman's wife.

He felt an enormous sympathy for her welling up, and said instead, 'How's your mother? Did she have her operation?'

She looked at him with relief and gratitude. 'No, they think she might not have to now. She's much better since they've put her on the new pills.'

'Good,' Slider said, nodding encouragingly.

'She asks after you,' Irene offered him, kindness for kindness.

'Well, give her my love next time you speak to her. If you think it's appropriate.'

101

'Of course. She'll be pleased I've seen you.' And now she was looking at him almost wistfully. 'I'm glad to see you, too,' she said in a small voice.

He met her eyes for an agonising moment, and saw in them the same look of bewilderment as in the children's. She was out of her place too; for two pins, Slider thought, she would ask him if they couldn't all go home again. And it was a tempting scenario, that was the damnable thing. It was always easier to settle for the familiar, however disappointing, than to get through the pain of change in the hope of something better. That weight of inertia was marriage's best friend. The words hung unspoken on the air – couldn't we forget everything that's happened in the past year and go back – sink back into our cosy frowst – it wasn't so very bad, was it?

Slider stiffened his sinews. Having got this far, he thought – and that reminded him that he ought to help things along a little, in case, apart from anything else, the ratepayer returned. Seeing his wife in Ernie's house was bad enough, but with Ernie present it would have been intolerable. There was a peculiar – given the circumstances – seed of possessive fury somewhere in him which he did not want to confront. He hardened his heart against her loneliness. She looked so little against Ernie's overstuffed furniture. 'So, you wanted to talk to me about the divorce?'

She chewed her lower lip, for a moment looking absurdly like Matthew, another thing he didn't want to think about. 'I wish I didn't have to, but things have to be sorted out. The thing is, I have to ask you if you're going to contest it. You see, we could arrange everything between us and then instruct a solicitor just to do the paperwork, and that way it could all be done as friendly as possible. I think what none of us want is for things to get nasty – I mean, especially with the children and everything, it would be so awful for them if we quarrelled.'

'Quarrelled?' He was almost amused at the inappropriateness of her nursery language.

'Over – well – money and things. I mean, you've been so good about all this – I just can't tell you how grateful I am that you've taken it so well – and I feel so guilty as well, all I want is for it all to be as easy as possible for everyone concerned.'

He had to put her at her ease. Her guilt reminded him too pointedly of his own. 'That's what I want too,' he said soothingly. 'And of course I won't contest it, as long as we can come to an agreement that satisfies us both.'

'Oh, I won't ask you for anything for myself,' she promised hastily. 'I mean, I want to be fair. And you can see the children whenever you want. There's absolutely no trouble about that. Ernie agrees with me. It's just a question of settling about maintenance for the children.'

'I'm sure we can come to an agreement without anyone getting angry,' he said. 'After all, there are always faults on both sides,' he said. 'A marriage doesn't break up through just one person's fault.'

She allowed her shoulders to drop in an exaggerated gesture of relief which was designed to conceal her very real relief that he was not out to seek vengeance. 'You always were a fair person, Bill. It's one of the things about you,' she said. 'Sometimes it used to annoy me, that you always saw both sides of every argument, but now—'

She was looking at him more meltingly every minute, and the hedgehog of guilt on which he was sitting was growing longer and longer spikes. He didn't want to meet her eyes, for fear of what he might be tempted to blurt out. She was the mother of his children, he had woken up beside her every morning for fourteen years, and even now he could have gone into the strange bedroom she was at present inhabiting and known exactly where she had put every item of her clothing. It was a huge dry bath-bun of knowledge to be swallowed down in one gulp.

'I've got a murder case on at the moment,' he said.

'You look as if you're not getting enough to eat,' she said.

As fine and evasive a pair of *non sequiturs* as you were likely to meet in a twelvemonth, Slider thought. He wondered what Joanna was doing at that very instant.

7

Sleepless on the Settle

Fiona Parsons lived in Chiswick, in that strange tangle of little streets between Chiswick High Road and the river, where Georgian country villas, Victorian workmen's cottages, and Edwardian clerks' semis jostle for proximity to the fabled real-estate values of the Strand on the Green. Miss Parsons lived on the top floor of a two-storey Victorian house which had been almost converted by the owner, who lived downstairs. The almost-conversion had made two separate dwellings within the house without separating them, which meant that when Norma rang the doorbell, the owner – a tall, vague, gangling, bushy-haired, media intellectual inevitably called John – opened the door onto the vista and smell of new buttermilk emulsion, and when asked for Miss Parsons, called up the bare and polished staircase like a husband, 'Fee, darling, it's for you!'

Fiona Parsons' voice floated back unintelligibly from somewhere above, upon which John smiled in a daffy, well-meaning way and said, 'She's upstairs. You'd better go on up.' Norma thought she had better, too, but had only got as far as the first step when John caught up with his thought processes sufficiently to say, 'Isn't that an awful, awful thing about poor Roger! Did you know him? Oh, I just couldn't believe it when she told me. Poor, poor Fiona. And she was actually *there*, poor thing! I can't believe anyone would do such a terrible thing. Such a sweet man!'

'Yes,' said Norma comprehensively, escaping up the stairs.

'She hasn't been to work since,' he called after her. 'It's totally *wrecked* her life.'

Upstairs the conversion had been carried out in the unengagingly dotty manner of the amateur, which meant that while the paint-clogged plaster of the elaborate vine-swag cornices had been painstakingly scraped, cleaned and restored to its full, crisp glory, there were bare wires hanging from the ceiling and the electric sockets were lying on the floor waiting to be chased into the walls; the handsome panelled doors had been stripped to the wood, but their hardware had not been replaced, so that presumably they could not be closed; all the floors had been filled, sanded and varnished, but the kitchen door was leaning against the wall out in the hallway and the hall window was broken.

While Norma was taking a quick peek in at the rooms, Fiona Parsons appeared from the bathroom handsomely wrapped in a fluffy dressing-gown and with her hair turbaned in a towel. She looked, Norma thought irritably, sensational, despite – or perhaps because of – the dark shadows under her eyes. She was the kind of woman who, rising from her bath, always looked like Aphrodite instead of a turbot like the rest of humanity; who naked and smeared with whipped cream would look like a sex goddess rather than just a mucky herbert.

Her mouth took on a downward curve when she saw Norma. 'Oh—!'

'I'm sorry, I was told to come up.'

106

'It's John – he's hopeless! My doorbell's never worked. D'you know, I've been here nearly a year and I've *still* only got a single ring to cook on. The trouble is he won't get anyone in. He insists on doing everything himself, in between writing his stupid scripts. I wish I'd never agreed to come here. I mean, the house will be lovely when it's finished, and he charges me hardly any rent, but I'd sometimes sooner pay the rent and have a bit of privacy. D'you want some coffee?'

'Will it be any trouble?'

'Oh no, I've got an electric kettle. I was going to make some for myself.' She turned towards the kitchen, and Norma followed. 'I don't do much cooking, I have to say. I take most of my meals out. I'd like to be able to entertain sometimes – or rather—' She stopped in confusion, and busied herself with her back to Norma making coffee with much clattering.

'Your landlord seems to have known Roger Greatrex,' Norma said.

'John?' she said with unnecessary insouciance. 'Well, everyone knew him, didn't they. John was a producer at the Beeb before he started freelance scriptwriting.'

'I think it was a rather more personal knowledge than that,' Norma said kindly. 'He's been here, hasn't he?'

Fiona turned with nervous eyes, and her voice came out rather high. 'Why d'you say that?'

It was so pathetic it was touching. 'You've got his picture on your bedside table.'

The eyes filled alarmingly with tears. 'Oh God – oh God—!'

In the end, Norma made the coffee, and by the time she carried in the two mugs to the sitting-room, Fiona Parsons had regained control, and was sitting on the sofa with her legs curled under her, a small alp of wet tissues beside her, ready to talk.

'How did you guess? I thought I was being so discreet.'

'I didn't really, I just thought it might be the case. It was you who asked for him to be on the show; and you went down to meet him in person.'

'But I did that with most of the guests. Phil and I shared the duty between us.'

'Not that night. You only met him, none of the others. And he was early. According to what I've heard, that was very unusual.'

She sighed. 'Yes. I did persuade Martin we ought to have Roger on the show – not that he needed much persuading, Roger's always good value – but Martin wanted to approach the question more from the government side. And he objected that we'd only had Roger a few weeks ago – although it was actually eight weeks, but it was still quite soon – so I pointed out that Roger and Sandal had both been in the news recently, and that we ought to have both of them. I said we could hardly have an arts-funding debate without them and in the end he agreed, and so that was that.'

'Why did you want him on the programme, though?'

'It was a chance to see him,' she said, and sighed again. 'I hadn't had a moment with him for weeks, and I'd hardly even spoken to him for days. It was so difficult to find time to be together, with both of us so busy, so it seemed too good a chance to miss.'

'You arranged the whole programme just to spend a few minutes with him?'

She blushed. 'Oh, I know that sounds awful and teenagery, but I just needed to be with him. Haven't you ever been in love?'

'Yes.'

Fiona studied her face as if to test how likely that was to be true, and then, apparently satisfied, said, 'Well, then, you'll know.'

'How long had you been seeing each other?'

'A year,' she said with faint pride, as though the length of time added legitimacy. 'Well, I've known him for ages, but it was just a year since we first – since we fell in love.' She looked defiantly at Norma as though she might challenge the phrase.

Obligingly, Norma did. 'Was he in love with you?'

'We were going to be married.'

Norma felt sad. She had heard this bilious tale before. 'But he was already married.'

'Yes, but he didn't love her. It was all over between them, really – had been for years. Just a marriage of form. They didn't sleep together or anything.'

'So she knew about you?'

'Well – no. He had to keep it secret from her. I mean, he was going to tell her, but he had to wait for the right moment. You see, everything was in her name – the house and everything – and if she wanted to be vindictive, she could have made it very difficult for him.'

So could you, Norma thought, marvelling yet again at the unquenchable silliness of even the most intelligent women in the quest for *lerve*. 'And in the meantime, you and he slept together, when he could spare the time.' When it was said, she wished she hadn't, for she didn't want to alienate her.

'I suppose it's your job to put the worst gloss on everything,' Miss Parsons said with dignity, 'but I can assure you that Roger and I were in love and were going to be married. It's just—'

'Yes?'

Fiona hesitated, evidently unwilling to spoil the picture she'd painted. 'It was difficult for us to get time together,' she said as if it were the beginning of a sentence.

Norma finished it for her. 'And just lately it had got more difficult?'

109

'Yes.'

'You began to wonder whether he was avoiding you?'

'Yes. No! Well, yes, all right. I did wonder if he was cooling off a bit.'

'Seeing other women.'

'He wouldn't have done that. He loved me. But – but I did wonder if he was trying to back out of marrying me. He didn't like discussing it. Sometimes he got angry if I brought the subject up. We had rows. He said it spoilt our time together, arguing about it, and I suppose it did, but somehow when I thought he was trying to avoid the subject it seemed to be the one thing I couldn't get out of my mind.' Norma nodded encouragingly. 'It was wonderful at first. He used to come here – John was sweet about it – and it was bliss, he's a wonderful lover, and then we'd go to a restaurant – there are lots of really great ones in Chiswick – and we'd talk about where we'd live when we were married and what we'd do, and then we'd come back here and he stayed quite late, sometimes all night.' She sighed. 'We had a terrible row about three weeks ago. I wanted us to go on holiday together. I'd been talking about it for ages, and he'd sort of not said yes or no, so I assumed it was all right, and I got the brochures and everything, and when I showed him and tried to get him to agree on a date, he told me it was absolutely out of the question. And I flared up, and all the old stuff came up again, and we quarrelled – and—'

'And after that you didn't see him and he was offhand on the phone and you were afraid he was going to drop you. So you thought if he was invited on the show he'd have to come and you'd have a chance to talk to him,' Norma finished for her. Fiona, looking shamefaced and much younger than her years, nodded.

'It sounds awful, doesn't it?' she said in a small voice.

'We've all been there, love,' Norma said sadly. 'So tell me what happened on the night.'

'I'd asked him to come early, and I was so pleased when he did. I went down to meet him, and I could see straightaway he was in a good mood. We went up to green, and as soon as we were inside with the door closed he started kissing me. I tried to talk to him, but he kept stopping me by kissing me, and in between he said, "No talking tonight, all right? Let's just be happy like we used to be." And then he said, "I've missed you, darling Fee. Let's have tonight to remember."'

'What do you think he meant by that?'

'I don't know. I didn't want to think. It sounded so final, I thought maybe he meant to drop me.' She raised appalled eyes to Norma's. 'You don't think he meant that he was going to kill himself, and that it would be our last time?'

'No, I don't think he meant that.'

The appalled voice was down to a thread. 'It wasn't suicide?'

'I don't think so. Do you?'

'I didn't want it to be,' she said voicelessly. 'But if it wasn't – who could have killed him?'

'I was hoping you might tell me,' Norma said with grim humour.

'You don't think – *I* did it?' Fiona stared. 'You can't! I didn't. I wouldn't! Why would I?'

'It was one way of stopping him leaving you. After all, this way he'll never belong to another woman. If you weren't his first love, at least you're his last.'

Fiona Parsons did not burst into tears, for which Norma liked her better. She seemed, rather, puzzled by the accusation.

'But I could never have done that. However angry I was with him.'

'And were you angry?'

'I suppose – yes, I was underneath. He was treating me

111

like an object. I mean, I loved our lovemaking, but he kept stopping me from talking. He wouldn't discuss things with me. He wasn't treating me like an adult.'

'So where were you between seven o'clock and twenty past? Where were you during the time Roger Greatrex was out of the greenroom, supposed to be going to make-up but never arriving there?'

She was still staring, her brain evidently working behind her stationary eyes. 'You think—? Oh but that's absurd!'

'Where were you?' Norma insisted.

'Well, with him, of course.'

Norma was wrong-footed, but caught herself up quickly. 'Naturally you were. But where with him?'

Now Fiona blushed richly. 'In the properties room on four. I had the key, and there was a chaise-longue in there. I said I'd meet him in there. He said he'd make sure he went up to make-up alone, and instead of going up he'd come to me.'

'So you were making love with him on a chaise-longue in the properties room while Philip Somers was scouring the building for him, and you never thought to tell us?'

'I – I couldn't – I didn't like to—'

'Where is this properties room?'

'It's on the left just past stairway five. That's left out of the greenroom and past the stairs. Past—'

'Past the gents where he was found.' She nodded painfully. 'Let's have some times, then. You met him when? And left him when?'

'I don't know exactly. I went to the props room when I left green, and he arrived a few minutes later. And we made love, and then straightaway he went. I wanted to talk, but he just smiled and put his finger on my lips – like this – to stop me – and he went. And that's the last time I saw him.' She was fighting tears now.

'So how long were you making love? Ten minutes? Fifteen?'

'*I* don't know. How long does it take?'

Norma was afraid any minute something gagworthy about eternity might be said, and let it go. Clearly Miss Parsons was not going to put her lover against the clock, but Norma betted it was on the shy side of a lingering experience, to judge from the peripheral mood that had been described. 'When you came out of the props room, was he anywhere in sight?'

'No. The corridor was empty.'

'And you went—?'

'Down stairway five to the ladies on three, and then to the studio.' She bit her lip to keep it from trembling. 'I dodged around a good bit in the studio, so that no-one would know where I'd been. And also because I didn't want to speak to anyone. I was too upset.'

'I should think you were,' said Norma. Then, remembering Slider's last minute instruction to her before she left the station, she asked, 'What form of contraception did you use?'

She blushed furiously. 'What business is it of yours?'

'Believe me, it's important. I'm not asking for thrills. What did you and Roger use?'

'I'm on the Pill,' she said.

'Despite the fact that he was sterile?'

'He wasn't,' Fiona said, indignantly, as though it was a slight.

'One of his closest friends says he was sterile, that he and his wife couldn't have children.'

'They *didn't* have any,' Fiona said – evidently she didn't know about Jamie – or didn't know Norma did – 'but that's because he didn't want them. He told me so. He said his wife had always wanted a family, but he hated the idea, so he took precautions.'

'He told you that – but you don't know it for a fact?'

'Why would he lie?' she asked simply. 'In fact, we used condoms at first, but he hated them so much he made me go on the Pill. If he was sterile, why wouldn't he have told me so?'

Pride, Norma thought; but Fiona had a point. Maybe he hadn't been lying. Maybe Palliser had got it wrong. Maybe it wasn't all that important anyway – except that the guv'nor wanted it asked, and he usually had his reasons.

'Well,' Norma said at last, 'my guv'nor won't be happy with the fact that you've been withholding information. You've wasted a lot of our time.'

'I couldn't talk about it. It's too important to me to have you people picking over it like ghouls. I knew you would make it sound sordid.' The eyes were filling again.

Quickly Norma asked, 'Were you ever in the Girl Guides?'

'Yes, I was. Why?' The surprise of the question had the effect of stopping the tears in their tracks.

'Oh, I just thought you might have been,' Norma said shortly. She'd taken quite a dislike to Miss Starry-Eyed Parsons.

McLaren put his head round the door. 'Did you call me, guv?'

Slider looked up. 'Why would I call you guv? I'm the boss.' McLaren didn't quite roll his eyes, but it was close. 'What's this note on my desk? I can't read it. I wish you people would learn to write clearly.'

'Victim of child-centred teaching methods, guv,' McLaren said smartly, in the manner of one asking for two bob for a cup of tea. He studied his note for a moment with frowning concentration. 'Oh, yeah, it's about the audience lists. It might be nothing, but there's a discrepancy between the names the tickets were sent to, and the names we took up in the hospitality room.'

'I imagine there'd be some no shows.'

'There were eight. But this is something else. There was a

ticket sent to a Mr James Davies, spelt "ies", but the name he gave in the hospitality room was John Davis, and spelt with an "is".'

'Could be a mistake. Who actually took it down?'

'I haven't worked that out yet. I don't recognise the hand-writing, and there were a lot of them up there. But it's SOP to check spellings, so I thought I'd better mensh.'

'Whoever it was might have misheard, or even heard it right and written it wrong. These things happen.'

'Yeah. All the same—' McLaren said hopefully.

'Of course, check it out. It's the unturned stone that gathers the moss,' Slider said. 'No luck from the search parties, I suppose?'

'No, guv. But they've still got the big outside bins to check.'

'Joy to the world. And no witnesses?'

'It's hard to find out who was actually in the building at the time. I'm glad I'm not their security chief.'

'We really need some more general appeal.'

'TV? *Crimewatch?*'

'I think it's early days for that. Anyway, I didn't mean that general. I'd like to leaflet every BBC employee but that's out of the question, both from the time and the expense point of view.'

'Sandwich board, then, in reception?'

'Yes,' Slider said. 'That might be best.' The difficulty would be to persuade Honeyman to it. Once you went public, the stopwatch started ticking, and your performance was under scrutiny. 'Check out this Davis, anyway. Clear as you go along. On the subject of which, Somers and Palliser are both supposed to be coming in to give their fingerprints. Ask the counter to let me know as soon as they arrive.'

'Rightyoh.'

★ ★ ★

'She obviously thought telling me was letting herself off,' Norma said in the canteen, hunching forward over her cup of tea with the urgency of persuading him, 'but she could still have done it. Reading between the lines, what Greatrex was after that night was a quick dip, not extending of the frontiers of sensuality. I reckon a few minutes, ten at the outside. There was still time for her to kill him afterwards and tidy herself up.'

'Whoever killed him,' Slider pointed out fairly, 'did it after he left her, so there must have been time.'

'Right, guv. And, you see, I was thinking: what's the first thing a man does when he's finished making love?'

Slider pondered. 'Goes home to the wife?'

'Very funny,' Norma said loftily. 'He goes for a pee, doesn't he? It's the most natural thing in the world. Greatrex bonks her, says goodbye, then heads for the make-up room, popping into the loo on the way. It's the first one he'd pass. It explains why he went there, and not the one upstairs nearest to make-up. And Parsons, furious with being treated like a substitute Mrs Palmer, follows him straight in there and whacks him. It makes sense, doesn't it?'

'So far.'

'And she admits she deliberately foiled her own trail in the studio. So she's got no alibi, and she had the motive, and we know she was in the vicinity. A big, strong, baseball-playing girl,' she reminded him.

'Yes,' Slider said. 'But you're talking spur of the moment, not slow burn—'

'Both. She'd been building up a fury for weeks.'

'But she'd have had to bring the knife with her. That means planning.'

Norma leaned towards him so eagerly that one or two others in the canteen ostentatiously didn't look at them, in case it was an assignation. 'I had a thought about that, and it makes her very attractive for the frame. The knife could have been lying about in the properties room where they had their hump. Or she could have got it from any of the props stores. She started at the Beeb as a properties buyer – who better than her would know? And those places are full of junk – you just never know what's in 'em. And they're not locked – anyone can walk through.'

'I wish you hadn't said that,' Slider complained. 'Now someone will have to check whether such a knife is missing.'

Norma's face fell a little as she realised the work involved. 'I doubt whether you could ever say conclusively it wasn't,' she said. 'Even if anyone knows what should be there, they wouldn't be able to say what never had been.'

'I get your drift. But what about the blood?'

'I've been thinking about that, too – need there have been that much? Standing behind him, reaching round, and making one quick, hard slash – I wonder if there'd have been more than a bit of blood on the hands? Remember she was wearing three-quarter sleeves. And she says herself she went to the ladies before going back to the studio – she could have washed and checked she was all right there.'

Slider sighed. 'It's all very plausible, but you know that's not enough, don't you? We've got to have evidence.'

'Yes, guv. I'll check out the properties to start with for the knife. And we could ask for her watch and bracelet – even if she's washed 'em, there might be traces of blood in the links.'

'It's possible. All right, you can ask her.'

'Thanks, guv.' She jumped up energetically, and then thought of something. 'By the way, why did you ask me to ask her about Greatrex being sterile?'

'Oh, just a little stream I was meandering along. Probably leading nowhere.'

117

'Never mind,' she said comfortingly, 'we might still find a witness.'

Palliser did not show up, but Somers came in, looking more ill than ever, and allowed his fingerprints to be taken, observing the operation as though it were happening to someone else. Slider took the opportunity to question him more closely about exactly where he had been to look for Greatrex, and whether he had passed anyone on the way, but he was of little help, seeming to have slipped into a deeper state of shock than he was in on the night in question.

Slider showed him out. Nicholls, the sergeant on duty in the front shop, let Slider back in behind the counter and said, 'That bloke – I know him from somewhere. What's his name?'

'Somers,' Slider said, pausing to look at Nicholls with interest. Nutty had a capacious memory for detail. 'Philip Somers. One of the witnesses in the Greatrex case. He found the body, in fact.'

'Somers. That name rings a bell. I'm sure I've seen him before.' Nicholls pondered.

'I've checked his record. He's got no previous,' Slider said. 'I had 'em all checked. Greatrex himself was nicked a couple of times for possession of cannabis in his young and heady days, which is just what you'd expect, but everyone else is as clean as a whistle.'

'Och, don't worry, it'll come to me. Somers – Greatrex.' He tapped his forehead. 'It's all in here somewhere. The mind's a computer, Bill – a computer of fabulous power.'

'I know that. But remember, the first rule of computers is rubbish in, rubbish out.'

'And we get to deal with all the rubbish,' Nutty said in an undertone as the shop door opened and a lean man in a stained fawn mackintosh came in. He had the sort of hair

118

that looked as though he'd been playing with live wires, and carried a plastic bag ominously full of documents. His face wore the monomaniac intensity of the intellectually disrupted, and Slider beat a hasty retreat, hearing Nicholls behind him say with massive patience, 'Yes, sir, can I help you? It's not the CIA tapping your phone again, is it?'

Slider was woken from a heavy sleep by a kiss on the cheek, and struggled up through layers of black flannel to find Joanna hunkered beside him, smiling. She was still in her coat, which was over her long black dress; she smelled of outdoors, with a faint whiff of cigarette smoke from her hair.

'What are you doing, sleeping on the sofa?' she said.

'I wasn't sleeping, I was thinking.'

'You're an awful liar,' she said kindly. 'Why didn't you go to bed?'

'I don't like that bed when you're not in it,' he said feeling foolish.

'You don't mean you've slept on the sofa ever since I went away?'

'Not at all. I just haven't slept,' he said with dignity, struggling into a sitting position. 'What are you doing home so early?'

'I couldn't wait to be with you, so I didn't even go to the pub.'

'You smell of the pub.'

'That was the interval. Don't you want me? Shall I go away again?'

'I wasn't sure you were coming back tonight. I thought you might stay with your parents again,' he said.

She eyed him cannily, resting her elbows on his knees and her chin on her hands. 'What's the matter?' she asked.

'Nothing,' he protested. He expected her to wheedle it out of him, but instead she got up and went out of the room, and he was afraid she had taken offence – afraid and annoyed. He could hear her moving about, and after a bit got up and followed her. She was in the kitchen. She'd taken off her coat and was making cheese sandwiches by the simple method of cutting wedges of cheese and folding a slice of unbuttered bread round each. He sniffed the air for her mood, but she said in a normal voice, though without turning round, 'I'm starving. Have you eaten? D'you want one of these?'

'No thanks.'

She flicked a look at him over her shoulder, and said, 'I want a whisky. Have one with me? I wish you'd lit the fire – I've been looking forward to a Laphroaig in front of the fire all the way up the M23.'

'It didn't seem cold enough,' he said, hoping his voice sounded natural to her, because it didn't to him. He collected the bottle and two glasses and led the way back into the sitting-room. He sat on the Chesterfield, and she got into the opposite corner with her legs tucked under her so that she was facing him, what he thought of as her interrogation position. The thought that he knew so many of her gestures made him smile inwardly, and she saw it.

'So, what's the matter?' she asked again. 'Did seeing Irene upset you?'

He was surprised. 'No! Well, yes, it did, I suppose, but I'd forgotten all about that. There's nothing wrong, really. I've missed you, that's all. I don't like it here without you, but I've got nowhere else to go.'

'And?'

He gave an embarrassed sort of smirk. 'If you must know, I was jealous.'

'Jealous?' She sounded incredulous.

'There you were, in the Trevor, drinking pints, having fun—'

120

'I was working.'

'—with all your friends around you.'

'You had nothing to be jealous of. On the other hand, I've had a hellish time thinking of you going to see Irene.'

'You can't be jealous of Irene,' he protested.

'But I am. She had you for all those years. Her interest in you was legitimate. You shared your life with her, she knew everything about you.'

'It was never the way it is with you, with her,' he said.

She grinned. 'I'm glad to hear it. But even knowing that doesn't help. I'm not talking rationality here.'

'I'm glad to know you do get jealous. I find that comforting. When I think of you surrounded by all those men – and musicians at that! What are you laughing about?'

'I've spent all my spare time for the last two days in the company of Clive Barrow, principal cello, and his friend John. They're wonderful company.' Slider raised an enquiring eyebrow. 'We call them the Botty Celli. You had nothing to worry about.'

'If lack of opportunity is the only assurance I've got—'

She put her plate down, reached for his neck, and pulled him to her to kiss him. 'There's no pleasing some people. And when I came home early especially to give you something.'

'I've got something for you, too,' he said.

'Oh? Oh, so you have.'

Fortunately it was not until about fifteen minutes later that the telephone rang. 'It's bound to be for you,' Joanna said, struggling into a sitting position and pushing the hair out of her eyes.

It was. 'Ah, Bill – did I get you out of bed?' It was Tufty.

'No, I'm still up.'

'Lucky pup. Wish I was.'

'What are you doing still on duty?'

121

'Looking after your interests. I had a swiftie with Bob Lamont earlier, and I bullied him into having a look at your fingerprints. He's just come through to tell me he thinks the thumb on the wallet is the same as the set you sent through today – Philip Somers. He's got to go over it again in the morning in more detail, but he mentioned in passing he's pretty sure it's the man, so I thought I'd mention it to you, in case you wanted to go and surprise a confession out of him.'

'At this time of night?'

'Best time – catch him unawares. A few sharpened matches under the fingernails—'

'We don't do that in the CID.'

'No? Oh well, suit yourself. At least it'll give you something to chew over in the stilly watches.'

'There's plenty to chew,' Slider said.

'Mastication is the thief of time,' Arceneaux warned.

'I wish you hadn't said that.'

'Said what?' Joanna asked as he returned to her.

'My prime suspect's just been and got primer,' he said, gathering her into his arms. 'God, you feel nice! I'm tired. Let's go to bed.'

'Not one of those sentences goes with another,' she complained.

8

Relative Values

They arranged to meet Atherton for breakfast at the Dôme down by the river at Kew Bridge.

'How's it going between him and Sue?' Slider asked on the way there.

'How does he say it's going?'

'Don't you start getting evasive,' Slider complained.

'Like that, is it? Well, as far as I can see, they're very interested in each other, and each is trying to advance their relationship by pretending not to be.'

'That's helpful,' Slider said.

'It's a problem,' Joanna said seriously. 'Sue's had a couple of lousy relationships, so she's not going to be the first one to show her hand. And from what I can gather, he seems to want her to make the running. It isn't fair.'

'He has more to lose than her,' Slider said absently, and drew down a storm on his head. 'I only meant that he's quite happy being single, whereas she—'

'Happy? Much you know. And I tell you something else – if Jim doesn't sort himself out soon, he's going to end up a very sad case. If you're his friend you should tell him so. Sue's the most generous person in the world, and she'd give him everything, but she's not going to parade herself like a concubine while he lies back on a divan and plays the sultan. It's for the man to make the first move, always has been and always will be.'

'I love it when you play the traditional woman,' Slider smiled. 'Can't you see my chest swelling?'

Joanna looked sideways at him. 'I know how to handle men,' she said modestly. 'Flatter their egos and they're putty in your hands.'

'I don't like those plurals,' Slider objected.

'That's exactly what Sue says.'

They found Atherton sitting alone in a patch of sunlight like a contented cat, reading *The Observer*.

'Make you go blind,' Slider warned, pulling out a chair for Joanna. 'No Sue?'

'She's got a rehearsal. She's doing a concert tonight – Verdi's Requiem at Woburn Parish Church.'

'Bad luck,' Slider sympathised.

Atherton shrugged. 'Her family lives in Woburn Sands, so it's a chance to see them.'

'At least it's the Verdi,' Joanna said. 'It's the only choral piece anyone really likes doing. We call it the Okay Chorale.'

'Anyway, she needs the money,' Atherton added repressingly.

'Who doesn't?'

'In the midst of life we are in debt,' said Slider. The waitress arrived and they ordered, and the conversation wandered off on the trail of breakfast generally, and where you could get the best hash browns in New York – a subject on which Slider had little to say, since he'd never been there. So it was not long before they reverted to the case, some of the details of which were new to Joanna.

'From a professional viewpoint I can't be sorry he's dead,' she said. 'Critics like him do nothing but harm. They know nothing about music – often their crits are the purest bunkum. I've read a crit in a serious paper that said the playing was "off-key". What the hell does that mean, "off-key"? And they perpetuate all sorts of ghastly snobberies and one-uppishness about which composer's "better" than another, just because it's this year's fad. And they never give *us* credit, even though we do all the work. It's because of them soloists and conductors can get such humungous fees.'

'Don't sugar-coat it,' Slider advised. 'Tell us what you really think.'

'How can you say they know nothing about music?' Atherton said indignantly, from the vantage point of an arts page reader.

'Because I've read what they've said about concerts I've played in.'

'You just don't like criticism.'

'*Informed* criticism I can take. But look at what Roger Greatrex said about the *Don*, for instance – praising Lupton's "incisive conducting", for a start, without mentioning the fact that every single evening he follows us for the first sixteen bars because he hasn't the faintest idea how to cope with that opening.'

Slider listened indulgently, having trodden these paths before in Joanna's wake. 'Well, perhaps whoever murdered him was a music lover,' he suggested lightly.

'You said you had a prime suspect?' Joanna veered obediently.

'We've several,' Slider said. He told Atherton about Tufty's telephone call.

'I'm not sure where that gets us,' Atherton said, 'except that it proves Somers interfered with the body. Which means he's lied to us. But what did he want from the wallet? He didn't take money or credit cards.'

'Whatever it was he wanted, it suggests he may have had a motive for the killing.'

'Anyone *may* have had.'

'He was the only person covered in blood, the only person we actually know had contact with Greatrex's essential fluids,' Slider said; but his tone was dissatisfied.

'What?' Atherton asked. 'You prefer Palliser or Parsons?'

'Or Person or Persons Unknown,' Slider said. 'The trouble is we haven't found an explanation that fits all the circumstances yet. All we're doing is eliminating this and that. What about that religious tract card, for instance? How does that fit in?'

'Maybe it doesn't,' Joanna said. 'Maybe he picked it up somewhere out of curiosity, or did it for a joke to give to someone. Or maybe some nut shoved it at him in the street and he put it in his pocket absent-mindedly and forgot about it. There could be any number of explanations that've got nothing to do with his death. I wouldn't like to take bets on the odd stuff you'd find in my pockets after a day on the tubes or in the streets. I was given a flyer for an evangelist meeting at St Martin-in-the-Fields last week, and just stuck it in my pocket. If I'd been killed next minute you'd be hanging around the Crypt looking for a killer in Jesus boots.'

'True, if unhelpful.'

'Which takes you straight back to your prime suspect.'

'Of course, we don't *know* that Somers had a motive, just because he messed with the body,' Atherton said. 'He might just have been exercising an unpleasant curiosity.'

'But he did say something to Fiona Parsons about not wanting to have anything to do with Greatrex,' Slider said. 'According to Dorothy Hammond he said he wouldn't share the same planet with him if he could help it.'

'It doesn't mean he had the drive – or the balls – to kill him,' Atherton said. 'Now Sandal Palliser, he's a different class of a man, as O'Flaherty would say. He's mean and he's tough, and we know he's concealing something from us. That's suspicious behaviour.'

Slider sipped his coffee. 'Sandal Palliser said *cherchez la femme.*'

'That alone should be enough to condemn him,' Atherton said. 'Anyone who uses cliché like that—'

'French cliché, which is even worse,' Joanna added.

'I should like you to follow up Somers,' Slider said. 'See what frightening him with the fingerprints will do.'

'Whatever you say, captain,' Atherton said. 'What about you?'

'I'm going to see Palliser again – after I've made a couple of phone calls.'

'I thought you didn't think it was Palliser?'

'That's why I'm bringing an unbiased mind to it.'

'Clear as you go, that's what you always say,' said Atherton, getting up.

'Are you staying here?' Slider asked Joanna.

'Might as well,' she said, and to Atherton, 'Leave me the paper?'

'I'll phone you later,' Slider said. 'I don't expect I'll be late today.' It still seemed odd to be saying that to Joanna instead of Irene. Odd, but nice.

Sandal Palliser seemed resigned rather than surprised to see Slider. 'Can't I even have my Sundays to myself?' He was looking tired, and some of the steel had gone out of his frame. Age had crept up a bit closer to him over the weekend.

'I'm sorry,' Slider said without regret. 'There are some things I want to ask you about your movements on Thursday. There are still some gaps to be filled.'

127

'Dogged type, aren't you?' Palliser sneered. 'I've told you all I intend to tell you. Unless you want to charge me.'

'Oh, I don't want to do that,' Slider said calmly. 'Not yet, anyway.' Palliser was still blocking the door, and Slider glanced past him and said, 'Can I come in?'

Palliser had looked at him carefully after the penultimate words, and said at last, more soberly, 'Oh, very well. You can talk to me all you like. I don't promise to answer you, that's all.'

'Is Mrs Palliser in?' Slider asked, following him into the passage and closing the door behind him – there was not room for him to pass and let Palliser do it.

'No, she's gone to church.'

'You don't accompany her?'

'I'm not of her persuasion,' Palliser said coldly. 'You'd better come up to my study.'

Upstairs, Palliser turned his chair from his desk so that he was facing the window, and gestured Slider to the other. The room was chilly with the sun off it, but outside the garden romped and burgeoned and seeded itself as nature intended, and Palliser fixed his gaze on it, as though it comforted.

'Very well,' he said. 'Talk away.'

'I've been trying to get to the bottom of the relationship between you and Greatrex and Mrs Greatrex,' Slider began.

'What the hell business is it of yours anyway?'

'A man's been murdered. I'm afraid that means a lot of things become my business, whether I want them to or not. Frankly, I'd just as soon not delve into your private life' – Palliser gave a grim little smile in acknowledgement of the touch – 'but you haven't been very forthcoming, Mr Palliser. You've refused to answer some questions. And you've told me lies.'

Palliser stared at the garden. 'Oh really?' he said indifferently.

'For one thing, you told me that Roger Greatrex was infertile. Now that just wasn't true.' Palliser did not move or answer. 'I checked with his mistress. I checked with his GP. And this morning I checked with his wife.'

Now Palliser shot him an angry look. 'You can leave Caroline out of it.'

'Well, no, I can't do that,' Slider said gently. 'But she confirmed what I had already been told by someone else – that their lack of children was because he wouldn't, rather than because he couldn't. Now, I can't help wondering why you would tell me such a thing – unsolicited – when it wasn't true.'

'It's what he told me. I can't help it if he lied to me.'

'Oh, but I don't think he did. It just isn't a lie a man would tell without a good reason, and he had no good reason. And if you and he went woman-hunting together in earlier days, it's something that would have been on your minds – the fear of unwanted pregnancies. No, I don't think Greatrex would have lied to you on that score; so I come back to the question, why would you tell me such a thing? And more importantly, why would you want to believe it?'

Palliser's face looked yellow, but it might have been the cold northerly light from the window. 'For God's sake—' he muttered, and stopped.

'The other thing you told me that relates to the subject is that Greatrex's son Jamie is not really his son,' Slider went on, watching him closely. 'If that was the case, whose son is he? You don't answer. Well, it was meant to be a rhetorical question. Because unless you're suggesting that Mrs Greatrex was inclined to run around with other men, you must be wanting me to think that you were the father.'

Palliser jumped up angrily. 'Oh shut up!' he said, fists clenched by his side. 'Shut up! Shut up!' But he didn't move, either to threaten Slider or leave the room. Slider had seen that rage before in his own son – the ineffectual rage of helplessness – of pain and guilt that can't be escaped.

'It all begins to make sense,' Slider went on, 'when a few other facts are added. The fact that you and Mrs Greatrex were fond of each other before her marriage, and that you went on being "devoted to her" – according to my source. You were always ready, even longing, to help her. You felt she demeaned herself by marrying Greatrex. You hated him for being unfaithful to her. When she ran away from him that one time, you went to her to comfort her; and it was after she returned to him that she announced she was pregnant—'

'Shut your mouth! If you say one more word—!'

Slider ignored him. 'I'm not sure whether you really thought you were the father of the child, or if you only wished you were, and gradually convinced yourself. But at all events, you liked to keep an eye on the child, and on Mrs Greatrex. Letters, phone calls, little presents. And any slight to either the boy or Mrs Greatrex from Roger Greatrex you regarded as a cause for anger on your part.'

Palliser was trying to regain control of himself. He sat down, facing Slider but not meeting his eyes. 'You seem to have quite a talent for fiction. Well, as long as you're enjoying yourself—' he said, trying for lightness and managing only to sound brittle. The muscles of his mouth were trembling. 'Though I can't imagine where you think it will get you, or what you think your fairy tale has got to do with Roger's death—'

'Well, you see, I had to account to myself for two things in particular,' Slider said helpfully. 'Your quarrel with Greatrex on Thursday, and the telephone call you said you made. They were the two things you wouldn't tell me about, so I couldn't help wondering whether they were connected. Fortunately, you used your mobile phone, and all calls on mobile phones are logged by the phone company. It was quite simple for me to find out what number you called.' Palliser was definitely yellow now. 'Didn't you realise that? Oh dear. Well, it turned out to be a Petworth number – the number of a home for retarded children.'

Palliser said nothing. He looked at his clenched hands which rested on his knees, and he looked very, very old. Slider felt almost sorry for him.

'One other telephone call I made added the last bit of information. It was to St Catherine's House – that's where they keep the register of births and marriages nowadays, what used to be Somerset House when we were younger. Doesn't have quite the same ring to it, does it? Anyway, it turns out that Thursday was Jamie Greatrex's birthday, one of the three occasions during the year when Roger always went to visit his son. Went rather reluctantly, according to Caroline, but still, he did his duty. Only last Thursday he didn't go. He called it off. Told the lad he was too busy. But he wasn't, was he?'

Slider had hoped for but not expected an answer, but Palliser gave him one. 'No, he wasn't busy,' he spat. 'He was with a woman. His new one – not that pathetic Parsons cow – even she didn't know about her. He boasted to me about it – boasted! He—'

Palliser stopped abruptly, and Slider said, 'Oh, it's all right, you haven't told me anything I didn't know. That's what you quarrelled about, wasn't it? You were furious that he'd let the boy down. He told you to mind your own business. You asked how he would make amends. He laughed and said one day was like another to Jamie, that the boy wouldn't notice whether he visited him or not. You were interrupted before the argument could go further. Later you went out of the room to get

131

a little privacy to telephone Jamie, though you'd already phoned him earlier in the day, your usual birthday call – oh yes, the lady I spoke to at the home was most helpful. And you discovered that Jamie was very upset about the missed visit – she told me that, too.'

Palliser put his hands to his face and rubbed his eyes. He seemed almost dazed. 'You've been busy,' he said. 'You don't really need me to tell you anything. What did Caroline say?'

'That Jamie was Roger's child,' Slider said. 'That you had no reason to think otherwise.'

His face sharpened. 'There was reason,' he said quickly. Then he sighed. 'It was only the once. She was desperately unhappy and turned to me for comfort; but she never forgave herself, or me. It was the only time she was ever unfaithful to Roger. She's of the old school, and very strict with herself. Ironic, really, when you think what she married. But Jamie was the only child she ever had, and he was born nine months after our – our one time. What would you think?' Slider declined to answer. 'I don't care what Caroline says, Jamie's mine – and she knows it, though it doesn't suit her ideas to admit it, not even to me – perhaps not even to herself. He's mine – but for her sake I'd never say anything, or let the boy guess – of course I wouldn't. I'm just his Uncle Sandy,' he said bitterly, 'and that bastard Roger was Daddy. I'd have given him a home – Phyllis would have accepted him for my sake – but bastard Roger shut him up in an institution, and only spared him three visits a year – and even then only if it didn't interfere with his *pleasures*. I hope he rots in Hell!'

'Yes,' Slider said. 'It's no wonder you were angry. Especially after you found out how upset the boy was. I expect you wanted to kill him, didn't you?'

Palliser looked at him, and bared his teeth in what might have passed for a smile. 'Oh no you don't! I'm not simple-minded. I can see where you're going, but it won't wash. Besides, I've got my alibi now, conveniently ferreted out by yourself: I was on the telephone. You've established that.'

Slider shook his head. 'The call was logged from seven-oh-three to seven-fifteen. That still left you time to find Greatrex and kill him, I'm afraid. Unless you want to tell me where you were after you rang off?'

'I – don't know. Not exactly. I walked about a bit. I was very upset, I needed time to compose myself.' He seemed suddenly to have come to a realisation of danger.

'Where did you walk?'

'Just – around. Along the corridors. I don't know exactly.'

'And did you see anyone? Did anyone see you?'

'I don't know. I don't remember.' The game had been abandoned, the pretences put aside. He looked at Slider helplessly. 'Are you going to arrest me?'

Slider let him wait for a long minute. Outside, the birds shouted in the tangled garden. He thought of Mrs Palliser's complex web of pain, of how much she must know and how much she would have to guess about her husband's obsessions; and he made it a good long minute. Then he said, 'No. But don't leave the country, will you?'

Palliser saw him out in a rather depressed silence. At the door, Slider said, 'When you told me you were not of your wife's religion – you're a Catholic, aren't you?'

'Why should you think that?'

'Oh, a guess. If Lord Chirnside is a devout Catholic but found you an acceptable companion for his children, it seems likely that you were one too.'

Palliser studied Slider's face, seeming almost puzzled. 'You're oddly perceptive for a policeman,' he said.

'We're not all Mr Plod, sir,' Slider said, parodying. Palliser was silent. 'Well, are you?'

'Lapsed,' he said tersely.

Philip Somers still lived with his parents, a little to Atherton's surprise, in a house in The Fairway in East Acton. The door was opened to him by a smart, pretty young woman of around twenty, framed by a narrow hallway with unforgivable wallpaper and a carpet which was obviously new and must therefore, hard though it was to believe, have been intentional. There was the sound of a wireless in the background and a level of voices and clashing crockery which suggested a large number of people somewhere inside; and the air was heavy with a complex aroma of roast beef, roast potatoes, Bisto gravy and cabbage.

Atherton showed his ID and introduced himself. The girl smiled brightly, like a well-trained receptionist. 'Hakkun a hip yey?'

'I would like to speak to Philip Somers, if he's in. Would he be your brother?'

'That's right. I'm Mandy. I s'pose you'd better come in.' She turned her head to yell, 'Mu-u-um!' on three cadences, and then stepped back from the door and almost bowed. 'Do come in.'

Atherton advanced far enough to see through the first door a sitting-room crammed with furniture and knick-knacks, a brown cut moquette suite of early seventies vintage, another new carpet with swirls of brown and cream on a coffee background, and a television the size of a Fiat Uno dominating the corner beside the imitation York stone fireplace. A second door just beyond presumably led to the dining-room, for it was from there that the sounds of voices and clashing came, and straight ahead was a narrow kitchen, filled with steam and women.

One of them detached herself – a grey-haired woman in an apron, worn over a tight Sunday dress Atherton recognised as quintessentially Marks and Spencer – and approached him with polite enquiry. The fingers of her hands were thick as sausages and shiny with years of food preparation and housework; the features of her face were blunted and blurred with years of wife – and motherhood. Atherton adored her on sight.

'Mrs Somers?'

'That's right,' she said, the faintest hint of Irish in her voice almost eroded by time.

Atherton introduced himself. 'I'm awfully sorry, I'm afraid I've come at a bad time. You're just about to have dinner.'

'It'll be a half an hour yet,' she said. She scanned his face anxiously. 'Is it Phil you've come to see? He's not in trouble, is he?'

'I just want to ask him a few questions,' Atherton said soothingly.

She seemed reassured. 'Ah, well he's not back yet. He plays football on a Sunday morning. He should be here any time, though. You're welcome to wait.'

'If I won't be in your way,' Atherton said humbly.

'Not at all. Come on in. Will you have a glass of sherry? Mandy, get that bottle of sherry out o' the sideboard, and one o' the best glasses. Come on in, Mr Attenborough. Everyone's in the back, now.'

The second room, to the rear of the house, was evidently not only the dining-room but the gathering place. There were French windows giving a glimpse of a tiny garden and the backs of all the houses round about, a large table in process of being laid, and a massive oak sideboard almost invisible under a drift of framed photographs and ornaments. On the wall above it was a highly-coloured framed print of a revoltingly anatomical Sacred Heart of Mary which might

135

have come straight out of *Pathologist Weekly*. On the far side from the door a pair of splay-legged Contemp'ry armchairs flanked an electric fire. In one of them a small man in a clean shirt with no tie, and a shinily shaved chin, sat in his braces reading the *News of the World*. Two large young men with thick hair still damp from bathing and a thin one with glasses were crouched before a Roberts radio on the other side of the fire, and two handsome young women and a sulky girl of fifteen were laying what looked like a vast number of places at the table. It reminded Atherton of a scene out of *Bread*.

The one called Mandy reappeared with a tot-glass decorated with flamenco dancers, filled with brown syrup. 'There you go,' she informed him brightly. 'Would you like a bag of crisps, atawl?'

'Oh, no thanks,' Atherton said, and seeing many eyes on him, he bravely sipped the sherry and smiled and said, 'Very nice. Thank you.' The faces all beamed with accomplished hospitality and the eyes were removed.

'So, you'll have come about that dreadful business at the BBC, I suppose?' Mrs Somers said. 'Poor Phil's been in a narful state, though what he thinks he could have done about it I don't know. The man was already dead when he found him. And his clothes were ruined.' She folded her lips in disapproval. 'I threw the shirt and the undies away, though it was a wicked waste, but the trousers were nearly new. I've washed them three times, but I don't suppose they'll ever be good enough for best again. And all for that wicked man!'

'Mum,' Mandy said warningly.

'God rest his soul,' Mrs Somers added perfunctorily. 'I must get back to the kitchen, if you'll excuse me, Mr Attenborough. Make yourself at home, now.'

She hurried away, and Atherton turned to Mandy, who

was idly picking at the edge of a raffia table mat, her eyes down either in boredom or discomfiture.

'Why does your mum think Roger Greatrex was a wicked man?'

'Oh, Mum thinks everyone outside the fam'ly's wicked. Permissive society and all that, you know. We're never allowed to do anything. Dad's as bad. They never even let me wear make-up until I was fifteen.'

'But you don't need it anyway,' Atherton said, and she brightened visibly at the compliment. For Atherton it was rather pleasant to be in a household that didn't view him as the enemy, that gave him sherry rather than spitting at him.

Mandy had evidently decided that tall and handsome was tall and handsome, whatever trousers it came in. 'It must be exciting being a detective?' she cooed, almost batting her eyelashes at him in her eagerness to please.

'Sometimes,' he said, and since he had to wait, he spent the next few minutes being agreeable to Mandy and playing her game. Only when he had downed the last of the execrable sherry and was trying to convince Mandy that he couldn't have any more because he was on duty did he hear the welcome sound of a key in the front door.

'Oh, that'll be Phil,' Mandy said brightly, and darted into the hall. Atherton followed her quickly, wanting the first look at the face when Somers saw him. He was looking thin and worn, though still red in the face from the game and the subsequent shower; he was carrying an Adidas bag, and listening distractedly to his sister as he tried to shut the door when, evidently before he had understood her words, he caught sight of Atherton standing in the passage. His face drained so suddenly that Atherton found he had moved instinctively forward to catch him in case he fell. Even Mandy noticed,

137

and looked from her brother to the policeman in sudden apprehension.

'I just want to ask you a few questions,' Atherton said. 'In private, if that's all right.'

Somers seemed to pull himself together. 'You'd better come in the lounge,' he said; and seeing his sister's questioning look, added, 'It's all right, Mandy. Give this to Mum, will you,' pushing his bag at her. 'I won't be long.'

The part of the sitting-room Atherton had not seen from the door was a wall covered in framed family photographs; and in the far left-hand corner beside the window, on a little table, the largest photo of all, in a silver frame, of a pretty girl of about seventeen, with a vase of flowers beside it. Somers sat down on the edge of the seat of the large brown sofa, so Atherton sat at the other end, facing him.

'I'm afraid I've crashed in on a special occasion,' Atherton began. 'You seem to have all your family here.'

'It's just Sunday dinner,' Somers answered automatically. He seemed a little dazed.

'It must be lovely to be part of a big family. How many of you are there?' Atherton asked pleasantly.

'Well, there's me and Kevin, Eileen, Denise, Mandy and Katy at home, and Patrick and Sheila are married, but they come every Sunday with their husband and wife.' The line of questioning seemed to soothe him, and he volunteered, 'Mum moans a bit that she hasn't got any grandchildren, and she goes on at us to get married, but she likes having us at home really. She'd hate it if we all left and she didn't have anyone to fuss over and cook for.'

Eight people living in this tiny house, Atherton thought, which could hardly have more than three bedrooms. For an instant he tried to imagine the bathroom rota in the morning, and then desisted.

'It must be a lot of work for her,' he said. 'Nice to have company, of course, but I suppose you must all get on each other's nerves sometimes.'

'Not really,' Somers said, looking wary now. 'We're used to it.'

'Still, tensions build up, don't they, even in the happiest families?'

'Look, what is it you want to ask me?' Somers said abruptly. 'Mum'll be dishing up soon.'

'Yes, I wouldn't like to keep your mum waiting,' Atherton said. 'All this must have been a shock for her.'

'All what?'

'Roger Greatrex being murdered. She knew him, didn't she?'

'Of course she didn't. Why should she?' But the eyes were watchful.

'Well, she just described him to me as "that wicked man", which doesn't sound like the judgement of a complete stranger.'

'Everyone knew about his reputation as a womaniser,' Somers said, fairly fluently. 'She doesn't approve of that sort of thing.'

'Is that what you had against him? That he was a womaniser?'

Somers almost answered and then caught himself back. 'Why should you think I had anything against him?'

Atherton felt it was time to lean a little. 'Oh, come on, Mr Somers, don't waste my time. You hated him. You were violently against having him on the show. You told Fiona Parsons you wouldn't have him on the same planet if you could help it – and now your wish has come true. I'd just like to know why you hated him. It's hard for me to believe it was just a general dislike of a man who slept around a bit.'

Somer's lips were compressed with fury. 'A bit!' escaped him before he could clamp them down.

'So why didn't you want him on the show?' Atherton pushed when no more was forthcoming.

'I didn't think it was a good idea. He and Sandal didn't get on. I didn't want there to be a row. We are a live show, you know.'

'But controversy is the life breath of a live show, surely? What better than to have a genuine argument on air? Lift your ratings no end.'

'You don't know what you're talking about,' Somers said scornfully.

'All right, then,' Atherton said, 'tell me instead why you went through Roger Greatrex's pockets – once he was dead, that is.' Somers stared, as if trying to gauge how much he knew. Atherton smiled unlovingly. 'It might save time all round if I tell you that we've found your fingerprints on Roger's wallet, so it would be a waste of breath to deny it. Fingerprints in his blood, I should add. Now I'm sure you weren't after his money, so what did you take out of there?'

'Nothing. I didn't. I don't know what you're talking about,' Somers gabbled.

'Whatever it was you took out of his wallet, I think it was something you knew was there. You didn't go through his other pockets, after all. And whatever it was, if it was important enough for you to take it from his dead body, it was probably what you killed him for.'

Somers groaned and leaned forward, clutching his stomach, his face so white that Atherton moved his feet back sharply.

'Come on, Mr Somers, much better to get it off your chest,' he said, though it wasn't his chest that looked the likeliest candidate at the moment. 'Tell me everything, clear your conscience. You know we'll find out in the end. Why did you kill him? By all accounts he was a bit of a bastard anyway, no great loss to humanity. Why did you do it?'

'I didn't,' Somers moaned. 'I didn't kill him. I wish to God I had, but I didn't.'

'What had he done?' Atherton coaxed. But Somers shook his head, still hugging himself and rocking. 'You'd better tell me. You're only making it worse for yourself.'

The door opened at that moment, and Mandy looked in. 'Mum says—' She broke off, staring at her brother in concern, and then at Atherton. 'What's going on? What've you done to him? Did you hit him?'

Atherton stood up, exasperated. He'd get nothing out of him now. 'I'm afraid your brother doesn't feel very well. I think I'd better go. I'll call again some other time and talk to you, Mr Somers,' he added, 'unless you change your mind and want to talk to me. You know where to reach me if you do.'

Mandy saw him to the door in a half-resentful silence. As Atherton stepped out into the open air, she said, 'I don't know what all this is about, but Phil hasn't done anything. He wouldn't. He'd never do anything that might upset Mum.'

'Say goodbye to your mother for me, will you? And thank you,' said Atherton.

9

The Wife of Acton's Tale

'Hello! What are you doing here?'

'There's a nice greeting. Aren't you glad to see me?'

'I didn't say I wasn't.'

'That's all right then,' Joanna said. 'I got bored on my own, that's all. I thought I'd come and see if you were going to have lunch. How did it go this morning?'

Slider told her. 'What a sad story,' she said. 'Do you think he really believes it's his kid?'

'I'm sure he does, at least on one level,' Slider said. 'But people can easily believe several conflicting things at the same time – though you can't say that in court. In court you've got to present a nice, simple world where everything's black or white and people behave consistently. Fortunately,' he backed out from the cave of gloom opening before him, 'juries are amazingly sensible on the whole. They generally get it right, whatever antics counsel get up to. It's the one great argument for the jury system.'

'And do you think Sandal Palliser is your man?'

'I'm not sure,' Slider frowned. 'I hoped when I got on the

trail of the telephone call that I'd be able to put him out of the frame, but I can't, entirely. He still had time to do it, and a better motive you couldn't want. Real, world-class resentment—'

He was interrupted by Atherton's arrival. 'I've just been comprehensively tortured by the smell of the Traditional English Sunday Lunch. Anybody ready for a bite?'

'We can get a sandwich upstairs if you like,' Slider suggested, more to Joanna than his partner. 'How did you get on with Somers? Get anything?'

'*Nada*. But he's definitely on the run now – gasping at the surface like a holed fish. I think he'll break soon. And there was an atmosphere of tension in the house. I think the mother knows something, or suspects something, at least. She mentioned Greatrex in uncomplimentary terms and then frightened herself and ran away. But what a household,' he added happily, and described it to them. 'In other circumstances it would give you renewed faith in society – a whole family living together and keeping up the traditions.'

Slider told him about his morning, and Atherton brightened. 'Maybe Palliser's our man after all. I'd sooner it was him than Somers. Somehow I can't see Somers cutting Greatrex's throat in that determined way. He'd have hacked about and made a mess of it.'

'Those quiet ones can be the most determined when they screw themselves to the sticking point,' Slider said.

'He couldn't screw himself to the wall. No, it's Palliser for me,' Atherton said cheerfully. 'Mystic Meg has spoken. I see a tall man with a warped mind – oh no, that's the mirror.'

Slider wasn't listening. 'But what did Somers go into Greatrex's pocket for?' he said with a dissatisfied frown. 'I wish you'd found that out. All we can do in a case like this is—'

'Clear as we go,' Atherton finished in chorus with him, and grinned at Joanna.

'Do I really say that a lot?' Slider asked.

'It's just a phrase you're going through,' Atherton said soothingly. 'What about that sandwich?'

But the phone rang from the front shop. 'Excuse me, sir, there's someone here who wants to talk to whoever's in charge of the Greatrex case. Says she's got some information, won't give it to anyone but the top man.'

Slider relayed this to Atherton. 'Don't tell me we've got a witness at last?'

'We can but pray,' said Atherton.

Joanna stood up. 'I'll go and leave you to it. Where are we eating tonight?'

'You notice she doesn't ask when,' Atherton said. 'You've got her trained.'

'I'll give you a ring before I leave,' Slider promised, and she stepped aside and let him pass, seeing his mind had already gone ahead of him, and she was forgotten.

As they passed through the charge room Nicholls, who had just come on and was still in his anorak, making tea, put out a hand to stop him.

'Oh, Bill, just a minute. That guy we were talking about – it's just come to me, where I knew him from.'

'Philip Somers?'

'That's right. Though strictly speaking, it wasn't him I remembered, it was his sister.'

'You'll have to do better than that,' Atherton said with a grin. 'I was round his house this morning, and they come in six-packs.'

'Is that a fact? Well, her name'll come to me in a minute. Anyway, the Somers business – it was about eight, nine years

144

ago – you can check it out with the Thames Valley records. It was while I was at Maidenhead. Oh yes, Madeleine! That was her name. Madeleine Somers. She was about seventeen, bright, pretty girl.'

'I asked Somers about his family, and he didn't mention a sister Madeleine,' Atherton said.

'I imagine not,' Nicholls said. 'Sister Madeleine was going out with Roger Greatrex.'

'What!'

'S'right,' Nicholls nodded. 'I don't know all the details of the affair, but one night Greatrex was driving her back from a hotel in Bray where they'd been making the beast with two backs, and they were involved in an RTA. He wasn't hurt, just cuts and bruises, but she went into the windscreen, suffered head injuries, and died a couple of hours later in hospital.'

'The photograph!' Atherton said. 'I should have realised the significance: there was one photograph on its own on a table with flowers. Pretty girl of about seventeen.'

'The memorial corner,' Nicholls nodded. 'Nice old-fashioned custom. They do it in my part of the world.'

'The mother's Irish,' said Atherton.

'But what about Philip Somers?' Slider said impatiently. 'What was your contact with him?'

'I remember him from the inquest,' Nicholls said. 'I had to give evidence, seeing I was on traffic patrol at the time and I was one of the first on the scene. Anyway, your man Somers maintained Greatrex was to blame for the accident, made quite a scene in the coroner's court. Said he'd been drinking – well, he undoubtedly had been, but we breathalysed him on the spot and he was below the limit, and there was a lot of black ice about that night, so nothing came of it. It went down as accidental death and that was that.'

'Was it, indeed?' Slider mused.

'So it seemed. But it occurs to me that people are much less forgiving these days than they used to be. There's no such thing as an accident any more. We're all encouraged to think someone must be to blame.'

'And some of us don't need much encouraging,' Atherton said. 'There's the motive, hot and strong! And we know Somers still resented Greatrex, because he tried to keep him off the programme.'

Nicholls watched the two of them with intelligent interest. 'Well, make of it what you will. It'll be in the records, as I said, though there wasn't a big splash in the papers as you'd expect. I think Greatrex must have had friends in high journalistic places, and used his influence to play it down.'

'Did the rest of the family share Somers's view?'

'I dunno, Bill. I only saw the mother in court, and she kept quiet. It was Somers who did the shouting. I think they'd been particularly close, as I remember.'

'Well, thanks, Nutty. That's a great help,' Slider said.

'N't'all. By the way, you did know there's a customer in the shop for you?'

'That's where I was going. Better not keep her waiting any longer.'

The customer was a stout, motherly woman in a cheap coat and even cheaper perfume, whose fantastically wrinkled face was explained by the equally fantastic nicotine stains on her fingers and the yellow streak across the front of her grey hair. She was sitting with a suffering expression under one of the No Smoking signs, and stood up as Slider approached.

'You the boss?' Slider introduced himself and Atherton. 'Gor blimey, you don't half make it hard for us smokers these days. I'm gasping for a fag. Can we go somewhere I can get one on, 'fore I passes out? You a smoker, dear?'

146

'I'm afraid not. But there's an interview room over here we can use. You've got something to tell me, I understand.'

'About that murder at the BBC,' she said. 'Well, I did see something, dunno if it's important.' She slid her eyes about. 'Don't want to make a song and dance about it, dear. Walls have ears, y'know.'

Slider nodded wisely and led the way to the small interview room. The woman fumbled in her bulging handbag, lit up, and sucked on the burning stick with an almost sexual ecstasy. 'Aaah, that's better!' she sighed like a genial dragon, smoke billowing from her nose and mouth and, Atherton fantasised, her ears too. 'Gor, I thought I'd had it, waiting all that time without so much as a puff. I dunno what the times are coming to, when a respectable woman can't even light up in her own local p'lice station.'

'I'm afraid it's all to do with the insurance company,' Slider lied gently, 'Mrs—?'

'Dorothy Edna Reynolds, 19D Mandela House, South Acton,' she supplied smartly. 'But that's between you, me, him, and the furnicher, all right? I didn't like the look of that bloke, and I don't want him coming round my house, supposing he *is* the one.'

Slider's soul thrilled to her words. An orchestra entirely composed of strings struck up somewhere. 'You saw somebody you think was connected with the murder?'

'Blimey, yes, what d'you think I come here for?' She sucked again, wriggled herself comfortable, and began. 'Thursday night, right? I come on six o'clock – six till eight, I do.'

'Do?'

'Cleaning. Just the offices and the lavs. Corridors is done by a contract firm during the night. Don't ask me what happens to the stoojos. Anyway,' she gathered her audience's attention in a thoroughly professional way, ''bout quarter past seven

147

time, going on har past, I finish floor five and come down the stairs with me box to do four.'

'What staircase?'

She looked approval at the question. 'Well, it was number five, wannit?' she answered rhetorically. 'That's the one right next door to where it all happened, which is what made me think. Not at the time, see, because I didn't know nothing about it at the time, but after.'

'Quite,' Slider said encouragingly.

'All right, so I come out the swing doors on four, and there's this bloke just come out the gents next door and stood in front of the lift.'

'Did you actually see him come out of the gents?' Atherton asked.

'Well,' she looked bothered and fortified herself with another suck of smoke, 'I been thinking about that, and I can't honestly say if I axshully *seen* him come out, but I know in me mind that's where he come from.' Her brow furrowed, sending fault lines of wrinkles racing in all directions. She seemed genuinely puzzled by her own inability to be sure on the point.

Slider said, 'Maybe you saw the door just closing. Those doors with the hydraulic hinge on the back do close very slowly.'

He expected her to leap at the explanation, but she didn't, only went on puzzling and puffing. 'I dunno,' she said at last. 'I dunno why I know, but if you'd asked me right then where he come from, I'd've said the gents, certain as I live.'

'All right,' Slider said, 'never mind that now. What did the man do?'

'Well, he stopped at the lift and pressed the button.'

'Up or down?' Atherton put in.

She shook her head. 'I dunno. I think, down, but I can't be sure. I mean, it was on'y just a second I looked at him as

148

I come out through the swing doors, because I turned the other way, see, to start with the offices down that end—'

'You turned right out of the swing doors?'

'Yeah, that's right. But I looked at him and he looked at me, and that's what sort of burned on me memory, otherwise I wun't have thought twice about it. Because he looked at me, right into me eyes, and he looked—' she paused again, rummaging through her memory or her vocabulary, or both, for the right description.

'Afraid? Anxious? Startled?' Atherton offered when the pause lengthened. She made a distracted movement of her hand and Slider stilled Atherton with a glance. This was a good witness. She knew what she knew.

At last she shook her head. 'I can't describe it. But it wasn't a nordin'ry look. That's what took me attention, see?'

'So he rang for the lift, and looked at you, and then you turned and went away – and that's the last time you saw him?' She nodded. 'Can you describe him to me?'

She fixed her eyes on the wall, the better to rifle her memory. 'He was medium height,' she said at last. Atherton converted a snort into a slight cough, and she glanced at him. 'Not so tall as *you,* and not so short as *you,*' she said indignantly. 'What would you call that, if it's not medium?'

'Thin? Fat?' Slider prompted.

'He was what I'd call a big man,' she said thoughtfully. 'Not fat, really, but, like, well-fed. Meaty. He looked strong. And he was really dark, with one o' them blue chins, and black hair and dark eyes. Sinister, I'd call 'em. And a beauty spot on his cheek, here.' She pressed the inner curve of her cheek just beside and below the corner of her left nostril.

Slider could feel Atherton seething with disbelief beside him as this Boy's Own description reeled out, but he knew a good witness when he met one. 'Age?' he asked.

''Bout fortyish. Give or take.' She grinned lasciviously at Slider. ''Bout your age. My fav'rite.'

'How was he dressed?'

'Oh, just in a suit an' tie. But he was carrying a bag, one o' them nylon bags, what d'you call 'em, flight bags, is it? Like with a shoulder strap, only he was holding it by the handles. Blue, it was, just plain blue.'

'Did it look full? Did he carry it as if it was heavy?'

She seemed distracted by the question. 'I dunno. He was just holding it, down by his side. I didn't notice it, except it was there.'

Slider could feel that Atherton was longing to ask questions, but was too good a subordinate not to ignore the silencing look he had been given. 'Did you see anyone else in the corridor at the time?' Slider asked.

'No, there was no-one around. I never see anyone going either way. I went straight down to the office at the end of the corridor and went in and started cleaning, and I never see anyone at all until about a half-hour later when I got nearly up to stairway six and found the whole place roped off and a copper standing there like he was stopping the traffic. So I says what's going on, and he says never you mind, there's nothing to see, and you can't come this way, so I says, it don't matter to me, I can go the other way, and I do, and that's that, because it was my time to knock off anyway. Six till eight I do.'

'Can you pin down the time any closer for me, the time you saw the man by the lift?'

'Well,' she said regretfully, 'I didn't look at me watch right after, but it's got to've been between quarter and twenty past, 'cause it was coming up to quarter past when I finished the gents next to stairway six on five, and I'd only just walked along to stairway five and down two flights.'

150

'Why didn't you use stairway six?' Atherton asked, unable to restrain himself any longer. 'Why walk back?'

'Because stairway six and seven was full of the aujence for *Questions of Our Time* going up to the canteen,' she said with just a hint of triumph. 'I wasn't up to pushing me way through that little lot.'

There was a pause while Slider digested all this; and then he said at last, 'So, this man you saw rang for the lift and looked at you, and you went away. Now what made you think he had anything to do with the murder?'

'Well, because of coming out of the gents where the poor bloke was topped,' she said.

'But you didn't actually *see* him come out of there?'

'Not to say, *see* him,' she said reluctantly, 'but I'm sure in me own mind that's where he come from.'

'And that's all?'

'And the look he give me. I wouldn't want to meet *him* again in a dark alley.'

'And that's all?'

'And the blood,' she said, as though affirming something already agreed.

'Blood?' Atherton exploded, unable to prevent himself.

She looked reproachful. 'I was just coming to that, if you'd a give me half a chance. See, when he put his hand out to press the button, his sleeve like kind of pulled back and I see his hairy wrist an' his wristwatch and the end of his cuff, and he had blood on it, on his cuff. Not a lot, but it was red, so it must've been fresh, mustn't it? And I thought at the time he'd cut himself shaving—'

'At that time of night?' Atherton protested.

'With his sort of beard he'd have to shave more'n once a day,' she told him scornfully. 'You thank your lucky stars you're nice an fair, my lad. My first 'usband had that sort of

151

beard – wicked on the razors, it was. Three I've had, counting this present one – buried two of 'em – and five sons, one of which was a sailor, so I know a bit about beards. And my first – he was one o' them blue-chin ones. If we went out of an evening, up west dancing or down the dogs or anything, he had to shave again afore we went, and by the time we got home and went to bed he was like a coconut mat again. You could've sanded down doors with his chin. Now my boy Reggie—'

'Did you see blood anywhere else?' Slider asked, drawing her back from this primrose path.

'No-o,' she said reluctantly. 'That's all I see. I didn't see no cuts on his face, anyway.'

'So why has it taken you so long to come forward?' Slider asked, but still gently. He didn't want to rouse her resentment.

'Well, I never thought of it,' she said. 'It went straight out of me head, and it was only yesterday when I went in to work I found out it was *that* lav that the poor gent was killed in. So that was what made me think of it then, and the blood an all.' She looked at Slider wide-eyed for once. 'D'you think that was him, the murderer?'

'It's possible,' he said cautiously.

She gave a shudder. 'Fancy, I was that close to him,' she said. 'I lived in St Mark's Road when the Christie murders was going on, and my mother reckoned she'd stood at the same bus stop with him. She said he had 'orrible eyes, like a dead cod. And now I've met another one. It's like fate, innit?'

'The most important thing, Mrs Reynolds, is, do you think you could recognise him again?'

'What?' she said derisively. 'Printed on my brain, he is! I'd know him anywhere.'

'And you'd be willing to come in again and look at an identity parade for me, if necessary?'

'Oh, I'd do that all right,' she said, 'but I want your word that my name'll be kept private. I don't want it all in the papers that I'm the key witness or nothing. Because you haven't caught him yet, have you?' She looked from one to the other and did not require an answer. 'That's what I thought. See, I don't want my life being at risk, if this bloke finds out I'm the only person what can pick him out. I want witness protection.'

The effects of watching too much television, Slider thought. 'I can assure you that if protection is needed, you'll get it,' he said. 'And for the moment, there's no need for anyone but us to know your name. But you mustn't tell anyone about this either, you know. That's the way these things usually get about. A witness tells a friend in confidence, and the friend tells another friend, and so on.'

'I'm not a fool,' she said briskly. 'I haven't told no-one any of this – not even your bloke at the desk,' she added with a flick of her head. 'I know how to keep my mouth shut. Careless talk costs lives – and it's my life we're talking about.'

'It won't come to that,' Slider said. 'I'm sure you won't be in any danger, even if this does turn out to be the man we're looking for.'

'You didn't see him,' she snorted. 'He looked capable of anythink to me.'

'Well, what do you think?' Slider asked Atherton.

'I think it's a load of old Tottenham,' he said robustly. 'You heard what she said about her mum standing at the bus stop with Reg Christie. She's a sensation-seeker, wants to be important, so she invents a sinister-looking man at the scene of the murder covered in blood and giving her threatening looks.'

'Hmm,' said Slider. 'Well, she didn't say covered in blood, did she? Just a little bit on his cuff.'

153

'You believed her,' Atherton discovered.

Slider paused. What he thought was that sometimes in this game all you had to go on to decide between what mattered and what didn't was a policeman's instinct; and something in his scalp had prickled when Mrs Reynolds started talking. If she was genuine, even following what he had come to think of as the Honeyman theory, the Man by the Lift, if he had come out of the gents, might at least be able to help pin down the time a bit more accurately and would therefore qualify for following up and tracking down.

What he said was, 'If she had been attention-seeking, she might well have said he was covered in blood. And if she was attention-seeking she'd have surely said that she *saw* him come out of the gents loo.'

'And that's what convinces you? That she hasn't told us anything useful?'

'I think she's telling the truth, and I think she's an observant person and not given to embroidery. It doesn't mean to say the man she saw was our man, of course.'

'Her description doesn't sound like Somers,' Atherton complained. 'And we'd just got him the perfect, hand-cut crystal motive.'

'It doesn't sound like Palliser either.'

'Maybe it was Parsons,' Atherton said recovering his sense of proportion.

'She didn't see anyone else in the corridor, so she must have come down the stairs before Somers discovered the body, or he'd have been standing at the door. So if the man she saw *had* come out of the loo, either he was the murderer, or—'

'Or he wasn't,' Atherton finished with grim humour. 'The trouble has always been that we haven't any exact times.'

'What we have got now,' Slider said, 'is the bag to look for.'

'You think the bag's important?'

Slider grinned suddenly. 'Me? Think? In this case? I think either the bag's been dumped somewhere near the scene—'

'Or it hasn't. God help us, what a case! When this is over it'll be hols all round at the Latex Hilton. Still, we've got something to work on with Somers, at least. Shall I go back and confront him, guv, see if he breaks down and confesses?'

'No, not today,' Slider said. 'I want to get the full report on his sister and Greatrex before we go any further with him. It's always best to lead from strength.'

'I thought you didn't know anything about bridge.'

'I can't help knowing the language, can I? Anyway, it won't do any harm to let Somers stew for a bit. You can go and roust him tomorrow morning, if the report's come through.'

'Thanks. So what now?'

'What now? Food, rest, recreation. Remember those?'

'All right for you, you've got a woman to go back to,' Atherton complained.

'You can come too.'

'Thanks, but won't you want to be alone?'

'Oh, no, it's all right. We did all that last night – the reunion, the heartsearching, the confessions, the forgiveness—'

'Stop it, you're getting me excited. What confessions?'

'I had a fit of jealousy to explain and get over,' Slider said.

'Oh,' said Atherton wisely, 'she told you about it, then? Sue seemed to think she wouldn't. We had quite a discussion about whether it was best to tell or keep silent.'

'Tell? Told me what?' Slider said.

'About this old flame of hers turning up.' Atherton looked at him. 'Wasn't that what you meant? Oh, sorry, I don't mean to pry.'

'What old flame?'

'Oh, blimey, guv, me and my big mouth! Have I gone and put my foot in it?'

'Stop clowning. What old flame?'

Atherton looked serious. 'Look, there's nothing to tell. It's some bloke she had a do with years and years ago turned up at the orchestra as a substitute for someone who was sick. That's all. End of story. She didn't know he was coming. Hasn't had any contact with him in years. Sue was just debating with me whether it would be better for Joanna to tell you he'd been there, and risk your feeling jealous over nothing, or not tell you and risk your finding out later and thinking there was something to be jealous about simply because she hadn't told you. And now,' he added, striking his brow, 'I've gone and given her the worst of both worlds.'

Slider pulled himself together. 'No you haven't. Don't be so dramatic. There's nothing to tell, as you so rightly said. So are you coming back with me to Joanna's?'

Atherton hesitated, wondering whether he would really be welcome. 'I'm not finished,' he said.

'Then I'll disregard the rumours,' Slider said kindly. 'Come on, make your mind up, I've got to phone her.'

'Well, if I really won't be *de trop*.'

10

Into Each Wine, a Little Leaf Must Fall

'By the way, did you hear the news?' Joanna said. 'Laurence Jepp was attacked in his home last night and killed.'

'Laurence Jepp?' Slider said. The name sounded vaguely familiar.

'Singer,' Atherton supplied, dabbling his last chip in the salty vinegar which had accumulated at the bottom of the bag. A sudden longing had overcome Joanna for fish and chips, and Slider had gone along with it on condition that they ate them out of the paper, anything else being a spineless compromise.

'He sang Leporello in our *Don Giovanni,*' said Joanna. 'It's terrible. I can't believe he's dead – I was standing just behind him in the coffee queue in the Courtyard only last week.'

This sounded uncomfortably like Mrs Reynolds. Slider said, 'It's always a shock when it's someone you know.'

'Well, I knew him to say hello to, that's all,' Joanna said, reaching for a sense of proportion. 'Its a good job the *Don's* finished now. He was a terrific Leporello, and the understudy was very weak.'

'I saw his *Pagliacci,*' Atherton said. 'It's a sad loss to music.'

'Was he married?' Slider asked.

'Apparently not. He lived alone, anyway – in Ealing. They showed it on the news – one of those big houses on the Green. Really enormous. I expect he only had a flat in it, though. I can't believe he was that rich – I mean, not in the Pavarotti class. None of the English singers are.'

'What happened?' Atherton asked.

'They didn't say much. Someone broke into his house while he was asleep. A burglar, I suppose. Apparently he had a panic button beside his bed and he must have pressed it before he got clobbered, because the alarm went off and the police were there within minutes, but it was too late.' She leaned over to top up the glasses with hock. 'It's a bummer, isn't it? Poor old Larry.'

'As you say, it's a good job the *Don* is finished,' Atherton said lightly. 'Jepp wasn't in anything else, was he?'

'Not that I know of, but I'm only in *Traviata* now.'

'Who's singing Violetta?'

'Sonia Morgenstern,' Joanna said, and Atherton made a face. 'Well, all right, she's a bit ripe and fruity—'

'I wouldn't mind that, but she's got so much vibrato she never gets within a tone of the note she's aiming at. And her coloratura—'

'I thought that was wallpaper,' Slider complained.

'No, that's Coloroll,' Atherton corrected. 'But you weren't far off. They're both decoration—'

'Yes, thank you, I don't want a music lesson,' Slider interrupted. 'Can we talk about something else? I'm up to my navel in culture these days.'

'You're the boss,' Atherton shrugged. 'Who d'you fancy for the cup, then, sir? Booked anywhere for your holidays?'

'Did you read that story in the newspaper the other day,'

Joanna said, 'about the girl who worked in the unisex hair-dressers? She was clipping round the back of this middle-aged bloke's neck when she saw his hand going up and down under the cape, so she thought that's enough of that nonsense and whacked him quite hard on the head with the clippers. And it turned out he had his glasses under there and was cleaning them on his tie.'

They sat late in Joanna's garden, drinking wine under the terminally blighted oak tree that took up most of the space, listening to the sounds of the evening and talking. When the wine was finished and Atherton had gone, ranging out into the night like a lean cat with the flattest of eyes and demurest of goodbyes, Joanna returned to Slider and gave him a brooding and not entirely friendly look.

'What was all that about, then?' she asked.

'What was *what* about?'

'Don't be tiresome. I'm talking about your performance tonight.'

'My performance?'

'Snapping at everyone. Making sarky remarks about opera and music. Playing the poor beleaguered Essex Man surrounded by pretentious Islingtonites.'

Slider stared in amazement. 'I didn't. I wasn't. I was a bit surprised by your performance, though – since you coined the word.'

'I didn't coin it, I only used it. Please try to be accurate. I thought it was part of your job.'

'You're doing it again, you see.'

'Doing what again?'

'Making pointed remarks about my job. It doesn't matter so much about sneering at me, but Atherton's a policeman too, you know.'

'Leave Atherton out of this—'

'I'd love to, but it was me who was being left out by you two, yakking on and on about music. It was perfectly obvious which of us you found the better company—'

'And I was right, wasn't I? The way you've been behaving tonight, you weren't fit company for anyone.'

'You should have stuck with him while you had the chance, then.'

'And what's that supposed to mean?'

'Work it out for yourself!'

'Oh, we're back to that are we? I thought we'd come to it sooner or later. It never fails – as soon as a man thinks he's got you, he starts throwing your past in your face, complaining that you weren't a virgin when he met you. You're such hypocrites, all of you!'

Slider opened his mouth to snap at her, and then shut it again as the echoes of the last few exchanges came back to him. 'What are we doing?' he said at last, appalled. 'This isn't us.'

'Why should we be different from anyone else?' she said grimly, but the heat had gone out of her, too. She looked at him for a long moment, while the grimness slowly gave way to wryness. 'You want to tell me about it?'

'About what?' he said defiantly.

'About what's wrong,' she said, and seeing the denial in his face said, 'I take back everything I said up to this point. But there is something wrong, isn't there?'

'Not with you, with me,' he said unwillingly.

'Is it the case?'

'Oh—! No, not directly.'

'What, then?'

He sat down abruptly, and she sat too, facing him across a little strip of patio that seemed suddenly as daunting as the

Mojave Desert. He licked his lips nervously. As an until-recently married man, he wasn't used to this talking to each other business. Better, though, as he was always telling reluctant criminals, to have it out in the open. 'Atherton told me that – that there was an old flame of yours down at Glyndebourne.'

A faint smile. 'What lovely language. An old flame.' But that was all she said.

'Well, was there?' Slider asked after a minute, feeling foolish, truculent and insecure in about equal proportions.

'Little tattle-tail, isn't he?' she said without affection. 'What business is it of his, I'd like to know? Well, since you ask, a person I knew a long time ago and haven't seen for years turned up, called in as a sub in the orchestra, that's all.'

'A person you knew,' he repeated. 'More than knew, surely?'

She looked at him with some deep unwillingness, but what it related to he couldn't be quite sure. 'I used to live with him.'

Damn, Slider thought; though he had feared as much. 'And?'

'And what?'

'Why didn't you tell me about him before?'

'I don't have to discuss my past with you. I don't ask you about yours.'

'I haven't got any,' he said bitterly.

'That's beside the point—'

'It is the point. You aren't going to spend your life tripping over people I've been to bed with.'

'Oh—!' She got to her feet in a movement of frustration and suppressed rage, walked a few steps, and turned back to him, her fists clenched with the effort of keeping her temper and being reasonable. 'The past is past. It's gone and dead and over, and it's none of your business anyway. What happened to me before I met you is *mine* and you can't have

161

it – not because I won't give it to you,' she hurried on, 'but because there's no way you can possess it. So just leave it alone, or you'll destroy what we have.'

'What about when it isn't over and dead? When it gets up and walks back in?'

'I'll tell you when it does.'

'You didn't tell me about this bloke being at Glyndebourne.'

'There wasn't anything to tell. I can't control who gets booked to play at the same dates as me.' She met his eyes steadily. 'You've got to trust me, Bill. We're going nowhere if you don't trust me.'

He knew that was true, but he had been stinging for days. 'It isn't a matter of trust. I do trust you – but I can't help feeling jealous.'

'You've *got* to help it. Do I spend all day fretting over what you might be up to? Do I worry about the gorgeous women you might be meeting every day who are just cra-a-azy over policemen, in or out of uniform, and who'd do anything for a little squint at your truncheon?'

'What about Irene?' he said.

'That's different,' she said after a moment. 'She's not out of your life.'

He stood up and stepped towards her, but something in her face stopped him touching her. 'Why didn't you tell me about this bloke?'

'There's nothing to tell,' she said wearily. 'He turned up, that's all.'

'But you went for a drink with him. He was there in the Trevor when you phoned me.' This was a guess, but an easy one.

'Everybody goes to the Trevor,' she said. His heart sank at this confirmation. He'd rather hoped the bloke went somewhere else.

'What's his name?' he asked, almost against his will.

'You don't want to know his name,' she said, and her eyes were suddenly humorous.

He resisted her. 'I do. What's his name?'

'Andrew,' she said.

She was right. He didn't want to know it. He felt a bit sick. He began to turn away, and now she moved, grabbed his hand, pulled him back.

'Nothing happened,' she said. She lifted his hand, kissed it, put it to her head. 'Not even in here.'

By its own will his hand cupped round the side of her skull, fingers in her short, rough hair.

'I love you,' she said. She was always generous, always made the first move. He drew her against him, held her head against his cheek. It was like coming home, the touch of her body. It was something he couldn't do without. He sighed. 'Into each life a little rain must fall,' she said. 'It's hell, isn't it – jealousy?'

'Now I know how Irene used to feel,' he said. He was aware immediately he said it that he should not have introduced another name at that particular moment, but he couldn't take it back once it was out, so instead he said, 'I love you, too.'

'Let's go to bed, then,' she said, and it seemed to him like an excellent idea.

There was nothing like an emotional scene before bedtime for making you wake up early. Slider woke feeling unrested to the sound of the dawn chorus. Joanna's bed, in any case, had been old when he met her, and was beginning to sport the scars of vigorous usage. There was a spring which caught him just under one hip. They ought to buy a new one, but he didn't know how to approach the subject, given that they had never actually discussed their future together, and he had never officially moved in to her flat. It had been merely diffidence on his part – or so he had thought until last night. Now he realised that however much they loved each other, they were both nervous about making so serious a commitment as to mention aloud what Palliser had called the M-word. In these post-feminist, modern times, it had become the love that dared not speak its name. Suppose he asked her and she refused? It was one thing to live with her like this, unmarried and undeclared, face not merely saved but never even staked; but to live with her unmarried after they had spoken of a permanent attachment would not do. He would always wonder what her reservations were, whether he had failed to measure up in some way, or whether she was holding back in the hope that someone better might come along. Besides, there were his children to think of, and the example he set them. Sooner or later, if he and Joanna stayed together, they would have to meet her, and he didn't want them thinking of her as 'Daddy's girlfriend', with all the tacky connotations of the phrase.

If they stayed together? What was he thinking? There could not be a question about it – could there? He pushed himself up on one elbow to look down at her, still sleeping and curled on her side with her hands under her cheek Shirley Temple-style. She looked so complete, as people sleeping often do, that he felt shut out from her. After all, she had managed without him all these years – without anyone. She had her own career, money, establishment, interests and friends: what could she need him for? He thought back to their first weeks together, and the time he had taken her to visit his father. She had said that a woman on her own for long enough became a sort of stray dog – a man might play with it in the park, but would never think of taking it home. And he saw that it was true. That completeness of hers might not be

164

something she liked or enjoyed, might not be what she wanted, but it existed none the less. He had no idea what either of them could do about it.

To avoid thinking about these imponderables, he thought about the case, and immediately experienced a rush of blood to the head that had him out of bed. He went into the sitting-room to use the phone there so as not to wake her.

The leather of the Chesterfield was chilly to his bare behind. He rested his elbows on his knees and looked down with detached curiosity at his own feet, legs and dangly bits. God's supreme joke; His way of cutting Man down to size. There was nothing laughable about the back end of a horse or even a dog, but the human male's wedding tackle was essentially ridiculous.

Fergus answered. 'What are you doing up so early?'

'Contemplating my navel,' Slider said. 'The feminists are right, y'know. If God was a man, He'd never have put the balls on the outside.'

'Izzat what you woke me up for, to tell me that?'

'I thought you'd like to know.'

'You're tryin' to think on an empty stomach, that's what's wrong wit you. A plate o' bacon an' eggs'll get your brain functioning right,' O'Flaherty said wisely. 'What *do* you want, anyway?'

'Is anyone from my team in?'

'I got Mackay standing beside me this very minute. Will he do?'

'Perfectly,' said Slider. When Mackay came on he said, 'I've got a job for you. I want you to go to the TVC for me. Go to the lift right next to the loo where Greatrex was killed. Inside it there must be an inspection hatch in the ceiling – get up there and see if there's anything hidden on the roof of the lift.'

'Now, guv?'

165

'Yes, now. You'll need someone with you to give you a boost.'

'Am I looking for anything in particular?'

'Well, I hope you may find a bag there containing blood-stained clothing. That would be my favourite result.'

Mackay was enlightened at last. 'Oh! Right! Nice one, guv. Why didn't we think of that before?'

We? Slider thought. 'Get on with it,' he said. 'I'll be in in about twenty minutes.'

When he returned to the bedroom, Joanna was awake and watching the door.

'I didn't mean to disturb you,' he said.

'This phone pings when you pick the other one up,' she said. 'Who were you calling?'

Was there something cautious about the question? 'Just the factory,' he said. 'I had an idea about where the bag might be hidden. I don't expect anything will come of it, but a man can dream.'

'Are you going in now?'

'Yes,' he said. He sat down on the bed beside her and stroked the hair back from her brow. Touching her head brought a rush of feelings through him, as though he had plugged in to something. 'About last night—'

She rolled onto her back to free her arms to reach up to him. 'Let's forget it. We wouldn't quarrel like that if we didn't love each other.'

He bent and kissed her. 'Could we find some other way of showing it in future, do you think?'

Her hand ran up and down his flank. 'You don't want to fight? What sort of a man are you, anyway?'

If he showered and dressed like lightning afterwards, he thought, there was just time to show her.

* * *

Half the force seemed to be gathered around a single desk in the CID room when Slider arrived, and it parted in a Red Sea of smiling faces before him to lead him to a rather dusty blue nylon flight bag sitting on Atherton's desk.

'Just where you said it'd be, guv,' Mackay gloated.

So his instinct about Mrs Reynolds had been right after all.

'I had inside information,' Slider said modestly. He didn't yet quite understand his own thought processes, but something was going on in the back of his mind. 'Let's have a look at it.'

Or more importantly, in it. The outside yielded nothing but a quantity of dust and an oil stain which probably came from the lift cable, but inside the bag was a pair of bloody surgical gloves and an elderly mackintosh with blood-soaked sleeves, bloody smears down both front coats, and an almost round bloodstain further down where, Slider surmised, the wearer had gone down on one knee.

'Oh Tufty,' Slider murmured, 'you lucky, lucky lad.'

The one person not pleased with the discovery of the bag was Mr Honeyman, whose doll face did not quite manage to express disapproval, but whose unchuffedness was evinced by the silence with which he received the news, a long silence during which he searched his mind for a budget-friendly reason for the bag to be found where it was. He had managed to believe that the bruising to the chin was not convincing evidence of foul play, coming up with the alternative – in both senses – theory that Greatrex might have bruised himself shaving, but this was harder going. He did not go so far as to suggest Greatrex might somehow have managed to conceal the bag in the lift after cutting his own throat but before collapsing, but he did say, 'You will check that the blood group is the same as that of Greatrex, won't you?' – as though it might be that of a clumsy, DIY-loving lift maintenance engineer with a strict wife.

'Of course, sir,' Slider said patiently – so patiently that Honeyman was recalled reluctantly to reality.

'Well, I suppose this changes things quite considerably,' he said. 'I suppose I must tell Mr Wetherspoon that we have a murder investigation on our hands.'

Slider had no mercy. 'Yes, sir.'

'You realise what this means, don't you?' Honeyman said irritably. 'If the murderer wore protective clothing, it could be anyone, anyone at all. There were hundreds of people in that building.'

Yes, there were, Slider thought as he walked back to his room; but whoever murdered Roger Greatrex must have planned it beforehand, to have brought the gloves with him, and must therefore have had a grudge against him. So it could not have been just anyone amongst the hundreds. The prime suspects were still the same three people who had had good reason to want to kill him; or someone else with a beef they hadn't unearthed yet.

But why didn't the murderer carry the bag away out of the building and dump it somewhere far from the scene? Because he couldn't leave the building just yet? Because he had to go back and join a group of people – like those in the greenroom, for instance – who would notice his absence?

And where had the bag been before – or rather, where had the mac been? Those nylon bags hadn't much bulk to them – it could have been stuffed into an overcoat pocket, for instance – but the mac couldn't have been concealed. It must either have been worn or carried over the arm – unless it was already in the building somewhere. Damn! There were going to have to be a lot of questions asked about that mac.

And why had the murderer hidden the bag in the lift? It was a good hiding place, provided you could get it up there in the first place. You'd need to be athletic to jump up, hold onto the ledge round the top of the lift, and hang there by one hand while you used the other to push the inspection hatch aside and swing the bag up into place. Athletic and tall. Well, all three of their suspects were tallish, and even Sandal Palliser was skinny and strong-looking.

The big drawback to the lift was that even if you happened to find it empty in the first place, you were just as likely as not to be interrupted by someone getting in or out, whereupon you might find it hard to explain why you were dangling about from the ceiling like an ape on whacky baccy. The lift couldn't have been essential to the plan, must surely have been a spur-of-the-moment thing. Perhaps being surprised by Mrs Reynolds, he had decided it was safer to hide the bag than go on carrying it about.

But Mrs Reynolds' description of the man at the lift didn't match any of the best suspects. If he wasn't the murderer, how did the bag get onto the lift roof? And if he was the murderer, then it wasn't Palliser, Somers or Parsons.

No, Slider sighed, he'd have to face the fact that they had been barking up the wrong street and pursuing red herrings down blind alleys all this time. His whole pack had been cur-dog hunting, and the fox must be two valleys away by now.

Still, clear as you go, that was the thing. A piece of the bloodsoaked raincoat material must be sent off to Tufty, Mrs Reynolds must be called in to identify the bag, and the forensic team must be dispatched to see if there was any trace of anything useful left in the lift. And the ground team would have to go back in and start asking everyone whether they'd seen anyone answering the description entering or leaving the lift, or entering the building wearing or carrying the mac.

The only good thing was that now he would not have to fight Honeyman for the manpower.

Atherton seemed as little pleased as Honeyman when he arrived and heard the news about the bag.

'It could still be Somers,' he said doggedly. 'He had every opportunity to plan the murder, bring the bag in at any time beforehand, and hide it again afterwards. He was only next door, and he's the only one who can say exactly when and how the body was discovered.'

'And why would he go to the trouble of putting on protective clothing and hiding it, and then go and dabble in the blood?' Slider said patiently.

'Well, we know he went into Greatrex's pocket for something. Suppose he did the murder in the protective gear, stowed it away, and then remembered whatever it was in the pocket. He had to go back for it, and then, seeing he'd got blood on him after all, he had to make the best of it by being the one who found the body. That would account for the state he's been in ever since – his perfect plan went astray, and now he's terrified he's going to get caught.'

'But—'

'And he was the one who had longest to brood over his wrongs and plan the thing. All those years of resentment, and then a couple of weeks of knowing Greatrex was going to be on the show and available to him.'

'But he doesn't answer the description of the man by the lift,' Slider managed to get in at last.

'We don't know he was anything to do with it. There could be a thousand reasons he had blood on his cuff.'

'He was carrying the bag,' Slider pointed out.

Atherton fought a noble rearguard action. 'It might not be the same bag. They're as common as blackberries. Or maybe Mrs Thing was mistaken. Or maybe she's confused the man she saw with somebody else.'

'You know you're beaten. Why don't you just admit defeat gracefully?'

'Show me the man who laughs at defeat and I'll show you a chiropodist with a warped sense of humour.'

'That's no answer.'

'Can I at least ask Somers about the mac?' Atherton pleaded.

'Of course you can, dear,' Slider said soothingly. 'In any case, you've got to clear up what he went into the pocket for. When you tell him he's out of the frame for the murder he'll probably come across. But the mac—' he shook his head. 'That's not a young man's mac. It's old, but it was once very expensive and very conservative. It's a stuffy mac. It's a wealthy, middle-aged, establishment sort of a mac.'

'It could have been bought second-hand,' Atherton pointed out.

'So it could, of course.'

'Or borrowed.'

'Quite. It's going to be no help at all.'

Mrs Somers opened the door to Atherton and drew a quick little breath. Her eyes searched his face for information, and, liking her, he said at once to relieve her, 'I know about Greatrex and your daughter.'

Her expression hardened, but there was still fear in her eyes. 'Phil didn't kill him. He deserved to die, but Phil would never do a thing like that.'

'I know,' Atherton said gently. 'Can I talk to him? There are some details he hasn't told us that are getting in the way of finding out who really did do it.'

171

She hesitated only a moment, and then stood aside to let him in. 'He's having a lie-in. He's not been well since this happened, so I told him to stop in bed. I'll go and get him up.'

'No need, I can talk to him in his room.'

She bristled. 'You can not! You'll sit down in the front room, and when I've called Philly, I'll make you a cup o' coffee. D'you take sugar?'

Philip Somers appeared at last in trousers, shirt and bedroom slippers, pale, unshaven, seedy about the eyes, and definitely apprehensive. His fingernails, Atherton noticed with distaste, were bitten to the nub.

'Mum says you want to talk to me,' he said, though from the sulky tone Atherton reckoned it was rather Mum says I've got to talk to you.

Atherton, who had been standing by the window, took a step and picked up the photograph from the corner table. 'Is this Madeleine?'

'Put that down,' Somers said sharply. Atherton took his time about complying.

'She was very pretty,' he said. 'Why did you hold Greatrex responsible? The inquest said it was an accident.'

'I didn't kill him,' Somers said sickly.

'I know,' Atherton said, and saw relief register so strongly on Somers's face that he wondered for an instant whether his own beloved theory was right after all. Somers sat down with involuntary abruptness. 'So tell me,' Atherton said again, 'why did you hold Greatrex to blame for your sister's death?'

'He was to blame, even if it was an accident,' Somers said fiercely. 'She was there because of him, she was in the car in that place at that time because of him. If he hadn't seduced her, she wouldn't have died. She'd be alive now, properly married, to a decent bloke, probably with children of her own.

172

Mum would be a grandmother, like she always wanted. Now – maybe she'll never be.'

'There's plenty of time, isn't there? And she has plenty of children.'

Somers shook his head. 'It affected us all. You don't understand. Maddy was the life of the family. She was the bright one, the funny one, always on the go. She was the one who made us do things. She was the one who made Mum and Dad buy this house when the council put it up for sale. She introduced Patrick to his wife. Without her—' He lapsed into a trembling silence.

'How did she meet Greatrex?'

'She was a voluntary steward at the Festival Hall, and he was always there, of course, being a music critic. He just saw her and decided he had to have her.'

'She was pretty,' Atherton commented.

'She was beautiful!' Somers cried. 'He had to have her, to spoil her. Whatever was fresh and good and clean he had to spoil. He seduced her and ruined her, taking her to cheap hotels—'

'That one in Bray wasn't exactly cheap,' Atherton said mildly.

Somers glared at him. 'Are you condoning what he did?'

'Well, you know, she was over age – what he did was no crime. She could presumably choose for herself, and most people don't regard having a sexual relationship with someone as disgraceful any more.'

'Most people! What do you know about most people? Maddy would never have gone to bed with him if he hadn't forced her – telling her lies, making her promises. I begged her to give him up, but she wouldn't. She said he meant to marry her. Marry her! He was degrading her! She was getting worse and worse, doing things she'd never have dreamed of

173

doing before. But I could still have got her back, if only I'd had the chance. Now she's dead, and lost to us for ever. He did that.'

Crackers, Atherton thought. He's as mad as a fish in a privet hedge. 'You wished he was dead,' he suggested lightly.

'Yes,' Somers said fiercely. 'But I didn't kill him.'

'All right, tell me about it.'

'When I found him there like that, I thought he'd killed himself. First of all I was glad. Then I was angry that he'd escaped so easily, without ever realising what he'd done to us. I'd wanted him to feel remorse, and now he never would. I was furious. I took him by the shoulders and shook him, I was so angry. That's how I got blood on me. And I kicked the knife across the floor, sort of in temper.' Atherton nodded encouragingly. 'And then – then I realised that it might look bad that I'd got blood on me. I'd been out looking for him, and here I was alone with him, and it might look as though—' He stopped, staring at his fearful memories. 'I – I suppose that's how I got it on my face. I must have put my hands up to it, like this.'

He cupped his face in his hands, and his long fingers reached into the hair at the edges of his ears.

'So I lay him down again, to try to make him look natural. I would have fetched the knife back, but I had blood on my shoes, and I knew I'd make a mark if I went to pick it up. I thought if I raised the alarm, I could explain the blood on me by saying I'd examined him to see if he was dead. Anyway, I reckoned no-one would think I had any reason to kill him. And then I remembered—'

'Yes,' said Atherton. 'You remembered what he kept in his pocket.'

Somers nodded slowly, seeming relieved that Atherton knew about it. Atherton waited, hoping for enlightenment.

At last he was forced to ask, 'How did you know it was there?'

'He'd showed it to me once. Years afterwards, when he was on a programme I was working on. He recognised me, and came up to talk to me, showed it to me, said that it proved he'd really loved her. I wanted to kill him then,' he said, trembling. 'I wanted to. It wasn't only Maddy, you see. There were others. They were all there, all the girls he'd seduced.'

Oh, I doubt it, Atherton thought – unless his boasts had far outstripped reality.

'I couldn't leave her there – part of his *harem*,' Somers said bitterly. 'Degraded into just one of his conquests. So I took it.'

'And where is it now?' Atherton asked, still flying by the seat of his pants.

Somers put a slow and reluctant hand into his trouser pocket. 'I thought you'd ask to see it,' he said unhappily, drawing out and handing over what looked like a leather wallet. Atherton took it and opened it. Inside transparent pockets on both sides were photographs. Photographs! Why didn't he think of that? 'That's Maddy,' Somers said, pointing.

'Yes, I recognise her,' Atherton said. The smiling face of Madeleine Somers gazed back through the plastic from the far side of death.

'Will I be able to have it back?' Somers asked in a small, defeated voice.

'Yes, of course, when we've completed our investigation,' Atherton said.

'I couldn't leave her there,' Somers said again. 'There's no knowing who those others were. And besides—'

'If the picture had been found, people might have thought

you killed him,' Atherton said. 'Quite. But why did you put the card in his pocket?'

'Card?'

'The religious card. The tract – a Bible quotation.'

Somers shook his head, puzzled. 'I don't know what you're talking about.'

'You didn't put anything into his pocket?'

'No. I took out this wallet, that's all. I got the wrong one first – his money wallet. He had – you-know-what's – in it,' he added in disgust. 'I put that back and took this one. I'd have taken Maddy's picture out and left the rest, but I was getting nervous, I thought someone might come in and find me. So I took the whole thing and went outside to raise the alarm. Luckily Dorothy was coming along the passage.'

'And you stood guard to stop anyone else going in until the police arrived. Why did you do that?'

'Well, that's what you do. I've seen it on the television. You're not supposed to disturb anything.'

'But you already had disturbed things. Wouldn't it have been better from your point of view if a few other people had done it too?'

'But I hadn't done anything wrong. I thought he'd committed suicide. I wanted to make sure the police would see that.' He looked at Atherton pleadingly. 'Don't you think he did? It could be suicide, couldn't it? I mean, now you don't think I killed him.' Atherton didn't immediately answer and Somers plunged on in alarm. 'You don't think I did, do you? You do believe me, what I've told you? It's the truth, I promise you. He was dead when I found him, and all I did was take the photos.'

'Yes, I believe you,' Atherton said, and only he knew how disappointed he was to be saying that. 'But you've given us a lot of trouble by not being honest with us from the beginning.

176

You've wasted a lot of our time, and my guv'nor's not going to be pleased about that.' Somers looked suitably cowed, and Atherton went on, 'I shall have to ask you to come down to the station and make another statement. And this time, please don't leave anything out.'

'Will it have to come out – about Roger and Maddy?' Somers asked pathetically. 'We kept it from the younger ones at the time. Kevin and Mandy and Katy don't know – what Maddy did. They think she was working with Roger the night she was killed.'

Like fun they do, Atherton thought. This man was a dreamer. 'I don't see why it should,' he said aloud. 'Provided you've now told us everything, I don't see why the matter of the photograph need be raised again.'

'Thank you,' Somers said. 'Mum'll be so glad. The shame of it nearly killed her at the time.'

Atherton would have thought rather that the grief nearly killed her; or the shame of having a son as spaced out as Silly Philly might do it.

11

Deliver us from Ealing

'Well, I'm not going to blow any sunshine up your skirts,' Slider concluded. 'We've now got a very long haul ahead of us, but you can comfort yourselves that this is what police work is really all about.'

With a sad smile in response to the irony, the troops dispersed. Slider called McLaren over. 'How have you got on with that discrepancy over the names on the lists? Davis or whatever it was?'

'Well, guv, the address Davis gave doesn't exist – Bishop's Road, SW11, which is Battersea of course. There isn't a Bishop's Road in Battersea. There's a Bishop's Park Road in Fulham and one in Mitcham, but he doesn't live in either of them. There's a Bishop's Terrace in SE11, but he doesn't live there. And there's four other Bishop's Roads in various places, five Bishop's Avenues, four Bishop's Closes, one Bishop's Court, and one Bishop Road without the "s". I haven't got round to checking them yet.' He looked up from his list. 'Doesn't the word "Bishop" start to look funny when you stare at it a long time?'

'What about the other name, the one that was on the ticket list?'

'Oh, that address is all right – Oakley Square, that's round the back of Mornington Crescent. Flats and bedsits, a lot of students and singles. But we knew that address must be all right anyway, because that's where they posted the ticket to.'

'And have you checked to see if Davis lives there?'

'Not yet. I was doing the other one first.'

'Well get onto it now,' Slider said, restraining himself nobly. 'Find out what the score is, whether he went to the BBC that night and if not, who did. And have you checked the no-shows?'

'All but one, and he's apparently abroad. His firm says that's pukka. The others seem genuine enough, but only one of them still had the ticket – the rest threw them away.'

'I don't think that's going to be important.' He turned to Norma. 'We need to get Mrs Reynolds in to identify the bag. Liaise with Atherton, see if you can get her here at the same time as Somers comes in to do his statement, and let them pass each other, just to see if she recognises him. I don't think it was him, now, but he was always our best chance. No harm in running him past her.'

'Yes, boss.'

'And then take Mrs Reynolds along to do a photofit.'

'Are you going public?' she asked with interest.

'That's up to Mr Honeyman, not me, thank God. He's having a press conference this afternoon, by the way, so he'll want as many things cleared up as possible before then. Let's snap to it.'

The later edition of the paper had a report of the Laurence Jepp incident. Slider was surprised to read that Jepp had not been beaten to death, as he had been imagining, but had had his throat cut. Any mention of throat-cutting immediately caught Slider's attention these days – like seeing your own name on a page, it was the thing that jumped out at you. It was not usually the preferred method for a surprised burglar, in his experience, and not a particularly common method of homicide overall. It was a long shot, but could there possibly be any connection between the Jepp case and the Greatrex murder? Greatrex was a music critic, after all, and he had reported on the *Don Giovanni* in which Jepp had been performing.

It was worth checking up on, at any rate, he thought. For want of a nail, and all that sort of thing. Probably there was nothing in it, but—

McLaren looked round the door. 'I think I got a result, guv,' he said.

'Davis?'

'Yeah. The one with the "e".'

'Come in.'

McLaren sidled in with his notebook in one hand and the stump of a Mars bar in the other. 'Well, guv—'

'Leave the chocolate outside, please. Last time you got it on my telephone, God knows how.'

McLaren looked at his left hand in surprise, as if he hadn't known the confectionery was there. 'I forgot I was eating that,' he said, and shoved it whole into his mouth. Slider averted his gaze. McLaren screwed up the paper and lobbed it accurately into the bin. 'Well, guv,' he resumed, bubbling a little, 'I got hold of this Davies guy. It turns out he's got an interesting story.'

Slider gestured McLaren to sit down. 'Did he go to the show on Thursday?'

'He went to White City, but he never went into the building. While he was queuing up outside with the rest of 'em, this bloke comes up to him and asks if he's there on his own. Davies says yes, and this bloke spins him a story, says he and his wife always come to these things together, only this time this bloke thinks he's working so his wife gets a ticket to come on her own, then at the last minute it turns out he's not working but by then there's no tickets left. So he says to Davies he really wants to go to this thing with his wife, and asks if Davies will sell him his ticket. Well, you don't pay for these tickets in the first place, and Davies isn't that struck on the show, really – he only goes 'cause he hopes to meet some-body—'

'Somebody?'

'He's a bit of a sad-act, this Davies guy. Unemployed, no money, no bird – no friends either. So he goes to a lot of these free shows at the BBC. It's a way of passing the time, which he's got a lot of, and he reckons it's his best chance of meeting birds, though they'd have to be desperate to fancy a legover with a pathetic nerk like him. Still, you get a lot of left-wing birds at the political ones like *Questions of Our Time* and they might see it as social work. The BBC's like a free dating agency to him.'

'I see.'

'So anyway, he asks this geezer how much and the geezer says a score, and Davies reckons for twenty quid he can go to the pub for the night and pick up a tart there, so he says okay and hands it over and the bloke gives him a twenty note, nice as pie. He's just walking off when the bloke asks him his name – says he'll need to know it at the door for the security check, which is true, which Davies knows it is – and Davies tells him Jim Davies, and off he goes.' McLaren leaned back in the chair with satisfaction. 'Geezer must have misheard the Jim for John; and not knowing the spelling went for the simplest version.'

'The man didn't tell Davies his name, I suppose? No, we couldn't be that lucky.' Slider thought a moment. 'Did Davies believe his story?'

McLaren shrugged. 'He didn't say he didn't. He told it to me as if it made sense to him.'

'Did he see the man's wife?'

'He says he didn't notice him at all until the bloke spoke to him. And when he'd got his score in his hand he shoved off fast, case the bloke changed his mind. Saw a bus coming and ran across the road and jumped on, and never looked back.'

'Did you ask him for a description of the man?'

'Yeah. He wasn't very helpful. He says he never really noticed. I s'pose he's standing there miles away and it's all over before he's on the ball. Probably more interested in the twenty than the bloke.'

'Well, what *did* he give you?'

'Middle age, middle height, clean-shaven, short hair but not bald. Brown or dark – not fair. Thinks the bloke may have worn glasses.'

'Clothes?'

McLaren shrugged again. 'A suit, he thinks, or possibly an overcoat. Not jeans, anyway.' He anticipated the next question. 'He doesn't remember if he was carrying a bag.'

Slider sighed. Davies had taken in merely an impression of a conventional grown-up rather than a shaggy youth. He could probably have told you the number on the bank note, though.

'All right, get him in, get a statement.'

'I've arranged that, guv. He's coming in today some time. D'you think it's the murderer?'

'It could be. Whoever it was was pretty determined to get in. I wonder why he picked on Davies, though?'

'He was right at the back of the queue, and on his own,'

182

McLaren said. 'And he sounds like a dozy git. Maybe he looks like he sounds. At least he probably looked as if he needed the money.'

'Fair enough. Well, see if you can get a better description out of him – maybe a photofit. Then we can compare it with Mrs Reynolds's efforts.'

'Rightyoh.' McLaren stood up. 'D'you think it's anything?'

'Anything could be anything. There could be any number of reasons why he wanted to go to this show, but—' He let it hang.

'Yeah,' said McLaren sympathetically. 'You gotta clear as you go.'

Slider determined never to say that again. He had always despised bosses who fell into tricks of speech and catchphrases. Mental laziness. That was one of the things he relied on Atherton for – to keep his mind perpetually on the hop.

DS Phil Hunt had been one of Slider's team, until he had got his stripes and gone to Ealing. He'd always been a bit of a pill. His one great passion in life was his customised red Escort XR3 on which he hung, screwed or stuck every new gadget that came out, like a crazed automotive Cophetua. No trouble was too great where his car was concerned. Slider vividly recollected a week during which his sole topic of conversation was a set of imported tyres he had ordered from a specialist dealer on the North Circular – how they brought the good pneus from Brent to Hayes, as Atherton had wearily put it.

The good thing about Hunt was that he did not realise what a dickhead he was, and had such an unshakeable sense of his own superiority that he never held grudges and was gracious to everyone. So when Slider rang to say he was in the area and asked if Hunt would like to slip out for a drink, he saw nothing suspicious in it, and met his former boss ten minutes later in one of the pubs in Madeley Road.

It was not difficult to get him to talk about the Laurence Jepp case. 'Ground-floor flat, conversion,' he said in his familiar, episodic style. 'One of those old Victorian piles down the side of the Common. Sash windows, no locks, of course – just the original catches. Child's play. Straightforward burglary, it looked like. Probably the bloke panicked when Jepp woke up and hit the alarm.'

'Anything missing?'

'Nothing obvious, but it's hard to say, with Jepp being dead, and living alone. He had a lot of nice stuff, if you like that sort of thing – antiques and pictures – but not what you'd expect a break-in for, not unless it was a proper daylight, front-door job with a van.'

'Opportunist thief, then?'

Hunt drew long and satisfyingly on his pint. 'Hard to say,' he said, wiping his foamy moustache with the back of his hand. 'It was a bit on the late side for a real kid, and a bit neat and tidy for a junkie. I thought maybe there was some really rare thing that someone was stealing to order. The way the catch had been slipped looked professional. But then, some of these addicts are virtually pros these days. My guv'nor reckons chummy was looking for something to sell, chose a big house in the hope, and then whacked Jepp when he woke up and hit the alarm.'

'So how was Jepp killed? Blunt instrument?' Slider asked casually.

'Throat cut,' Hunt said. 'Right through – hell of a mess in the bed. Amazing how far eight pints will spread.'

'Hard to cut someone's throat lying down,' Slider said.

Hunt gave a mirthless grin. 'Evidently that's what chummy thought. Jepp was lying face down with his knees under him.

184

Pathologist reckons the perp dragged him out of bed, turned him round, knelt him down on the bed, and cut his throat from behind. Knew what he was doing – you don't get so much blood on you that way.'

'He must have been strong.'

'Right. Though Jepp's only a little shorthouse – five foot five or six. But he cut his throat right through first cut – no haggling – so he must have been strong.'

Slider picked up his own pint so as to continue to look casual, but had to put it down again. He was afraid he'd spill it on the way to his mouth. He tried a wild shot. 'Was there a religious tract left on the body, or by the bed? A card with a verse from the Bible on it?'

Hunt looked surprised. 'How'd you know that, guv?' Slider jumped inside, but managed to keep still, as though it was matter-of-fact. 'Bloody hell, has somebody leaked? My guv'nor'll be right pissed off if anyone's been talking.' He evidently did not see the irony of that comment.

'What did it say on the card?' Slider asked casually. 'What was the verse?'

'Some bollocks about blood.' Belated caution visited Hunt. He narrowed his eyes. 'I don't remember exactly. Probably not important. Here, is that the time? I'd better be getting back.'

But Slider stood too. 'I think I'd better come and have a talk with your guv'nor,' he said.

Hunt stared in alarm mingled with resentment. 'What's all this about, guv? I thought you just wanted a social drink.'

'Don't worry, son, I won't get you in dutch,' Slider said.

'I never told you anything,' Hunt insisted.

'Of course you didn't. It's just that I've got a special interest in the late Mr Jepp.'

* * *

185

DI Gordon Arundel – known behind his back as Gorgeous Gordon or sometimes Glorious Goodwood – was a large and handsome man who left a trail of broken hearts and fractured marriages behind him wherever he served the forces of law and order. He had two ex-wives and seven children that he knew about and his maintenance payments were such that he could now afford to pursue only women who were independently wealthy, which had forced him dangerously high up the social scale. Stories about him were legion; he had now passed almost into legend. 'Did you hear DI Arundel had a nasty accident? He pulled out quick to avoid a child and fell off the bed.' 'Did you hear the Super's wife's up the club? It's a grudge pregnancy – DI Arundel had it in for him.' And so on.

He was also extremely jealous of his intellectual property, and Slider had much to do to allay his suspicion. Arundel would hardly admit the Jepp case existed, and would divulge nothing about what evidence they might have, though Slider gathered from the tone of his talk that it was not much. It took ten minutes of hard talking to persuade Goodwood even to let him see the Bible card. It was spattered with blood, which was appropriate to its text:

All things are by the law purged with blood; and without shedding of blood is no remission. Hebrews 9: 22.

'It was on the bedside table,' Arundel said. 'It's a misquotation, in any case. I looked it up. It should say *"almost* all things".'

'Not as punchy as this version,' Slider said, passing back the plastic bag in which the card resided. It was a disturbing quotation either way, especially taken in conjunction with the one found on Greatrex. 'I think,' Slider said cautiously, 'that it's just possible we may be looking for the same man. There seem to be similarities in the MO.'

'Well?' Arundel said impatiently. 'What are you saying, we've got a serial killer on the loose?'

'Not exactly.' Slider told him quickly about Greatrex. 'I don't know if there was any connection between them, anything specific, I mean, apart from music and opera generally. But it's possible someone had a grudge against them both.'

Arundel looked askance at him. 'It sounds like cobblers to me,' he said. 'Just because they both had a card with a Bible text on it. They could both have been given them by the same person. Or your bloke could have given it to my bloke, or vice versa, if they knew each other. Anyway, your man was done in a public place. Mine was done by an intruder. People's houses get burgled every minute of the day – especially old houses with sash windows.'

'And the MO?'

'A throat-cutting's a throat-cutting. Granted it was done professional, but they all know how to use a knife these days. They're tooled up by nine years old. If I was to be given a fiver for every kid walking about my ground who had a blade on him, I could retire a rich man. No, take my word, it was a burglary, plain and simple, some coke-head looking for something to sell.' He looked sidelong at Slider. 'I wouldn't like any of your lads trampling over my ground, Bill. Friendly advice. If anything comes up that might be of interest to you, I'll make sure it gets passed on.'

'Thanks Gordon.' Slider stood up. 'I know I can count on you.'

'Naturally,' Arundel said. 'And you'll help me in exactly the same way, of course.' It was meant to be ironic, Slider saw. It was a pity there were so many coppers who saw other coppers as opponents rather than oppos.

★ ★ ★

187

Norma brought Mrs Reynolds to Slider's office door on her way out.

'Mrs Reynolds has identified the bag, boss.'

'That's right, dear,' Mrs Reynolds said, not one to let someone else speak for her. 'It was that one, or one just like it.' Slider had stood up for her, and she gave a little nod of approval for the courtesy. 'But there's plenty around, aren't there? I mean they're not expensive.'

'That's true. But it's a help anyway, and we're grateful to you for coming in.'

'Oh, that's all right. Got to 'elp each other, haven't we? And I've enjoyed meself. Your young lady here has looked after me beautiful.' Behind her back Norma rolled her eyes.

'And you've made up a photofit for us of the man, have you?' Slider asked, more of Norma than Mrs Reynolds, but it was she who answered.

'Oh yes, I've done that. It was a queer feeling, seeing his face come together like that in front of me. I'll never forget him, nor the look he give me.'

Norma said, 'It looks faintly familiar, guv, but I can't place him. Not one of our front-row villains, though I've got a strange feeling I've seen him somewhere quite recently.'

Slider nodded. 'When you've got a minute, sit down with it quietly and go through your recent cases; and try it against the files. Perhaps you'd like to see Mrs Reynolds out now.' He gave his best boyish smile to the old lady. 'Thank you very much for coming in. We really do appreciate your help.'

He flicked a glance at Norma, who ushered the woman out, then asked her to wait in the corridor just a moment and popped back into Slider's office. 'No go, guv,' she said quietly, so that Mrs Reynolds wouldn't hear. 'I trundled her right past Somers in the front shop, and she didn't even glance. And the photofit she's done doesn't look anything like him.'

188

'Never mind, I didn't really think—'

He was interrupted by a breathless ejaculation from Mrs Reynolds – 'Oh, my good Gawd!' – followed by her hasty re-entrance from the corridor, clutching her bosom in alarm, her eyes wide with urgency. 'It's 'im! 'E's out there! Oh my Gawd, it give me such a fright!'

'Who?' Slider said and 'Where?' Norma said simultaneously.

'The bloke I seen by the lift!' Mrs Reynolds hissed. 'Go on, quick, 'fore he gets away!'

Slider gestured Norma tersely with his head and she crossed to the door and looked out. 'There's no-one there,' she said.

Mrs Reynolds extended her neck tortoise-like and peered round the door. 'You bleedin' blind? Down the end by the coffee machine!'

Norma looked at Slider, shrugged, and stepped out into the corridor. 'Mills!' she called. 'Can you come here a minute?'

Mills appeared opposite the doorway, plastic cup in hand, an enquiring expression on his face. Mrs Reynolds backed, clutching her coat to her neck in an instinctive gesture of alarm. 'That's 'im! Keep 'im off me!'

Slider stood up and went to her, laid a soothing hand on her arm. 'This is Detective Sergeant Mills, one of my team.'

Mrs Reynolds didn't take her fascinated eyes off Mills. 'I don't care. It's 'im all the same, the bloke I seen by the lift, with the bag.'

'Are you sure?' Slider said gently, with a glance at Mills. Mills was still looking at them with the mild enquiry of incomprehension.

'Course I'm sure,' she said scornfully. 'Look at 'im! You couldn't mistake that face, could you? That's 'im all right, sure as I stand here.'

★ ★ ★

'I suppose you haven't got a twin brother?' Slider asked hopelessly. 'Or a brother who looks a lot like you?'

Mills, sitting glumly on the other side of his desk, looked up from the contemplation of his hands dangling between his knees. 'I haven't got a brother of any sort. I'm adopted.'

'Oh yes, so you are. I'd forgotten.'

Norma smacked her forehead with a reproving hand. 'And there was I saying I thought the photofit looked familiar and I was sure I'd seen him recently.'

Slider was worried. 'That photofit is a real problem. She picked that out before she identified him in the corridor, which means she didn't just point a random finger.'

'Sir,' Norma said, 'Mills was there on the night on duty and she could quite easily have seen him. His face stuck in her memory for some reason, and she's confused him with the man she saw by the lift. If she actually did see a man by the lift at all. It could all be a figment of her imagination.'

'It could,' Slider agreed, 'but unfortunately she's a good witness – very sure and very circumstantial. She'll take some getting past. And she identified the bag.'

'She might have said yes to any bag we showed her.'

'She said beforehand it was a blue nylon flight bag. She could have said any colour. I'm afraid I have to take the bag as fact.'

Mills gave a tight smile. 'Nice try, Norma.' He looked at Slider. 'Am I in the clarts, sir?'

'Do you remember seeing Mrs Reynolds at all? Did you pass her in the corridor or speak to her or anything?' Slider asked.

'No sir, not that I remember. But she could have seen me, all the same. I didn't hide the bag in the lift. I've never owned a bag like that. And I didn't kill Greatrex.'

Slider sighed. 'I'm afraid it doesn't look very good, clartwise.

I shall have to take you off the case. And I shall have to tell Mr Honeyman. Whether he decides to go further is up to him.'

'Sir,' said Mills. He bit his lip, but did not look overpoweringly anxious, which was a comfort. Slider nodded to Norma to go. When they were alone, Mills said, 'You don't think I did it, do you, sir?'

'When I knew you at Charing Cross, I'd have bet my life on you. I suppose I actually did a few times. But I haven't seen you for ten years. And as I said, in all fairness Mrs Reynolds is a very good witness. She described you moles and all. It speaks volumes about my opinion of you, though, that I didn't identify you from her description.'

Mills seemed disconcerted by Slider's less than wholehearted endorsement of him; but he said, 'Thank you for being frank, anyway, sir. At least I know where I stand.'

Slider leaned forward. 'Off the record, Mills, I'd still trust you with my life. But I've got to keep an open mind, even if it is against my will. Did you have any connection with Greatrex?'

'No, sir.'

'Are you sure?'

'I'd never seen him before in my life, as far as I can remember. Well, not in the flesh, I mean. Of course I'd seen him on television.' He gave a strained laugh. 'It's fantastic. It's like asking me if I'd murdered Melvyn Bragg or Jeremy Paxman.'

'Ah, now we're talking wish-fulfilment. Well, I take your word for it. But you know we're going to have to investigate this, don't you? Go into your past life. Go through your drum.'

'I've got nothing to hide, sir,' Mills said, meeting his eyes steadily.

'Examine your movements,' Slider added on a more worried

note. 'For instance, I have to ask you again what you were doing at the TVC at all on Thursday night. You weren't on duty.'

'Ah!' It was a barely articulated sound of – enlightenment? Realisation of danger? Mills's dark eyes were full of understanding for an instant, and then he looked away from Slider, and answered neutrally, 'Like I've already told you, guv, I just happened to be passing and saw the mobile go in. So I followed out of curiosity, to see if I could help.'

'And what were you doing to be just happening to pass?'

'I'd been to see my auntie earlier. I didn't want to go home, it not really being much like home yet, so I was walking round the ground, getting my bearings again.'

Slider watched him for a moment, but he didn't waver. 'You're going with that, are you?'

'It's the truth.'

The trouble with the truth was that it was so often entirely unconvincing. A good, well-woven, colour-co-ordinated suit of fiction could always outclass it; but Slider could hardly say that to his subordinate.

'I'm very, very unhappy about this, Slider,' Honeyman said, like an enraged cairn terrier. No, strike that simile – it made Slider immediately envisage a small pink bow on the top of his boss's head, which wouldn't do at all.

'I'm not very pleased myself, sir,' he murmured, fixing his eyes on the bridge of Honeyman's nose, about which there was nothing risible, except its being part of Honeyman.

'It was bad enough having to announce that we don't think it was suicide after all, after four days of investigation—' He glared at Slider as though daring him to say he had favoured murder from the beginning. Kamikaze was not high on Slider's list of hobbies, and he kept a respectful silence. 'I was anticipating some upsetting analyses in the papers, though I did hope for sympathy from the BBC. At least they would understand the difficulties we were labouring under. But now this – this—!'

He slapped his hand down on the copy of the *Evening Standard* whose front page was half obscured by the thick black headline OWN GOAL and the only slightly smaller subhead MEDIA-STAR MURDER – COPS NAB ONE OF THEIR OWN. Slider didn't like to mention the later edition which had just come out, which Honeyman hadn't seen yet. It was on Slider's desk at that moment, and two-thirds of the page was now occupied by only three words: BILL THE RIPPER?

'At least they haven't got a picture,' Slider said comfortingly. 'In fact, they haven't even named Mills – just "a detective investigating the case".'

In fact, of course, in tabloids the size of the headline was always inversely proportionate to the amount of actual substance to the text. If there'd been enough story to fill the front page, they wouldn't have needed the heavyweight, scandalsized, 144-point scream.

'It can only be a matter of time,' Honeyman said. 'But in any case that isn't the point. The point is that someone has leaked, and on this of all issues, the most sensitive, embarrassing subject of all. It's going to make us look complete fools!'

For 'us', read 'me', Slider thought.

'I want to know who it was who gave the story to the papers! I want a full investigation, and when the culprit is found, I warn you, Slider, I shall have no mercy! This sort of thing has got to be stopped. I shall come down on him as heavily as I possibly can!' He stamped away a few steps and back again in uncontainable rage. 'What is Mr Wetherspoon going to think? What do you think the Divisional Commander's going to think? It'll be all over the dailies tomorrow, and there's no knowing how far it may go.' Honeyman's eyes bulged at the awful prospect. 'Imagine what the ADC's going to be reading over his breakfast marmalade!'

'I think it much more likely the leak came from the witness, sir,' Slider said. 'The fact that there's no name mentioned suggests that. She probably just said something to a neighbour and the neighbour's phoned the local paper with it, and it's gone on from there. But it hardly matters—'

'Oh, I'm glad you think that! I'm very glad indeed you think it doesn't matter that we're marked with sending a man out to investigate his own murder!' Honeyman moaned as the whole of his pension flashed before his eyes. 'We'll never live this down!'

'What I meant, sir, was that the important thing is to sort out what this accusation means. Recriminations can wait until later, but Mills's whole life and career are on the line here.'

'Career!' Honeyman ejaculated helplessly; but then he pulled himself together. 'Carver tells me you worked with Mills some time ago.'

'Yes, sir, for three years at Charing Cross.'

'And what sort of officer was he?'

'The best, sir. Quiet, efficient, conscientious.'

'You had no doubts about his honesty?'

'He was my bagman on several cases. I had complete faith in him.'

'I've pulled his record, and that's clean,' Honeyman said regretfully. 'And Colin Washbrook over at Epsom speaks highly of him. But that's his duty life. His private life is less satisfactory. He isn't married, you know. I don't like the idea of policemen who aren't married. And he's a loner. I prefer a policeman to be the sociable type. That way we all check up on each other.' He looked up. 'He had blood on his clothes, you say?'

'He said Somers had clutched hold of him, and the blood

came off on him. That's a reasonable explanation. And Baker confirms that Somers was hysterical and that Mills had a job calming him.'

'He might have grabbed hold of Somers deliberately to hide bloodstains he had got earlier.'

'But Mrs Reynolds doesn't say the man at the lift had blood on his clothes, only a little on his cuff.'

'Even that would be enough for him to want to hide. He wasn't to know that the woman had noticed, if they only saw each other for a second – or that she would come forward.' Honeyman's fingers drummed absently on the newspaper on his desk. 'The fingerprint on the religious tract card doesn't match, you say?'

'Bob Lamont says they are very similar, but there are certain distinct features which differ in Mills's.'

'Well, fingerprinting's not an exact science. You can always argue it either way. It's negative evidence at best. And that print could have got onto the card at any time, as we always knew. The most damning thing is the fact that he was there in the first place. It's going to be hard to get round that.'

Slider was silent. He knew that was true. It was the bit, on the whole, he didn't like; yet putting himself in Mills's shoes, he wondered if natural curiosity might not have made him act the same. Walking your new ground trying to get a feel of things, trying to assemble the knowledge on which your future success, possibly even life, would depend . . . Well, it was arguable, at the outside.

'You've checked with the mobile team – what were their names?'

'Baker and Morley, sir. They say Mills just appeared soon after they got to the scene of the murder.'

'Ah. And what about reception?'

'Mills says he didn't go to the desk, he just followed the

uniformed lads. No-one tried to stop him because the reception area was crowded with people – the audience going up to the show.'

Honeyman looked seriously at him. 'This could be crucial. If you can find anyone who saw him arriving, and pin down the time, we might have a defence.'

'Yes, sir,' Slider said patiently. 'We're on it.' The team was already re-contacting all the people who might have been in the reception area at the time to ask, rather hopelessly, if they had noticed the uniforms arriving and the dark-haired man following. It was not necessary to tell them how urgent the matter was; Mills might be new, but he was one of their own, and, loner or not, he was instantly likeable.

'For the time being, I have no alternative but to suspend Mills,' Honeyman said, and to his credit he sounded regretful; Slider hoped on Mills's behalf and not his own. 'On your recommendation I shan't take any further action yet, but of course Mills must be very, very careful and very circumspect. I've told Carver, and he thinks that as Mills has been working on your case, you should be the one to tell him.'

Oh joy, Slider thought. Thank you, Ron.

'One other thing, Slider – nothing's been said yet to the Complaints Investigation Bureau. I want to give you a chance to justify your faith in Mills. But I have to warn you, if he is named in the press, or if you fail to progress within the next two days, I shall have no alternative. And once Mills has been turned over to the CIB, it will be out of my hands.'

'I understand, sir,' Slider said. Forty-eight hours to get old Dark Satanic out of the brown and viscous. And to rescue dainty Eric Honeyman's career from an ignominious end. On the whole, he thought, I'd rather be in Philadelphia.

12

Close to Home

'You never got married, then?' Slider asked, sitting at one side of the table in the tiny kitchen while Mills sat at the other. Through the open door they could hear the soft sounds of Atherton searching the bedroom. Mills had a tiny flat on the top floor of a house on the bend of Stanlake Road, where it bumped into the edge of the New Park and swung away again. From the little window behind the sink you could see through the trees a bit of the park and the BBC building on the other side of it. It was much too close to the nick for a policeman to settle in permanently, but it had often been let for short periods to newcomers while they looked for a place – having the advantage that it was almost impossible to be late for work while living there. As Atherton said, you could almost smell the canteen from the door.

'Never,' Mills answered Slider's question, with a quirk of his lips at the word, as though it amused him in some way. He took a sip from his mug of coffee. Slider's sat untouched before him. He didn't like instant coffee anyway, and this was edging towards record-breaking awfulness. It was the colour of ditch water and smelt like a stale face-flannel, and those were only its good points. Odd that 'a coffee' had always been the accepted precursor to – and even euphemism for – a sexual encounter. But then, like sexual encounters, instant coffee was usually disappointing and often left a funny taste in your mouth.

'What happened to that nice girl you were seeing when we were both at Charing Cross? Dark-haired girl. What was her name?'

'Ruth.'

'That's the one. Scottish, wasn't she? She was a nice girl.'

'She married a nice man,' Mills said. 'With a nice job, nine to five and a company car and no hassle.'

'Ah. I'm sorry.'

'So was I.' Mills looked at him with a gleam of humour. 'There have been others. I'm not gay.'

'I didn't think you were.'

'For the record, then. But the longer you're on your own, the harder it is to get it together with someone. You know the problems – the only people who understand are police-women, and if you date a plonk from your own ground, it's like having it off in a goldfish bowl. No romance could survive that.' He shrugged. 'So I keep it outside and I keep it casual. Or it keeps itself casual. Women don't like taking second place to the Job.'

'Are you seeing someone at the moment?'

'There was someone in Epsom.'

'The girl you left behind?' Slider suggested.

Mills didn't smile. 'She was married. He was a sales director for an ice cream company. He didn't know. She didn't want him to. It suited her that way. Having her Arctic Roll and eating it.'

'And you? Did it suit you?'

He shrugged. 'She wasn't the one great love of my life.'

'So who was?' He didn't answer. 'Ruth?'

'I suppose – if it was anyone. But if I'd married her we'd probably be divorced by now. Statistics. Are you divorced, sir?'

'Not yet,' Slider said. He wasn't going to let Mills turn the point. 'So tell me about your family.'

'My Dad's dead – ten, eleven years ago. He was a lot older than Mum. Mum's getting a bit—' He rocked his hand. 'Well, she's pushing seventy. It's not Alzheimer's, apparently – something to be grateful for. But she doesn't always remember things. Gets confused.'

'She's in a home, you said?'

'Not a home. Sheltered accommodation. St Melitus's in Brook Green.'

'And you go and visit her?'

'That was mainly why I got myself transferred here, so I could get to see her more often. When I was in Epsom I couldn't just "drop in". It was too far. And when they get old like that, you don't know how long you'll have them. After Dad died – well, when it's too late, then you realise how often you missed the chance to visit them because you were tired or couldn't be bothered or whatever.'

Slider thought of his own father, and thought away again. 'Any other family?'

'Only Auntie Betty. When I was a kid there were some ancient uncles and aunts on my Dad's side that we saw occasionally, but they're all dead now, and I never kept up with the cousins. My mum just had the one sister. Like I said, she lives in Ormiston Grove.'

'And you visit her too.'

'I always called on her when I came to see Mum. But she was a bit cross about me transferring to Shepherd's Bush.

Told me she didn't want me hanging around bothering her.'
He smiled to show it was a joke. 'She was always very fond
of me. I loved going round her house when I was a kid. She
used to take me out places, tried to widen my horizons. She
took me to Covent Garden, the museums, the zoo – to the
Oval to watch Surrey—'

'You had an aunt who liked cricket?' Slider said in envious
tones.

'She was a very unusual aunt – an education in herself.
She really made me what I am. She and Mum never really
got on, but I will say Mum never tried to stop me seeing her.
I think she disapproved because Auntie Betty had a career
instead of getting married and having children, like a proper
woman. But it was nice for me. It meant I got all the attention and all the presents. It was Auntie Betty bought me my
first bike.'

'That's quite a present from an aunt,' Slider said.

'It caused a bit of a fuss at home,' Mills said with a rueful
grin. 'Mum and Dad didn't have a lot of money, they couldn't
afford to buy me stuff. I remember some pretty sharp
comments about that bike. I think Dad had half a mind to
send it back, but it would've broken my heart. I'd wanted
one for years. I suppose it was a bit tactless of Auntie, but
she had a good job in the Civil Service and no-one else to
spend the money on, and she was very fond of me.'

'She wasn't married?'

'Married to her career.'

'Like you.'

Mills shrugged. 'I'll be a bachelor like my father – that's
what I used to say. It used to drive Mum mad.'

'Did you know anything about your natural parents?'

'No,' Mills said firmly but indifferently. 'I never asked.'

'Weren't you curious?'

'Why should I be? I was happy as I was. My mum and dad were good to me, and as far as I was concerned they were my parents.'

'You must have heard something about the circumstances, though, over the years. How you came to be born.'

'I gathered my natural mother was unmarried and the bloke didn't want to know, that's all. The usual story. Of course in those days it was a serious thing, getting pregnant. A girl couldn't just keep the kid and live on the State like she can now. I mean, she needn't have been a bad lot. But she was nothing to do with me. How could she be? I was taken away from her at birth and adopted when I was a couple of weeks old. My parents didn't talk about it, and like I said, I didn't ask.'

'You grew up around here, you said?'

'You could hardly get a more local boy than me. Went to Ellerslie Road primary and Christopher Wren secondary. Supported QPR. Went dancing at the Hammersmith Palais. Got drunk for the first time at the General Smuts and fumbled my first girl in Wormholt Park.'

'Impressive credentials,' Slider smiled. 'And what made you become a policeman?'

'I suppose that was down to Auntie Betty in a way. Mum and Dad wanted me to go in for something like banking or accountancy, something respectable and secure in a suit. But Auntie used to talk about public service. She really believed that being a civil servant was doing something for your country, bless her. And she used to say, "You can't just live your life as if you were the only person on the planet." She was quite scathing on the subject of doing a job just to earn money. I think that was another reason she and Dad didn't get on. He must have thought she was criticising him all the time. I don't think she was – I think she was just tactless. But everything

201

she said and did must have looked as if she was saying the way Mum and Dad lived wasn't good enough.'

'Weren't you afraid joining the police would look like siding with her against them?'

'I never thought about it. Once the idea of the police took root in my brain, it was all I wanted. And anyway, there was never any open hostility between Auntie and Mum and Dad. It was just little things that, looking back, I can see now must have annoyed them. But they were always polite. And I don't think in the end they minded me being a policeman. Mum nearly died of pride at the passing-out parade – any time she saw me in uniform, really; and Dad was always trying to get me to come and talk to his Sunday school class.'

'Were they churchgoers, your parents?'

'Oh yes. In the Pillars Of class – though of course it wasn't so unusual in those days. If you were respectable people you went to church, and that was that. But they were quite religious. I was adopted through the Church. I suppose they might have been grateful on that account as well – it was quite hard even in those days for a couple with such a big age difference to adopt. Dad was twenty years older than Mum.'

Slider nodded. 'Was your aunt religious, too?'

Mills made an amused face. 'I don't know. I was never allowed to visit her on Sundays. But I rather doubt it. She was always a bit of a rebel, my Auntie.'

'Nothing,' said Atherton. 'Normality encapsulated. You couldn't get anything less Dark and Satanic. The only iffy thing in the house was a large collection of Barbra Streisand records; but I suppose it is possible for a Barbra Streisand fan to be a good man,' he added doubtfully.

'I once knew a thoroughly decent person who quite liked Barry Manilow,' Slider admitted.

'You just never can tell,' Atherton said wisely. 'So what about Mills?'

'I don't know,' Slider said. 'I don't believe he's a murderer, but you don't necessarily have to be a murderer to kill someone, do you? The question is, if it was him, why Roger Greatrex? There's got to be some connection. I can't believe Greatrex was dispatched completely at random, and if it wasn't robbery from the person, it was because of something he did, or was.'

'Or even everything he did and was,' Atherton said.

'Yes, perhaps,' Slider said absently.

'Well, what do we do now?' Atherton asked after a moment. 'Keep looking for some connection between Mills and Greatrex? Or accept that the old bird was confused?'

'We haven't got a lot of options. We'll have to do a full investigation into Mills, because if we don't the CIB will. That means someone will have to go to Epsom and try to find out who his friends were, what he did in his spare time, whether he had any cases that bear on the situation. And we'll have to try to trace his movements on Thursday night and since he's been back in the Bush.'

'This aunt might throw some light, I suppose?'

'We can only hope so. And meanwhile, we continue to act on the assumption that it wasn't him Mrs Reynolds saw by the lift. We keep asking questions, look for witnesses, show people the photofit and see if they recognise it, try and trace the bag—'

'Ha ha.'

'And the coat.'

'And the knife?'

Slider frowned. 'Mills said he was in the Scouts as a lad. And the knife is the sort of old-fashioned clasp-knife that Scouts used in those days. But it could have been anyone's,

203

and come from anywhere. I think the most likely thing is that Mrs Reynolds saw someone by the lift who was superficially like Mills; she'd seen Mills at the TVC without realising it, and compounded them in her mind when she saw him again at the station.'

'Sounds good to me,' Atherton said. 'And we've still got the spare Mr Davis to follow up. No need to despair yet.'

'How do you follow up someone you know doesn't exist?' Slider said rhetorically.

Miss Elizabeth Giles, Mills's Auntie Betty, turned out to be a tall, vigorous, chain-smoking lady in her sixties, whose intelligent dark eyes made her face look younger than her white hair suggested. Though thick and bushy, it was cut very short.

'Unseemly, I know,' she said, having made an apology for her 'skinhead crop' the opening gambit in their conversation, 'but I've let it grow out since I retired – I used to dye it, you see, sad effort to look younger than my years – and with the ends dark and the roots growing out white, I looked such a sight, like a skewbald pony. So I keep having them cut off. The last of it's gone, now, as you see, so I can start to resume the dignity due to my vast age. Except that I rather like the freedom.' She shook her head about. 'Like Jo, you know, in *Little Women*? No, delete that. *Silly* thing to say. What would a chap like you be doing reading *Little Women*? Even if you have a daughter, I'm sure the PC brigade will have banned books like that from sale.'

She occupied the ground floor of a tall terraced house in Ormiston Grove which showed, by its paper bell-signs, to have other occupants upstairs and in the semi-basement. 'I bought it years ago for an investment, in case I ever got married and had a lot of children, but what sort of man would marry a woman who owned a house large enough to have ten children in?' she said cheerfully. 'Don't attempt to answer that. In case you wonder, I've had plenty of offers of marriage over the years, but never from anyone I'd have dreamed of accepting. I suppose my trouble is I could never respect any man who'd want to be married to a woman like me. So here I am, all alone, except for the students in the basement and the bats in the belfry. I like to keep some young people about me, keeps me on my toes.'

'Bats in the belfry?' Slider managed to slip a question in.

'Oh, God love them, they're not really bats, of course, but one can't resist, can one? *Le mot juste* and all that. CICs they call them now, bless them – Care in the Community. I've got two upstairs, and you couldn't want better lodgers. Besides, it makes the tax position so much more favourable. God knows I've paid enough in all these years – not that I begrudge it. You have to do your bit, don't you? No man is an island. Would you like tea? Excuse the mess, I'm not one of nature's Little Housewives, and now I'm at home all the time, I seem to make ten times the mess. But it's all clean dirt, as my mother used to say. Do you mind dogs? Do you mind if I let mine out? I shut them in the scullery when I came to the door because they're off out into the street if they get the slightest chance. Can you switch the kettle on while I let them out? It is full.'

Slider obeyed, while Miss Giles picked her way through the cluttered kitchen and opened a coat-infested door at the other side, whereupon two small, hairy projectiles shot out between her feet and hurled themselves round the room like wall-of-death riders, making frantic love to each pair of legs as they passed them. After a moment they slowed down enough to resolve themselves into two grey schnauzers with very short haircuts and muscle-packed bodies who, for some reason, seemed to Slider to reinforce the view that people choose dogs that look like themselves.

'Loonies,' Miss Giles said affectionately, shoving the nearest one with her foot. 'You'd think they'd been locked in there for days instead of minutes. Now, tea. Where did I put the teapot? Oh, wait, I remember, it's got flowers in it, in the other room.' She smiled engagingly. 'I was sent rather a large bunch a few days ago, and had to press every vessel into service. Never mind, it's teabags anyway. Do you mind my being terribly vulgar and making it in the cup?'

'Not at all,' Slider said. 'Was it your birthday?'

'Good lord, how did you—? Oh, the flowers, you mean! Yes, my birthday, though at my age it would be more seemly to stop having them. But Steve always remembers, bless him. He's a good boy.'

'Have you—?'

'Do you want a cup or a mug?' she overrode him. 'The cups are rather twincey, you get more if you don't mind a mug. And how do you take it? Milk, sugar?'

'No sugar, thanks.'

'Right. We'll stay in here, if you don't mind. The other room is such a tip. Sit down, boys. No, no, we're not going out. Go and sit down. Basket!' She smiled through the steam. 'It always made me laugh when people shouted "Basket" at their dog. I started doing it as a joke, but of course they don't know any better. It works, though – a nice, sharp-edged, distinguishable word.' The two little dogs had certainly obeyed her, and were sitting side by side in the large, old-fash-ioned wicker basket by the back door. The kitchen was unreconstructed fifties, with a wooden table and chairs, a grey enamel gas stove, a porcelain sink, and a wooden cupboard with an enamel top for a work surface. The only modern thing in the room was a gleamingly large portable radio/tape recorder in the corner from which music and voices were issuing quietly. After a moment Slider identified it as probably a Mozart opera, and felt proud of himself. Apart from the books, clothes, newspapers and personal clutter washing about the room like a landlocked tide, everything was in pristine condition. Slider wondered if it had been like this when Mills visited as a child.

'Have you lived here very long?' he asked while she paused for breath.

'Thirty years. I must have been one of the first single women on earth to get a mortgage on my own salary, and even then I had to get a special recommendation from my boss to the building society. They assumed all women were going to marry and get pregnant, as night follows day. I've often wondered what he told them,' she grinned. 'Maybe that no-one would have me on a bet.'

'So it was here that Mills – Steve – used to visit you as a child?'

'Yes. Well, they lived just round the corner in Oaklands Grove.'

'Is that why you bought the house? I mean, bought it here rather than somewhere else?'

'Property was cheap here at the time,' she answered, and he thought there was something about that which was slightly less straightforward than her previous deliveries. She dealt with the teabags before she spoke again. 'I didn't mind living nearby. I didn't see much of Maggie and her husband, but it was nice to have Steve popping in. I suppose he's told you I was very fond of him as a boy?'

'He spoke very warmly of you,' Slider said. 'He said you took him to cricket matches and the opera.'

She laughed, and he saw that she must have been attractive in her youth, though probably overpowering even then. 'I had to do something to counteract the football culture. Arthur – his dad – used to take him to see QPR play most Saturdays in winter. His idea was to make Steve as ordinary as possible, as much like himself and everybody else as he could. Whereas I wanted him to be as individual as possible. I could see the boy had great potential. I introduced him to a wider set of horizons. I hoped he might be musical – my mother played the piano very well, and Father sang apparently. I didn't want Steve growing up thinking football and the Methodist Church was all there was in life.'

'How did his father like that?'

She looked at him sharply, and set his tea down with rather more of a bang than was strictly necessary. 'You mean his dad? You don't expect people like Arthur to appreciate other people's points of view. Their minds run on rails. Anything at all different from their experience is automatically suspect, and a criticism of themselves.'

'You didn't get on with him?'

The expression became veiled. 'Oh, I wouldn't say that. Arthur was a good, decent, Godfearing man. I dare say he found me irritating. And of course he hated the fact that I had a career. In his eyes, a woman's place was in the home. But he was a good dad to Stevie, according to his lights. I just felt I could offer him something he wouldn't get with Maggie and Arthur – but I tried to do it discreetly.' She met Slider's eyes, and gave a hearty laugh. 'Yes, I know! You don't need to look at me like that. And of course, I'm not the most tactful person in the world. But we all tried to put a good face on it and get along, for the boy's sake.'

'Your sister's older than you?'

'Eight years.'

'And there were just the two of you?'

'There were two brothers in between, twins, but they died

at birth. Poor Maggie was always very much the elder sister, running after me, trying to keep me out of trouble and getting the blame when she didn't. And then Father died untimely, and Mother went to pieces rather, and Maggie had to mother me. It made her old before her time, poor darling, whereas I could go on being disgraceful all my life, safe in the knowledge that I was the baby of the family. Wicked!'

'Were you? Wicked, I mean?'

'Oh – no, not really. It's just the mores of the time were against me. I mean, Arthur was a perfect example of the normality of those days. He thought it was disgraceful to see a woman smoking. And as for having my own bank account and cheque book – slippery slope! I often wondered why Maggie married him.'

'Why do you think she did?'

'Father replacement, I suppose. Move over Sigmund. But he was twenty years older than her – thirty in spirit. I suppose she was fed up with being Mother and wanted to become somebody's daughter again. Well, that's what we all want really, isn't it – someone to take responsibility for us? Some more than others.' The last words were muffled by the cigarette on which she pulled hard, blinking her eyes rapidly in the smoke.

'Were they very religious – your sister and her husband?'

'Well, quite, I suppose. Very, compared with me. But they weren't weird about it or anything like that. Straightforward Methodist. They went to church every Sunday, Arthur taught the Sunday school, Maggie did teas at various church dos, that sort of thing. Arthur was a bit old-fashioned about keeping the Sabbath, but then he was old-fashioned about a lot of things. Wouldn't let Steve eat in the street, for instance – not even an ice cream. Imagine, if the boy wanted a threepenny cornet, he had to bring it indoors and eat it sitting down at the table. Where's the fun in that?'

Slider smiled. 'My mother was the same. She wouldn't let us eat fish and chips out of the paper. We had to take it home and have it off plates. She said it was common to eat in the street.'

Miss Giles smiled broadly. 'I call that sheer cruelty! Was she a Methodist?'

'No, just the normal C of E.'

'Well, anyway, you can see why I felt I had to do my bit to introduce a little leaven into Steve's life. Thank heaven Arthur never had a daughter, that's all I can say.'

'They never had any children of their own?'

She shook her head. 'They wanted them, but nothing happened. I rather fancy Arthur couldn't, but it wasn't something that was discussed in those days – and in any case, Maggie would never have discussed it with me. Loyalty, you know. So they adopted.'

'Through the Church, I understand?'

'Yes.'

He waited for more, but she said nothing, sipping at her cigarette, her eyes fixed on the rising smoke.

'Was anything known about the baby's parents?'

'It was a private adoption, arranged by their minister,' she said. 'Because of Arthur's age they couldn't go through the usual routes. But it was all legal and above-board.'

She sounded defensive, and he said soothingly, 'I'm sure it was. I just wondered if anything—'

'Joshua Green was his name. I always think that sounds like a village in a children's book. Not that there was anything pastoral about him – he was a real, eye-flashing, fire-and-brimstone preacher. Had a terrific following in the flock. And he was a great organiser. Maggie used to say he could organise a cat into having puppies.' She puffed again. 'It wasn't the only adoption he arranged – Green. He was attached to a mother-and-baby home, financed by the Church. It was his pet charity, I believe. I suppose it was natural for Maggie to turn to him when she found she couldn't have a child.'

'But you think she knew nothing about the natural mother?'

'How should I know what she knew?' She sounded irritable. 'All I know is that they kept those things very discreet in those days. Once the woman had given the kid away, she was supposed to bow out for ever. Nobody in those days thought adopted children would ever be allowed to look up their past, as they can now. The Children Act, or whatever it was called. Retrospective law is bad law, that's what I've always been told. Fortunately most of them don't bother. In any case, what has it got to do with anything? Maggie was the one who brought Steve up. She's the one who moulded his character, if that's what you're enquiring about.'

'According to him, you had quite a lot to do with it,' Slider said smilingly.

She got up abruptly from her seat and went over to the sink, emptied the dregs of her cup and ran the tap noisily into it.

'I'm sorry, I didn't catch what you said,' Slider said when she turned it off.

'I said, what did you want to know specifically about Steve? What's he supposed to have done – or aren't I allowed to know?'

'There seem to be some irregularities in the conduct of a case in which he's involved,' Slider said carefully. 'I'm just trying to clear things up. I worked with Mills some years ago and I'd prefer to get it straight myself than to see it passed to an outsider.'

'You worked with him?' she asked, her gaze sharpening.

'Yes, wait a minute now, I remember your name. I thought there was something familiar about it. It was when he was at Charing Cross, wasn't it? He used to talk about you sometimes – thought you were a good 'un and destined for high places.'

'They don't always go together, I'm afraid,' Slider said. She was looking at him with interest and more friendliness now.

'Well, what's he supposed to have done? How can I help? What is this case?'

Slider told her; and explained how Mills had been seen at the scene of the crime at the wrong moment. 'I don't believe there's anything in it myself,' he said casually, 'but the witness seems a very steady sort of person, and she described him very well. She compiled a photofit picture for us, and it does look very like.'

She sat down slowly in her vacated chair. She stared at him as though she had thought of something. 'But he—' She tried to lick her lips, and then went into a coughing fit. At the end of it, drumming her fist briskly against her chest she said, 'Got to give these damned things up. You were saying – you don't think there's anything in it.'

'I think the most likely thing is that the witness saw him somewhere else, and simply remembered him in the wrong place. After all, he was there during the evening. But with such a positive identification, I have to follow it up.'

'Positive, yes,' she said, and she laughed strangely, as if at a private joke. 'Well, obviously, Steve isn't a murderer – if you've worked with him, you know that anyway. He did come to see me on Thursday afternoon, and he left about – oh, I don't know – half past six. Ish. I wasn't checking, but it would be somewhere around there.'

'Yes,' Slider said. That tallied with what Mills had said. 'Is he religious at all?'

'Religious? What a horrible expression! If you mean, like his mum and dad, no he isn't. But I'm sure he has an inner belief and an inner code, as most of us do. I don't think he could be a good policeman if he didn't believe in anything, do you? And he is a good policeman, isn't he?'

'I think so,' Slider said. 'But he isn't a regular churchgoer? Doesn't belong to any special groups?'

'Not that I'm aware of.'

Slider nodded, and went on chatting to her while his thoughts roamed. They hadn't found anything of a religious nature in Mills's flat, not even a Bible – though with an upbringing like his, Mills was likely to be *au fait* with the Bible, perhaps enough to be able to quote from it from memory. And as he was living in temporary accommodation, he might not have all his things with him. He must make a mental note to check that out.

He rose to leave. 'By the way, why didn't you want Mills to come back to Shepherd's Bush? I'd have thought you'd like to have him a bit nearer than Epsom, fond of him as you are.'

She was ready for that one. 'I didn't like to think of him tied to the apron strings of two old biddies like me and his mum. Especially now Maggie's going gaga. We could be a real drag on him, especially given his kind heart, and that's not what I ever wanted for him. He's got his own life to lead. I told him when he came round on Thursday that I didn't want him popping in to see me every five minutes. That's not the way to get ahead.'

'And you want him to get ahead?'

She looked at Slider with slightly narrowed eyes, though it might only have been because of the smoke rising from the freshly lit cigarette. 'He's the nearest thing I ever had to a son,' she said. 'Of course I want him to get ahead.'

13

Private Lives

Atherton knew that look. When Slider returned, he wore the expression of internal preoccupation, like a man who has just eaten rather too large a curry along with several pints of the Anglabangla's Super Mistral lager.

'What it is, guv?' he asked, but without much hope. At this stage his guv'nor often didn't know himself. It was just that something was trying to connect up inside his mind.

Slider merely shook his head and headed for his office. Atherton followed. 'No luck so far with the photofit, but it's slow work, of course, everyone being so scattered. Thirteen staff and about twenty of the audience have been shown it and so far only one has said it looks familiar, and even she's pretty vague – thinks she saw someone like that at some point but can't be sure. People are so unobservant,' he complained.

'Yes,' said Slider.

Atherton looked at him enquiringly. 'I can't quite work out whether we want people to recognise this mug or not. I mean, if people saw Mills knocking around the building – is that good or bad?'

214

'Has the photofit been shown to the man who sold his ticket?'

'Jim Davies? Yes, and he thinks it might have been the same man, but he's not sure. Still, at least he hasn't said absolutely not, which gives us the possibility that the ticket-buyer looks enough like Mills to have confused Mrs Reynolds, and that makes him the murderer and then we only have to find him.'

'Have you found out yet who actually wrote down the Davis name and address up in the canteen?' Slider said abruptly.

'Oh, yes, it was Coffey. D'you want to talk to him?'

Coffey, a young officer lent by the uniform side, came in looking shamefaced.

'Your handwriting's so bad you could have been a doctor,' Slider said. 'Did you think you were writing Davis or *Davies?*'

'It's *Davis,* sir, definitely. And I always check spellings like that. I know I did,' he added earnestly, 'because I'm a bit sensitive about names. Nearly everyone spells mine wrong.'

'So you remember this man?'

'Well, sir, no, not really.' Slider looked up sharply, and Coffey lifted his hands slightly in a gesture of surrender. 'There were so many people there, all milling about this sort of canteen, and we were sitting at tables writing while they came up one by one and sat down and gave their names and addresses. It was like a sausage machine. I just kept writing.'

'You've had a look at the photofit?'

'Yes, sir. Well, I suppose it could have been him, but I honestly can't say I remember. I suppose I must have looked up at the people when they sat down, but I didn't really take in any faces. I wasn't looking to recognise them, I was just trying to hear what they said. There was so much noise in there, you could hardly hear yourself think, and—' The sentence trailed off, and Slider could easily add the rest for himself – we were all cursing the guv'nor downstairs who thought we had nothing better to do than take the names and addresses of a couple of hundred punters. 'But the photofit is supposed to be Mills, isn't it, sir? I mean, I'd have noticed if he sat down in front of me, or someone like him.'

Slider wouldn't have bet on it, especially as Coffey could only have seen him for an instant downstairs. And as Atherton said, people were so unobservant.

He was about to go home when Norma put her head round the door and said, 'Mr Honeyman wants you, boss.'

'What's he still doing here?' Slider said wearily.

'It looked like the Maori Haka,' she said. 'Have you seen the paper?'

'Oh, don't tell me!'

'They've named Mills.'

'How the hell did that get out?' Slider cursed. 'Well, I suppose I'd better go and face it.'

Honeyman was very upset. 'This couldn't have come from your witness,' he said accusingly, rapping the paper with an admonitory finger. 'Someone in your team has leaked.'

Slider took the paper in silence and read.

The police officer in the Roger Greatrex murder case, who has been suspended over alleged irregularities of conduct, has been named as Detective Sergeant Steven Mills, 38. Mills, recently transferred to Shepherd's Bush, lives locally and has no previous disciplinary record. The Police declined to comment on the specific reasons for Mills's suspension.

Then it went on to rehash the details of the Greatrex murder. There was nothing else about Mills. But there was a picture – rather a bad one, but recognisable if you knew him.

'They don't really know anything,' Slider said, handing the paper back.

'It won't be long,' Honeyman grumbled. 'God knows how they got hold of the photograph, but now they have, some neighbour will recognise him and then they'll find out where he lives and it will be all over the six o'clock news. I'm very, very unhappy about this, Slider. I looked to you to keep your team in order. This is very unprofessional conduct, quite unacceptable.'

'It could have come from anywhere, sir,' Slider began, but Honeyman interrupted.

'The point is, it came from somewhere,' he said, silencing Slider admirably. 'This alters the situation. I shall have to inform Mr Wetherspoon. I imagine he will take it out of my hands.'

'Sir,' Slider said urgently, but Honeyman held up his hand.

'I know, I know. I will do my best to get you some time, but I can't promise anything. Have you made any progress?'

Slider looked frustrated. 'Only negatively, sir.' For an instant something flickered in his mind at the sound of the word, but he had no time to lay hold of it then. 'There's nothing to indicate any connection between Mills and Greatrex,' he went on. 'But—'

'It's not enough,' Honeyman said with vast regret. 'Well, as I said, I'll try and buy you some time. But my advice to you is to try to come up with something a bit more positive, and as soon as possible.'

Now what the Sun Hill does he think I've been trying to do? Slider asked himself glumly as he trod away.

★ ★ ★

Joanna knew that look, too. 'Are you on to something?' she asked as he leaned against the kitchen door, watching her with unseeing eyes.

'Mmm,' he said vaguely.

'A line on the case?'

'I don't know. Nothing makes any sense yet. I think I'm about to understand what I'm thinking, but I'm so far out to the side I can't see the play. What are you cooking?'

'Minestrone soup. Thick enough to trot a mouse on. It's nearly ready. Do you want any bread with it?'

'Umm,' he said unhelpfully.

'Was that a yes?' Joanna asked, but he had wandered away. She sighed, and then thought of Irene, and restrained herself. This is what it must have been like to be married to him all those years, and in Irene's case she didn't even have the comfort of knowing herself deeply loved and fancied rotten by him. The bread was a bit stale so she decided to toast it, and then thought it would be nice to make it garlic bread, so she took her time peeling and crushing two cloves of garlic and mixing them with salt and butter to spread on the warm toast. But for all Bill noticed she might as well have given him the table mats to dip in his soup.

Between mouthfuls she looked at the blank face opposite her and felt her brief peeve dissolve to be replaced by a rather wistful affection. The difficulty always was that you loved a person as they were, and you couldn't get rid of the annoying factors without changing who they were. Bill's job got in the way, but separate him from his job and what you had left was not Bill. She supposed he must feel the same way about her job – or would if he was given to introspection. He had been pretty annoyed and upset that she had not been around over the weekend, though she doubted if he would have got right to the bottom of his own feelings.

Apart from anything else, he hadn't had time to think about much but the case.

She wasn't at all surprised when after the meal he said apologetically, 'Look, I'm sorry, but I think I've got to go out again.'

She protested only because she felt he expected it, and might think she was indifferent if she didn't. 'It's my only evening at home this week. Does it have to be now?'

'I'm sorry,' he said again, helplessly. 'I'm up against the clock, and there's one of my own men in trouble as well.'

'Yes, I know – Mills. Do you think he did it?'

'It isn't my business to think anything. I'm supposed to collect evidence, whichever way it goes.'

'Yes, but do you think he did it?' she insisted, knowing him.

'I'm hoping to prove he didn't,' he admitted. 'You remember that attempted burglary of Christa Jimenez that I mentioned to you?'

'You think that's part of it?'

'It did occur to me to wonder, in the light of Laurence Jepp being murdered, whether there was a connection, whether it really was a burglary.'

'Because they were both in *Giovanni*? *You* think there's a curse on the production?'

'I haven't got as far as that. I just wondered if it was intended as an attack rather than a burglary; if so, it might have been by the same man. So I've asked Mills for a blood sample, and I've persuaded Ron Carver to let me compare it with the blood on the knife that Jimenez attacked her intruder with – because it's his case, of course. I'm waiting to hear from Tufty. Of course, it's negative evidence at best. There's no certainty that incident was any part of it. And there's still the identification to be got over.' He lapsed again into his thoughts.

She studied his face. 'Is that what you've been thinking about since you came home?'

'Not entirely,' he said. 'There's something else I've got by the tail, but even if I'm right, I don't see where it gets me. But you've got to do the next thing. It's the only way forward. The next step. Maybe I'll see more clearly when I've taken it.'

'Go,' she said. 'With my blessing.'

A slightly lightened look was her reward. 'Really?'

'A man's gotta do what a man's gotta do. You're no use to me anyway, in this mood.' She saw the doubt, and reached across to pat his hand kindly. 'I mean it. Really. Go on, I ought to practise anyway, and I'll never do it if you're here looking provocatively sexy all evening.'

He even managed a grin. 'Thanks.'

She came with him to the door, and kissed him so that the bit of his mother in him worried about what the neighbours might think.

'Anyone might be looking.'

'Poor things,' she said, and did it again, but this time he reached behind her and switched off the hall light. He didn't like feeling exposed in the spotlight like that – but then, unlike her, his life had been threatened more than once. Looking over your shoulder got to be second nature.

There were lights on in Miss Giles's flat and faint music, but no answer when he rang the doorbell. He thought of trying the top bell, but then remembering who she had said was living there, decided to try the basement instead. There was a noise of pop music inside, and after a while the door opened and a young girl with a towel wrapped round her head looked out.

'Oh, have you been ringing long? I had my head under the tap,' she said, looking at him with such an open and trusting expression that he thought of his daughter, Kate, and a fatherly sternness came over him. He could have been anyone, and there she was in a dressing-gown and completely defenceless.

'I'm a police officer,' he said quickly, though she evidently had no apprehension about him. He showed his brief, but she barely looked at it. 'You ought always to check when someone shows you an ID like that,' he admonished her, but she only grinned at him.

'Oh, I had a look at you through the glass before I opened the door. I could see you were all right,' she said.

'You can't tell from appearance,' he objected.

'I can,' she said simply. 'What's the matter, is there something wrong?'

'I hope not,' he said. 'I've been ringing Miss Giles's doorbell and there's no answer.'

'Oh, that's all right, she never answers the door at night.'

'Unlike you.'

'I might miss out on something,' she pointed out with unconscious cruelty. 'Did you want me to get her for you?'

'Can you?'

'There's an inside door to her flat. She always hears if I knock on that. Come in.'

He followed her, but said, 'You shouldn't let me in when you haven't checked my ID.'

'Why are you so worried about me?' she asked gaily over her shoulder.

'I've got a daughter myself. These are dangerous times.'

'You're sweet,' she said, looking back at him for an instant. He gave up. Maybe he shouldn't try to spoil that wonderful confidence of youth. Statistics were on her side; it was just the caution that was built in to the job.

The house had originally been all one, of course, and the stairs down from the first floor had not been removed when

221

it was made into three. The young tenant used them as display shelves, but there was passage through the middle to the door at the top. Slider stood at the bottom while the young woman rapped briskly, held a brief conversation through it, and then crouched down to field the schnauzers as the door was opened.

'It's all right, come up,' she said.

Miss Giles looked very different from when he had first seen her. She was dressed in an ancient red felt dressing-gown with a striped cord tied tightly about her waist, which probably didn't help, but she looked old, and very much less vigorous. Her face without make-up looked pale and lined, her lips without lipstick thin and blue. Even her silky white hair looked limp, and her freckled hands shook a little as she lit a cigarette from the stump of the previous one and put the pack back in the pocket.

'I don't answer the door at night,' she said. 'You hear such terrible things.'

'Very wise,' he said. She led him, as before, into the kitchen, where a one-bar electric fire was set up near the table, on which stood a bottle of Famous Grouse, a tumbler, and an ashtray already overflowing with stubs. He looked quickly round to see what she had been doing when disturbed, but there was no book, paper, letter. Perhaps she had just been listening to the music and turned it off when she heard the knock on the door. Or perhaps she had been sitting and thinking.

She sat down on the side of the table nearest the fire. 'D'you want a drink?' she asked, unscrewing the cap from the bottle.

'No, thanks, not just now.'

'Well I'm having one. Let me know if you change your mind. One advantage to retirement is that it doesn't matter what you look like the next morning.' She looked up and met his eyes; hers seemed apprehensive. 'Oh yes, I've had a few already. And I mean to have a few more.'

'Is there something on your mind?'

'Is there something on yours?' she countered. 'It must be something urgent to warrant a visit at night. Or do they pay you overtime?'

'Sometimes.'

'So what do you want? I've told you everything I know.'

He smiled. 'It would take a great deal longer than one short visit to learn everything you know.'

'You flatter me,' she said. 'But I've worked in many parts of the world in my time, and I wouldn't have lasted long unless I knew how to keep my counsel.'

'Every life has secrets,' he said. 'They're harder to keep at the beginning than at the end, though. They have a sort of energy when they're first born, and they wriggle and wriggle to get out. But once that's exhausted, they tend to give up and lie quietly. If you can keep a secret for the critical period, you can keep it for ever.'

'Very poetic,' she said.

'Unless it becomes important for some reason to let it out.'

'And what possible reason could there be?'

'Oh, if someone was in danger of some sort, for instance.'

She shook her head, puffing busily. 'I can't see it, myself. A secret kept absolutely and for ever couldn't hurt anyone. A secret no-one knows effectively doesn't exist.'

'Maybe you're right,' he said. One of the dogs came up and sniffed his leg, and then stood up with its front paws up on his knee, and he caressed its ears absently. 'It's probably the half-known things that are more dangerous,' he went on. 'They're certainly an irritant. They nag at your mind until you can't rest. Things you can't quite understand. Things that don't quite add up.'

She looked at him unhelpfully. Whatever he guessed at, it would be less than she knew, and he still didn't know where what he guessed at might get him.

'For instance,' he said, 'I made a phone call this afternoon to a very helpful friend of mine at St Catherine's House, who never minds looking things up for me. She told me that Margaret Rose Giles married Arthur Mills in September 1955.'

Miss Giles shrugged. 'I could have told you that, if you'd asked. It isn't a secret.'

'I didn't want to bother you,' Slider said. 'But the thing is, you see, that Steve Mills's date of birth in his records is May 1957, and he told me that he was adopted when he was just a couple of weeks old. That means your sister had been married less than two years when she adopted him.'

'What of it?' Miss Giles said with massive indifference.

'Well, it struck me, you see, that it was rather early days to decide you're never going to be able to have a child naturally and that the only course is adoption. Most couples wait five, six – even ten years before giving up hope.'

'You're forgetting Arthur's age. He didn't have ten years to wait,' she said, and Slider smiled inwardly. Once they start giving explanations, you've got them on the run. 'Maybe he'd had tests.'

'In 1957? It wasn't that easy on the National Health, and I gather there wasn't much money in the case. No, I think if you'd gone to a doctor in 1957 and said you hadn't become pregnant after less than two years of marriage, he'd have just told you to go away and try again.'

'Perhaps,' said Miss Giles. 'I've never been married, so I don't know.'

'It struck me as odd,' Slider continued, 'both that they should leap to that conclusion so early, and that they should have settled for adoption so quickly. Even after a couple despairs of pregnancy, it's usually a long time before they've talked enough about adoption to decide on it.'

'Well, it doesn't strike me as odd, but everyone to their own,' she said briskly. 'I don't see what it's got to do with me, anyway. They didn't confide their thought processes to me, however fascinating you may find the subject.'

'I'll come to that,' Slider said. 'I thought, you see, that if they didn't decide to adopt when they did because they'd exhausted all hope and all other channels, maybe the timing depended on the baby being available just at that moment. And if that was the case, then perhaps it was because they wanted to adopt not just any baby, but that particular one. That it was special to them in some way.'

She said nothing, but she kept on looking at him, in the manner of one who must know the worst.

'You were very fond of Steve when he was a boy,' Slider said gently. 'Unusually fond, perhaps, given that you and your sister didn't get on.'

'The boy wasn't to blame for that. And besides, he was very lovable.'

'Yes, I imagine so. But you loved the boy so much you even bought a house one street away to be near him—'

'That wasn't why—'

'Please. Bear with me. I'm just describing my thought processes. You bought this house, one street away, and the boy came to visit you, and you took him out places, interested yourself in his education, in the broader sense, encouraged him to make something of himself. And all this for the adopted child of a sister you didn't get on with married to a man you despised. And what was odder still, even though the sister and her husband disapproved of you, they let you take a hand in the upbringing of their son.'

She was silent.

'I also noticed that while you referred to your own father as "Father", you referred to Arthur as Steve's "dad". You even corrected me when I used the word "father" in respect of Arthur. And you're a woman, I've noticed, who uses words with skill.'

'You notice a lot,' she said acerbically.

'I noticed quite a few things you said. For instance, when you spoke of adopted children being able to trace their natural parents these days, you said, "Fortunately, most of them don't bother." That "fortunately" struck me as odd – as if it had personal relevance for you.' She didn't respond to that. 'And although you are not a churchgoer and seem rather contemptuous of your sister and brother-in-law's religion, you seemed to know an awful lot about the minister who arranged the adoption. Well,' he sat back from the table and put his hands down on it with a completing gesture, 'I thought everything over, and eventually I came to the conclusion that when you said Steve was the nearest thing you ever had to a son, you were having a little private joke at my expense.' He looked up from his hands. 'I'm right, aren't I? Steve is your son. He was your baby. Your knowledge of Minister Green and his mother-and-baby home came from first-hand experience.'

He wasn't sure what reaction he had expected from her – stubborn silence or even furious denial, perhaps – but he had not expected her to cry. It was painful and horrible for both of them, and there was nothing he could do to comfort her. He knew well enough that to touch her or offer her sympathy would compound his crime. After a moment of struggle she put her hands over her face and cried without grace, with the clumsiness of the unaccustomed, and with the tearing anguish of a lifetime of constraint and concealment. The dogs ran to her, looking up and wagging their tails curiously at the noise, and then began to grow distressed in their turn, running round her and trying to jump up. They finally settled for sitting at her feet crying in sympathy, occasionally pawing at her unresponsive leg.

'You can have no idea,' she said. Red-eyed, blotchy, and old, so old, she sat hunched at the table, smoking slowly. 'None of you men has any idea. Well, I can't blame you – I didn't have any idea either. I thought you could just have it and walk away. A baby you'd never seen – how could it mean anything to you? But it isn't like that. It's a part of you, you see. Oh, not your flesh, you can part with that. People don't hanker to know what happened to their amputated leg or whatever. But a part of who you are. And there's a bit of you that can't let go. However sensible and pragmatic you think you are. You can't – let – go.'

She smoked again, and he was silent. Now that she was talking, he must let her take her time.

'They took the babies away at birth. That was supposed to be the best thing for the mother. Kinder – the clean break. I don't know.' She shook her head. 'It seemed sensible to me at the time – beforehand. Maybe it is best for some people. A few months in the home, then into hospital, whisk the thing away like an appendix – that is a joke, you know, of a sort – and six weeks later you're back to normal and ready to take up your life again. That's the theory. But it wasn't that simple. Those girls in the home—' She was silent, lost in memories. 'They were so pathetic. All they wanted was to be able to keep their babies, but it wasn't allowed. Society didn't allow. You can't imagine how impossible it was then.' She looked at him for an instant. 'Nowadays nobody thinks twice about it. People even do it intentionally, when they don't have to, people who have the choice. "Starlet's love-child" and all that sort of thing. And if you haven't any money, the State pays.

But not then. You simply couldn't. It was impossible, and those girls knew it. But oh, how they cried! The matron said it was just their condition – hormones all shaken up – but it wasn't. God damn it, she didn't hear them at night! They cried from their souls upwards. It was a river, an unstaunchable flood of tears. Have you ever heard a cow calling for its calf? They cried like animals for their stolen children, those poor, ignorant girls! But they were trapped. Even if society had let them, Green and his Church wouldn't. That's why they took the babies at birth, you see, to give us no chance to change our minds. The Church had put down good money for those babies. Those babies were *capital*.'

'You mean they took money for arranging the adoptions?' Slider asked.

'Good God, no,' she said contemptuously. 'Green wasn't interested in money. His vanity was purely religious. It was souls he wanted. He placed the babies with good, churchgoing couples, in return for which the couples kept on being churchgoing, and brought up the kid to be, too. It was God's work – evangelism in its most practical form. Give me a child at an impressionable age – and so on.' She sucked on her cigarette and then snorted with unamused laughter. 'He used to preach to us, too. Not content with the babies, he wanted our souls as well. A lot of the girls were swayed – that *was* hormones. You feel quite sexy at a certain stage of pregnancy, and your mind is rather loose in the haft as well, easily unbalanced. And he was quite a man. They yearned for him, and thought it was religion. Poor saps!'

'What about the father of your child?'

'What about him? He doesn't come into it. He's dead now, long since. That's one mercy.'

'How did it happen?'

'How d'you think?' she said, and then relented. 'He was

228

my boss. Married, of course. I was just starting out on my career. I fell for his status and he fell for my earnestness. I have to say he behaved decently according to his lights. He was horrified when I told him I was pregnant – it would have been the end of him in those days, if it had got out – but he tried to do the decent thing. He arranged for me to have a sabbatical, and gave me money to keep me going. He was so glad when I said I was going to have it adopted. I think ideally he'd have liked me to have an abortion, but of course it cost the earth to have it done properly in Switzerland, and even he wouldn't have expected me to take the risk of an illegal in England. So Joshua Green's salvation plan for fallen women filled the bill perfectly.'

'How did your sister come into it?'

'Oh, she introduced me to Green, of course. It was her I turned to first of all, even before I told the father. She'd been like a mother to me, after all, so I naturally thought she could sort me out. But Arthur was horrified. His first worry was what would the neighbours think and what would the Sunday school think. He'd have thrown me out into the snow if he could, but Maggie talked him round. I think she must have suspected by then that he wasn't going to be able to give her a baby, and she wanted one so badly. And at least mine would share her genes – not that she thought in those terms, but the idea was there. And it was common cant that a woman who adopted often got pregnant soon afterwards, so she had nothing to lose. I don't know how she persuaded Arthur, but I think religion came into it. I was a fallen woman and past redemption, but the child could be rescued from sin and brought up by Arthur in the paths of righteousness, and wouldn't that be a good thing to do? Worth a gold star, ten points towards his halo at least.'

'And the minister, Green, arranged all the legal side, did he?'

'Yes. He wasn't too keen on the arrangement, really – didn't like the idea that an unmarried mother would know where her baby had gone. There was supposed to be an absolute cut-off and no contact ever after. He only agreed to it – and Arthur only agreed to it – on the condition that I kept out of the way while I was pregnant, and went right away afterwards and didn't come near Maggie and Arthur ever again.' She shrugged. 'I was happy enough with the arrangement. I wanted my career, I thought babies were revolting, I wanted to be a free-wheeling, hard-headed power-woman in a suit, get to the top of the Civil Service, and have no ties, and retire with a small gong and a large pension.'

'But it didn't work out that way.'

'Not entirely. I went away to begin with. I went back to work, kept my mouth shut and my head down and started to climb the ladder. But there was always the question mark. And Green was right in one way. Knowing where they were made it difficult not to go and take a look at them. So finally I gave in to the voices and bought this house and—' She shrugged again.

'I imagine Maggie and Arthur weren't too happy about it.'

'You imagine right. But there I was, like a mountain, and it was easier to work round me than try and remove me. I promised I would never tell Steve, or even hint at it, and I kept my word. Maggie knew I would, and I suppose she persuaded Arthur. Besides, I was the only one in the family who was ever going to have money, and he'd have thought by rights it ought to come to Stevie. But it galled him, I think, that he had the expense of keeping the child while I had the fun of taking him to the zoo. Like a weekend father.' She looked at him quickly. 'It isn't all roses being a weekend father.'

Slider nodded. Had she guessed? Statistically, it was a fair bet.

'But I'd made my bed, and I wasn't going to whine about it. And nobody has ever guessed until today, until you – damn you.' But she said it without heat.

'Are you sure?' he asked.

She searched his face. 'You mean, does Steve guess? No, I don't think so. Have you reason to think so?'

'No. Not really. I just thought—' He studied her. 'There is a resemblance, when you look for it.'

'But people don't,' she said. 'People never do. Those gothic romances where the heroine looks at a family portrait and realises it's her mother – it just would never happen in real life. Steve – Steve looks like his father. But even if he'd ever come face to face with his father, I doubt if he'd have noticed.'

Slider sat silent. Much more made sense now, question marks had been exploded and swept away. But it didn't get him any further on. He hadn't known where he was going with his doubts, and he still couldn't see daylight ahead. All he had done was to upset this woman and rip a secret out of her that she had taken a lifetime to bury under the foundations.

As if she heard his thought, she said, 'You were right about secrets losing their energy. If I was going to blurt it out to Steve, it would have been when he was about eight years old. I loved him so much then, and he was so fond of me, I used to think sometimes I'd done the wrong thing, that I should have kept him and tried to bring him up myself. But it would have been hell for all of us. The way it turned out was the best for him, and for me in every way but one.' She paused a moment, staring at the middle air. 'But after that, there was never any danger I'd tell, or let anything slip.' She changed her focus. 'You guessed because you were looking for something. Or maybe – maybe because you're unusually perceptive.' She sounded puzzled by the notion.

'I don't think I am,' he said. 'If I were I'd know what the hell was going on in this case, and I don't. I'm trying to clear your – your *nephew*, and the only way I can think of to do it is to solve the case, find who really did it. But I don't even know where to look.'

'Find out who did *what?*' she asked. 'What is he supposed to have done?'

'He's been identified by a witness.' He looked at her thoughtfully, wondering if the gravity of the situation would make her more or less forthcoming. 'It's a case of murder. A man carrying a bag which turned out to contain clothes stained with the victim's blood was seen and described by a witness, and she's picked out Mills as being the man.'

She was silent, but her face was drawn, her eyes seemed to have gone back in her head. After a moment she said, 'I saw – in the paper it said – it was a murder case. But I didn't know he was suspected. Oh my God.' He half wished he hadn't told her now. She seemed not just distressed, but terrified. After a moment she said, '*You* don't think – do you?'

'No. No, on the whole I don't.'

'But how can you have *any* doubt? He just isn't capable of murder!'

'I always maintain you can't say that about anyone. Anyone is capable of murder, if the circumstances are right. But I don't happen to think that Steve is capable of this particular murder.'

She said nothing more, though her eyes scanned his face urgently as if she was trying to glean more information from him without having to ask the questions. Or as if she was wondering if she ought to tell him something. He wasn't sure which. There was something on her mind, that was a fact. Did she suspect Mills of something, or know something about him she wasn't telling? Possibly, even probably on both counts.

232

But she did not divulge it, though it looked as though it was making her sick – by the time he left her, she was looking as crook as rookwood, so much that he felt constrained to ask if he ought to call someone for her, or ask the girls downstairs to come and sit with her a while. That suggestion at least aroused her to scorn, but it was on the surface, and didn't touch the undercurrent of preoccupation. He went away feeling vaguely anxious for her and vaguely hopeful for himself, for whatever was preying on her mind, he felt it could not prey there long, and that if he came back the next day she would surely let it out. She liked him, and if she was going to tell anyone, it would be him.

14

Death at Auntie's

Slider drove slowly and on automatic, running his mental fingers idly through the mass of facts, searching for inspiration. Something somewhere needed to connect up, was wanting quite urgently to connect up. When you were stuck, you looked for patterns and you looked for anomalies. Roger Greatrex – media star, chronic womaniser, neglecter of his wife and child, accidental killer of Madeleine Somers – was dead. Someone had reason enough to kill him; specifically, to cut his throat. There was something about that, something calculated, perhaps, or professional. It was not the enraged bash on the head with the nearest implement to hand. Someone had brought the knife to him. A swift and silent death, that – but you had to be determined. You had to be single-minded. Not every person could cut a throat like that.

Assuming it wasn't Mills, for the moment – what about Sandal Palliser? Slider thought he had the intelligence to plan it, and the determination to do it, and would be unlikely to be squeamish – but that left the question of the clothes in the bag. Yes, Palliser might well think of the lift roof as a good hiding-place, and he of all suspects would have had to hide them on the premises, since he had to get back to the green-room. But surely if Mrs Reynolds had seen a striking-looking man like him, even supposing she did not recognise him as the television star, she would have remembered him, and not confused him with Dark Satanic.

On a sudden impulse he did a series of left turns to reverse direction and drove towards Kensington. There were lights on in the house in Addison Road, but there was also a sense of emptiness, and it was so long before there was any response to his ringing that Slider thought he was not going to be answered. But at last the door was opened, by Palliser himself. He looked gaunt and grey and wild-haired, and somehow insubstantial, like a scarecrow with the stuffing removed. Slider had the impression that if he joggled the wrong bit, Palliser would collapse in an empty heap at his feet.

A look of dislike came over Palliser's face as he saw Slider. 'You again! Can't you leave me alone? Haven't you done enough damage?'

'What have I done?' Slider asked.

'My wife has left me,' Palliser said – blurted, rather. 'Phyllis has walked out on me, after thirty-two years. I mean, now, after all this time! It's unbelievable.'

Seeing how shocked Palliser was, Slider inserted himself into the house and closed the door behind him, and Palliser allowed the movement, obeyed the body language instruction and led the way into the kitchen. It was warm from the Aga, and as chaotic as ever, but lacking the smell of food which had given it its homeliness and purpose. Palliser sat down at the table and leaned on his folded arms in an attitude of helpless despair.

'She went yesterday, after church,' he said dazedly. 'She just came home, packed a bag, and went. Didn't even take her hat off.'

235

'Where did she go?' Slider asked. He hefted the kettle, judged there to be enough water in it, and pushed it onto the hot ring. Tea was in order, he thought. Always tea in a house of bereavement.

'I asked her that. I said where can you go on a Sunday, and she said there were plenty of hotels around, and they all had rooms on Sunday nights. I said, that's crazy, and she just shrugged. I said stay, talk about it, but she said she wanted to go, it had taken her two days to make up her mind and she wasn't going to unmake it again. She phoned later to say where she was, but I couldn't persuade her to come back.'

'But do you know why?'

'It's this business over Roger.' Palliser looked up resentfully. 'Murder is so commonplace to you, you never think how it affects ordinary people. She'd known Roger almost as long as she knew me. It's hard enough coping with someone dying naturally, but when someone's murdered, especially in that brutal way—'

'Is that what she said? That that was why she was going?'

'Yes. No. Not exactly. She said it had made her think a lot about things. She said – she's suspected about Jamie for a long time, but then when you and that other one came here asking questions and obviously thinking I'd killed Roger, it confirmed it in her mind. All those questions made her think – about everything, her and me and Caroline and—' He rubbed his face with his hands as though trying to rub normality back into his life. 'She said she'd just decided she'd had enough. After all these years. I mean, she was always happy enough. I gave her everything. She knew I'd never leave her.'

Slider made the tea. 'She'll come back,' he said comfortingly.

'You think so?' Palliser was eager for comfort, whatever the source.

'She probably needs a bit of time alone to think things out, that's all. She'll get her mind settled, and then she'll come back.'

'It's been unsettling for her. For all of us.'

'That's right. Your patterns have been disrupted – hers most of all, because she doesn't have a career, like you, to take her out of herself.' He brought the tea to the table, milked two cups, and poured. Even as he did it he realised he'd forgotten the tea-strainer, and cursed inwardly as the dark rush of leaves sprang into the first cup. Oh well. Important not to break the flow now, of tea or talk. He took the leafy cup himself and pushed the other towards Palliser. Making the tea had made him unthreatening. Palliser took it unprotesting, and looked at Slider without hostility.

'I didn't kill him, you know.'

'Didn't you?'

'I wanted to – that night most of all. But often. For what he did to us. But I didn't kill him. It isn't in me to kill another human being.'

'It's in all of us,' Slider said for the second time in one evening. 'That particular murder just wasn't your murder. But whose was it?'

'Don't you know yet?'

Slider shook his head. 'I was hoping talking to you might help me get there. You were the person who knew Roger best – better than his wife, probably. You were almost the last person to see him alive – probably the last to have a quarrel with him.'

A bitter expression crossed Palliser's face. 'Oh, that! I wish to God – you'd never have come here asking questions, but for that.'

'Yes I would, for the same reason I'm here now. What did Roger Greatrex do that made someone want him dead?' He asked it seriously, and saw that Palliser was thinking about it

237

seriously. He sipped his tea. Slider sipped his, incautiously, and got a mouthful of tea leaves, which he nobly swallowed rather than make a fuss and disturb the other man.

'What he did most of was writing and fucking,' Palliser said at last. 'I can't see anything in that to drive anyone crazy. Caroline was the person with most to object to about the fucking, and I'm sure she didn't do it. As to the writing – well, that brings it back to me, doesn't it? We had a well-publicised difference of opinion over his critical acuity.'

'I have it on good authority that that was manufactured for publicity purposes, to advance the careers of both of you.'

'I don't know whose authority you think carries weight,' Palliser said scornfully, 'but I can tell you it was a genuine disagreement. It wasn't manufactured – although, of course, we argued intellectually and not personally, if that's what you mean.'

'But you actually quarrelled in public, at Glyndebourne, over the *Don Giovanni*, didn't you?'

'Oh yes, but that didn't mean anything. I get heated over my opinions – so does Roger – but that's an intellectual exercise. An opinion isn't worth holding unless you're vehement about it. It doesn't mean I'd kill anyone for disagreeing with me. Only an intellectual pygmy would do that. Or a religious fanatic.'

A stillness fell in Slider's mind, a sensation like a great lump of white silence in the middle of his head, into which after a moment small, crystal-clear words were spoken very quietly. A religious fanatic. The *Don Giovanni* row: Greatrex had praised the production, had identified himself closely with it as his idea of a fine example of opera production. There had been a lot of talk in the papers about the production being blasphemous. And Greatrex had been murdered. Farfetched?

But Palliser had condemned the blasphemous aspect of it in print – and Palliser had not been harmed.

Laurence Jepp and Christa Jimenez – but then, why those two singers and not any of the others? Or, if other victims were intended, why those first? Because they appeared in the blasphemous scene? But Lassiter, the man who sang the Don himself, had not been attacked. Mere geography, perhaps, because the other two lived not too far apart? Or accessibility – maybe Frederick Lassiter was abroad, or had family or minions around him all the time, or had a terrific security system. The other two had lived alone, and in old houses with easy windows. Would a religious fanatic worry about such things? Well, why not? Maybe he had to. If he was working up to slaughter everyone connected with the blasphemy, maybe he would start with the easy ones. In which case—

'You've thought of something,' Palliser said. Slider realised he had been looking at him curiously for some time.

'Yes,' said Slider with an effort. 'It was something you said, reminded me of something.' A religious fanatic. It didn't do to underestimate the power of religion – especially these days, when there was so little of any other sort of power. But there was Mrs Reynolds to be got over, and her description of the man at the lift. Damn it, he'd got to get Mills out of the frame – or, reluctantly, into it. Because everyone was capable of some murder, and Mills was an unmarried man living alone, and Slider couldn't really swear on his soul that this was not Mills's. He had been brought up by deeply religious people, though he showed no symptoms of it himself. And all three attacks – if they were connected – had happened since Mills came to Shepherd's Bush. 'Tell me,' he said, reaching into his pocket, 'have you ever seen this man before?'

He handed over a copy of the photofit, and Palliser looked at it, turning it first for better light, and then taking a pair of

239

half-glasses out of his pocket. 'Yes, I have,' he said. 'Now, let me think, where do I know him from?'

He stared for some time, and Slider waited, wondering whether he hoped more than he feared, or vice versa. At last Palliser flipped the paper with the backs of his fingers. 'Well, of course! Why didn't I place him at once, considering we were only just talking about it? It was down at Glyndebourne, when Roger and I were having our famous disagreement in the foyer. Of course we gathered quite a crowd – and I won't say,' he added with a faint smile, 'that we weren't conscious of it, and that it would make good publicity. But he was saying his usual fatuous things about modernity and innovation and exciting new interpretation, and I must admit I got a bit heated, especially considering the exciting new interpretation he was so thrilled about had run to that completely gratuitous defiling of the altar, for which there's no textual authority, and which of course had only been put in to shock a few reviews out of people who might otherwise ignore the production, and to tempt the sillier element of the population to buy tickets out of mere prurience—'

'It worked,' Slider remarked.

'It always does,' Palliser snorted. 'Mainly thanks to reviewers like Roger who are so ready to be thrilled by the meretricious – but however,' he recalled himself to the task in hand, 'this man was at the front of the crowd and listening to every word. I noticed him because he really looked as though he was listening to the argument, as opposed to merely gawping with open mouth at the sight of two celebrities sparring, like the rest of the dinner-suited dross that infests opera audiences these days. Of course, Roger's reviews were addressed to just those people, which is why he made so much money. You can count the real music lovers in the average audience on the fingers of one foot.'

He ought to get together with Joanna, Slider thought. 'Are you quite sure this is the same man?'

'Oh yes,' said Palliser, quite surely. 'He tried to accost me afterwards, I suppose to carry on the argument, but I avoided him. It's a thing one gets quite good at.' Then, looking again at the picture, 'There is something different. Maybe he had his hair differently. But certainly this looks like the man I saw. I particularly remember this mole on his cheek.'

'Have you seen him anywhere else?'

'No, I don't think so. Not that I remember. When I noticed him at Glyndebourne, it wasn't as someone I had ever seen before, and I'm not aware of having seen him anywhere since.'

'Well, thank you. You've been a great help,' Slider said. There was no reason Mills shouldn't have been to Glyndebourne. His "aunt" had said she tried to interest him in opera and Mills himself had said she took him to Covent Garden. When he said it, Slider had registered it as the jolly place full of shops and jugglers it had now become, but of course in earlier days the name was synonymous with the Royal Opera House – and still was in some circles. Silly him. And if Mills had been at Glyndebourne that night, why shouldn't he have listened with more than average intelligence to the critics' row? Slider didn't know whether it helped the case or hindered it. He only knew that he had to get away somewhere and think, because the idea that had been struggling to be born an hour ago was still struggling. Something he had seen or heard somewhere had impinged itself on the pattern in his mind as out of place, and he needed peace and quiet to ferret it out.

'You're going?' Palliser said as Slider stood up, and he sounded quite disappointed. Perhaps he'd hoped Slider would cook his dinner for him as well as make his tea.

'I'm sorry, I have to,' Slider said. 'I've still got a lot of work to get through tonight.'

241

'I was going to offer you a spot of supper,' Palliser said. 'I – I'm not used to being in the house alone.'

He sounded so pathetic, compared with his former arrogant self, that Slider felt sorry for him. 'Why don't you phone her up? She's probably lonely too – especially if she's in a hotel. They're dismal places to be alone in.'

'Do you think I should?'

'I think you can hardly ever make something worse by talking about it,' Slider said, and Palliser nodded at these words of wisdom.

'Thanks,' he said.

And Slider thought of Phyllis Palliser, and reckoned that, sad as her life had been, it would be better to be sad at home in her own kitchen than in a cheap Kensington hotel; and that, being a sensible woman, she'd probably realise it for herself soon enough.

He drove back to the factory, for no other reason than that he wanted to be alone to think, and walked in from the yard to a warm reception.

'There you are! Christ, Billy, you got to start carryin' your little tinkler wit' you,' O'Flaherty cried expansively. 'Everyone's goin' mad tryin' to find you, and worryin' the bejasus out of your woman, phonin' there when she thought all the time you were here.'

'I left it on my desk,' Slider discovered again. 'Psychological. I hate that thing. What's happened, anyway?'

'A very nasty murder,' O'Flaherty said, and for once he was quite serious. Slider felt a chill in the middle of his back, because Fergus hardly ever spoke in that tone of voice. 'You were round the house o' Mills's anty earlier on, weren't you?'

'About an hour and a half back.'

'Yes, the girls downstairs said it was you. Ah sure God, it's a bad business.'

'You don't mean it's her?'

'Hacked to death. A frenzied attack.'

'For Chris' sake, Fergus—!'

'The girls saw a man goin' in. Described him, said he'd visited there before.' He shook his head, partly in wonder and partly in pity at Slider's frantic look. 'Don't take it to heart, Billy.'

'Where else am I to take it?' Slider said wildly.

The girls – the pretty one he had met before and her plain friend who had come in from a late library session shortly before the incident – had heard the thumps from upstairs, and a bit later the dogs howling and barking like mad.

'When they didn't stop, we thought something must have happened to her,' said Valerie, the prettier one, her eyes red with weeping. 'We thought she must have fallen over and hurt herself, so we went and knocked on the inside door, and shouted really loud. She always answered when we shouted at the door. But there was no answer.'

'We couldn't open it because we hadn't got a key,' said Sue, the plainer one, briskly. She was dry-eyed but very pale, determined to do the right thing and not let the side down. 'So I climbed up from the area to the back garden. There's some wooden steps down from her back door, and if you lean right over you can just about see into the kitchen. I could hear the dogs locked in the scullery, barking like mad. I could hear them scratching the door. And I could see—' She swallowed. 'I could see a chair was knocked over from the kitchen table, and what looked like a bundle of clothes on the floor. Except I knew Miss Giles's dressing-gown. So I told Val to call the police.'

Slider turned to Valerie. 'You say she had a visitor, after I left?'

'I didn't see him,' she hiccupped. 'It was Sue.'

'When I was just coming in,' Sue said. 'I was standing at our door getting my key out and I saw him pass the railings, coming from the Uxbridge Road direction.'

'Wearing?'

She frowned in thought. 'Trousers – not jeans – dark-coloured. An anorak, I think – dark blue maybe.'

'Shoes? His feet must have been more or less at eye-level.'

'I don't remember,' she said after a moment.

'Trainers?'

'I don't think so. I think it was shoes. But I'm not honestly sure. He just walked past. Oh – I think he was carrying a bag.'

'A carrier bag? Briefcase? Suitcase?'

'No, just a bag – like a sports bag or an airline bag, something that size.'

Slider nodded. The *modus operandi*. It was deliberate, then – can't walk back through the streets covered in blood. And where was the bag now? 'Did you see him go in?'

'No, I just saw him pass, but I heard his feet on the steps before I went in.'

'Didn't you say she never let anyone in at night?' Slider asked Valerie.

'That's right. She never even answered the door after about six o'clock,' Valerie said.

'So,' to Sue, 'why didn't you warn him he was wasting his time?'

'It was none of my business,' she said indignantly. 'I'm not her guardian. Anyway, she must have let him in, mustn't she?'

'Did you hear her doorbell?'

'No,' Sue said. 'Val didn't either. But we might not have noticed, if he only rang once. Or he might have had a key?'

244

'You'd seen him visit her before? But you said you only caught a glimpse.'

'Enough to recognise his face. Yes, I've seen him come to the house before, though I don't know that he was visiting her – he could have been for the upstairs people, it's the same door, though a different bell. I had an idea, actually, that he was a social worker.'

'Why do you think that?'

'I don't know really.' She seemed genuinely puzzled at her own perception. 'I suppose maybe – there was just something about him. I honestly don't know.'

'But he did visit her last week, one afternoon,' Val said, 'because I saw her at the door with him. I thought he might be a relative of some sort,' she added with an apologetic glance at Sue.

'Why a relative?' Slider asked.

'The way she was talking to him. And I can't think who else would visit her, anyway. She never had friends round. She didn't entertain.'

'That's right,' Sue agreed. 'She said to me once she lived too much like a pig to want anyone to see her house.'

'Do you remember which afternoon it was last week?'

Valerie screwed up her face with effort. 'It might have been Wednesday. Or Tuesday? No, I'm not sure. I think it was the middle of the week. Not Friday, anyway, because I wasn't in Friday afternoon.'

'So it could have been Thursday?' She assented. With a sense of inner weariness, Slider drew out the photofit print and offered it to the girls. 'Is that the man?'

'Yes, that's him,' Valerie said eagerly. 'I'm sure it is.'

Sue didn't answer at once. She looked at the picture very carefully, and said at last, hesitantly, 'I *think* so. It's so hard to tell from a picture, isn't it, unless you actually know

245

someone very well. I mean, pictures never really look like people.'

'Oh Sue,' Valerie said reproachfully.

'Well, I can't help it,' Sue said irritably. 'I can't swear it's the same man, all I can say is he does look quite like this.'

'You're right to be cautious,' Slider said. 'Identity is a tricky thing.'

Sue looked at him eagerly. 'I always think it's an interesting word – identity.' She obviously had a theory and was glad of the chance to expound it. 'I mean, we use it carelessly, but what it means is saying something is identical with something else, saying it is exactly the same thing, and therefore unique. And I can't say a picture is identical with a human being. I can't say that someone I've only just seen is exactly the same person as someone else I've seen, not unless I know them personally.'

'Oh, you always quibble,' Valerie objected. 'How you can talk about words when poor Miss Giles is lying up there—' and she burst into tears.

'*That's* no answer,' Sue said unkindly. Slider agreed, though it was not for him to say so.

'I didn't do it,' Mills said, with the calmness of desperation. 'How can you even think it? I loved her. She was like a mother to me. For God's sake—'

Slider remained impassive. It was hard to get out of his mind what he had seen in that now-familiar kitchen. Miss Giles had been lying on her back, half under the kitchen table, her eyes open. Her throat had been cut, severing the carotid artery, which had probably been the fatal blow, but she had been stabbed in the upper torso another seven times. From the blood distribution it looked as though she had been standing near the stove, facing the wall – perhaps putting the kettle on – when the first blow had been struck; had then been whirled around, struck in the back, which had made her fall forwards, knocking over the chair and hitting her head on the edge of the table; and then rolled over or been turned over to receive the other wounds from the front. One blow had been so forceful it had gone right through her torso and nicked the lino underneath. It was indeed, in the words beloved of police reports, a frenzied attack: as if the throat-cutting had been calmly planned, the rest of the blows the result of a rage of hatred.

A terrible wave of sickness and despair had overwhelmed him as he looked at the pathetic bundle of old clothes which only a few hours ago had been a vigorous and intelligent woman. The appalling waste – the stupid vandalism which could destroy in seconds a personality which had taken more than sixty years to create, a unique and fascinating personality that could never be restored – made him angry. And he felt a personal loss, as for a friend, for in the short time he had learned a lot about her; he felt she had given him more of herself than she had given to anyone for a long time. When someone gives you something of themself like that, you become guardian of it, and responsible. He was responsible. He ought to have foreseen this. He had seen that she was worried, even afraid, and he had virtually assured her that Mills was not the man, instead of putting her on her guard against him.

But he would not have thought it of Mills. He would not have thought it. He had been badly wrong, and Miss Giles had paid the price of his arrogance, which had led him to do what he was always warning against. He should have paid attention to the evidence, not tried to explain it away. Mills had put up a convincing show of bewilderment when he was brought in, so convincing that Slider was toying with the idea that he had shut the murder out of his mind completely, and

247

genuinely had no recollection of it. He had to force himself to be calm, and to ask the questions in the sort of matter-of-fact tone that eases out information that might otherwise be held on to.

'So, tell me, you let yourself in with the key, didn't you? You have a key to her flat.'

'No, I haven't,' Mills said, almost indignantly. 'Auntie Betty would never give anyone a key. She was a very private person. She wouldn't have liked anyone to be able to go there when she wasn't in.'

'But you were – her nephew. Very close to her. Probably the person she loved most in the world.'

'She still didn't give me a key.'

'So how did you get in, then? According to her tenants, she never answered the door at night.'

'No, that's right. If I wanted to visit her at night I always rang her from the nearest telephone box and said I was on my way, so she knew it was me.'

Slider nodded. 'And that's what you did tonight?'

'No! I didn't go there tonight.' Oh he was good, very good. Slider looked at the man he had once known so well, and his conviction faltered. Surely a man could not be so psychotic without something showing? 'I didn't kill her,' Mills said. He sounded bewildered now. 'I don't know what's going on here, boss, but you've got to believe me. I loved her. I wouldn't hurt her. And I was home all evening. I never left my flat.'

'Doing what?'

'Watching telly.'

'What programme?' Mills hesitated and Slider hardened. 'Come on, what programme?'

'I don't know. I can't remember,' Mills cried in a panicky voice. 'I dozed off while I was watching. Some investigation programme – *Panorama* or something. About computers. I dozed off and when I woke up it was a film. I didn't fancy it so I turned it off.'

'Look, Steve, why don't you tell me about it?' Slider asked. 'We know it was you. You were seen going to the house. She wouldn't have opened the door to someone she didn't know. She was killed by someone she offered tea to, someone she trusted enough to turn her back on.'

He shook his head slowly, like an animal in pain. 'Why would I kill her? Tell me that. Why on earth would I do such a thing?'

'Well, I don't know,' Slider said wearily. 'I wish I did. I hoped you might be able to tell me.'

'I don't understand any of this. Ever since I came back, everything's been weird. You've got to help me, guv. They want to stick this on me. And the other business, at the Centre. But you know I didn't do it. You *know* I didn't.'

'I wish I did.' Slider closed his eyes for a moment. 'Just imagine you did set out from your place tonight to walk to your aunt's house. Which way would you go? Describe your route.'

'I turn right out of the house, round the corner into Abdale Road,' Mills said, rather surprised, 'down Ellerslie Road, across into Halsbury, and then right into Ormiston Grove.'

'You wouldn't walk along Uxbridge Road, then, at any point?'

'Well, no,' Mills said, 'because she lives nearer the other end, the Dunraven Road end. There'd be no need to touch Uxbridge Road. It'd be a longer way round.'

'That's what I thought,' Slider said. 'I just wanted to be sure.'

'I'm holding you personally responsible for this, Slider. It was on your recommendation that I didn't act earlier. You were so sure your former colleague was innocent – and now look what's happened.'

'I'm not absolutely sure it was him,' Slider said hesitantly, and against his will.

Honeyman's eyes bulged. 'Not sure? He was seen going into the house. What more do you want?'

'Being seen at the house doesn't mean he was the murderer, sir.'

'Then why does he deny it? If he was there for an innocent purpose, he'd say so.' Honeyman shook his head. 'I'm sorry, Slider, I know how hard this is for you – a colleague, and particularly a close colleague from many years ago. I can see you're genuinely confused, and I would be the same. It's hard for all of us when one of our own goes astray. But that's the more reason to have no mercy. If he did kill his aunt, he's a very dangerous man. It was a frenzied attack, you know.'

'He seems genuinely to believe what he says, sir—'

'But that only makes it worse,' Honeyman interrupted heatedly. 'If he killed without remembering it, he might be subject to psychotic episodes. He could kill again. We can't take the risk. Can't you see the headlines, if we let him go and he struck again?'

'Sir, if we charge him, it'll be all over the papers, and he'll never live it down. He may be innocent. All we've got is one witness who admits herself she only caught a glimpse of a man passing. Can't we wait until we've got something more? He's not trying to run away. He's co-operating. He's given intimate samples.'

'For God's sake, man, I've already given you time to clear him of one murder, and now I've got another on my hands. Do you want a bloodbath, is that what you want?'

'His flat's been searched – not a drop of blood anywhere,

nothing on his clothes. And nobody saw him leave his house or re-enter it this evening.'

'Negative evidence is no evidence,' Honeyman said impatiently. 'I agree with you we haven't got a case against him yet, but the witness identification is enough to charge him. It's up to you to get the rest. Someone will have seen him at some point on the double journey. The bag will turn up, the knife, the stained clothing. Until then, we can't take any chances.' He looked at Slider's mute and puzzled defiance. 'You've been up all night,' he said quite kindly. 'You'd better go home. Things will look clearer when you've had something to eat. Get a couple of hours' rest, have a hot bath and a change of clothes. It's going to be a long day.'

'Yes, sir,' Slider said. 'Thank you.'

Nice advice from one to whom the length of the day would be voluntary. He was tired, but not ready for sleep. He had far too much to do, anyway.

Tufty telephoned. 'I've got some news for you, my old banana. Are you ready for this? I don't know if it's good or bad, but those last blood samples you sent – I think I've got a match for you.'

That was the Jimenez knife sample, and Mills's blood. Slider had been expecting no match – hoping for no match? He sat down heavily. 'Tell me the worst.'

'Oh, didn't you want it to be the same? Well, not to worry. The sample from the knife wasn't good enough for me to go the whole way. There was a variant in the lysate EAP of both samples which is fairly rare – only five and a half per cent of the population – but even that gives you a pretty big leeway.'

'Five per cent?'

'Well, old boy, Tufty said cheerfully, 'statistics is what you make 'em. If you *wanted* the match, you could say *only* five per cent and call it a practical certainty. If you don't want it to be the same you can point out that five per cent of the population still gives you going on two and a half million bods to play with.'

'What I wanted,' Slider said, 'was certainty one way or the other.'

'Ah! Well, you'll have to talk to God about that.'

'What about genetic fingerprinting?'

'I've sent the samples off for you already. You should have a result in about a week. But as I said, the sample from the knife wasn't too hot. Don't pin your hopes on it.'

Slider went down to see Mills again. Now he didn't know what to think. 'Have you got a cut on your left thigh?' he asked.

'A cut? No sir,' Mills said, too weary now to be much surprised by any question. He surveyed Slider's face. 'Do you want to see?' He stood up and lowered his pants.

'All right,' said Slider. 'Cover up and sit down.' When Mills had complied, Slider said, 'I've just got a few more questions for you.' He looked at him carefully for a long time, and Mills did not look away. Though tired, he seemed eager to answer anything that was asked him. Eager to explain. 'How did you like *Don Giovanni?*' Slider asked suddenly.

'What, Mozart? It's not one I know very well,' Mills said, and seemed a little embarrassed at admitting it. 'I like the lighter stuff, really. Puccini – the Three Tenors – you know, something with good tunes. But I like some Mozart. I saw *The Magic Flute* once—'

Slider interrupted. 'I meant the production of *Don Giovanni* at Glyndebourne,' he said.

'I haven't seen it,' Mills said, looking puzzled.

'You were there. You were seen.'

'Sir, I've never been to Glyndebourne,' he said. When Slider didn't respond he went on, 'I've always wanted to. But it's

252

one of those things you plan for when you're retired, isn't it, like going on the QE2. I mean, you'd have to be rich and idle.' Slider went on looking at him thoughtfully, a slight frown between his brows. Eventually, Mills said, 'Would you mind if I had a smoke, guv?'

'No. Go ahead.' He watched absently as Mills dragged his cigarettes towards him, extracted one and lit up. Then he asked in a neutral voice, 'You're left-handed, aren't you, Mills?'

'Yes, sir. You know I am. Well,' looking down at his own hands, 'I suppose I'm ambidextrous really, but I write with my left hand.'

'You perform delicate tasks with which hand?'

'My left, probably, for preference.'

'What about tasks needing strength? Right or left?'

Mills shrugged. 'It could be either. It would depend how I was standing, I suppose.'

'So you could, physically, cut someone's throat holding the knife in your right hand?'

Mills looked sick. 'Sir, I swear to you—'

'Answer me!'

'Yes, I *could*,' Mills said with deep reluctance. 'But then,' he added defiantly, 'you could do it with your left hand.'

'True,' Slider said. 'The question is, would I?'

'No more than I would.' Slider was silent. Mills studied his face and experienced a slight dawning of hope. 'Sir? Have you thought of something?'

'I don't know.' Slider said quickly. He got up. 'Mr Honeyman wants you charged with the murder of your aunt. Is there anything you want to tell me, anything at all? Think, man!'

'I've been thinking,' Mills said despairingly. 'I didn't do it. I was in all evening. What more can I say?'

Slider nodded briskly and turned away.

253

15

On a Clear Day You Can See Fulham

He went back with Atherton to his house for breakfast.
Atherton had a gentrified Victorian workman's cottage on the
Kilburn/ Hampstead border, two up, two down, and a tiny
garden about ten foot square at the back which generally
smelled of privet and cats, but today, in the early morning,
had that airy, ozony smell of young days that are going to
grow up to be hot. Slider sat by the open window with Oedipus
kneading bread on his knees and purring like a JCB.
Somewhere outside a sparrow was doing its best to be a
skylark, and from somewhere inside the heartbreaking
perfumes of fresh coffee and frying tomatoes came wafting
sweetly over him. Slider felt his mind ticking like the metal
of a cooling car, and knew he was in danger of drifting off,
but he had promises to keep, and miles to go before he slept,
and miles to go before he slept . . .

The phone had rung, Atherton had answered, and was now
saying, 'It's for you,' over his shoulder as he hurried back to
his kitchen. Slider removed fourteen stone of cat from his
knee and staggered over to the phone.

'Slider.'

'So where were you all night?'

Oh shit, Joanna. He'd forgotten her. 'I should have phoned you, shouldn't I?'

'Well, I think you should.'

'But they told you where I was?'

'Nobody told me anything. They rang me to find out where you were. And of course, I didn't know.' Her tone was reasonable, but he couldn't help knowing she was batey.

'There was another murder last night—'

'It's a bit late to tell me that now. I was worried about you. For all I knew, you could have been dead in a ditch.'

He groaned. 'Why do wives always say things like that?'

'I don't know about wives. I've never been one,' she said tautly.

'Sorry. But you know how it is. Don't make a big thing out of it.'

'I'm not making a big thing out of it.' Now she was really trying to be reasonable. Probably the wives taunt, though tactless, had struck home. 'I just think you could have let me know at some point that you weren't coming home, or asked someone else to let me know. What do you have all those minions for?'

'Yes, I'm sorry, you're quite right. I just forgot. I had a lot to think about.'

'So I understand.'

'Oh, come on, Jo, it's my job. I always thought you could cope with my job.'

'I do. I am.' A pause. 'After all, you have to cope with my job.'

'That sounds ominous.'

'Only that I've got to go now, and I'd hoped to see you again before I leave. I won't be back tonight.'

'Oh, Christ. Glyndebourne. I'd forgotten. Why can't you come home tonight?'

'It isn't worth it. There's an orchestra call tonight, and a rehearsal tomorrow morning. By the time I got home it'd be time to leave again.' That was not strictly true, but as if she heard him think that, she added, 'Besides, you don't even know if you'll be home.'

'I probably will be. Well, at some point.'

'You might be back, or you might not,' she corrected. 'I'm not doing all that driving just to spend the evening alone.'

'Who are you going to spend it with, then?'

'What's that supposed to mean?' she said irritably. He hadn't meant anything in particular by it, he'd just been being smart, but her reaction immediately made him think of the Old Flame.

'Will he be there? This Andrew person?'

'Oh, for God's sake. Yes, of course he will. He's doing *Traviata.*'

'The whole thing? So you'll be seeing a lot of him.'

'Not really. He sits behind me. Look, Bill, this is stupid, I'm not going on with this. I've got to go, anyway. I'll see you tomorrow – if you're home.'

'All right.' He didn't want them to part on a sour note. 'Drive carefully.'

'In Sussex? You betcha. Good luck with your case, Inspector.'

'Good luck with your rehearsal.' He was going to add, 'I love you,' but she had put the phone down. He stared at the receiver for a moment, wondering what the hell had got into him recently, why he was feeling so peculiar and suspicious. But was it all him? She seemed tense and irritable. Maybe something *was* wrong, and he was picking up subliminal signals.

Atherton came through with plates. 'Sit,' he said, putting them on the table. He cocked an eyebrow at his boss. 'Trouble at t'mill?'

Slider gave him a weak smile. 'I wish you hadn't told me about the Other Man. Now I keep wondering.'

'I wish I hadn't told you, too. Honestly, Bill, the woman's nuts about you. She has eyes for no-one else. I should know.'

'What does that mean?' Slider asked indignantly of his retreating back.

In a moment Atherton came back with the coffee. 'It's just first-night nerves, that's all,' he said. 'It's a big step – for both of you. It'll take time to get used to it.' He nudged the plate in front of Slider. 'Eat. You're tired, your sugar levels are down, and you're not thinking straight.'

'My sugar levels can't have been down continuously since Sunday.'

'No, that's just hormones,' Atherton smiled. 'If I were you I should just relax and revel in it. Feeling jealous is a luxury commodity, you know. You have to have someone, and be in love with them, to feel jealousy. When you live hand to mouth like me, you'd be grateful for a bit of it.'

'You do talk such bollocks,' Slider said, sitting down, but he felt comforted all the same. And the food revived him, so that he felt the renewed sensation of blood flowing about him, and the thoughts began to bubble up in his mind, like coffee percolating.

With the plates pushed back and the second cups before them, they went over the case notes, the photographs and the transcriptions.

'We've got to keep a grip on this,' Slider said. 'Try to look at it logically. Mills looks like a good suspect for Miss Giles, because of the witness ID and because he was the closest person to her. He doesn't look quite such a good suspect for

Greatrex, because we can't find that he ever knew him, but there was still the witness ID, and Palliser says he saw him down at Glyndebourne, which Mills denies.'

'As he would.'

'Indeed. But I think whoever killed Miss Giles also killed Roger Greatrex.'

'Because the MO is similar?' Atherton said.

'And because of the timing. Why else should she be killed, if it wasn't something to do with the investigation?'

'Beats the hell out of me. But it's a short walk if that's where you're going.'

'Bear with me. Greatrex was killed. Laurence Jepp was killed by the same method. Both had a Bible tract card on or near them, though Greatrex was lapsed Jewish and Jepp was a lapsed atheist. The fingerprint from the card was similar to Mills's, although as Mr Honeyman pointed out, finger-printing is not an exact science. There was also a query attempted attack on Christa Jimenez. These three had in common that they all had to do with the *Don G* production at Glyndebourne. Tufty says the blood on the knife with which Jimenez attacked her intruder is not incompatible with Mills's. And Mills has no satisfactory alibi for any of the three times in question.'

'Nor had I, for that matter. That's the trouble with living alone,' said Atherton. 'Did Mills have a cut on his leg?'

'I looked—'

'Lucky you.'

'—but I couldn't see anything. But the Jimenez incident was almost a week ago, and we don't know how deep the cut was. It could have healed in that time.'

'Without a trace?'

'It's possible. We might know more when the genetic test comes back.'

'But meanwhile we've got to get on with what we've got. Why would Mills kill or attack all those people?'

'I don't know. The only connection I can come up with is the Glyndebourne one.'

'Religious fanaticism, you mean?'

'There is something very biblical about the throat-cutting. The one strong cut from behind – like a sacrifice at an altar. And a religious fanatic would be cold-blooded enough, or at least single-minded enough, to do it first time like that.'

'Then why Miss Giles?'

'Because I'd been talking to her, and she knew something that might be dangerous to him.'

'Is Mills religious?'

'Not that I know of,' Slider said. 'But of course he could be. I haven't seen him for years. And they say at Epsom he was a bit of a loner. I thought I knew him, but how much do you ever know people?' They were both silent for a while. 'It seems to me that Mrs Reynolds's evidence is the real hair in the custard,' Slider sighed at last.

'The what?'

'The thumb in the gravy – the unpleasant detail that can't be ignored. It was such a definite identification. Without that, we wouldn't be looking at Mills at all.'

'But as you say, you can't ignore it. And what about the girl who identified him going to his aunt's house?'

Slider tapped his notes. 'She didn't identify him. She only says he looked quite like the photofit.'

'A distinction without a difference. Anyway, nobody ever really looks like a photofit unless they've got a bolt through their neck,' Atherton grumbled. He looked at Slider. 'What is it?'

Slider was staring hard at the empty air, evidently in labour. Then he rummaged through the papers and brought out Mrs

Reynolds's statement and a copy of the photofit. He read the former, and then tapped the latter with a forefinger. 'Look, look at this. She's put the mole on the wrong side.'

'You'll have to do better than that,' Atherton said. 'Mills has got more moles than M.I.5.'

'This one,' Slider pointed to the large mole on the curve of the cheek, half an inch below and to the side of the nostril. 'His most distinguishing one. She's put it on his left cheek; but it's on his right.'

'Are you sure?' Atherton frowned, trying to visualise. 'No, it's on his left, surely.'

'Trust me. I know Mills's face very well.'

'Let's see her statement.' Atherton read it through. 'She says left cheek. Well, if you're right then she's wrong. So what?'

'So what? What d'you mean, so what?'

'She just made a mistake. Left, right, what does it matter? The rest of the description fits, and he's *got* a mole. Who cares which side?'

Slider shook his head slightly, thinking rapidly. 'Damn it, I can't remember. I think it was on the left, but I'm not sure.'

'You just said right,' Atherton complained, but Slider wasn't hearing him, rummaging through the photographs.

'The one thing we haven't got a photograph of! I'll have to go and check.'

'Check what?'

'The lift. No, wait, maybe you remember.' He focused belatedly on Atherton. 'The lift next to the men's room where Greatrex was killed – the lift where Mrs Reynolds says she saw the man – do you remember it?'

'What's to remember? A lift is a lift.'

'Visualise it! Which side was the control panel? The buttons? On the outside, I mean – out in the corridor.'

'On the left.'

'Are you sure?'

'Yes.' Atherton, good subordinate, didn't ask again what did it matter. He waited. Slider went on thinking.

'And Auntie Betty's dead, damn it,' he said at last. 'The one person—' He hit his palm softly with his fist. 'Maybe that's why! God, I hope so! That poor woman.'

'Guv, can I know what it is?'

Slider looked at him for a moment. 'Not yet. I'm so far out on the branch on this, it won't take the weight of two. You'll have to trust me for a bit.'

'*I* trust you,' Atherton said with delicate emphasis. 'Can I do anything to help?'

Slider thought for a moment. 'Not yet. Just cover for me – I'm going to stay out of reach of the office for a bit. I'll ring you the moment I've got something to work on.'

'All right.' Slider was already on his feet. 'Keep your mobile with you, then.'

'Yes.' A brief smile, like sunshine between fast-moving clouds. 'Thanks.'

First things first. Clear as you go. He went in search of Mrs Reynolds, who lived in one of those high-rise flats in Bollo Bridge Road. A complex community of streets and little houses had been erased to create the windy veldt on which the towers were erected, which accommodated slightly fewer people than had lived in the same space before; but, by golly, the ones on the top floor had a terrific view.

The door was opened by a tiny, wizened man whose trousers had obviously been bought to last before age had shrunk him. He wore them now hauled up so high by his braces that the waistband came under his armpits. He also wore a white shirt, buttoned up but without a collar or tie, tartan bedroom

261

slippers and a tweed cap. The saddest looking roll-up Slider had ever seen was stuck magically to his lower lip, and he breathed so badly and his nose was so blue that Slider feared the slightest extra exertion would see him off. Perhaps he ought to tell him to answer by blinking his eyes – one blink for yes, two for no.

But Mr Reynolds Mark Three seemed quite cheered by the visit and impressed by Slider's official status. He actually took the ID from him and caressed it with an orange thumb before returning it. 'Dolly's in the front room, having a lie-down,' he wheezed. 'She's not too clever s'morning. Jwanna come in?'

There were few things Slider wanted less, but in the line of duty he had sometimes to risk life and limb. There was no air inside the little flat, not a cubic centimetre: it had all been displaced by cigarette smoke. In the 'front room' an electric fire was on, heating up the smoke to rival the atmosphere of Los Angeles on a summer afternoon. The television was on, tuned to a breakfast show on which people with the air of having been up all night and knowing their mental agility to be impaired by the experience sat on a hideous sofa and desperately tried to keep talking until the adverts came on. On an equally hideous sofa in real life, Mrs Reynolds reclined, her sparse hair in small, tight curlers. She was covered from the waist down by a tea-stained 'honeycomb' blanket evidently stolen from a hospital, with an ashtray in her lap, a cigarette in her fingers, and a depressed-looking dachshund on her feet.

'Oh my good Gawd!' she said as Slider came in, and clapped her hand to her bosom. 'You arf give me a fright – I thought it was the council!'

'Not allowed to keep dogs,' whistled her husband sadly. 'She's always afraid they'll find out. I told her—'

'He says they don't care slongs we pay the rent,' she took

over for him. 'But I told him – I've told you,' she swivelled her head to her husband, 'they'd dearly like us out of here, and put immigrants in.'

'No they don't. Thass cobblers.'

'The social lady said.'

'She never. She said they'd move us if we ast to, on *account* o' them.'

'It's the same thing.'

Slider knew a single-track line when he saw one. 'Mrs Reynolds, there's something I'd like to ask you,' he said. Before my breath runs out, he added silently.

'Course there is, dear. I didn't think you come 'ere for the pleasure o' my company,' she said archly. 'Not but what—'

'Concerning that night at the BBC Television Centre. I want you to think back to the moment when you saw the man at the lift.'

'Yes, dear.'

'You came through the swing doors, he was there by the lift, and you said in your statement you saw him press the button to call the lift.'

'Thass right.'

'Picture it in your mind. The lift buttons are on the left side as you face the lift. The man puts his hand out and presses the buttons—'

Her face was screwed up in the smoke as obediently she visualised the scene. 'Yeah, I got it.'

'Which hand is he using?'

'His left,' she said promptly.

'So he's holding the bag in his right hand?'

'Thass right.'

'Now, you said in your statement that you saw blood on his cuff – that's on his left cuff, correct?'

'That's right, dear.'

'You saw his hairy wrist, his watch, and the end of his cuff sticking out beyond his jacket sleeve.' She nodded. 'You're quite sure about that?'

'Why shouldn't I be?' she sounded slightly annoyed now.

'It's just that the detail is very important on this point – I can't explain to you why, but it matters very much. You definitely saw his left wrist, with a watch, and blood on the cuff, reaching for the lift buttons?'

'I said it, and I meant it,' she said firmly. 'And if you want me in court, I'll swear Bible-oath to it.'

'Thank you. That's very satisfactory.' She smirked through her cigarette. Slider was getting black spots before his eyes from lack of oxygen. Oh no, that was just the pattern on the carpet. 'One other thing, now. Can you visualise the man's face? You said in your statement he had a mole on his left cheek, here.' He tapped his own face. 'Now are you sure it was his left cheek and not his right?'

She thought for a moment, and his heart misgave, but then she said, 'Yes, o' course I'm sure. Because that's the way he was facing. That's the side of his face I could see, wannit? His head wasn't turned right round towards me, it was more, like, three-quarters, and it was his left side nearest me, see?'

'Thank you,' said Slider. 'You've been very helpful.'

'Will you ave a cuppa tea, sir?' Mr Reynolds asked courteously.

'Oh my Gawd, ain't you put the kettle on yet, Bert?' Mrs R exclaimed, struggling to extricate herself from her blanket. The movement stirred the comatose dog, which lifted its head mournfully for a moment and emitted a just-audible hiss from the other end. 'I'd a made you one meself first off if I hadn't been feeling a bit iffy this morning. Only *e's* not been so clever either, with his chubes—'

'No, really, thanks, no tea for me. I must go,' Slider said, backing hastily. 'I've got an awful lot to do today.' He was almost sure a bit of the pattern on the carpet had moved, and he really didn't want the chance to find out for certain.

The next part would be harder. He could not ask Mills without revealing the true nature of his relationship with his Auntie Betty, which, if he was innocent of the murders, Slider was almost certain he did not know. And Auntie Betty was now silenced – an image of her face, bloodied, staring, slid out from his memory. He imagined a stumbling step, the jolt of a knife in the back, and just time enough to know betrayal, to the background clamour of hysterical dogs, before the darkness came up. He shook the thought away violently. Whatever it took, he had a duty to her now. He got into the car and drove towards Brook Green.

St Melitus's was a low, two-storeyed block in yellow brick, with picture windows over a rather severe patch of garden which sported grass with a military haircut and two oblong flowerbeds in which bedding geraniums, salvias and begonias kept rank or else. An utterly lovely seventy-foot London plane grew up from the pavement near the front gate, with languid limbs trailing scarves of leaves like Isadora Duncan, but it was evidently out of the gardener's jurisdiction, or it would surely have been pollarded to within an inch of its life to make it smarten its ideas up.

Inside there was a central sitting-room – regrettably called an 'association area' – with high-backed, high-seated armchairs ranged round the walls as in a hospital waiting-room, where old people, women to men in a ratio of about eight to one, sat facing forwards and waiting for something to happen – the tea trolley or death, whichever came first. A rosy-cheeked, black-haired woman in a blue nurse's dress fielded Slider as he came through the door.

'Come to visit someone, have we?' she enquired cheerfully with a hint of Irish. 'I don't think we've seen you before. Now, which one did you want?'

'Are you the – er – matron? Head person?'

'Superintendent,' she helped him out. 'No, that's Mrs Maitland. Is it about a vacancy? We haven't any at present—'

Slider didn't like the idea of that 'at present'. Some of the old people were dozing with their mouths open, and looked too close to supplying a vacancy for Slider's comfort.

'No, not that. I'd like to speak to Mrs Maitland about one of your residents, if I may. I'm a police officer. Detective Inspector Bill Slider, Shepherd's Bush.' He spoke quietly and made a discreet gesture towards his ID, in case the police presence alarmed any of the frail folk, but the cheery one laughed aloud.

'Oh my God, have you come to arrest one of them?' she cried in extremely audible amusement. 'What've they been up to now? I'll bet it's our Cyril looking up ladies' skirts again – you wicked old divil!' The only man in the direction she threw the witticism was one of the fast-asleep ones, but the ladies on either side of him seemed to appreciate the jest. One broke into whispery laughter, and the other made a riposte so broad that Slider realised even twenty years in the police force had not prepared him for communal old age.

'Come along, Inspector,' said the nurse, noting his embar-rassment with amused sympathy. 'This is no place for you. I'll take you to the office.'

Mrs Maitland turned out to be disconcertingly young, very smart, and wearing a bright yellow suit, presumably to make her easily visible. It had a very short skirt and she didn't quite have the legs for it, but it certainly made her a more cheering sight for a matron than Hattie Jacques in NHS blue and a lamb chop frill on her head.

'Mrs Mills – Margaret – we like to use first names here,' she confided unsurprisingly. 'Yes, she's in flat 5. She's been here for years – quite able-bodied, spry really, but she gets a bit confused sometimes.'

'Is she aware of what's going on? Her son's name has appeared in the newspapers.'

'I don't know about that. They do get various papers here – the *Mail* and the *Mirror* and the *Evening Standard*. They're put out in the association area – but whether she will have read about it I can't say. Of course, some of them buy their own papers too, but Margaret doesn't go out very much. Hardly at all, really, except to church sometimes, when one of the others takes her. We don't encourage her to leave the premises alone. She spends a lot of time in her own room, in fact. A bit solitary. Sometimes we have to positively chase her out. It isn't good for them to sit alone too long, especially the confused ones.'

'Does she know about her sister?'

'Not as far as I know. I didn't know about it myself until you told me. Murdered, you say?' She shook her head. 'I'd rather you didn't say anything about that. It's a bit too upsetting. Can't you ask her what you want without mentioning that?'

'She'll have to know sooner or later that her sister's dead,' Slider pointed out.

'Yes, but I'd sooner one of us told her. We know them, you see, and we're trained to deal with these things. You never know how the shock might affect them.'

Slider was beginning to take a dislike to Mrs Maitland, and was forced to restrain himself from pointing out that all of these old people had lived through one war, some of them two, and had probably experienced worse things than Mrs Maitland could imagine without the aid of a video. He didn't like the idea that this pert young thing called the old people by their Christian names – probably without asking permission – and referred to them as if they were a species, like starfish or algae, with generic attributes. But he reminded himself that he did not take care of even one old person full time, let alone thirty or forty, let further alone not related to him, and bit his tongue.

'Can I talk to Mrs Mills, then?'

'Yes, of course. I'll get someone to take you up, and stay with you while you have a chat, if you like.'

A middle-aged woman in a white overall dress and surprisingly peroxide hair took him up to the flat. She rang the doorbell, simultaneously putting the key hanging by a chain from her belt into the lock, and called out, 'Maggie, it's Joyce. Can I come in, dear?' as she opened the door. She looked in and then nodded to Slider, preceding him into a tiny room, furnished in early MFI, of which every surface was covered in china ornaments and plaster knick-knacks whose only virtue was that they were small, and therefore of limited individual horribleness. Cumulatively, they were like an infestation. Little vases, ashtrays, animals, shepherdesses, tramps, boots, tobys, ruined castles, civic shields of seaside towns, thimbles, bambis, pink goggle-eyed puppies sitting up and begging, scooped-out swans plainly meant to double as soap-dishes, donkeys with empty panniers which ought to have held pin-cushions or perhaps bunches of violets – all jostled together in a sad visual cacophony of bad taste and birthday presents and fading holiday memories, too many to be loved, justifying themselves by their sheer weight of numbers as 'collections' do. Maggie's collection of china ornaments. What can we get for Maggie? Oh, get her one of those Chinese horses – she collects things like that. That thimble with the arms of Bexhill-on-Sea – that ashtray with the Spanish dancer painted on it – that bulldog with the Union Jack waistcoat – they'd never be looked at again, they were just there, swelling the numbers, like the forgotten sleeping oldies downstairs. And when Maggie died, they'd be shovelled into a cardboard box and sent off to a misnamed Antiques Fair in a scout hall somewhere to be the things left on the stall at the end of the day.

Mrs Mills was sitting in one of the high-backed chairs by the window, her hands resting on the arms, looking out, away from the ugliness and confinement and clutter, out at the beautiful tree. She turned her head as they came in and said, 'Go away.'

'Now then, Maggie, don't be like that,' Joyce said coaxingly. 'I've got a visitor for you. This gentleman's a policeman, dear, come all this way to talk to you.'

Mrs Mills looked at Slider, and said, 'He can stay. I don't want you, though. Go away.'

'Ooh, we can be rude when we try,' Joyce said archly. She turned to Slider. 'She's a bit – you know,' she whispered perfectly audibly, tapping her temple. 'And a bit unsociable. Unsociable,' she added loudly, 'aren't you, Maggie? All right, I'll leave you alone with your boyfriend.' She lowered her voice again. 'There's a button over there by the fireplace if you have any trouble. Let Mrs Maitland know when you leave again, won't you.'

When they were alone, Mrs Mills looked at Slider, and then poked her tongue out at the closed door. 'I was rude, wasn't I? Can't stand them, stupid bitches. Think if you're old, you're daft. Wait till they're seventy, then they'll see. What did you say your name was?'

'Slider. Bill Slider.'

'Well, sit down then. There's a pouffe over there. They only give you one chair – afraid you might have company in your room, enjoy yourself or something. Bitches.'

Slider fetched the pouffe and sat on it in front of Mrs Mills. She looked down at him with a gleam of malicious pleasure, presumably at his reduced elevation. 'Can't see out from down there, can you? I like to look out. Sit here and look at the tree. You get birds in that tree. You'd be surprised how many. Watch 'em for hours. Did they tell you I'm gaga?' She didn't wait for him to answer. 'Well I'm not. But I let them think it – saves me having to listen to their rabbiting. What do you want, anyway? What did you say your name was?'

'Inspector Slider,' he said, with less confidence.

'What, police are you?'

'That's right.'

'My boy Steve's a policeman. Well, a detective.'

'I know. I used to work with him years ago. That's what I've come to talk to you about.'

She looked at him sharply. 'He's in trouble. I saw it in the newspaper. They think I don't know, just because I don't talk about it. I wouldn't talk to *them*.'

'I think your boy's innocent, Mrs Mills, and I want to prove it,' Slider said.

'Course he's innocent. He's a good boy, my Steve. Always been a good son to me.'

'That's why I've come to see you. I want to talk to you about your sister.'

'He's in the police. Out in Epsom. I never see him now. Too far to visit. But he's always been a good son to me.'

Slider leaned forward a little and tried to catch her eye. 'I want to talk to you about your sister – about Betty.'

She sharpened. 'Betty? What about Betty? Is she dead? Is that it?'

Alarmingly prompt – but at her age, you must hear a lot about death. Slider hesitated only a moment. 'Yes, I'm afraid so.'

Mrs Mills seemed to think about it. 'Comes to us all. But she was younger than me, you know. Still, she didn't lead a pure life. She smoked, drank – had affairs. Men!' She snorted. 'I could tell you a thing or two! She was always a wild one, even as a girl. I had to be mother to her, after Father died and Mother went a bit gaga. I always said she'd get herself into trouble one day – and she did! But she'd never listen to me. Oh no, I was just boring old Maggie, good enough to come to when she wanted something, but take advice – huh!'

'When she got into trouble,' Slider inserted, gently but urgently, 'she went into a home, didn't she? A mother-and-baby home.'

'I'd have had her with me,' Mrs Mills said, not as if she was answering, but as if following her own thoughts. She was not looking at him. 'I mean, blood is thicker than water, and I was fond of her in a way. But Arthur wouldn't have it. He was a good man, mind,' she added sharply, as though Slider had argued, 'but she made fun of him. I told her, the Devil laughs at the virtuous, and you'll laugh on the other side of your face when you go Downstairs. I told her that. But she liked to make fun of him – until she wanted his help. Then it was a different story, oh yes! Well, he was a good man and he helped her, but as to having her in the house – never, and I couldn't blame him. He was right, too,' she added with a wise nod, 'because she broke her word. She promised to go right away afterwards, but she came back.'

'Why do you think she did that?'

'To show off, of course, because she had money and we didn't. Always buying him things, taking him places, trying to set him against his own parents with her money and her outings and I don't know what. Arthur couldn't stand her – painted hussy, he called her. They had some set-tos! But then just when you thought she'd gone too far, she'd come round

271

and apologise, really handsome, and bring Arthur something, a book or a present, something he really wanted, and talk to him so nicely about church and the Scouts and Sunday school and everything, it made you wonder why she couldn't be sensible like that all the time. He had to forgive her. She had charm, you see, when she wanted to use it. She wasn't really a *bad* woman – just wild.'

'Was that why you let the boy see her?'

'Well, he was a fair man, was Arthur. She never appreciated him, really, because he had his funny little ways and he could be a bit ridiculous sometimes, I have to admit, but he loved the boy and he'd have done anything for him. And Steve really loved *her*, and Arthur said, he said, after all – you know.' She nodded wisely. 'And he said the boy must come first, we can't put our pride before his happiness.'

'That was very noble of him,' Slider said, but she took it the wrong way and looked at him suspiciously.

'What's it to you, anyway? Who are you?'

Slider didn't bother with the introductions. 'The mother-and-baby home your sister went into – do you remember where it was?'

'She's not in a home. She works for the Civil Service – did very well for herself,' Mrs Mills said. But she seemed to be tiring, and he knew he had to get on.

'When she was a girl, when she got into trouble, she went into a special place. It was run by your minister, Mr Green, wasn't it?'

'Mr Green? Mr Green? He was here the other day.' She looked rather dazed. 'He keeps a friendly eye on the boy. Always did. I think he's afraid she might steer him wrong. She was never one for religion. But she'll think on the other side of her face when she goes Downstairs.'

'Mrs Mills, I really need to know,' Slider said urgently.

'What was the name of Mr Green's home for girls in trouble? What was the address?'

'Out in the country, that was, to keep 'em out of harm's way. Talk about hate it! She never liked the country. Nothing but mud, as far as the eye could see – mud and potatoes, she said afterwards. That's all the country is – mud and potatoes. Five miles even to get a packet of cigarettes. Essex, I think it was. Or Kent. Some village.'

Wonderful, Slider thought. Only two counties to search. He could see she was tired now, and thought he had failed, but suddenly she spoke again out of her thoughts, quite sharply and lucidly.

'*He* lived in East Acton, though. Shaa Road. House on the corner. Just up the road from the church. They've pulled that church down now, building a block of flats instead, sacrilege I call it. He was a great big man, great big hands and a deep voice. Joshua Green,' she said, shaking her head. 'Betty always said it sounded like someone off *The Archers.*' She looked at him, seeing him suddenly, and frowned. 'She's dead, isn't she? That's why you came. Policeman, aren't you? Betty's dead.'

'Yes, I'm afraid so.'

She sighed. 'I always knew I'd see her out. She was younger than me, but she led a wild life. I expect my boy will see about it, the funeral and that. My boy Steve. He'll see to everything. He's a policeman. Well, detective really. What did you say your name was?'

16

Negative Evidence

In the nature of things, there were likely to be four corner houses to Shaa Road, and even if he found the right one, he didn't expect Green would still live there, if he still lived at all. But Slider hoped to catch hold of the end of a chain which might lead him to the information he wanted. This was something he could hand over to the team, but he wanted at least to find the right house to begin with, to see it with his own eyes.

As it happened, he hit the right one first shot. A neat, thirties-style urban villa with a red-tiled bay window and stained glass in the front door yielded to his ring at the doorbell a neat, small woman in her late fifties, wearing a nylon overall. Just behind her on the hall table a pair of rubber gloves, a duster and a tin of Mr Sheen stood where she had put them down; the smell of the polish mingled on the air with a slight threat of oxtail soup and that particular odour that some boarding houses and small hotels have – something of cheap carpets and institutional food gently ripened in a centrally-heated, double-glazed airlock.

'Good morning. I'm looking for a Mr Green,' Slider began. 'He—'

'If it's about a wedding, I'm afraid he's retired now,' the woman interrupted with a sweet smile.

'Oh – no,' Slider said, beguiled. Did he look as though he wanted marrying? 'He does live here then, Joshua Green? I have got the right house?'

'Yes, that's right.' The woman waited patiently. Clergy wives were first filters, had to cope with all the nuts.

Slider reached for his ID. 'Would you be Mrs Green?'

'Not for all the tea in China,' she said with unexpected wit. 'I'm the housekeeper. Mrs Hoare.'

Slider blinked, and stopped himself asking why she had never thought of changing her name. 'Detective Inspector Slider,' he said steadily. 'Is Mr Green at home? Could I have a word with him?'

'I expect you could. Come in. He'll be *reading* in his study at the moment.' One of her eyelids dropped and rose again with oiled smoothness. 'I generally wake him up for lunch, but it won't hurt him to be disturbed for once. Just wait here.'

She went off round the corner and Slider waited, listening to the sound of a clock ticking, looking at the row of cacti on a shelf along the hall window, the neat piles of pamphlets and tracts on the hall table, the capacious umbrella-stand, the carpet chosen for its ability to take wear and hide marks. The walls were decorated with framed reproductions of Canaletto views of Venice, and there was a hideous Edwardian mahogany hallstand, complete with mirror and numerous tiny what-not shelves, which sprouted coat-hooks upon branched coat-hooks like a ten-point stag. It was a home that was a public place, and vice versa. It must be a rotten life being a priest, he thought – especially these days when you couldn't even enjoy the satisfaction of a hearty malison when provoked. On the subject of which, he drifted closer to look at the tracts, but they were pre-printed on shiny paper with coloured colophons, and their messages had the kick of a pair of suede sandals. No more swords, wrath and vengeance for the Church, no blood, wine, betrayal and agony in the garden – just little homilies about being more understanding, helping Oxfam, and loving your brother regardless of race, colour, creed or sexual orientation. Slider wondered what the prophets of old would have made of that – what Joshua Green, if he was really a fiery preacher in his youth, made of it. It was all very restful, though. Maybe the Church Militant had been an aberration, and this was what God had wanted all along.

Mrs Hoare reappeared and beckoned to him. 'He'll see you,' she said, leading him where she had gone before. 'He's just a little deaf, but if you talk clearly and straight at him he hears all right. You don't need to shout.' She opened a door. 'Here's Inspector Slider, now,' she announced, and stood back to let Slider pass, saying to him, 'Do you prefer tea or coffee?'

'Oh, tea please. Thank you.'

The small room had French windows onto a very dull garden, and one whole wall was covered in bookshelves. The rest of the available space was taken up with a large old-fashioned desk with a much-buttoned leather wing chair on one side of it, and a depressed-looking row of wooden upright chairs on the other. Green was seated on the master's side of this arrangement, and gestured Slider towards the supplicants' position. He made a gesture of standing up, but did not actually rise, and seeing how upright he sat and the large-knuckled deformity of his big hands on the chair arms, Slider suspected arthritis and did not blame him.

'It's good of you to see me, Mr Green. I do call you Mr?'

'Yes, yes, that's all I am now – a retired soldier in God's army – or perhaps I should say a reservist? Ha!' He gave a single shout of laughter which Slider guessed had become a mannerism over many years, a jocularity designed to show that a man could be a devout Christian and yet *not at all dull*. 'One never knows when one might be "called up" again.' He marked the waggish inverted commas in his speech by speaking the words more slowly and in an even deeper voice. 'And what do I call you? Inspector, is it?'

'Mr will do,' Slider said, taking the middle seat in Penitent's Row.

'Very well. "Mr" Slider. Puts us on equal footing, eh? Ha! Now, what can I do for you?'

He made a curious movement of his hands across his midriff and back to the arms of the chair, which Slider recognised as an attempt to steeple his fingers, thwarted by their crookedness. He had not yet grown used to his disabilities. Slider could see how he must have been 'a great, big man', and he was tall still, though age had shrunk him somewhat. He still had a fine head of hair, worn brushed back so that it framed his head like a lion's mane; his bushy eyebrows had stayed black, and jutted out like rock formations over his dark eyes, hinting at the charismatic figure he must once have cut. Slider would have put his age at around eighty, but it was a vigorous eighty which might just as easily have been ninety or seventy. His features still had strength and firmness, though there was something rather ugly, Slider thought, about his mouth – very wide and very thin, with an unexpectedly red lower lip and no upper lip at all.

'I've come to raid your memory,' Slider said. 'I am here concerning the case of Elizabeth, or Betty, Giles—'

'The case? Is she dead, then?' Green interrupted sharply.

'She was found dead at her home last night,' Slider said carefully, looking at the man with interest. 'You were very quick on the uptake.'

'You'd hardly have called her a case otherwise. I doubt she was "drug smuggling" or organising "a rave" at her age. She must be—' He paused as if to work it out, but in fact left it to Slider. When Slider didn't help, he concluded, 'An elderly woman.'

'You do remember her, then. Even though it was such a long time ago.'

'Her sister was one of my flock, and her brother-in-law ran my Sunday school most competently for very many years. Naturally I remember her.'

'And her son?'

The eyes were cautious under the bushes. 'Her son? I was not aware that she ever married.'

'She didn't. Come, Mr Green, let's not waste time fencing. Miss Giles herself told me the story only yesterday. Steven Mills, who was adopted by her sister Margaret, was her illegitimate child.'

'Well, you astound me,' Green said emphatically.

'Surely not. It was you who arranged the adoption – amongst many others.'

'If you know that, then you must know that I am not at liberty to disclose the circumstances surrounding any adoption. The children I placed are entitled to my absolute discretion – as are the adopting parents.'

'I appreciate that,' Slider said. 'But in this case, Miss Giles herself told me half the story, and would have told me the other half today if she had not been silenced. She was murdered last night, Mr Green, brutally murdered, and her son Steven, whom she loved, is under suspicion.' Green's face was impassive, but he was listening hard. 'Now I worked with Steve for some time a few years back, we were friends, and I was pretty close to him. I think I know him, and he's a decent, good man, and he loved his Auntie Betty and would

278

never have harmed a hair of her head. I need your help to prove that.'

'There is nothing I can tell you,' Green said, but Slider could hear that he was weakening. He attempted to steeple his fingers again, and instead raised them to his lips. It wasn't quite the magisterial gesture it ought to have been. It looked more as if he was sucking both thumbs at once.

Slider went at it again. 'Nothing you tell me can harm Miss Giles any more. Arthur Mills is dead and Margaret Mills is in a home and, I'm afraid, mentally confused. Steve Mills, whom you helped once as an infant by placing him with good, loving parents, needs your help again. In those circumstances, it would be quite wrong of you to refuse information. It's your duty as a citizen, but I think also as a Christian, to answer my questions.'

Green was silent for a few moments. Then he removed his hands from his mouth and said, 'You are very persuasive, Mr Slider. You should have been a minister.'

'I suppose I'm a fisher of men in my own way,' Slider said, with a smile to show he was joking. 'But my job is to go after the sharks.'

'Ha! A useful occupation all the same. Well, then, well then—' He paused a moment. 'I suppose you are right. Betty Giles. You want to know about Betty Giles.'

'You obviously remember the whole family very well. Did they stick in your mind for any particular reason?'

'I remember all the adoption cases I handled. I've kept in touch with many of them: the children are like my own children, in a spiritual sense. I like to keep a distant but fatherly eye on them – and their adoptive parents. Not the unfortunate girls, of course – they would not wish to be reminded by me of what they once were. In those days, you know, society punished them very severely, condemned them for ever on the grounds of one sin – which sometimes they were too ignorant to realise was a sin. It's quite different now. I think we have gone rather too far in the other direction these days. We are supposed to hate the sin and love the sinner. Nowadays we don't even hate the sin.'

'I'm sure you're right,' Slider said anodynely. 'Please go on.'

'Of course. Well, my idea in those far-off days was to offer a safe, clean, Christian home to these girls during their pregnancy, and afterwards to place the babies with Christian couples of my acquaintance, and to help the girls find respectable employment. But for them to begin a new life free of the taint of their error, everything had to be conducted with the most complete discretion. No-one must be able to point a finger at the girls afterwards; and for the sake of the babies and their new parents, the girls must never know their identity. So we rented a house in a village called Cooksmill, near Chelmsford – it was real countryside in those days, very remote and out of temptation's way for the girls, but also out of the public eye. The girls could "disappear" there, and it was unlikely they would ever meet anyone afterwards who had seen them there. When the time came they went into the hospital in Chelmsford, and the baby was taken away at once, usually without their ever seeing it, certainly before they had any opportunity of forming a fondness for it. Afterwards they spent six weeks recuperating at the house, and then they were placed in suitable work.'

'What happened if they wanted to keep the baby?' Slider asked.

Green looked as though he had said something mildly offensive. 'That was not possible. The social climate in those days made it impossible for an unmarried girl to bring up a child alone.'

'But if they were determined?'

Green looked his loftiest. 'It was a condition of our helping them that the child was given up. We could not have operated on any other basis.'

Slider thought he understood. 'How did you choose the couples who adopted the babies?'

'On the grounds of their Christian commitment and moral probity. We were very thorough – otherwise it would have been "out of the frying pan and into the fire" as far as the poor infants were concerned.'

'But how did *they* find out about *you?*'

'Through the Church, or by word of mouth, usually. Sometimes couples were referred to us by doctors or almoners. But there was never a shortage. Childless couples are very determined about seeking what they want.'

'Did they pay you?' Slider thought the bluntness of the question might shock something out of Green, but he had evidently faced this ball before, and played it straight down the wicket.

'There were expenses involved, and the applicants made a contribution to that. It was not a fee. Some paid more and some less, according to their resources.'

'What if they were really poor?'

'If they were unable to afford any contribution, it is unlikely they could have afforded to bring up a child in the proper manner. We did not,' he added, lowering the brows sternly, 'consider couples where the woman went out to work. A woman's place is in the home, nurturing her child and caring for her husband.'

Slider thought of Joanna's version of that adage: A woman's place is in the wrong. He was getting quite a clear picture of the frying pan and fire the 'unfortunate girls' alternated between. At that point the housekeeper brought in a tray, with a cup of tea, a cup of milky coffee, a sugar bowl, and a plate on which reposed two Nice biscuits, two garibaldis, and two bourbons. She placed everything within reach, looked the two men over carefully, as if gauging whether they were likely to come to blows if left alone again, and went.

Slider took up his teacup and said, 'Tell me about the case of Miss Giles. That was rather different, wasn't it?'

'It was,' Green admitted, as though seeing now it had been a mistake. 'The identities of all the parties were known to each other, which was dangerous.'

'And Miss Giles was not a common, ignorant girl. She was bright, ambitious, career-minded.'

'She was very difficult, from beginning to end,' Green said gloomily. 'It was her sister who brought her situation to my attention. I had met her once or twice at the Mills's home, and did not like her. She struck me as what we used to call in those days "fast". It did not come as a surprise to me when Margaret came to say that her sister had got into trouble.'

'Did Mrs Mills know about your activities in that field?'

'She knew I had arranged adoptions for other couples, and I think she had a vague idea that I was connected with some kind of home. What she asked, that day she came to see me, was simply whether I could help Elizabeth. I asked in what way, and she said, "Betty doesn't want the baby. I'm afraid she might try and get rid of it."'

'By that you understood abortion?'

'Some girls found it preferable in those days to the shame of being an outcast,' he said sorrowfully. 'It was another reason for our operation.'

'So it became not just a matter of saving Elizabeth from her predicament but of saving the baby too?'

'Its life as well as its soul,' he nodded. 'I told Margaret that I could only help Betty if she placed herself entirely in my hands, and did exactly as I said. She said she would talk to her. But by the time they both came to see me on the next occasion, the plot had been hatched between them. Margaret had some fear that she could not have a child of her own, and would rather adopt her sister's baby than a stranger's. Elizabeth would sooner know what sort of a home her infant was going to. I said in that case they had no need of my services and could arrange matters between them. But they insisted,' he finished gloomily.

'What did they want you to do?'

'It was a matter of maintaining secrecy. Elizabeth had a career which would be damaged by her shameful condition. She needed to be able to go somewhere discreet where she would be looked after. On their side Margaret and Arthur wanted an arrangement which safeguarded them, a proper, legal adoption, and no chance that Elizabeth would go back on it at the last moment.' He sighed. 'I warned them of the hazards, I told them it was not an arrangement I could recommend, and suggested alternatives, but they were adamant. Margaret had set her heart on having the baby, and Elizabeth wanted to be rid of it as conveniently as possible, and Arthur was in the middle hoping to keep everything respectable. So I helped them.'

Slider said encouragingly, 'I expect you did the right thing. It might have turned out much worse if you hadn't.'

Green inspected him for irony, and then nodded. 'I think you are right. I did my best to build in safeguards. Any breach of the rules by Elizabeth while she was at Coldharbour House would terminate the agreement. The baby was to be taken from her immediately as with the other girls and she was to sign the adoption papers before leaving the hospital. And after her convalescence she was not to contact her sister again or go anywhere near the house. But of course she broke the agreement on every count. She was a troublesome inmate at Coldharbour, flouting the rules and disturbing the other girls. And she not only contacted her sister, she returned to live almost next door and to insist on contact with the child.'

'She never told him she was his mother, though,' Slider said, feeling driven to Miss Giles's defence. He remembered what she'd said about the weeping girls in the home, and the 'kindness' of having the baby taken away at birth. Green, he thought, must have been a Mr Brocklehurst to them. 'Steve doesn't know even now what their relationship really was.'

'I'm glad to know she had even so much decency,' Green said stiffly. 'I hardly think she was a good influence on the boy. And she made Margaret and Arthur very unhappy – good, decent, Christian people.'

'It was a difficult situation,' Slider said, needing to placate him as they approached the tricky part. 'I'm sure on reflection you must be satisfied that without your help it would have been much worse.'

'Perhaps,' he said, unwilling to be seduced. 'So, Mr Slider, have you the information you required?'

'Not quite,' Slider said. 'I need to know what happened to the other one.'

'The other one?' The words came out naturally enough, but the body had suddenly become still, watchful.

'The other baby. There were two, weren't there?' Green did not answer. 'Twins,' Slider said helpfully. 'Miss Giles had twin boys, didn't she?'

'You are mistaken,' Green said stiffly. 'I can't think where you have your information, but you are quite mistaken.'

'Come, now, Mr Green, it's pointless denying something that can so easily be proved. The hospital records will show it. I would sooner not have to go to the trouble, but I can get the documentary evidence and bring it to you if you insist. Don't make me waste my time.'

Green looked almost dazed. 'Nobody knew. It was the most absolute secret. Of course, there were no scans in those days, and the girls were all as ignorant of these things as each other. The matron was under my instructions, and even Elizabeth herself knew nothing until she actually gave birth. If it could have been done by Caesarean section, as I wished,' he added bitterly, 'she wouldn't have known even then. But the hospital wouldn't play ball. They said the decision must be made by the doctor, and for medical reasons only.'

Slider looked at him in amazement. 'Why? Why did you want to keep it a secret?'

There was a flash of the power that must have once made him a formidable man. 'To save something from the wreck! I knew the arrangement could never work, that Elizabeth would not keep her word. The child the Millses took would be in constant jeopardy. But I thought that if I could place the other as it ought to be placed, with neither side knowing the other's identity, something good would have come out of it. It would not all have been in vain.'

'And so what happened to the other baby?'

Green was silent a moment, seeking escape. 'It died.'

'No, I don't think so,' Slider said gently. 'You see, I've been puzzled by a number of things recently that didn't make sense; someone I kept crossing the path of, someone who was so like Steve Mills people were willing to swear to his identity. But as someone pointed out to me, identity means actually being the same person, not just looking like them. And I found myself wondering about a person who looked like Steve; whose fingerprint was similar to Steve's but not exactly the same; who had the same blood-group; but who was right-handed where he is left-handed. My Steve Mills, like other

285

left-handed people, wears his watch on his right wrist. The Steve Mills I was looking for wears his watch on his left wrist, like the majority of the population. And there was the matter of the moving mole – a mole on Steve's right cheek that suddenly wandered over to the left cheek.'

Green was watching him warily, but following everything with an air of waiting for the inevitable blow to fall. Perhaps he had known what was coming. Perhaps he had been waiting for this blow for years.

'It does happen sometimes,' Slider went on almost conversationally, 'that zygotic twins are mirror images of each other, like left hand and right hand.' He lifted his hands and put them together to demonstrate. 'And unless you see them side by side, you are not likely to notice the differences. It also happens that a tendency to have twins runs in families, and I knew there had been twin brothers in Miss Giles's family. So when a friend of mine at St Catherine's House told me that Miss Giles's mother was also one of a pair of twins, I started to put two and two together, if you'll pardon my little joke.'

Green didn't look as if he would. He said, 'What exactly is it that you suspect?'

'I think that you placed the other baby with a couple, that the adult that child became now lives somewhere not too far from here, that he has committed a crime, and that he knows, because he read it in the newspaper, that his twin brother is suspected of the crime and is happy enough to let that ride. I know a few things about him. He is very religious, fond of music, probably interested in scouting or something of that sort – an athletic, outdoor type. Probably unmarried. He is intelligent, too, a planner, not easily flustered. But a man of strong feelings and strong convictions.'

Green looked shaken. 'You seem to know a good deal.'

'Am I right, then?'

'How should I know? You are telling your own story.'

'You haven't corrected any of it. Where is the twin now?'

'I placed an infant for adoption almost forty years ago,' Green said loftily. 'How should I know where it is now?'

'But you said yourself that you liked to keep a distant, fatherly eye on them. Your children – in the spiritual sense. And you must have been particularly proud of this one – your success story, snatched out of disaster.'

'Leave me alone,' Green said suddenly in a weak voice, the last thing Slider would have expected. 'Don't mock me.'

'I'm not mocking. Just give me what I want, and I will leave you alone.'

'What do you want?'

'I want to know what happened to Elizabeth's other baby.'

Green gripped the arms of the chair and breathed hard, as though he had been running and was distressed for breath. 'I placed him with a couple – a very good, pious couple, churchgoers, total abstainers, very strict. The best start he could have had.'

'And did Elizabeth know? Did she ever find out?'

'Not from me. But I think – I suspect – *he* may have found *her*. There was a break-in – some of my papers, records, were taken from my files. They were returned later. The details of that adoption were amongst them.'

'You suspect he was the one who took the papers?'

'He had asked me several times who his natural mother was. I had always refused to tell him, and he got very angry.' He swallowed. 'He wasn't a bad boy, but very determined. Very – single-minded. He felt it was his *right* to know.'

'So he broke into your house and stole the papers.'

'He returned them later. And he would not have done anything like that unless he felt he had good reason.'

'How old was he when this happened?'

'Eighteen – nineteen perhaps.'

'You had kept in touch with him all that time?'

'I – he – I looked upon him as my special trust. I felt almost like a father towards him. I watched him grow up, and took a delight in seeing how he developed.' He stopped abruptly, frowning, as though some memory did not please him.

'So he found out who his mother was, and went to see her?' Slider prompted.

'I don't know,' Green said forcefully, looking at Slider now. 'I think he may have, but I don't know. I never spoke to him about it, and Elizabeth certainly never said anything on the few occasions after that when I met her. But he was not the sort of boy *not* to act. He liked to be *doing* – a very practical Christian. He was a leading light of the Boys' Brigade, loved camping and mountaineering. Later he ran adventure holidays for disadvantaged boys and young offenders. He's a *good* man. Whatever you suspect him of, you are quite wrong.'

'What's his name?'

'I won't tell you,' Green said heatedly. 'You want to persecute this good man to try to get your friend off the hook.'

'He can't be persecuted, or even prosecuted, if he's done nothing wrong. If he is a good man as you say he is, he has nothing to fear.' Green said nothing, his thin mouth pressed shut. 'Mr Green, Betty Giles has been savagely murdered. It's very important that we get the right man into custody, in case he attacks again.' Silence. 'I believe she was killed because she was in a position to tell me the secret of the existence of a twin brother to Steve. How many other people know that secret? How many others are at risk?'

'You don't know,' Green cried, 'that he has done anything! You are only guessing! For all you know it could be someone else entirely!'

'All the more reason, then, for me to find him and ask him some questions, so that the shadow of suspicion can be lifted from him. What has an innocent man to fear?'

'Nothing.' Green swallowed. He looked shaken. 'Nothing, of course. Very well, his name is Gilbert, Geoffrey Gilbert.'

'And his address?'

'I don't know.' He set his jaw stubbornly. 'That's the truth. He used to live in Acton, but he moved about ten years ago, and I haven't seen him since. We had a – a disagreement at about that time and I haven't had any contact with him for years. I've no idea where he is now.'

The door opened again at that point, and Mrs Hoare came in. She gave Slider a stern and significant look, and then said to Green, 'I'm going to have to disturb your little talk now, because you know the doctor said you hadn't to sit still all morning, so if you're going to have your walk before lunch—'

Green seemed happy to take the excuse of dismissing Slider. He became almost courtly in his relief. 'You'll excuse me seeing you out, I hope. The weight of years, you know. I hope I've been of some help. It was pleasant meeting you, though it was sad news indeed to hear of poor Miss Giles.'

'I'll just see the gentleman out, and then I'll come back and get you ready for your walk,' Mrs Hoare said, and hustled Slider away. Alone with him in the hall she said, 'You'll forgive me disturbing you, but I knew you'd get nothing more from him after that. He's as stubborn as a donkey, and I don't want him upset for nothing.'

'You were listening?' Slider said, half-shocked, half-amused.

'At the door.' She bridled a little. 'I always listen. He's an old man, and we get some very funny customers in here. I have to protect him.' She looked at Slider with grudging approval. 'You did all right with him. You're good at handling people. But when I heard that tone of voice, I knew you'd

289

not shift him any further. You've got your job to do of course,' she added sympathetically. 'You might get more out of him another time, but you'd have to wear him down. Isn't there some other way you can find out what you want to know? Surely an address shouldn't to be too hard, with all your computers and everything?'

'When all you have is a name,' Slider said, 'and the whole country to search – the whole world, for all I know.'

She made an impatient movement of her head. 'Whole country, nothing! When he moved from Acton, he went to Askew Road. If he's not there still, you can trace him from there, can't you?'

'Does Mr Green really not have any contact with him now?'

'Not for many years. They quarrelled. Too much alike, you know, each thinking he knew best. And between you, me, and the bedpost, the Gilberts had done too good a job with the boy. If ever there was a pair of smug, self-righteous bigots! Well, I thank God I'm only a housekeeper, so I don't have to forgive everybody. Hard, that's what they were, holy and hard, and they made him hard too. I heard him once telling Mr Green what they'd done to punish him for having a – well, not to put too fine a point on it, a wet dream – and I tell you, even Mr Green was shaken, though he's heard some things in his life. That was why he tried to keep contact with the lad, if you ask me, to be a bit of a softer influence on him, though God knows he was a firebrand himself in his younger days, though you wouldn't think it to see him now. But Geoffrey was beyond softening, and I wasn't sorry when he stopped coming here. I didn't like him upsetting Mr Green. And he had funny eyes. I didn't like the way he looked at *me* sometimes. I've had plenty of comments in the years I've been housekeeper here, and they're water off a duck's back to me, but Geoffrey looked as if he wasn't going to say anything, he was going to do it.'

'What number Askew Road?' Slider asked.

'Ah—' She thought, and shook her head. 'I don't remember. It was a high number. Seventy-six? Sixty-seven? No, I don't remember.'

'Wouldn't he have it written down somewhere?'

She opened her eyes wide. 'How should I know that? You aren't suggesting I should look through his things, I hope?'

Slider felt he had nothing to lose. 'Yes.'

'I couldn't do that,' she said firmly. 'No, if you can't find out any other way, you'll have to come back and ask him again. But I'd sooner he wasn't upset. He's an old man, and his heart's not too good any more. I'm sure you'll think of something.'

Slider allowed himself to be thrust out into the day, and walked back to his car, feeling that unreal sense of not quite touching the ground that comes from having missed a night's sleep. So he had been right! It had seemed so improbable before, that it was only because it had also seemed so obvious he had had the courage to pursue it. Now he felt as if he had been struck rather hard on the head with a padded bludgeon. He had been right. Steve Mills had a brother. A doppelgänger. And maybe, just maybe, he was within smelling distance of the fox.

291

17

Bishop's Move

After driving rather hopelessly up and down Askew Road, Slider parked down a side street and went into a corner newsagents. A tall and chubby Asian man stood behind the loaded counter. Further in, a short, stout white woman was serving sweets and gossiping to a bosom pal, and neither looked round as Slider came in to a tinkling of the doorbell.

Mindful of the niceties, he bought a newspaper and a chocolate bar from the man, who bemused him rather because he had parted his hair straight down the middle and oiled it, in a style Slider had not seen outside of nineteen-thirties' photographs, and also wore a Fair Isle pullover. The effect, combined with the dark, overstocked chaos of the shop, made him feel he was time-travelling. Pocketing his change, Slider drew out the photofit print, which was becoming rather dog-eared. 'Do you know this man?' he asked.

The man took it and looked at it briefly before scrutinising Slider rather more thoroughly and asking, 'Are you police?'

Slider produced his ID. 'I've reason to believe he lives somewhere near here. Have you seen him before?'

'Yeah. I know him,' the man said, still searching Slider's face for information. 'What's he done?'

'I can't tell you that,' Slider said. 'Does he live near here?'

'He's one of my customers. Binden Road, is it? Or Bassein Park Road?'

'I was hoping you'd tell me.'

'Oh, d'you want me to look him up? Half a mo, then.' He dragged out a large black ledger from under the counter and began to turn the pages, which were covered with elaborately loopy handwriting and many crossings-out and insertions. 'Oh yeah, here we are. Bassein Park Road – d'you know it? It's just up there on the left. He has the *Guardian* every day, plus the *News of the World* and the *People* on Sunday, plus he has *Opera* monthly, *Music* magazine which is also monthly, and *Scouts and Scouting,* which is quarterly.' The bosom friend departed, passing behind Slider's back, and the stout woman turned her face in their direction. 'Very good customer. Mr Gilbert, his name is. I call him the Bishop.'

'Who's that, Mr Gilbert?' the woman chimed in, sidling nearer. 'He's a very good customer. Very nice man.'

'Been coming in years.'

'My husband knows him very well.' She slipped her hand through the man's arm, seeming eager for a share of any kudos forthcoming from the acquaintance.

'Why do you call him the Bishop?' Slider asked.

'Oh, that's just his silly joke,' the woman said anxiously. 'He doesn't mean anything.'

'He's very holy, is Mr Gilbert. Always talking about God and religion. Says he wanted to be a reverent once, only it didn't work out for some reason. He talks like a bishop an' all. Posh and snooty.'

'He does not,' the woman urged.

'If he'd been a reverent, he'd've been a bishop by now. Never comes in without having a chat to me about the state of the world and what he'd do if he was in charge.' He grinned. 'Tried to get me to give out religious stuff to my customers once – I mean, me!'

'What sort of religious stuff?'

'Cards with religious stuff printed on them – from the Bible and that. Wanted to leave a stack by the till for me to give out.'

'It does seem to suggest a lack of touch with reality,' Slider said.

'I said no. But still—' The man shook his head in wonder at the idea. 'Anyway, he reckons to be holy and everything, but he buys *Knave* and *Fiesta* when he thinks I'm not looking.'

'He does not!' the woman said, removing her hand to signify her complete detachment from this judgement.

'Yes he does, Reet,' the man insisted. 'When Barry's at the till on a Saturday and I'm up the other end doing the bills. He waits till he thinks I'm not looking and he slips them under a *Dalton's Weekly* and takes them to Barry. I've seen him do it.'

'Oh, you!' the woman said, furiously.

'What's up? Nothing wrong with that. It's all good clean fun. Mind you,' he turned to Slider, 'he looks a bit funny to me sometimes. He comes in in shorts, which isn't natural in a man his age. And he has a funny look sometimes. Barry says he's gay.' The woman tutted vigorously and moved away, to distance herself further from the views being aired. 'I wouldn't be surprised if that wasn't why he didn't become a vicar or whatever you call it. Got himself into trouble. With a boy scout, eh?' He gave Slider a grin and moved his elbow in a rib-jabbing gesture.

'Do you know what he does for a living?' Slider asked.

'I think he's a social worker or something, isn't he? Rita?'

The woman, appealed to, stopped pretending not to be listening and said, 'He's a counsellor, I think they call it. Down the advice centre in Acton High Street.'

'Have you seen him around lately?'

The man frowned. 'Now you come to mention it, no. And I didn't see him in here Saturday. He always comes in Saturday morning. Reet?'

'I never saw him. But I was in and out.'

'It was pretty busy,' the man added apologetically. 'Maybe he's been ill. He's not been in for a day or two, anyway.'

'So I might catch him at home now, then?'

The man assented, and watched him with shining eyes, evidently longing to know what the Bishop had done. Slider extricated himself, seeing out of the corner of his eye how the couple flew together as soon as the door was closed to engage in eager speculation, and went back to the car. He radioed in to ask for Geoffrey Gilbert's police record to be looked up. He expected a negative, but after a lengthy wait Norma came on.

'Guv? There's quite a bit of it. Nothing for the last twelve years, but the seventies and early eighties there's all sorts of things. Do you want me to read it out to you?'

'Summarise a bit.'

'All right. There's a whole scad of burglaries and thefts, small stuff, some affrays and resistings – oh, here's one, early on, riding a bicycle without lights, that's what probably turned him into a wrong'un. Who is this guy?'

'More recently?'

'June 1979 fined for behaviour liable. Another in December 1979 for assault and resisting arrest. January 1982, three months' suspended for conspiracy to wound—'

'Is that the most recent?'

'No, there's December 1982, two years for ABH. I looked that one up. It was a youth who was disrupting a scout meeting he was holding. He went for him like a madman and did him over a treat. Served nine months, came out in January 1984. After that he's been clean.'

Slider was silent. That would be about the time he moved away and severed relations with Green. Probably lost his scout troop over it. Fines and suspended sentences he could have hidden from the authorities, but an actual spell in the pokey would have obliged them to make an example of him. Whatever fires raged in him must have gone underground.

'Is Atherton there?' he asked.

A pause while presumably she looked around. 'He was here a minute ago. Must have just popped out.'

'When he gets back tell him to meet me at this address.' He gave the address the shopkeeper had given him.

'Right, boss. Anything else?' Even over the telephone he could hear her curiosity.

'No. Is everything all right there?'

'Everyone's upset about Mills. Mr Carver's been doing his pieces. I think he thinks you ought to have warned him.'

'Warned him of what?'

Norma heard the chill. 'I don't think Mills is guilty either,' she said hastily. 'Is that what you're working on?'

'I'll let you know when I know. Get that message to Atherton.'

'Okay, guv. Be careful.'

'I always am,' Slider said, and signed off. He drove the short distance to Bassein Park Road and parked across from the house. He watched for a while, but there was no movement at any of the windows. The house had an unkempt look, with paint peeling from the window frames, a chunk of stucco fallen from the façade, the front gate missing, the brown paint of the front door old and dirty. Unlike its neighbours it had no nets at the windows, and in the gap between the dark red curtains at the front ground-floor bay a large clear-plastic cross was stuck to the pane on the inside with one of those transparent sucker-caps. Nothing like nailing your colours to the mast, he thought. He got out of the car and walked over, and after a brief internal debate, rang the doorbell. He couldn't hear it inside, so in case it was broken he knocked long and loudly. There was no sound of movement within. Gilbert was probably at work, establishing his alibi. When Atherton arrived they could pursue him there.

He moved across and looked in at the front window. The room was empty except for a wooden kitchen table on the far side on which was a pile of books and several of what looked like pamphlets, and two wooden chairs against the left-hand wall. The floorboards were bare and dusty and the wallpaper pale brown with age; there was an open fireplace with a spotted mirror above the mantelpiece, but the hearth and grate were littered with waste paper, sweet wrappers and apple cores.

Still no sign of Atherton. Slider was feeling light-headed with fatigue now. He went on round to the side gate, which was falling to pieces as side gates so often are, hanging by one hinge and a rusty nail, and propped half-open. There was a damp, mossy passage down the side of the house, leading to a square of unkempt grass littered with bits of broken furniture and metal of unimaginable purpose, and a large, stout and fairly new garden shed. The back door, presumably the kitchen door, had frosted glass at the top. The kitchen window was high up and had extremely dirty brown check curtains, and what had once been French windows from the back room onto the garden had, oddly, been bricked in and reduced to an ordinary-sized window, which had dark red curtains drawn across it.

It was all horribly drab and depressing, not the sort of thing you would associate with a Christian or a scoutmaster. Slider knocked at the back door, and then idly tried the handle and found to his surprise that the door was unlocked. He opened it cautiously and stepped in.

'Hello! Is anyone at home? Hello, Mr Gilbert?'

The house was silent. Slider looked around the kitchen. It was furnished with cheap units in dark brown melamine, the electric stove was encrusted with burnt fat, and there was fawn and brown chequered lino on the floor, though little of the pattern showed through the ancient spillages and general dirt. The air smelled of mould and boiled fish. The sink was an old, chipped earthenware one, brown with years of having tea leaves emptied down it, and a heap of used enamelled tin plates and mugs sat in an inch of greasy water, awaiting the day of reckoning. The cupboard door under the sink was half-open, forced out by an overflowing waste bin, from which an eggshell, some toast crusts and an empty packet which had once held Bachelors Savoury Rice had already escaped onto the floor. Other used saucepans and more plates lay about the worktops, remembrances mostly of meals featuring toast toppers, baked beans, fried things, and one of boil-in-the-bag cod and bottled sauce which had added its perfume to the stale air. This was not the scouting way, Slider thought. Even if he had nothing but a running stream and a piece of twig, a scout cleared as he went. Gilbert had certainly let standards slip.

By the door into the rest of the house was a cork notice-board, and Slider padded over to it, each footstep sticking slightly to the gunky floor and coming up with a little sucking sound. To the notice-board were pinned a number of news-paper cuttings, mostly just headlines from the sensational Sundays. MAN SHOT WIFE AND LOVER CAUGHT IN ACT. BISHOP'S SECRET LOVE-CHILD. 'QUIET' MAN GOES BERSERK WITH AXE – FIVE DEAD. PC'S HAND SEVERED IN MACHETE ATTACK. ROCKER VICAR'S KNICKER SHOCKER. REVENGE KILLER BLOODBATH HORROR. There was also the cutting about the Greatrex murder with the picture of Mills and the news that he was being questioned about irregularities, and a cutting from a shiny magazine which was a review of a recording of *The Damnation of Faust* with Lupton conducting the RLP – Joanna's orchestra – with the CD serial numbers marked with shocking pink highlighter.

This was one disturbed dude, Slider thought – but the cutting about Mills was real evidence. It was too good an opportunity to miss. He opened the door and stepped out into the hall. The floorboards were bare, and a bicycle stood between the stairs and the front door, an ancient sit-up-and-beg bike with black paint and chrome mudguards which, unlike everything else he had seen so far, was clean and shinily well-kept. He walked past the open door to the front room he had seen through the window, and went lightly up the naked stairs. There was a bathroom on the mezzanine which he looked into and quickly out of, and three small bedrooms which were all empty – unfurnished and with no floor cover-ings. Puzzled, he went downstairs again. Gilbert must live and sleep in the only other room left, the ground-floor back.

He opened the door cautiously. The room was in half-darkness because of the curtains drawn across the window, but he could see well enough. It had a frowzy smell of feet and stale bedding and sweat and dust and general uncleanness that made Slider want to gag; certainly, this was where the man lived and moved and had his being. It was horribly ugly and comfortless – underfoot a variety of dirty old rugs of different sizes and colours almost concealed the original carpet, and a naked light bulb dangled from the centre of the ceiling. The room was almost square. Along the left-hand wall was a narrow divan bed, the bedclothes thrown back and rumpled, the linen grey with use and the blankets old and stained, and on the floor beside it were further used plates and mugs. Beyond it was an old armchair littered with clothes, and in the corner a hand basin, with a shelf bearing a clutter of half-used toiletries and a mirror above it.

Under the window was a table covered in papers and books, amongst which Slider could see some London telephone directories, a *London A–Z,* and a couple of foolscap student's pads closely written.

Behind the door on the right was a paraffin stove standing on a tin tray, and next to it a wicker chair, on which he noted coats and jackets were piled. On the right-hand wall was an enormous old-fashioned wardrobe with a mass of boxes and bulging bags on the top, and next to that, between it and the window wall, ran a wooden bench. It looked handmade, a plank seat, thick, stout square legs, and a tongue-and-groove back screwed to the wall with heavy coach bolts. Slider looked at it reluctantly, for it had plainly been customised for some purpose he did not want to imagine. A semi-circular piece had been cut out of the front edge of the seat in the middle, and two thick iron rings – the sort you might tether horses to in an old-fashioned stable – had been screwed into the seat, one at either end. A piece of dirty rope lay on the bench and a crumpled piece of cloth which might have been a pillowcase; underneath it was stacked an impressive collection of soft-porn magazines. Slider swallowed saliva and moved his gaze elsewhere. The wardrobe. What was in the wardrobe?

The door hung half-open, and he pushed it a little wider. The hanging section was stuffed with clothes, suits, trousers, jackets, shirts, coats, some newish, even tolerable, others old, scruffy, smelling dirty. In the bottom a jumble of shoes gave out a strong but cold smell of feet – oddly enough not a pair of trainers amongst them, but two pairs of black plimsoles, one with holes where the big toes had worn through. There was also, significantly, a shoebox which proved to contain several packets of surgical gloves. The shelved section was stuffed with pullovers and underwear, all but the bottom three shelves, which contained scouting clothes – shorts, shirts, a Baden-Powell hat which must be an antique – and insignia, all clean, pressed, and neatly folded. It might have been poignant in other circumstances.

God, this was a hellish place! Slider was beginning to feel sick, though whether from fatigue or the smell he was not sure. He had no doubt now that he had found his man; in his mind he compared this dismal, grim den and the normality of Mills's rooms. If ever there was an example of nurture versus nature, this was it. Gilbert was obviously an abnormal and possibly dangerous man, and coming home to these surroundings night after night would be like marinading meat to increase the flavour. Slider wondered how he managed to keep up a normal life outside at all, which he must do if he gave advice at the centre, unless his customers were even further spaced out than him.

Slider knew he must get out of here to wait in a safer and pleasanter place for reinforcements and the return of the householder; but he had one more small hunch to play. He crossed to the table and flicked through the London telephone directories. Yes, it was as he thought: both Jimenez and Jepp were listed. Not only that, but, joy of joys, their addresses had been marked with highlighter. Gotcha, you bastard, Slider thought. And Greatrex was not listed, nor was Lassiter, nor Lupton; rifling his memory Slider came up with the name of one other singer, Connie Malcolm, and the producer Ben Edgerton, and they were not listed either. The answer, then, to why those particular people had been chosen was one of simple access. How the campaign would have progressed he could guess from some of the things lying on the desk – the Musician's Union directory, a list of what seemed to be agents' addresses and telephone numbers, and a copy of the programme from Glyndebourne for *Don Giovanni*, carefully dissected, with the cast list and the stars' profiles laid out separately. He had meant to get them all, given time and reasonable luck.

The thing now was to get a search warrant. There was plenty of stuff here that he could see, and probably more that he couldn't, maybe even bloodstained clothing – for Gilbert must be believing himself quite safe, knowing that Mills was under suspicion and that Mills had no idea he had a twin. Presumably that's why he had killed Miss Giles, because she was the only one who was likely to give away the secret to Slider. He felt miserably guilty for her death. The thing now was to get the evidence before Gilbert had a chance to destroy it.

Slider left the room, closing the door carefully behind him, and retraced his steps, feeling an enormous weight of oppression lift as he breathed the comparatively fresh air outside. He walked back down the side of the house, reaching for his mobile to ring Atherton and find out where the hell he was, why he wasn't here yet. He had to stop for a moment still short of the side gate to disentangle the clip from the torn edge of his trouser pocket (would Joanna mend that if asked, or would that be tactless?) thinking that it was odd that there had been no religious stuff in the house, nothing except that cross in the front room, which given that he—

The smell of sweat – sharp, rank as nettles in a ditch but much less reassuring – warned him an instant before the single footfall he actually heard. He swung round, his hand holding the mobile going up instinctively as though to defend himself, to see a man wearing Mills's face but certainly not Mills's expression, holding a piece of lead piping – how traditional! – in a surgically-gloved hand – how odd! – but not just holding it, swinging it. Too late to dodge. Slider heard the smack of the blow, felt the sickening thud of it at a level that was beyond or at least outside pain, felt his stomach rise up nauseously, and saw a brief confusion of ground coming up to meet him and old-fashioned black plimsoles (quiet) (*another* pair?) before he fell through the ground and surprisingly and completely out of the world altogether.

He came to himself to the awareness of a headache – mother, father and both grandparents of a headache which precluded any other sort of thinking just at first. It was a smashing, sickening sort of pain; as he adjusted to it, other, lesser pains faded in, a deep ache in his neck and shoulders, a stinging, raw pain in his cheek, sharp bands of it round his arms and legs. He had no idea what had happened to him, and was aware that the first priority was to open his eyes, but this he was deeply reluctant to do, from a sharp certainty that it would hurt, and from a duller suspicion that he would not like what he saw.

It was at that point that someone grabbed his hair at the back of his skull and dragged his head up. It seemed an unkind thing to do. Simultaneously he smelled rank, horrible sweat and surprisingly the sweet perfume of wood shavings. A voice above him said, 'You're awake. Come on, stop pretending.'

Memory flooded back, his muscles tensed to leap for escape, and he realised he was tied up and couldn't move. Now he opened his eyes. He was inside the garden shed, which accounted for the smell of wood, and he inwardly cursed himself for not having thought of looking in the shed which was so anomalously new and smart. Now he was in deep, deep shit.

The sweat factory released his hair and came round from behind him to sit on a wooden stool between him and the door. The man with Mills's face (yes, there was the mole on the wrong side) wore his hair without a parting, brushed straight back, but otherwise looked startlingly like Mills, in general size and shape as well as features. He was wearing a khaki short-sleeved shirt with large dark rings under the armpits and down the middle, tucked into khaki shorts, and his thick muscular legs (there was a very fine red mark on one thigh, the last trace of a healed cut) bulged out from below them to disappear into olive green socks and the black plimsoles. These things Slider was sure Mills would never wear. The other really serious difference from Mills was that this man was holding in his right hand a large and glittering combat knife.

The true depth of the trouble he was in caught up with Slider's dazed mind and for a moment pushed the headache into the background. He was sitting in a very heavy wooden chair, like a one-seater garden bench except that there seemed to be a hole cut out of the seat, commode-style, the edges of which were cutting into his buttocks and upper thighs. The size and squareness of the chair made it very stable. His ankles were tied to the front legs, his arms behind the seat back, and there was a cord round his thighs and the chair seat, all of which accounted for the bands of pain he had registered. The cords were tight and a covert wriggle convinced him that the knots were good.

As though he heard the thought, Gilbert smiled. 'Don't

waste your energy, I know how to tie a rope. They used to teach you knots in the Scouts, you know. Not any more. It's all environmental awareness and cultural sensitivity.'

Slider said nothing. The shorts, the knife and the smile added up to bad, bad news; he was frantically searching the situation for some escape, but the headache made it hard to think. Gilbert had hit him on the temple, possibly fractured his skull. He could feel the stickiness of blood on his left cheek where presumably it had trickled down. His right cheek was also painful, stingingly so, and after a second he realised he must have been dragged to the shed, scraping his face on the ground. That also accounted for the pain in his shoulders and neck.

Gilbert must have been in here, in the shed, all the time – that was why the back door was unlocked – saw Slider come out and crept up on him. What had he been doing in here? Slider now realised that the shed contained some odd things. Under the window, to his left as he sat facing the door, was a wooden workbench, on which was an old manual typewriter, some Letraset sheets and a stack of white cards printed with a cross at the top, a very large Bible and various other religious books – one a luridly coloured children's picture storybook called *Bible Stories for Children*. There were various wood-working tools, and a set of brass weights of the sort used with old-fashioned kitchen scales; the largest, the 2lb weight, had a thin piece of cord knotted through its ring with a thick elastic band on the other end. There was also a set of powder-paints ready mixed up in jars, and another jar full of brushes. On the wall to either side of the window could be seen the fruits of the brushes, a series of paintings pinned up, of simple, highly coloured Bible scenes, presumably copied from the children's book. Abraham about to sacrifice Isaac, Moses and the Burning Bush, Absalom caught up in the thicket. How

305

innocent and sweet, except that they had been painted by a man of thirty-eight.

On the blank wall to his right was a less beguiling collection, of ropes and cords of different thicknesses, textures and materials, all carefully rolled up and tied, and hung from nails. The ropes were interspersed with various ceremonial knives and swords, many of them with decorative sheaths, and the whole was arranged in a pattern, as sometimes old shields and battle-axes are hung up in stately homes.

And there were crosses everywhere – wood, plastic, raffia, metal, ivory – all different sizes, probably a dozen of them at least, with the largest on the back of the door straight ahead. What had Gilbert been doing in here? Not painting – nothing was wet. Reading? Praying?

'So, what were you doing here,' Gilbert asked suddenly, 'snooping around my house? Up to no good, that's obvious, or you'd have called at the front door like an honest man.'

'I did call at the front door,' Slider said – his voice came out in a croak and he had to adjust it. 'I rang and knocked but there was no answer.'

'So you came round the back.' Gilbert was not looking at him. He was looking at the knife which he was turning back and forth softly against his bare thigh, almost as if he was stropping it.

'Yes,' Slider said. 'To knock at the back door.'

'To ask the time? Or did you want a drink of water?'

'I wanted to speak to Mr Gilbert. Is that you?'

'And what did you want to see me about?' Gilbert cooed, smiling.

Slider was watching the knife. That dreamy, preparatory movement terrified him. In his imagination it had already flashed out to open a slit in him. If he said the wrong thing – but what was the right thing the say to a five-star nutter?

306

I'm sorry, Mr Gilbert, I'm not very good at pain. Can we skip this bit? This isn't what I joined the police for. 'I heard you were an expert on opera,' he heard himself say, and immediately regretted it as he saw Gilbert begin to move. Oh shit, oh shit—

But Gilbert stood up and laid the knife down on the workbench. Slider's relief was so intense he'd have slumped if the ropes allowed. 'Opera?' Gilbert said. 'You're fond of opera, are you?'

'Well, I don't know much about it, but I'd like to learn,' Slider said, trying to sound conversational.

'Would you like to hear some?' said Gilbert, crossing behind him. 'I've got just about everything here. Oh, of course, I beg your pardon, you can't see, can you? I've a very nice sound system, and everything on CD.' Slider heard various small sounds and clicks interspersed with Gilbert's breathing which he could easily follow in his mind's eye as a CD was selected and put into the machine. In a moment a chorus roared out from speakers just behind him, and was immediately turned down, though not by much. It was still loud, and Slider recognised it without welcome as a bit of *Don Giovanni*.

'I come out here to listen because I can have it on as loud as I like without the neighbours complaining,' Gilbert said, still behind him. His mouth approached Slider's ear as at the same time his arm came out past Slider and picked up the knife again. 'It will also do nicely to cover any noises you might make,' he said, warm, wet and close. He put an arm round Slider's neck and laid the blade delicately against his throat. 'And now suppose you stop playing silly games and tell me what you really came here for, Detective Inspector Slider. I've been through your pockets, you see. I know who you are.'

Slider felt the tickle of the cold metal on his skin, and had a vivid image of exactly what the inside of his neck would look like. He had seen the inside of Roger Greatrex's and Elizabeth Giles's recently enough to remember. 'If you know who I am, you must know what I'm here for,' Slider said. Oddly enough, though, it wasn't so bad now as when he could see the knife at a distance. At least now he knew where it was aiming. Maybe throat-cutting wasn't too painful. Freddie said death was almost instantaneous when done by an expert. And this man was *good*.

'Not quite,' said Gilbert. 'I want to know how much you know.'

'I know everything,' Slider said, 'so if anything happens to me, someone else will come after me, and someone else. You'll never get away. So it won't do you any good to kill me.'

'It won't do *you* much good, either,' Gilbert said logically. Out of sight, he even sounded quite a bit like Mills. 'So if you know everything, why are you here alone, snooping around?'

'I'm only the scouting party,' Slider said. 'The others are on their way.' Atherton! he thought suddenly. Praise be, of course someone *was* on the way, and would be here any minute. Why the hell wasn't he here already? 'The others will be arriving any time now,' he went on, and something in the changed tone of his voice must have carried conviction because the knife was removed from his throat and Gilbert came back round, first to look out of the window, and then to sit down again facing Slider and looking at him thoughtfully.

'I don't believe you,' Gilbert said at last. He began that evil stroking of the blade again. 'Tell me what you know, and then I'll decide what to do to you.'

Slider didn't like that preposition. *With* you would have been kinder. He decided to be bold. 'I know about the three people you killed and the one you didn't manage to, and I know why you did it.' Gilbert watched him quizzically. 'You

308

were shocked and outraged by the blasphemy you witnessed – and by society's calm acceptance of it. Why, Roger Greatrex even praised it! He was symptomatic of the whole sickness of the modern world – slick, clever, evil. And his private life was as bad as his professional one – everyone knew what sort of a man he was. That's why you decided to start with him.'

'Go on,' Gilbert said. He sounded pleasantly interested, and the knife now lay still on his knee. Everyone likes hearing about themselves, Slider thought. If he could keep the talking going until Atherton got here—

'The difficulty was getting near him. You didn't even know where he lived. Then you saw in the paper that he was going to be on the television programme, *Questions of Our Time*, which goes out live from White City. You went along there on the evening and picked out somebody scruffy-looking at the back of the queue who'd be glad to give you his ticket for twenty pounds. Once inside, it was easy enough to slip away from the rest – it's always chaotic in there.'

'My, you do know everything, don't you?' Gilbert said ironically, but he didn't seem angry, only fascinated.

Slider went on, trying to sound conversational. 'The one thing I don't know is how you managed to find Roger Greatrex – or was that just luck?'

'Not entirely. I'd been to that programme before – when they had religious or ethical questions – so I knew the routine. And I went on a guided tour of the centre years ago with my school, so I knew the layout. The difficulty was going to be getting him on his own. I hid on the staircase and watched the greenroom through the glass. I couldn't believe my luck when he came out alone. But then he went into another room.'

The knife was now being tapped briskly against the kneecap. Slider swore if he got out of this alive no-one over whom he had any influence would ever wear shorts again.

'I went to the door,' Gilbert said, 'and listened. I thought if he was on his own—' He stopped.

'But he wasn't. He was with a woman,' Slider said.

Gilbert glared. 'I heard them – the filthy animals! I heard him slaking his filthy lust – just wherever it took him, like a dog. Oh, I knew then I was right to kill him. He came out at last and went into the men's room. I was going to follow when the female came out and I had to dodge back. I thought about putting her down, too, but I wanted Greatrex. She could wait. When she'd gone I went into the men's and there he was. Do you know what the filthy creature was doing?'

'Yes, I think I do,' Slider said. 'He was washing himself.'

'As if water alone could cleanse him of that!' Gilbert paused a moment and looked at Slider thoughtfully. 'Are you a Christian?'

'Yes,' Slider said, grateful he could say it with some conviction.

'Churchgoer?'

'When I can. When I'm not working.'

'You shouldn't let work interfere with your duty to God,' Gilbert said sternly. 'That's no excuse.'

'Go on about Greatrex,' Slider said weakly. He licked his lips and tasted blood. His head was bleeding again. 'When you found him in the men's room—?'

'I went up behind him, held him, read him his sentence. Ezekiel, chapter 18, verse 24. *"When the righteous turneth away from his righteousness, shall he live? In his trespass that he hath trespassed and in his sin that he hath sinned, in them shall he die."* He didn't struggle. Unlike the dumb beast, he knew what was coming to him, and he knew what for. I saw the understanding in his eyes as I looked at them in the mirror. Then I put the card into his pocket, caught him by the chin, and *cut*.'

Slider had never known there could be so much emotion

310

in such a small word. It was a sharp-edged, lip-smacking, blood-filled word. The music behind him boomed, sounding distorted, he felt very sick and there were specks before his eyes. Concussion, he thought. He struggled to keep hold of his consciousness.

'Afterwards,' he said. 'Tell me what you did afterwards.'

'I thought you knew everything,' Gilbert said, sharply suspicious.

'You went up in the lift – to the canteen – mix with the others,' Slider said with difficulty. 'Hid – hid the bag – on the roof of the lift.'

Gilbert relaxed. 'I was sorry to part with that raincoat, but the blood would never have come out.'

'But the knife,' Slider said. 'Why did you leave the knife?'

'He knocked it out of my hand as he fell, and landed on top of it. I didn't want to move him. It always shows, doesn't it, when someone's been moved?' Slider nodded and then wished he hadn't as lumps of pain went rolling about his head like rocks. 'The only thing I did was to put his *thing* away. I couldn't leave him like that. The knife – well, that didn't matter. I've got plenty of others. I collect knives,' he added, looking dreamily at the display wall. 'There's something beautiful and pure and simple about a blade – that's why they talk so much about them in the Bible. Especially as an instrument of God's vengeance. Draw the blade across the taut flesh, and let the soul out in a great gushing fountain of redness. That redness which is man's animal nature, his sin. The thirsty earth drinks the sacrifice, and is quenched. And his soul goes to God for judgement. So simple, so easy.'

Slider blinked as a trickle of blood stung his eyes. He was losing his grip on things. 'Why,' he croaked, 'did you kill your mother?'

Gilbert's dreaminess disappeared, his expression sharpened.

311

'My mother died ten years ago, of cancer. The good woman who brought me up, she was my mother. The whore who bore me was nothing to me. She was lewdness and filth, she was Babylon—'

'She was the only person who knew about you and your brother. She knew you were going to let your twin brother take the blame for what you'd done. She reproached you, didn't she? And you couldn't stand it. She said you ought to take your punishment—'

Gilbert moved with astonishing swiftness for such a large man, and the knife was against Slider's throat again, his head being pulled back agonisingly by the hair, the stink of sweat almost overpowering. 'Punishment? Don't you think I know about punishment? I learnt about it at my mother's knee. Scourge thou the flesh that the soul may be made clean. In suffering is salvation. Scourge the back with rods and flails – as my father did for me, out of his love for me. Beat the devil out and let God in!' He flung Slider's head down and walked away, marching about the confined space to the beating music. 'The flesh is just an envelope for the soul, an envelope with no address. The flesh is a snare and delusion. But the temptations of the flesh are strong, oh yes. So strong! You have to punish, punish every day, crush out the lewdness and the evilness. When the Devil stands up, you have to force him down again.'

Through the waves of nausea, Slider suddenly realised what Gilbert had been doing in here, what the kitchen weights were for, and the hole in the chair seat. He groaned, unable to help himself. This man, he thought dimly, is seriously bonkers. He is probably also going to kill me – but it was getting harder to care. He wished Mozart would shut up. How long can you hang out a death scene? His head hurt so much. But he thought the end was very near.

And suddenly Gilbert stood still, frozen in mid-stride and

mid-rant. He would have looked ridiculous in those shorts and socks if it hadn't been for the knife. Slider couldn't see the knife any more. Was it somewhere in him? No, surely he'd remember that. What was up with Gilbert? Slider's chin was sunk on his chest, and with a great effort he lifted it up, raised the throbbing football and peered through the blood and sweat that blurred his vision. Gilbert was standing by the door, listening, every line of his body taut. Then suddenly he flung it open. A breath of heavenly fresh air came in, and Slider saw Atherton standing there – elegant, fragrant Atherton. The cavalry.

Atherton said, 'What the—' and his eyes widened with surprise for an instant as he recognised the face in front of him. 'How did you get here?'

Slider tried to warn him, but he couldn't make a sound. It was all he could do to keep his head up. He saw an instant's struggle as Gilbert thrust Atherton violently aside and ran. Atherton reeled sideways, briefly out of sight against the side fence, and Slider saw beyond Gilbert, oh blessed sight, the dark blue-black of uniformed police coming up the side passage. Atherton had thought to call out the infantry too, probably when Slider didn't answer his mobile. The lads didn't need telling to catch Gilbert – to bring down a running man is the most basic of a copper's instincts. They were on him like the hounds of Hell on winter's traces – hounds of fell – felon—

Atherton reappeared in the doorway, a puzzled expression on his face, his hands clasped over his stomach like a post-prandial bishop. Slider desperately wanted to say something – he'd thought of a really wonderful bishop joke, about long time no see – but all the talk had gone out of his tongue. Atherton unfolded his hands and looked at them, and the palms were red, and there was red all over his shirt. While

Slider was trying to puzzle it out, Atherton said, quite conversationally, 'Oh shit,' went down on both knees like a shot ox, and fell gracefully sideways.

A DCI BILL SLIDER CASE

Cynthia Harrod-Eagles

Killing Time

Detective Inspector Bill Slider is back at work with a thumping headache, courtesy of the last villain he apprehended. But he is minus Atherton, a friend and colleague, who's still recovering from his injuries.

Slider was hoping for a quiet week, but a murder at a night club plunges him into the underworld of entertainment to question table-dancers, prostitutes, pimps and cabinet ministers. And when it appears that this murder could be linked to another unsolved case, Slider is left with more questions than ever.

What with Atherton's slow recovery and his replacement's unhealthy interest in Slider, the DI has enough to fuel his headache for the foreseeable future. But the old grey matter won't be denied; doggedly and with a whimper, Slider starts to unravel the truth . . .

*

'An outstanding series'
New York Times Book Review